Unforgiving Ghosts

Written by

Candy Ann Little

Published by

Sacred Grounds

(books of a different spirit from
Inknbeans Press)

©2017

Cover art by Shatzie Lee
©2013 Candy Ann Little, and Kingdom Kastle Publishing
© 2017 Candy Ann Little and Sacred Grounds (books of a different spirit from Inknbeans Press)

ISBN 13: 978-1-946841-01-8 (Sacred Grounds)
ISBN 10: 1-946841-01-3

Inknbeans Press
25060 Hancock Avenue
Bldg 103, Suite 458
Murrieta, Ca 92562

To my daughter - Megan Candace Little - you will always be in my heart and soul.

Chapter 1

Megan's heart burst into tiny fragments. The dark clouds loomed overhead, as if mocking her. The gray, dreary day seemed to mirror her mood. The bright balloons waving solemnly in the wind looked out of place against the field of gray stones. The silver Mylar balloon with 'Happy Birthday' inscribed in bold letters further aggravated her misery. It reminded her of the birthdays missed. The parties never thrown, gifts that wouldn't be unwrapped, cake never eaten - but mostly the absence of a candle marking another year.

"I miss you." She laid a hand against the cold marble, the chill sinking deep into her soul. A shiver raced through her body, as the wind whipped her long blond hair around her face.

Tears flowed, coursing a path down her cheeks, making her blue eyes red-rimmed and dim. The grief was so heavy it felt like a rock sitting on top of her heart. The pain and memories fighting their way to the surface. "I'm not strong enough to handle this," she told herself. Closing her eyes, Megan tried pushing back the memories, rubbing her pounding head, as if physically trying to force the doubts back into the dark recesses of her mind, back where they belonged, back where she could control them.

Her breathing became more erratic, each breath harder to take. Her heart thudded louder than the thunder now rolling in the sky. The gray shadows slowly turned into a black abyss. She inhaled a few short breaths, as raindrops pelted her face.

"Not again," she wheezed. Why did she always have a panic attack when she tried to remember? It had been a year and she still couldn't face the ghosts of her past. She wanted to scream at God, to ask where He had been in all this turmoil but right now it took every ounce of her concentration just to breathe normally.

The sky threatened to open, pouring wet misery and drenching any hope. She had to get to the car and make it home before the storm broke, but her legs wouldn't move. And then the rain started, a gentle caress that chilled the back of her neck.

The steady tattoo of raindrops beating against the headstone kept perfect time with her heartbeat. The pain slowly crept up, drowning her soul. "I have to leave," she sobbed. "I can't live with the memories anymore."

After sidestepping a bustling group of passengers, Megan made her way to the rows of monitors showing the times of the planes' departures. There were hundreds – even thousands – of locations around the world, but she didn't know where she wanted to go.

A loud commotion behind her ended with what felt like an elbow in the middle of her back sending her flying forward to trip over some luggage.

"Pardon me, ma'am." A large hand was extended to help her up off the floor. "I'm so sorry. I tripped over the blasted suitcase and fell right into you."

"It's all right. I'm not hurt." She stood, straightening her long wool coat. "Guess I lost a button, though."

"Again, my apologies."

"It's not a big deal. I can sew it back on if I find it." She scanned the floor.

"Is this it?" He bent and picked up a shining black disk.

"Yes. Thank you." She slipped it into her pocket.

"I see you're dressed properly for the weather."

"When you're born and raised in Illinois, you learn to dress appropriately, or suffer the consequences."

"So, you are from this wonderful state?" His Southern accent dripped with sarcasm. She nodded, with a slight smile. "Tell me one thing, little lady. Is it always this cold and rainy in October?"

"No." She laughed softly. "Sometimes it snows."

"Well, then. Perhaps I shouldn't complain too much."

"Why don't you have a winter coat?" Her tone turned parental.

"I'm on my way to California for business. Didn't think I'd need one. Guess I should have figured the layover into my wardrobe." Taking off his Stetson hat, he shook some droplets from the brim. "My suit jacket didn't do much for me against the cold."

"You were outside?"

"I needed a cigarette. Since this is a smoke-free building I had no choice."

"You always have choices." Megan choked back the doubts flooding her heart. "The problem is making the right ones."

3

"Very true. Well, if you'll excuse me." He tipped his hat. "Good day."

She waited until he had taken a few steps before asking him, "By the way, what part of California are you headed for?"

"Santa Barbara. It's beautiful this time of year." He waved, turned on his heel and disappeared into the crowd which seemed quite a feat, since he stood over six feet tall.

"Santa Barbara sounds perfect," she mused aloud, and now with a bit more purpose, she strode to the ticket desk.

After purchasing her ticket and receiving her boarding pass she found Gate 10A and waited. She had one hour to change her mind. *No, I can't change my mind*, she told herself firmly. Leaving would be the best thing. She had to start her life over again.

Megan fidgeted in the chair, crossing and re-crossing her legs, folding and unfolding her arms. Finally, she stood up, and walked over to the large window to watch the motorized vehicle deliver luggage to the plane.

Although the earlier downpour had turned to drizzle, a roll of thunder banged in the sky. Megan jumped, her heart racing. Would her apprehension lead to a panic attack? Inhaling deeply, she waited for the onset of an attack, but her lungs drew in the air easily. Only the memories seemed to cause the attacks.

Her heart ached. Leaving behind everyone and everything she loved was the hardest thing she'd ever done. Hesitation surrounded her heart. Would she be able to start over again? Was she doing the right thing? Would the pain ever go away? The doubts and fears flooded her mind. One memory after another crashed like waves beating against steep, rocky cliffs. *Oh, what am I doing?* she asked herself.

When her flight started boarding, she got in line. A quick scan of the crowd showed that no one had come to stop her departure. She tried to stomp the resentment down. After all no-one knew about her plans to leave.

The line behind her shuffled impatiently, waiting for her to move up. She couldn't stall any longer - taking one last look, she somehow found the strength to take the final step.

Megan boarded, and walked down the narrow aisle searching for her seat.

"Well, if it ain't the pretty little native." The man with the black hat stood up from his aisle seat.

"I don't believe anyone has ever called me that before." She squeezed into the seat next to the window with the broad-shouldered stranger on the other side.

"Happy to be the first." He smiled. "By the way, my name is Tex." His deep, booming voice seemed amplified in the small space. She found the strong Southern accent a bit sexy, too.

"Hi, I'm Megan." She shook his offered hand.

"Figured we might as well be on a first name basis. I can't call you 'pretty little lady' the whole flight." He winked at her. "Not that it isn't true."

Megan smiled, but said nothing. She had never known how to handle compliments with grace or style. After fastening her seat belt, she listened to the flight attendant go over the safety instructions. The idea of oxygen masks, and using the seat cushion for a flotation device did little to ease her fears - in fact, it intensified them.

"First time flying?" Tex asked.

"Is it that obvious?" she said, through gritted teeth.

"Well, most people usually wait until the plane is airborne before tearing the arm rest to pieces."

Megan uncurled her fingers and laid her hands in her lap. Looking up, she noticed a pair of dark blue - almost black - eyes, watching her from under the Stetson hat. "I guess I am a little nervous. I've never been on a plane before."

"Most people are a bit nervous their first time up, but it gets easier the more you fly. Soon it's just like riding in a car." He chuckled. "Heck, you should have seen me and the armrest on my first flight. I almost ripped the whole thing right off the seat."

His broad shoulders and muscular arms left no doubt that he could indeed rip the armrest out with one thrust of his brawny hands. An amused smile crossed her lips as she pictured this rough, rugged cowboy turning into a scared little kitten.

"Do you mind if I ask you a personal question?"

"Not at all. Seeing as how I plowed into you and knocked you over earlier and ripped the button off your coat, I think it entitles you to one personal question."

"Are you from Texas?" She didn't really care where he lived, but the conversation kept her mind off things. Being seated next to him seemed like a miracle. They'd already broken the ice, so conversation came more naturally. His incredible good looks and flirtatious manner could make the trip more fun.

"No, ma'am, I'm from Louisiana. But a lot of people mistake me for a Texan. That's how I got my nickname. Tex." He winked again. "My turn. Are you going to California on vacation?"

"Something like that." Her blue eyes darkened.

The engines roared to life and the plane taxied down the runway, lurching forward and pressing her against the seat. She took a deep breath, giving Tex a weary smile. As the plane ascended, the air pressure in the cabin shifted and Megan felt her ears plug up. She swallowed hard and felt her eardrums pop. *If I don't die in a plane crash, I'll be deaf,* she told herself. Her hands once again wrapped tight around the armrests. "Dear God, please help me," she whispered before holding her breath.

"You can breathe now," Tex teased her.

Megan exhaled with a loud gasp, and unfastened her hands from the armrests once again.

"Taking off is the hard part. It'll be smoother now." His dark eyes winked at her again.

She ventured a glance out of the window, which revealed the storm had passed. The gray clouds scattered displaying golden streaks through the dark blue sky that looked like the fingers of God. She could make out small patches of color on the ground woven together like a patchwork quilt.

Tex had his laptop out and was busy typing away. Megan dug out her pink music player, put in her earbuds, and listened to her favorite love songs. Perhaps this wasn't the best choice of music as she headed away from home however, country love songs were all she had loaded onto the player. She tried to ignore the tugging of her consciousness.

No turning back now. No matter how much her heart hurt, her head said it was the right thing to do.

Three hours later the plane touched down in sunny Santa Barbara. Tex – as a true Southern gentleman - offered to help her with her luggage. "This place can be a madhouse," he said, pushing his way through the throng of people waiting to collect their luggage. After securing a taxi for her he smiled and said, "Have a nice time in California, Megan."

"Thanks for all your help."

"No problem, little lady. You take care now." He tipped his hat.

"You, too." She slipped into the cab, watching over her shoulder as he strode away.

"Where to, miss?" the driver said softly.

"A cheap hotel that is in a safe neighborhood, I guess."

"I know just the spot." He smiled, revealing a gap between his front teeth. "It ain't fancy, but it's cheap." She watched as the scenery slipped by, noticing the differences between her Illinois home and this part of California.

The driver pulled up to an L shaped building with 5 doors. A wooden sign hung from a large palm tree that read "The Ocean View Hotel." The faded blue paint was pealing and gray, weathered wood showed underneath. White shutters hung crooked and a few were missing completely. The driver set her luggage on the front porch and asked, "Anything else I can do for you, miss?"

"No, thanks. I can handle it from here." She tried to sound confident but was unsure if she could handle anything. So far, messing up her life had been her biggest accomplishment.

She walked across the old, tattered wooden porch, and opened the door, which protested with a loud screech. A whiff of dusty, stifling air hit her as she stepped inside. Noting how the interior decorating contrasted the exterior though, she breathed a sigh of relief. A large rug lay in the middle of the wooden floor. Plain white walls and a ceramic tiled counter completed the look. Though it wasn't fancy decor, it felt quaint.

The lady behind the counter looked startled. "Oh, my! I was so deep in my book I didn't hear your car." She marked the page and set the book on the counter. "What can I do for you?"

"I need a room." It came out shyly and softly.

"You're in luck, we have one." She laughed. "How long will you be staying?"

"I'm not sure, maybe a couple of weeks. Will that be a problem?"

"Heavens, no. It's not like we're that busy around here." She shuffled through some papers. "But we'll want half of the payment in advance. Name?"

"Megan Black."

She wrote in a ledger. "Will that be cash or check?"

"Credit card."

"I'm sorry, we don't have the machine." She held up the ledger. "We haven't updated to the 21st century yet. We still do everything the old-fashioned way."

"I guess I'll have to write a check." Megan felt a pang of guilt for using this account, but what else could she do? Besides, it would only be for a little while. She hoped to get a job soon, then she'd have her own money.

"Can I see the ocean from my room?"

"Heavens, no. The ocean is about half a mile that way," she pointed. "Not too far, just a short walk.

We wanted to fit in with the surroundings, so we used the word 'ocean' for the name."

"I see." She didn't know why she felt disappointed about this hotel being so shabby. She wasn't used to fancy hotels or elegant restaurants. After all, this was the first time she'd been outside Illinois.

"We give the *Santa Barbara News-Press* to each guest." The clerk handed Megan the newspaper. "Enjoy."

"Thanks. That saves me the trouble of going out and buying one."

"Don't mention it." She waved a chubby hand. "I'm always glad to help. And if you ever need any supplies there's a mom and pop shop down the street. And a block the other way is a small café, which serves the best BLT in town."

Megan opened the door to her room with the key she'd been handed, and surveyed her new surroundings. They would - she decided - be home for the next few weeks. The double bed took up most of the space in the small room, with a round table next to the bed and an antique dresser on the opposite wall, next to the television set. She sat down on the bed and ran her hand over the blue and burgundy puffed quilt. Eyes closed, breathing deeply, she remained sitting for a few moments.

Feeling tired and drained, she decided to unpack later, and stretched out on the bed. She looked through the classified section of the newspaper, chewing her lip, as she looked through the jobs offered. Though she didn't have much experience, she managed to circle a few jobs where there was a slight potential.

Suddenly she saw something of interest. "I can do this," she said to herself. Sitting up with excitement she read aloud, "Prominent executive and his family seek full-time creative chef for private residence in Santa Barbara. Must be able to handle small dinner parties as well as family occasions. Excellent salary/benefits." She pulled out her cell phone and punched the number in.

A woman's voice answered. "Peterson residence."

"I'm calling about the job for a cook."

"Hold on one moment, please." A minute later another voice came on the line. "This is Delores Peterson. How may I help you?"

"Has the position for a cook been filled yet?"

"No, it hasn't. I'm setting up interviews for tomorrow. Can you make it?"

Megan let out a sigh of relief. "Yes, that will be fine."

She gave her the address. "I'll see you tomorrow at nine."

Megan hung up and flopped down on the bed again. A quick glance at the time on her phone told her it was four o'clock. However, in Illinois it was six. Closing her eyes, she had just started to drift off to sleep, when her phone vibrated next to her. She looked at the number, guilt filling her heart. She pushed ignore and cried, "What have I done?" Tears sprang from her eyes as she went into her contacts and blocked the number. She wiped the tears away, resolving to be strong. The pain and memories silently crept up like invisible ghosts, reaching inaudible hands around her thoughts, tugging and pulling, until she felt unable to control her feelings. Overpowering, conflicting emotions convulsed through her, forcing her mind to shut down. She couldn't think, and didn't want to feel. She wanted the pain to stop. *If only someone could make it stop!* she cried silently.

Sitting up and wrapping her arms around herself, she tried to shield herself from the anguish. Somehow, she found strength, and forced the pain back inside the tightly guarded compartment of her heart. It felt as if it would burst under the strain, but she had to do it - otherwise, she would lose her sanity.

Wiping away the tears, she started unpacking. It didn't take long to empty the suitcases, although it felt like it had taken forever to fill them. With that done, she looked around the room - everything was neat and tidy.

Hoping a walk would help her recover some self-control, she changed into a pair of black knee-length leggings and a lavender turtleneck sweater. Pulling her long hair into a ponytail, she headed out the door.

She thought about grabbing a bite to eat, but still felt queasy from the plane ride. Her emotions were too raw to even consider food right now, so she headed towards the beach - after all, that had been her main reason for choosing California. Her whole life, she'd dreamed of seeing the ocean. Picturing the seascape had been one of the mental tasks that had helped get her through the flight.

The roar of the ocean called to her like a lullaby. With anticipation building, her feet traveled faster and faster, until she broke into a trot, then a sprint. She followed the intriguing sound, and moments later stood face to face with the magnificent Pacific Ocean.

The blue-green water extended out as far as she could see, and the bright blue sky stretched over the ocean like a blanket, with the setting sun a giant orange ball to be tossed on the white caps of the waves. Megan's eyes widened in amazement at the spectacular sight. The view was more breathtaking than any picture she'd ever seen. Closing her eyes, she inhaled the salty mist that stung her face, while a cool breeze played with her hair.

Absorbing the sights and sounds for several minutes, Megan felt transported a world away from the monotonous farm fields of Illinois. The waves lapping against the shore beckoned like an invitation. Slipping off her shoes, she tentatively walked to the edge of the shore, she squealed as the cold water washed over her bare feet. As the tide receded, a strange sucking sensation tickled her feet. Feeling as carefree as a child she ran along the shore jumping over each wave that crashed on the beach.

Breathless and exhausted, she found a soft spot to sit and rest while watching the sun set. Burrowing her now numb toes into the faintly warm sand, she watched as the bright ball aligned itself on the horizon where the water and sky met.

For the first time, Megan observed the presence of other people and felt a little embarrassed as she wondered if anyone had noticed her hopping and skipping along the shore.

"Beautiful, isn't it?" A voice interrupted her thoughts, disturbing her.

"Yes, it is." A tall, thin man, clad in jeans and a blue polo shirt, towered over her. She looked around to see where this stranger had come from, and spotted a small group a little way down the beach, lying on blankets, with rock and roll music blaring from an iPod and speakers. "I've never seen anything so beautiful," she added.

"I have." His brown eyes admired the child-like image she presented. The setting sun cast an amber glow that made her look angelic.

"What?"

"You." He sat down next to her.

"Do you get a lot of women with that line?"

He shrugged. "A few."

Megan looked skeptical. "You can't come up with something more original?"

"That *is* original."

"Oh, and next you'll be asking me if I come here often."

His thick, blond brows shot up in amusement. "Well, do you?"

"No, this is my first time at the beach." His intense stare made her feel uneasy, so she turned her attention back to the sunset.

"I'd say it's my first time too, but I've lived here my whole life." Looking at the blazing display he sighed. "This is my favorite spot in the whole world."

"I can see why."

He studied her pointed profile for a few minutes, and finally asked, "So what's a lovely girl like you doing in a place like this?" His laughter echoed around them before being swallowed by the ocean.

"Watching the sunset." The indifference in her tone strongly contrasted the way his boyish smile made her melt. She desperately tried not to be taken in by his charm. However, it had been a long time since anyone looked at her like that.

"Can I buy you dinner?" He decided to take the direct approach.

Megan studied the stranger with sun-kissed blond hair and bright brown eyes. *It would be nice to make a friend*, she thought. But the last thing she needed was another complication in her life. "No, thank you."

A gust of wind whipped some tendrils of hair lose. Without hesitation, he gently tucked them behind her ear, reluctantly pulling his hand away from the soft, silky strands.

A shiver tingled down her back. From his touch or the wind? She couldn't tell, and she couldn't give in to this attraction she felt. "Before we get to the cliché, 'your place or mine', I should be going." She stood, brushing the sand off herself.

He jumped up, trying to think of something to alleviate her apprehension. "Can I at least buy you a drink?"

"No, thank you." Megan almost felt tempted to accept. "I've had a long day and I'm really tired."

"You wouldn't have to go far. We have a cooler right over there." He pointed to the group she'd spotted earlier.

"I don't drink, anyway."

"We have sodas."

"You're persistent, aren't you?"

"Persistence is my middle name." He flashed a brash smile, his perfectly straight teeth gleamed, forming a contrast with his tanned face.

"And 'no' is mine."

His smile faded but it seemed he wasn't going to give up that easily. "Oh, come on - what will one drink hurt?"

Her patience had worn thin. Going out with him would be a mistake, and she'd made enough of those lately. "Look, mister. I don't want to have dinner or drinks with you. Please leave me alone."

His brown eyes darkened. "You're tired? Is that the best excuse you can come up with?"

She didn't want to fight, having done enough of that in Illinois too. This stranger might be handsome but his forceful personality seemed to be pushing all the wrong buttons. "Look, I don't know what your problem is but—"

"My problem?" he erupted. "I don't have a problem. You're the one with a problem."

"Yes…my problem is you!" Megan poked his chest. "I came to the beach to be alone. I'm not a trophy to be picked up by some shallow playboy."

"Shallow playboy!" He tried to sound offended, however, couldn't deny it. He hadn't been serious about a girl in years but resented her throwing it in his face. "Well, aren't you Miss Conceited?" he fumed. "You're not the only pretty girl in town. I can find any number of women waiting to go out with me. And they won't be as frigid as you."

"Since you seem to have a harem following you, I won't be missed." She picked up her shoes she stomped away.

He absently raked his hand through his wind-tousled hair, bewilderedly staring after her. No woman had ever given him such a cold shoulder. "Ice queen," he muttered and joined his friends.

"Ouch! Crash and burn," his buddy laughed.

"I don't believe it, Steven the Great, turned down," another teased.

"Mark it on the calendar," a girl joined in, "it must be a first." Her smile however held more than amusement. Satisfaction glowed in her eyes.

Megan sat in a booth at the small café, absently stirring her glass of iced tea while waiting for her food.

Who does he think he is, anyway? Irritation welled up, turning her pale face red. *He acted like a spoiled brat.* She sipped her tea. *Oh, what do I care? It's not like I'll ever see him again. After all, Santa Barbara is a big city. What are my chances of running into him again?*

The waitress brought her food to the table. "Here you are. One tuna salad, fries, and an extra pickle."

"Thank you"

"Anything else I can get you?"

"Not right now."

Megan nibbled on the sandwich and a few fries, but started to feel nauseated. She did manage to devour both pickles and finish her iced tea.

"Is everything okay?" the waitress asked a little while later, seeing the food left on the plate.

"Yes, the food's fine. I'm just not feeling that well."

"Hope you feel better, soon." Handing Megan the check, she cleared away the dishes.

The cool night air did wonders for her stomach and her attitude, as she walked the couple of blocks back to the hotel. She felt better physically, but felt exhausted emotionally.

Putting on her favorite cotton nightgown, she climbed into bed, praying that sleep would come soon, but as usual, she only tossed and turned. Why should tonight be any different? In fact, tonight was worse. She had never felt so empty and alone.

Alone. The word rang through the silence of the night.

Fatigue finally took over and she drifted off to sleep, only to be awakened a few hours later by a nightmare. Screaming, she sat up with a jerk, brushed her hair back with a shaky hand. The panic attack overwhelmed her, making her throat squeeze shut. She tried inhaling a few deep breaths. It didn't help.

Oh, God please help me. Once again, she tried to drag a breath into her lungs. The constriction forced it back out. Nothing ever calmed her any more, not even praying.

She mentally went down a list of positive things in her life, and soon found breathing came easier. Listing things that made her happy helped with the panic attacks, but never took away the pain. If she could only find some peace from this perpetual nightmare, maybe, just maybe, she could find happiness again.

Would God ever allow her happiness again?

Chapter 2

Where am I? Megan thought groggily as she watched lines dance on the unfamiliar rug as dust motes floated in the beams coming through dingy Venetian blinds. She stretched and yawned, sitting up in bed. "Why does my body feel like I've been hit by a truck?" she asked aloud. She unsteadily remembered the interview as reality slowly dawned on her.

"The Petersons. Nine o'clock." She glanced at the clock: 7:50 glowed in neon green. Jumping out of bed and nearly knocking the lamp off the table she stumbled into the bathroom for a quick shower. Forty-five minutes later, she assessed her appearance in the mirror. The conservative black pants and long white sweater made her look smart and competent, without being overdressed. Her bangs gently twisted under as her long hair softly curled about her shoulders. She slipped on her shoes, grabbed the Petersons' address, stuffed it in her purse, and then headed out the door.

She purchased a steaming cup of coffee and two cinnamon rolls from a small store, and a few minutes later she stood with a small group of people waiting under the black and yellow MTD sign. Thankfully the owner of the hotel had known which bus to take. The bus was much cheaper than taking a taxi. After she devoured the sweets, her stomach stopped the tap-dancing routine it had begun earlier in the morning. The bold aroma of coffee penetrated her senses, and after a couple of sips, her body stirred back to life.

When the bus finally arrived, she boarded with the other passengers.

"How much is the fare?"

"One seventy-five, little missy."

"I need to get to Cliff Drive."

"Well, now, this bus doesn't go that far, but I can write you a ticket that will allow you to transfer to another bus. The voucher won't be good for your return trip, you understand. It only allows you to change buses and not have to pay again."

"I understand."

"If you want to take the seat behind me, I'll write up your voucher in a minute.

She rubbed her shoulder, where a knot had started to form, and leaned back against the hard seat, watching the other passengers pay and head to the back of the bus.

"Here you are, missy." He handed her a slip of paper. "Are you headed to the Petersons?"

"Why, yes. How on earth did you know that?"

"I'm psychic." He chuckled. "Not really. They're the only ones who live on Cliff Drive. It's a very private estate. I take it you've never seen it before."

"No."

"Well, you're in for a treat. They are the wealthiest people around here and believe you me, the mansion shows it. It's a good tourist attraction for out-of-towners like yourself."

"How'd you know I'm from out of town? Oh, let me guess. It's the psychic thing again."

"I'd like to claim I'm psychic, but the truth is anyone who's been here more than a couple of days know who the Petersons are."

"I liked the psychic bit better. Then you could predict if I'll get the job."

"Don't worry, little missy. I'm sure you'll do fine."

"I hope so."

"Well, you couldn't ask for better people to work for."

"Do you know them?"

"Not personally, but I know of them. They're the owners of the Peterson Corporation and they've done a lot for the community. They're good people."

She thought about life, about how things can change so quickly. A few days ago, she had been in her normal routine on a farm. Now she was headed toward a mansion. If all went well she may be working there.

A chime on the bus prompted the driver to say to her, "Your stop is next. Just look for the bus with the same number on the ticket. It will take you to the bus stop a few blocks from the estate."

As the bus squealed to a stop, he added. "Okay, little missy, here's your stop. Good luck with the job."

"Thanks."

Megan stepped down from the second bus into an unmistakably wealthy section of town. Huge houses towered over her, each with beautiful landscaped gardens and manicured lawns. Walking the few blocks helped calm her nerves, but her mind continued to work overtime. She'd never dreamed of being employed by the most influential people in Santa Barbara. *What do I know about working for wealthy people?*

She turned down the lane marked "Cliff Drive" and soon stood in front of the most magnificent houses she'd ever seen.

The white, castle-like structure was breath-taking and extravagant, yet exuded an elegant ambience. The rounded wall stretching between the two rectangular sections of the house was covered with rows of long, thin windows, which gave an almost chateau impression. A garage was attached to the left of the house and a smaller, flat addition extension to the right. A red tile roof covered the entire place.

The massive lawn stretched out in deep shades of green, while orange and grapefruit trees dotted the property. A huge palm tree reached its branches over the top of the garage, shading a portion of the roof. Brightly colored flowers in beds, planters and gigantic clay pots completed the look. No detail went un-attended: the care of the property was as elaborate and perfect as the house.

Megan felt even more apprehensive than before. Anxiety gripped her stomach with a white-fisted death grip. The few jobs she'd had in high school and college had been at fast food joints and supermarkets. They weren't going to be much preparation for this job interview.

She had turned to leave, feeling unready for the ordeal ahead, when a familiar scent drifting on the breeze caught her attention. The smell brought a sense of security, and the assurance that some things never change, no matter where you are. Fresh cut grass smelled the same in a ritzy estate in California as it did on a small farm in Illinois.

She inhaled deeply, filling her lungs until they felt as though they'd explode. With the familiar scent of the grass came new-found confidence. Deciding to go ahead with the interview before that confidence disappeared, she walked over to the black iron gate and pushed the buzzer. The heavy gates swung open smoothly, and Megan walked up the long, winding driveway to the front steps. She had barely pushed the doorbell when the door opened, revealing a slightly plump woman in a black dress, with a starched white apron. Her long black hair was streaked with gray and wound up in a bun. Dark brown eyes intently examined Megan before she flashed a quick smile, as if approving of what she saw, and greeted Megan in a thick Mexican accent, "*Buenos días.*"

"*Buenos días* to you, too."

"You know *español*?"

"Just a little."

"*Hola*, I'm Rosa." Her smile looked bright white against her dark complexion.

"Hi, I'm Megan."

"*Señora* Peterson is waiting in the dining room."

Megan's eyes widened in apprehension, and her heart rate picked up. She wiped her sweaty palms on her black slacks as she followed the maid through the massive, elaborately decorated rooms. They entered the dining room, where an elegant refined lady with short-cropped salt and pepper hair was sitting. Small square-framed glasses were perched on her nose as she read the paper in her hand. Other papers were scattered across the long, cherry wood table. An exquisite golden chandelier with crystal teardrops and glass votive cups hung above, providing a gentle light.

"*Señora* Peterson. Megan Black is here for her appointment."

Mrs. Peterson stood, and took off her glasses. "Thank you, Rosa." Looking at Megan with kind blue eyes she added, "Won't you have a seat, dear?"

Megan forced her legs to move, shaking the extended hand, and swallowing hard. "H...hello, I'm Megan...Megan Black."

"It's nice to meet you. I'm Delores Peterson, but you already know that, don't you?" She played with a string of pearls that hung around her neck.

Megan gave a faint smile and gratefully sat down, noticing how Mrs. Peterson's rounded features looked incredibly young - in fact, her wrinkled hands were the only indicators of her age.

"Now, I know your name is Megan. Why don't you tell me more about yourself?"

"I'm afraid there isn't much to tell." In truth, she had a lot to tell but didn't want to get into all of that. "I moved here from Illinois."

"That would explain your accent." She smiled. "Have you lived there long?"

"All my life. I grew up on a small farm."

"Did you attend college there?"

"For two years, but... then I had to drop out... for......personal reasons."

"Oh, I see." Delores cleared her throat. "I'm sorry I have to ask this, but how old are you?"

"Twenty-five. I know I don't look it, but I have my driver's license if you want proof." She fumbled for her purse.

"No, that's all right. I believe you. It's just that you look much younger."

"I hear that a lot."

"What experience do you have? And do you have any references with you?" She held up a few of the papers she'd been reading.

"I hadn't thought about references." She'd never get this job now. Who would hire a college dropout with no references? "I...I don't have any professional experience, not really."

"What makes you think you can handle this job?"

"Well. I...umm...I grew up cooking for my family."

Delores laid a comforting hand on top of Megan's. "Do you have a large family?"

"Yes, I'm from a family of seven."

"Oh, my! Seven. I had a hard time with two!" Delores laughed. "I bet that was a lot of work. But then again, God only gives us what we can handle, doesn't he?"

"I guess." God had certainly given her more than she could handle.

"Farming sounds like a hard life."

"It wasn't easy but we all helped out. Pitched in to get the chores done. We had fun too." Megan smiled, remembering her childhood. "I guess the good times outweighed the bad. And the hard work paid off in later years. I think it builds character."

Delores smiled satisfied with her answer. "That it does, dear. I have a feeling that you have a lot of char-acter. I can see it in your eyes."

Megan had never characterized herself as being strong. The past year had been proof of that.

"What brings you to California?"

"I needed a change." Megan said, tensing up.

"Well, I hope the change is relaxing." Delores patted her hand as if to say everything would be all right from now on. "As I told you on the phone, we need someone right away. Rosa has been filling in, but I'm afraid with the holidays approaching, the burden will be too much for her." Her pale blue eyes filled with compassion as she looked at Megan. "The job is yours, if you want it...but..."

"I got the job!" Megan exclaimed, and jumped out of the chair.

The sudden movement startled Delores. "Oh my, do sit down, dear."

"I'm so sorry." Megan slid back into the chair. "I don't know what came over me."

"That's quite all right. I like to see enthusiasm in my employees." She paused. "As I was saying, I know good people when I see them, and I have a good feeling about you. My instincts are never wrong. However, I must inform you that this job is only temporary. Our cook is coming back in January and we need someone to fill in for the holidays."

"Oh, I see." Megan felt like a balloon that had been pricked with a pin, the air slowly leaking out. "I was hoping for something more permanent."

"Most people are. That's why we haven't been able to fill the position yet."

Megan sorted out the details in her head for a minute. She needed a job now, and they needed a cook. If she took this job she would have a reference for the next job, and what better reference then the Petersons? She'd never find someone else who'd hire her based on her character.

"I can take the job."

"Oh, that will be wonderful!" Delores lit up like a string of Christmas lights. "When can you start?"

"Right now."

"I knew I was right about you." Delores patted her hand one more time. "Why don't we get you settled in the kitchen?"

The spacious kitchen had been artfully decorated in an old world Italian-meets-modern Mediterranean style. The dark wood cabinets and tan granite counter tops contrasted with the light tranquility of the turquoise painted walls. A large island stood in the middle of the room with four white bar stools on one side. The floor was covered with the same terracotta colored tile as the entryway. The light streaming in from the round wall of long rectangle windows bounced off the stainless steel appliances.

"It's usually just me and my husband – sometimes our daughter and her family join us. Although our son lives in the addition, he usually has his own plans for dinner." Delores paused, noting Megan's pale face. "Are you all right, dear?" She laid a consoling hand on Megan's arm.

Megan looked down, hoping to hide her insecurity. She felt less confident about this job position by the minute. *What do these people like to eat*? *I can't cook fancy dishes. Maybe I should have looked for a job at a fast-food joint*. "This place is just so big."

"I know it's overwhelming, but after you've been here a while it'll feel like home."

"I think my whole house would fit in here," Megan stated in awe.

"Don't fret yourself, dear. Once you know where things are you'll feel more comfortable."

"I guess."

"Now, why don't you familiarize yourself with the kitchen? I'll be back in a little bit to check on you." Delores left.

Megan stood in the middle of the kitchen, looking around. She decided to start with the refrigerator.

"Do you need any help?"

Megan spun around to find Rosa standing there. "I didn't hear you come in." She turned back to the refrigerator. "I need some ideas."

"Mr. Peterson has been getting sandwiches for the past few weeks." Rosa winked.

"That shouldn't be too hard to top."

"No, it shouldn't."

Megan found some potatoes. They were old with sprouts growing out of them, but they didn't have any bad spots.

"What are you doing with those?" Rosa asked.

"Peeling them. I can't make mashed potatoes with the skins on."

"Actually, you can. I like them better that way."

"I've never heard of that." Megan paused then asked, "Do the Petersons eat potatoes with the skin on?"

"I don't know. Cookie just uses instant."

Megan wrinkled her nose. "They aren't the same."

"No," Rosa agreed. "But they're easier."

"True, but I'm making homemade ones. Do you want to peel or make biscuits?"

Rosa took the potato out of her hand. "I don't know how to make biscuits."

After Megan made the biscuits, and cut them out, she put them in the oven, and then turned her attention to making sausage gravy. As Megan hurried around the kitchen, she almost tripped over the leg of a high chair. The mere sight of it caused her heart to beat faster and her chest tighten. Closing her eyes, she willed the memory away, refusing to let it take control. But that little four-legged chair cut her to the quick, magnifying the hole in her life.

"Sorry. I thought I put that away." Rosa moved the chair into a corner. "It's for their granddaughter, Crystal."

"How many grandchildren do they have?"

"Two. Billy is four and Crystal is one. The high chair will get a lot of use when Cookie comes back." Rosa paused. "Did Mrs. Peterson tell you why she's off?"

"No."

"Well, now, Cookie is pregnant and developed some complications in the pregnancy and had to be put on bed-rest until she delivers."

"It's good she's taking care of herself. That's the most important thing." Megan's voice sounded strained even to her own ears.

"*Sí.* Do you have any children?"

"No." The pressure intensified, causing a sharp pain to explode behind her eyes. She squeezed her eyes tighter as her thoughts drifted back. Back to her life on the farm and all the sadness that had prompted her to leave. The sound of a buzzer ringing brought her back to the present. *I can't dwell on the past now,* she chided herself. *I have to finish making lunch.*

After Rosa finished helping, she showed Megan to the family dining room. They entered a charming room with a comfortable and casual feel. The Mediterranean decor had been continued, in shades of tan and pale yellow. The chairs were placed about a round oak table with a flowery design carved into the edge. A matching ornate China hutch stood in the far corner. The floor had cream titles and the large, round rug underneath the table was blue with yellow triangles and green palm trees. Small potted palms were arranged in the corners and lots of hanging plants gave a fresh feel to the room.

"The china is in the hutch, and the silverware is in the top drawer. Now, if you don't need anything else, I should get back to my other chores."

"Thanks for all your help."

"*De nada*," Rosa walked away.

Megan was setting the table when Delores entered with a tall, distinguished looking gentleman, with a square jaw and deep-set brown eyes. He was dressed in a three-piece gray suit, which perfectly matched his silver hair. He wore his authority like his suit - it was palpable, and he silently demanded respect.

"Megan, this is my husband, Grant."

"It's nice to meet you Mr. Peterson." She shook his hand, ducking meekly.

"Good to meet you, Megan. So, what's on the menu?"

"Sausage gravy. It's one of my specialties." She was careful to keep her eyes cast down.

"I've never had that. But it sounds interesting." Megan excused herself and came back with the biscuits, potatoes and gravy. After making sure they had everything they needed, she busied herself with cleaning the kitchen. She reappeared a while later to clear the table.

"If I keep eating like this, I'm going to get thick around the middle," Grant patted his stomach. "I'm too stuffed to go back to work."

"I wish you didn't have to go," Delores pouted.

"I know, darling, but I have meetings this afternoon that I can't miss." Looking at Megan he added, "Thanks for lunch. It was delicious."

Megan blushed, and began clearing the table.

Grant kissed his wife and left.

As Megan loaded the dishwasher, Rosa walked in wearing a smile. "The Petersons sure were impressed by you."

"Do you think they really liked the meal?"

"*Absolutámente.*"

"That means absolutely, right?"

"*Sí.* Not only the meal - they like you too. When Mrs. Peterson starts talking about her feelings, she has usually found a keeper. I heard them say you're going to make a fine employee."

"Really?"

"*Sí.* I, too, can tell you will make a good addition."

"How can you tell that?"

"You don't think *Señora* Peterson is the only one with intuition, do you?"

"You have telepathy also?"

"*Sí.*" Rosa laughed as she walked away.

Megan grinned and went back to her work feeling more confident. *Things might work out, after all.*

Megan dressed in a pair of jeans and a blue sweatshirt, braided her hair and left for the bus stop. It was already becoming a routine, and Joe, the bus driver, was now a familiar friendly face.

"Good morning, little missy."

"Good morning, Joe." Megan handed the bus driver her fare and took the seat directly behind him. "I see you forgot my name again."

His round belly jiggled when he laughed. "I didn't forget, Megan. I call all the pretty girls 'missy'."

"Is that so you don't mix up all your girlfriends' names?"

He roared even harder and slapped his knee. "Only you can be so witty this early in the morning."

"I'm just trying to keep up with you, Joe."

"Nah. You have me beat by a mile. It must be that Illinois blood that makes you so sassy."

"Either that or being the second youngest of seven kids. I had to hold my own against my older siblings."

"Well, it certainly prepared you for California life. You fit in real good."

Megan looked to the back of the bus where a young boy sat dressed in black leather. His yellowish-blond hair was spiked up like nails, and he had more metal in his face than a tackle box. "Seeing some of the weirdoes around here, I'm not sure that's a compliment."

"Take it however you want, little missy. But you seem to have settled right in."

"Of course, landing the job with the Petersons helped."

"I told you they were good people."

"You were right."

"Hey, have you checked out the mall yet?" Joe asked impulsively.

"No. I haven't had time."

"The Santa Barbara Bluffs are real pretty too."

"Giving me the run down on sightseeing again?"

"Why don't you do something fun? Have your boyfriend take you out."

"I don't have a boyfriend."

"Well, I'd be more than happy to escort you myself, but I don't think my wife would approve."

"I don't think so, either."

"I have a friend who's divorced. I could set you up with him."

"No, thank you. Romance is the last thing I'm looking for."

"You left your heart in Illinois."

"No. I believe my heart is here beating for you." She put a hand over the left side.

"Oh, Megan. You're too much." His brown curls danced when he shook his head. "So, you're not going home again."

"I believe my stop is coming up."

"All right, I'll let up on the questioning. Someday you're gonna have to fill me in on all the details."

"Maybe." *Just not right now*. She'd dealt with so much lately, that keeping her emotions intact was getting harder to do. Would she ever be able to put the past behind her?

Slipping in the back door, she started a pot of coffee, then mixed the batter for pancakes. "Good morning, dear."

Megan jumped slightly as the voice surprised her. "Oh, good morning, Mrs. Peterson." She poured a cup of coffee and handed it to her new boss.

"Thank you, dear."

She figured they would drink cappuccinos, espressos, or some other fancy blend, but they drank plain old-fashioned coffee, just like everyone else. Actually, she'd been surprised by a lot of things. She had also assumed they would be stuffy, old, ruthless people, who cared about nothing except making money. On the contrary, they seemed to be the kindest, most generous people she'd ever met.

Delores sipped her coffee and watched Megan for a couple of minutes. "I see you're finding your way around here with no problems."

"Yes. You were right, it almost feels like home." Remembering how terrified she'd been four days earlier almost made her laugh. She moved through the kitchen easily and liked working with the modern appliances that made her job quick and easy.

"I was hoping to have a family dinner in two days. Do you feel comfortable handling it?"

"Yes. Of course." She didn't really feel confident, but didn't want to look incompetent.

"Nothing fancy. It'll be Tiffany and William, Steven and his latest date, I'm not sure if Tiffany will bring the children. I'll get back to you on that." Delores fidgeted with her pearl necklace.

Megan breathed a sigh of relief. She could handle a dinner for six. "Your necklace is beautiful."

"Grant bought me this over forty years ago."

"Wow, that's a long time."

"We were still in college, and he worked part time as a bagger in a grocery store. He saved up for months and put these under the tree at Christmas." She smiled wistfully.

"That's so romantic!"

"It also helps me remember the times when we didn't have money. It keeps me grounded."

"I have never met anyone as grounded as you and Mr. Peterson. Guess I haven't thought about you not having money before."

"Oh, yes, a long time ago. Grant worked hard to get where we are today." She smiled. "But I wouldn't trade those years for anything."

"I know what you mean."

"I suspect you do. You remind me a lot of myself when I was younger."

"I do?" Megan sounded shocked. "How? Why?" She didn't feel her life compared to this wonderful woman at all.

"You've had a tough life and you're not afraid of hard work. Most people grow up feeling cheated and bitter about early hardships. You, on the other hand, took that experience and bettered yourself."

"I'm not sure I had much of a choice."

"Oh, you had a choice. It just doesn't seem like a choice because you've always known the path you wanted and worked towards it."

Her path certainly didn't seem clear now – it hadn't for a long time. "I just deal with what life gives me."

"I do know that hard work prepares you for the road of life. It gives you strength to overcome the bumpy parts."

"There are some things in life that nothing can prepare you for." Unwanted tears started to well in her eyes.

"Is there something wrong, dear?"

"No." Megan walked to the cabinet and took out a skillet.

"Are you sure?"

"I really don't want to talk about it." Her tone turned defensive, more so than she'd intended.

"Is there anything I can do to help?"

"There's nothing anyone can do." Megan fled the kitchen, wiping at her eyes. She bumped into Grant in the doorway. "Sorry," she mumbled and continued on her way.

"Good morning, honey." Grant gave his wife a kiss. "What's wrong?"

"I'm concerned about Megan. Something is bothering her."

"Did you ask her about it?"

"Of course, but she didn't want to talk."

"She'll talk when she's ready."

"I know, but you should have seen how sad she looked. Something is wrong. I only want to help."

"I did see she was upset. Sometimes you can't do anything. Some things people have to work through on their own."

"You're probably right," she sighed.

"Stop worrying." He filled his cup and headed to the dining room, where he took his position at the table and opened his newspaper.

Rosa walked in. "Good morning, everyone."

"Good morning, Rosa." Grant said from behind the paper. "Grab a plate and get some of Megan's delicious pancakes while they're still warm."

Megan blushed slightly. She was not accustomed to all the compliments.

"Don't mind if I do - they smell wonderful." Rosa got a plate and sat down.

It seemed so natural for her to be eating with her boss. Megan assumed that she'd done it before. She, on the other hand, kept arguing that she should eat her meals in the kitchen so they could be alone. Both Grant and Delores insisted she eat with them. They treated their employees as part of the family.

"Where is *Señora* Peterson?" Rosa asked.

"I'm right here." Delores walked in, then took her seat at the table. "I was going over menu for the family dinner."

"Is Steven bringing his new girlfriend?" Rosa asked.

"I don't think he keeps them around long enough to be considered girlfriends," Delores groaned. "He just wants to play the field. And he's getting too old to be running around still. He isn't a teenager anymore, you know."

"I know, dear." Grant lifted his shoulders and arched his eyebrows in amusement. Megan tried to refrain from laughing, but a small smile escaped.

Delores took a deep breath and said quietly, "I wish he'd find a nice girl and settle down."

"He will, dear. Give him time," Grant soothed.

"Time! How much time does he need?"

"You know Mrs. Peterson, getting married is a big step, and some people need more time to prepare for it. You wouldn't want him to make a rash decision and regret it later." Megan offered with a small smile.

"Megan is right," Rosa agreed. "Steven just hasn't found the right woman yet."

"Is this your way of telling me to butt out of his life?"

Megan tried to hide another smile, but when she locked eyes with Grant they both started laughing. For a few moments, Megan felt like part of a family. It also felt good to laugh.

Megan felt totally exhausted by the time she reached her room. The memories had been especially strong, constantly tugging her thoughts back into the past. She filled the tub, hoping that a long soak would ease the stress. Flipping the radio on, she scanned the range until she found a classical station. Her emotions were too undisciplined to listen to the country music that she normally enjoyed. The love ballads made her life seem more pathetic, while the lovelorn songs hit too close to home. These songs wouldn't cut it tonight - no castles in the sky, no love forever, no heart-breaks, and especially, no roads leading home. It was much safer listening to music without any lyrics.

The warm, soothing water enveloped her as the bubbles snuggled against the curves of her body. The scent of lilacs filled the air. Her muscles began to relax and her eyelids felt heavy. Closing them, she rested her head on the ledge, feeling the stress evaporate with the steam. The symphony of music quietly playing helped her indulge in a pleasant reverie of happier times. Even though the past year had been a nightmare, it hadn't always been that way. She'd had a normal and fulfilling life on the farm.

Although her childhood had been defined by hard work and discipline, she'd also learned how to have fun. Playing games, swimming, and camping in the summer. Building snowmen and riding sleds in the winter, then coming in to thaw out over Mom's home-made hot chocolate. She loved the lazy afternoon walks in autumn, when the leaves would slip from the treetops, floating down to cover the ground in intricate designs of rust, red, and gold. There were the spring picnics after church. The entire family would go to the lake, park, or some other shaded spot, where they could enjoy nature after a long winter.

Remembering her senior prom brought a smile. She'd felt like a princess in the pink satin gown. It may have been a hand-me-down from her cousin, but at least it hadn't been the old, tattered, blue dress that her three older sisters had worn. Roger had looked so handsome in his tux.

Roger. The name drifted through her thoughts. *I wonder what ever happened to him.* They had dated most of her senior year. She'd received her first real kiss from him, but they'd gotten into a fight and she'd broken up with him. Funny how she couldn't recall what the fight had been about, only remembering her animosity and how she'd stubbornly ignored him until he left for college.

Her own quest for learning landed her in Illinois Center College, but the scholarship had been canceled after her sophomore year. The two years of education, however, had introduced her to astronomy and her love for the outdoors extended into the twilight. She'd met...

No. She stubbornly shook her head, determined not to go there. She wouldn't let the oppressive memories take control. She may have felt lonely sometimes, but she'd always been happy. Only in the last year had the anguish and grief insinuated themselves into her quiet life, waiting patiently in the back of her mind and heart, ready to pounce whenever her guard slipped. Keeping a tight rein on her emotions, she forced her thoughts back to the good times.

"Good morning, Megan." Grant smiled briskly as he entered the kitchen.

"Good morning, Mr. Peterson. How do you want your eggs?"

"Over easy would be nice."

She set the skillet on the stove then went to the refrigerator for the eggs. "Do you know how Mrs. Peterson likes her eggs?"

"I hope I would after forty years of marriage."

Megan looked at him thoughtfully and asked, "How have you guys managed to stay in love that long?"

"I don't know. Determination, I guess."

She couldn't comprehend how two people could stay together by sheer determination. If she'd had more determination, maybe she could have stayed in Illinois. *What's done is done,* she sighed.

"What is that sigh for?"

"I was just thinking about the family dinner tomorrow."

"Don't fret so much. Everything will turn out fine." Grant offered an all-knowing, reassuring smile.

"I hope so." Megan muttered as he left. "My future is depending on it."

Chapter 3

Megan woke up feeling sick. Every movement made her feel nauseous. *How am I going to handle the dinner party?* She wondered. *I'm too sick to move. Lord, please help me get through this day.* She hadn't done a lot of praying lately. God had stopped listening to her, or so she thought. Yet her belief in a sovereign God still existed, even if she was angry with him. She needed the strength of the Almighty to make it through the day.

A long shower helped her feel better. She dressed in the black and white outfit that matched Rosa's, then wound her hair into a bun and secured it with a matching white cap. Although Rosa wore her uniform every day, Mrs. Peterson had said Megan only needed hers on special occasions.

She checked her appearance in the mirror. "It'll have to do." She sighed, and then headed to the bus stop.

"Good morning, little missy." Joe greeted in his usual enthusiastic tone.

"It doesn't feel very good."

"What's wrong? You look like you have one heck of a hangover." He laughed.

"I don't know what's wrong." She handed him a dollar. "But I can assure you it's not a hangover."

"I think you've been holding out on me." He winked. "Tell me the truth. You had a wild night of partying, didn't you?"

"You've got me, Joe. Under this clean, quiet facade is a party girl."

"Go take a seat and try and behave, will ya? I run a clean bus here, little missy."

"I'll try, but can't promise anything." Megan walked to back of the bus. "Hey, Joe," she yelled. "Try to miss the bumps, okay."

"Sure thing, missy."

"Why are you so nervous?" Rosa poured coffee into her cup. "It's only family. They aren't food critics." She took a sip. "This *café* is *fantastico*. Did you buy a different brand?"

"No, I added a little cinnamon to it."

"You're a genius." Rosa winked. "You really should stop worrying over this dinner. If you can transform simple *café*, then you won't have a problem with the food."

"Thanks, Rosa."

"*De nada*." She left Megan to finish the last minute preparations.

"Tiffany is here. Why don't you go meet her?" Rosa suggested.

Megan entered the dining room where she saw a lovely, sophisticated looking lady sitting at the table with Delores. Her dark hair was piled on top of her head, and her thin, rounded features resembled her mother's. Her tailored red suit had a short skirt, which made her long legs look like they went on forever. She seemed more materialistic than her parents, having accented her outfit with several gold chains with rubies and diamonds dangling from them. She also wore a large gold bracelet, and matching hoop earrings. Her long, thin fingers were adorned with jeweled rings and her manicured nails had been painted the same bright red as her outfit. The differences between the two women didn't stop with style - it also extended to personality. Delores was comfortable and easy to be around with a smile and a kind word for everyone. Tiffany, on the other hand, was more rigid and arrogant. Something about her sent a chill up Megan's spine.

"Megan, dear, come in," Delores said, smiling at her reassuringly. "This is my daughter, Tiffany."

"Nice to meet you." Megan smiled stiffly.

Tiffany studied Megan with cold blue, sharp assessing eyes. "So, this is the new cook you've been raving about." Her scrutiny made Megan feel invisible and worthless.

"Would you like something to drink?" She shot a frightened glance at Delores.

"Yes, that would be nice." Delores smiled, trying to ease the tension. "I'll have a cup of coffee."

"What else is there?" Tiffany snarled.

"Iced tea and lemonade."

"I want hot tea with a slice of lemon."

"Yes, ma'am." Megan went to get the drinks, thankful to be out of that room. Tiffany made the temperature drop ten degrees. Megan wondered, as she headed back into the safety of the kitchen.

"How did it go?" Rosa asked.

"I don't want to go back in there. Does Tiffany have ice running through her veins?"

"I know she can be rather abrasive. But she'll warm up to you. Don't worry - the rest of the family is nice." Rosa smiled. "You'll like them, especially Steven."

"Great. I get to meet both kids in one night." She dreaded meeting the son after her brush with the daughter.

"Steven isn't like Tiffany, although he can be quite a handful." She winked, "if you know what I mean. Just don't take him too seriously."

"I have no intentions of taking anyone seriously. From my understanding, he's never been serious about any girl."

"*Sí*. It has been a long time, but he was in love once. It ended badly. I think he's too hurt to ever trust anyone again."

"That's too bad. We all get hurt sometimes. The trick is to get over it and move on with life." Megan said it more confidently than she felt, knowing she hadn't dealt with the pain in her own life. She kept avoiding it, hoping it would go away. "Maybe some-day," she whispered softly.

"What?"

Megan cleared her throat. "Maybe he'll get over it someday."

"*Sí*. He just needs to meet that special person, someone who can mend his heart."

"Yeah," Megan agreed. That's all *she* wanted, peace in her heart once again.

As if on cue, an unfamiliar voice carried into the kitchen. "Where's my Rosa?"

Rosa tossed Megan a wink and replied, "Coming, Steven."

Megan took a deep breath and followed Rosa into the dining room. Upon entering she watched as a tall, well-built man picked Rosa up in a bear hug and twirled her around until his back was to Megan. "You're beautiful as always." His smooth voice filled the room.

"Oh, Steven, you lie through your teeth," Rosa laughed. "But don't ever stop."

Delores gave her son a hug. "It's about time you had dinner with us."

"I know, Mom." He kissed her cheek. "You're looking great."

"That silver tongue won't work on me."

"I'm hurt!" He clutched his heart. "I'm not giving you a line. You really do look great. Besides, I have your genes. For me to look good you have to look good."

"Always the vain one." Delores laughed, reaching up to ruffle his blond hair.

"It's part of my charm." He ran his hand through his hair to straighten it. "Anyway, I just closed some business deals, now I'll have more free time."

"Monkey business?" Delores laughed.

"No, Mom, I swear." He crossed his heart with his finger.

"Steven, I swear, you're never going to grow up."

Voices drifted in from the hallway. Tiffany entered, talking to a beautiful, large-breasted, brunette.

Grant followed behind both women. "Look who I found in the hallway," he announced. He set his briefcase on a small table by the door.

"Mom. Dad. This is Priscilla." Steven introduced them, his back still toward Megan.

"I'm pleased to make your acquaintance." She looked like a supermodel, but had an unfortunate nasal whine that grated on the nerves.

"How do you do?" Delores raised a questioning brow to Steven as if to say, where did you find her?

Although Megan was curious to see Steven's face, she felt content standing in the corner, watching the family. Even though Rosa had joined in the conversation, Megan felt like an intruder. She didn't know what the protocol was for this situation.

However, Grant eliminated the problem when he noticed Megan standing in the shadows. "Why are you hiding in the corner?"

"I didn't want to interrupt." Megan quietly stepped forward.

Steven turned around and Megan's heart plummeted to her stomach. His smile and brown eyes sparked a flame of recognition. "You!"

"Ice queen?" He blinked, making sure the vision was real and not a dream. "Well, isn't this a small world?" He appeared to recover his composure.

Megan felt dazed and her knees began to wobble. "Excuse me." She made an exit to the kitchen.

"Wait!" Steven followed, not wanting her to get away again.

Delores and Grant looked at each other, and then turned to Rosa - the one person who knew everything that happened in the house.

Rosa shrugged her shoulders. "I haven't a clue as to what's going on."

Steven watched Megan lean against the counter for support, pressing her lips together so tightly that they looked white. He couldn't tell if she was shocked or angry. Finally breaking the silence, he said, "So you're the new cook."

"What if I am?"

"Hey, I didn't follow you in here to fight."

"Why did you follow me?"

Steven casually walked over, leaning his hip against the counter. "I wanted to get your name." He flashed that smile that most people found hard to resist.

She stiffened her back and replied, "I thought you already figured that out."

"We never exchanged names," he said, confused.

"Ice queen."

A chuckle slipped out before he could stop it. "Look, I'm sorry." Noticing the animosity of her stare he continued, "I shouldn't have called you that. But you must admit that you were pretty cold to me."

"I believe you used the word frigid."

"Okay. Yes, I did. I'm sorry about the whole incident on the beach. I handled your excuse badly, and I apologize."

"Tired. I told you I was tired." Megan repeated aggravated. "If you took it as an excuse that's your problem."

"Call it whatever you want, it still means the same thing."

"So what? You've never had a girl turn you down before?"

"Actually, I haven't." His seductive smile was back. "In fact, most women find me irresistible."

"Like your little doe-eyed Bambi in there."

"Her name is Priscilla."

"I'm surprised she can remember a three-syllable word name."

"Do you like fights? Because you seem to pick a lot of them." His easy-going smile seemed to ignite her anger even more.

"You started it." She crossed her arms defensively.

"You called me a playboy first."

"Are you familiar with the terms conceited, arrogant, or self-centered?"

"All right." He held up his hands to stop her. "I don't want to fight. I already apologized. Since you work for my parents, I propose that we should at least be on a first name basis." He tried making it sound logical.

Megan pressed her lips together and bit her tongue so hard she tasted blood. There were a lot of things she wanted to tell him, but her name wasn't one of them. "Don't you have enough girls' names to worry about? How do you keep them all straight, anyway?"

"I said I didn't want to fight." His soft voice took a sharp tone. "I live here. Am I supposed to call you *the cook* whenever I see you?"

Realizing that making an enemy of her boss's son would be a big mistake if she wanted the Petersons to give her a good job recommendation, she swallowed her pride and reluctantly said, "Megan Black."

Steven clasped her small hand in his. It felt soft and warm. "Pleased to meet you, Megan. I'm Steven Peterson." He brushed a light kiss across her hand.

His soft lips scraping across her knuckles sent shivers through her body, leaving her knees weak. *What's wrong with my legs?* They didn't seem able to hold her up tonight. "It's nice to meet you too, Mr. Peterson."

Mr. Peterson. The displeasure passed briefly in his eyes, but never extended to his smile.

Megan withdrew her hand, grabbed the pot holders off the counter, and took the roast out of the oven. "I have to get dinner on the table." What she really needed was some distance.

"Megan, could you do me a favor?"

"That depends on what it is?"

He continued cautiously. "You don't have to be so formal with me. My friends call me Steven."

"I hardly know you. I wouldn't consider us friends."

He planned on rectifying that situation. "Could you call me Steven, anyway? Mr. Peterson is my dad."

"If that's what you want." Megan started mashing the potatoes. "I guess that would make you Steven 'Persistent' Peterson.

He chuckled. "And, you would be Megan 'No' Black."

Her smile seemed to melt him on the spot. Intrigue grew until it rooted itself deep into his heart. What was this fascination? It went beyond beauty, even beyond the sexual attraction he normally felt for most women. There was a strange feeling in the pit of his stomach. An aching? A need? He didn't know what, just that he'd never felt it before. Something stirred inside his chest.

Megan didn't like the way he watched her. Even with her back to him, she felt his eyes tracking her every movement. Needing some time to think, she asked, "Can you take the potatoes and roast to the table?"

"Sure." He took the platter of meat she held. Then, sliding his left arm around her waist he stepped so close she could smell the faint scent of musk and see his muscles flex under the white dress shirt. Her heart felt as if it were beating in her throat. Unintentionally holding her breath, she jumped back when his chest brushed against her. She wanted to run away but the stove halted her progress. His lips came so close to her face that she noticed how the upper lip was slightly thinner than his bottom one. *What is he doing?* he frantically wondered.

"Are these the potatoes?" He whispered, holding up the bowl he'd taken from the counter next to the stove.

"Umm, yes." Her thoughts were all jumbled with him standing so close.

"I'd better get the food out there."

Megan nodded in agreement.

Steven muttered a curse to himself as he walked away. The slightest caress of her body sent him into a tailspin. He knew he would have to proceed with caution - not just for his sanity, but because he noticed fear in her eyes.

Megan exhaled a sigh of relief as she watched him leave. "What is wrong with me?" she chided. "One touch from him and I jump like a scared rabbit." She couldn't afford another encounter like that. *Who does he think he is, anyway*? He had no right invading her personal space, boss's son or not. He was baiting her. Waiting to see what she'd do. Well, next time she'd do more than...*nothing.*

"Steven tells us that you know each other." Delores smiled.

"We...uh, ran into each other on the beach. I'd hardly say we *know* each other." She glanced over and saw the amusement in Steven's eyes. "I'd describe it as more of an encounter."

Priscilla stiffened, shooting her a look that seemed to be warning Megan to stay away from her man.

"Whatever it was, can we eat?" Grant asked.

Everyone was enjoying the meal, which made Tiffany skeptical. Her parents were raving about the bread.

"It's my mother's recipe." Megan informed them as she sliced it.

"Is her name D'Angelo?" Tiffany elevated her small round nose a few degrees.

"Who's that?" Priscilla asked perplexed.

"D´Angelo Bread on Gutierrez Street." Tiffany rolled her eyes. "It's the best bakery in town."

"I don't shop much for bread," Priscilla confessed. "I'd rather shop for clothes and shoes." Running a manicured hand through her long, dark hair, she added, "I need to be dressed in the latest fashions if I want modeling agencies to take me seriously."

"You have a live one there, don't you, little brother?" Tiffany said.

Priscilla - missing the sarcasm - flashed into an award-winning smile. "People are always saying how smart I am for a model."

Steven, sensing an open door for a rude remark by Tiffany, decided to intercept, "You don't need brains with a body like yours."

Delores groaned and rolled her eyes while Tiffany laughed. Megan tried to hide a smile as she loaded the slices of bread into a basket.

"Looks just like the bakery's bread." Tiffany said as she passed the basket.

"Tiffany, why must you be so rude?" Delores asked.

"I'm not being rude. I just don't see what the big deal is about the bread."

"You're the one making it into an issue," Steven remarked, passing the basket to Priscilla.

"No thanks, I'm counting carbs. I have to watch my figure," Priscilla passed the basket while leaning over, giving Steven full view of what was inside the low-cut dress. "Steven likes his women thin."

"Steven likes any type of woman that will date him," Tiffany snorted.

"Where is your husband, Sis? Did he get tired of hearing your nagging?"

Tiffany glared. "You know he's been sick. He wasn't at work today either."

"Really...you two still squabble like five-year olds." Delores reprimanded.

"Let us eat our dinner in peace," Grant said.

After dinner Rosa and Megan brought the desserts to the table. Rosa's presence helped eliminate some of the tension from Tiffany.

"Everything is delicious," Delores said.

"Megan, you have outdone yourself." Grant smiled.

"Unbelievable!" Tiffany snarled. "What is this stuff on top of the apple pie?"

"A crumb topping made with oatmeal and brown sugar."

"Well, I like regular pie crust."

"Then try one of the other pies," Delores said.

"Mom, you know I don't like blueberries or cherries."

"How about some mousse?" Rosa offered.

"Chocolate breaks me out."

"Of course, all sugar is out for me." Priscilla put her hand on Steven's knee. "Did you make anything with Splenda? That is the only sweetener I like."

"No. I wasn't aware of any special dietary needs." Megan inhaled a shaky breath. Between Tiffany and Priscilla, this dinner was turning into a disaster.

"It is your job as the cook to be prepared for these things," Tiffany chided.

"Yes, ma'am."

Megan watched as Priscilla leaned closer to Steven. Her hands seemed to be all over him. Steven had put his hand under the table as well. She couldn't tell if he was holding her hand, or trying to stop hers from roaming.

Megan finished serving dessert then returned to the kitchen. She fought back the tears. She'd worked hard on this dinner, wanting to prove she could handle the job. Now, because of the Tifanizer and Barbie's sister in there, everything was ruined. She'd be lucky to keep this job, let alone get a good recommendation.

Arriving the next morning, she started the coffee then went to the pantry to retrieve the waffle mix. Walking back to the island, she noticed Steven standing by the counter half-asleep, watching the coffee brew. The blue velvet robe gaped open, revealing small patches of blond hair scattered across his chest. The clinging material defined his tall, slender physique. He was a handsome man, she couldn't argue with that.

"Megan?" He sounded surprised. "I didn't know you were here."

"The coffee will be done in a few minutes. I just put it on." She took a bowl from the cupboard, measuring the mix into it.

"Mom is usually the designated coffee maker." He yawned and stretched, "Then, again, Cookie never comes in this early."

"So I've been told." She got the milk and eggs.

Steven watched her work. "How can you be so perky this early in the morning? What time did you get up?" he asked with another yawn.

"Five thirty."

"That's awful early. I have a hard enough time getting up now. I stay out too late to be a morning person."

"You're a night owl."

"I guess. What does that make you?"

"An early bird." She poured some batter into the hot waffle iron.

"But, why get up that early?"

"To get the worm."

"What?"

"'The early bird gets the worm.' Don't tell me you've never heard that expression."

"No, but then again, I don't want any worms."

"No one really gets worms." She rolled her eyes. "It means if you want something, you have to be there first to get it."

"Sounds too intellectual for me. At least let me have a cup of coffee before you start getting so deep."

"You asked."

"No. I just wanted to know why you get up so early." He poured the coffee into his cup.

"I'm just used to it. You have to be up early on a farm. There's a lot of work to be done."

"You're a farm girl?" He had trouble picturing this petite, beautiful, babe as farm material.

"Do you have a problem with that?" She stiffened. "If it weren't for us farmers you wouldn't have food to eat. I realize that on the pay scale we're lower than you, but..."

"No! I didn't mean that." Steven tried to defend himself. "I just meant that..."

"You're better than farmers."

"No," he snapped. "If you could quit telling me what I think long enough to let me explain..."

"What's the racket in here?" Grant asked as he entered the kitchen. "I can hear you two all the way upstairs."

"I don't know. Why, don't you ask the ice queen? She won't listen to anything I say."

Megan glared at Steven as she got a mug, filled it and handed it to Grant. "I'm sorry, Mr. Peterson."

"Thank you, Megan." He took the cup, noticing his son's clenched fists.

"I better get ready for work," Steven stated. "It's too early in the morning to be fighting." Grabbing his coffee, he stalked out of the room.

Megan remembered the waffle. She lifted the lids, noticing the brown was a little too dark. *Great!* The confrontation with Steven not only irritated her, now it had her running late. How was she supposed to concentrate on work with him hanging around? She threw the burnt waffle away and finished the rest. She took the food to the dining room table.

Steven walked in and announced, "I'm going to work."

"Don't you want to eat first?" Delores asked.

"I'm not hungry this morning, Mom." He scowled at Megan, then left.

"First time he's been on time, let alone early," Grant snickered. "Things are going to get interesting around here."

They finished their breakfast in silence, Grant stood, thanked Megan for breakfast, and gave Delores a kiss.

Megan wondered why he always thanked her for the meals. After all, that's what he paid her to do. She was the cook, and *only* the cook, according to both of his kids. If she didn't stop letting Steven get to her like this and find a way to control her temper, she might get fired. What was it about him that set her on edge? "My life is getting complicated, again," she muttered. *Lord, why can't anything ever be simple?*

"Good morning, Rosa."

"How did it go last night? I got the impression that you and Steven know each other." Rosa couldn't hide her curiosity.

Megan knew she had to fill her new friend in on all the details. Rosa would more than likely find out, anyway. She always knew everything that went on in the house.

"Well, what happened?" Rosa asked eagerly. "Come on, I need details."

"It's really no big deal."

"Oh, yeah?" Rosa arched a dark brow.

Megan filled her in on the story.

"That's incredible!"

"Our meeting again?"

"No, that you turned him down in the first place."she laughed.

"Rosa, you're incorrigible."

"I like to think of myself as a hopeless *rómantica*."

"I'll go for hopeless," Megan replied. "But I don't know about romantic."

Rosa threw a dishtowel at her. "You probably took him by surprise when you rejected him."

"Whatever." Megan sighed.

"Still, I find it *fantastical*, the way you met again. Almost like fate."

"I don't find it romantic or fantastic. I find him irritating," Megan fumed. "Do you know he had the audacity to call me frigid because I wouldn't have dinner with him?"

"I told you he's a handful," Rosa said.

"Among other things," Megan snorted. "He's also a spoiled, inconsiderate, and selfish..." she stopped abruptly. Rosa had worked for the Petersons a long time, and was very loyal to them.

"You don't have to be concerned about what you say. It will stay between the two of us - after all, we are friends, no?"

"Yes, we're friends." Megan smiled. "But I don't want to put you in the middle."

"Don't worry about that," Rosa reassured her. "I like being in the middle."

Delores stood in the doorway of the kitchen, without making a sound. Megan noticed her as she put the casserole in the oven. "Mrs. Peterson, I didn't hear you come in."

"I know. I didn't want to give you the chance to escape." Delores pinned her with a sharp stare. "Is there some reason you're avoiding me?"

"What makes you think I'm avoiding you?"

"Because you haven't said more than five words to me and every time I come in the room you make a quick exit."

"I've been busy, that's all. I didn't mean to hurt your feelings."

"My feelings aren't hurt, but I want to know what is bothering you."

Here it comes, Megan silently groaned. The line of questioning she'd been trying to avoid. She didn't know what to say. She couldn't blurt out, *your beloved son is a big pain in the butt!*

"Does it have something to do with Steven?"

Megan had too much respect for her to lie, but complaining about her son wouldn't be a good career move. "Look, I don't want to step on any toes, so..."

"There are no toes being stepped on." Delores said adamantly. "If Steven is bothering you, I'll have a talk with him."

"It's not that he's bothering me. We just don't seem to get along."

"If he's behaving inappropriately, I'll put an end to it."

"He hasn't done anything inappropriate." Megan assured her.

"Sometimes Steven can be very persistent. And his actions can be misinterpreted."

"I'm sure Steven is always a gentleman. He just irritates me."

"Honey, welcome to the club. He's been irritating me since the day he was born." Delores laughed.

Megan pondered this warm, caring mother. She clearly loved her children, but didn't have any illusions about their shortcomings. Still, Megan couldn't figure out how two of the sweetest, most generous people she'd ever met could have raised such spoiled, inconsiderate, and selfish children. Hadn't they inherited any of their parents' good qualities?

"Megan, I don't want you walking on eggshells around us. If you and Steven aren't getting along, or if you're getting along famously, that is your private business. It won't affect your job."

"Thanks, Mrs. Peterson, I needed to hear that." It was amazing how comfortable she felt around the Petersons. In a way, she felt closer to them than her own parents. Although her parents had been good providers, they had never established a strong emotional bond. Was that what was lacking in her life?

Steven walked in to the kitchen, stopping in the doorway to watch Megan as she prepared a salad.

She looked up to find him standing there. "Oh, I thought you were..."

"My mom."

"Yeah."

If Steven had any sense, he'd let her stay angry, but for some reason commonsense seemed to be lacking these days. "I don't know what I said this morning to upset you, but I didn't mean to imply anything negative or demeaning about farmers. I certainly don't think I'm better than anyone else is. My sister has the corner on the market." Steven paused, unfamiliar with apologizing to anyone, he now found himself doing it twice to the same person. "I just wanted to tell you I'm sorry if I offended you."

Do you know why I got upset?"

"No."

"How can you properly apologize if you don't know what you did?"

"You could tell me." He waggled his blond brows.

Megan stopped tossing the salad and stared at him. "For one thing, I didn't like your tone. Secondly, I'm not a girl. Although I assume that's what you're used to dating."

"So, are you mad at my tone of voice or the type of women I date?"

"I could care less who you date, but you're not going to treat me like one of your lovesick, air-headed supermodels who swoon at everything you say."

"If I didn't know better, I'd say you were jealous."

"Jealous!" Megan snorted. "You're so full of yourself."

"Me? Seems to be the other way around."

"How absurd!" She couldn't be jealous, could she? "I don't like being called a girl. I'm not a girl."

Steven's eyes slowly raked over her body. Starting with the old worn out tennis shoes, and traveling up her long blue jean-clad legs. His eyes swept past her shapely hips and flat stomach resting briefly on the folded arms underneath the large curve of her breast. His eyes seductively roamed over the blue, cotton fabric up to the creamy white skin on her neck. He wanted to taste that spot. It reminded him of white chocolate. His gaze flowed past the hollow of her throat and up to her titled, pointed chin. Sliding past soft pink lips, and a small perky nose, his eyes finally stopped roaming, staring into her dark blue eyes. He could stay lost in those pools forever.

"Oh, sweetheart, I'm well aware of the fact that you're not a girl." His hushed voice raced along every nerve ending causing her to flinch.

"Then, don't call me one again." She tried sounding in control, but heard the quiver in her voice. "And, I'm not your sweetheart."

"I'm sorry, it won't happen again." Recovering his emotions, he asked, "Will you forgive me?"

His mere presence disturbed her. She felt it would be safer staying mad at him. Yet his apology seemed sincere. And she did work for his parents. "All right, let's call a truce."

"Not so fast." Steven held his hands up. "We can't have a truce until both parties have a compromise."

"What do you want?" she asked, realizing that was a loaded question.

You, his heart screamed, but he replied, "I promise not to call you girl or sweetheart, and you quit picking on my girlfriends."

He was right; she had no business saying anything about the women he dated. It's his life. "All right. I'm sorry I said anything negative about your girlfriends. It won't happen again." She gave him a sappy sweet smile.

Steven smiled. "Good business deals need to have some kind of contract to finalize them."

"Like what?"

He knew he should stay away, but something pulled him toward her. "We could seal our deal with a kiss?" He took a step closer.

Megan grabbed the salad bowl, blocking his advance. "Why don't you take this to the table and I'll get the casserole." She smiled triumphantly. "Your word is good enough for me."

Steven took the bowl, staring at it, mumbling under his breath. Every time he made a move, she blocked him.

Chapter 4

Megan spent the next couple of days trying to get into a new routine which included one more person in the kitchen. Although Steven's easy-going personality and light-hearted laughter pulled at her heart strings, she had to keep a distance. One thing about a big kitchen was that she could create diversions and move away from him whenever he got too close.

Megan thought Steven looked like a hunter tracking his prey. Good thing she was quicker and smarter than him. She assumed Steven had little experience in *chasing* anyone, whereas she was a pro at avoidance.

Steven helped Megan carry the food to the table.

Delores looked at Steven while taking her seat. "I think Megan should start giving you cooking lessons. You might as well make yourself useful since you're in there all the time."

Grant choked on his iced tea. "Steven in the kitchen? He doesn't know the difference between a spoon and a spatula."

"Like you do?" Steven said.

"I know my way around the kitchen."

"Sure."

"I do," Grant insisted. "I used to cook your mother dinner when we were dating."

"A lot has changed since the dinosaurs died." Steven laughed. "It's been years since you were in the kitchen."

"Maybe so, but I can cook circles around you."

"Is that a challenge?"

"Are you up to it?"

"You bet I am." Steven met the challenge head on. "Are you up for giving some cooking lessons, Megan?"

What? She needed to spend less time with him not more. Why on earth would Mrs. Peterson suggest such a thing? However, she didn't want to look incompetent. "As your mom said, you might as well help out instead of just taking up space."

"Feisty little thing, isn't she?" Grant chuckled.

"Yeah, she's a real fireball." Steven smirked.

"I thought I was the ice queen."

"You've thawed out some."

"Thawed out!" Megan laughed. "You make me sound like a frozen steak."

"Only top grade." Steven winked. "I like steak when it's done over a flame. It comes out hot, tender, and juicy."

"But if you leave it on too long it gets burned."

Steven's heart lurched at the triumphant smile spreading across her face. Her lips were parted ever so slightly, and he yearned to kiss them, just one time. "It takes getting burned a time or two before you get it right," he reasoned. "But when you do, the burns are worth it."

"If you want to keep getting your fingers burned, all the more power to you. I, on the other hand, stay away from flames that are too hot to handle."

"I've never seen a fire that a man couldn't get under control," Steven said.

"You need to watch the news more. They're always covering fires that burn for days or even weeks, ruining everything in their path."

"They eventually get put out. Don't they?"

"Eventually," she admitted. "But there's a lot of damage left behind."

"The damage can be repaired. Even Mother Nature replenishes herself. No impairment is forever." Steven's gentle tone tugged at her damaged heart.

"I'm not so sure about that." Sadness replaced her smile. "Some damage is too severe for anything to recover."

"I agree with Steven." Delores responded. "I think time heals all wounds."

"Maybe, but I'd just as soon stay away from something that would hurt me." Megan looked directly at Steven. "And that includes fire."

"There is no fire involved in this contest." Noting the tension in her tone made him wonder if she believed he would hurt her. "Just teach me in the manner most comfortable to you."

"That's the problem," Grant teased, trying to lighten the conversation. "She doesn't feel comfortable with you in the kitchen at all."

"What are you trying to imply?" Steven questioned. "That I'll burn the place down?"

"You're the one talking about fire."

"When is this contest taking place?" Delores interceded.

"As soon as our son learns to cook." Grant chuckled. "That may be never."

"Laugh while you can, old man, because when I get done with you, you'll wish..."

"Now, boys. Play nice," Delores warned.

"How soon do you think you can teach him to cook?" Grant inquired.

"That depends on how fast he learns," Megan said.

"In that case, it'll be next year," Grant taunted.

"Ha, ha. Very funny," Steven cocked his head. "I'll bet that in three weeks I'll cook better than you."

"Oh, no. Three weeks is Thanksgiving," Delores reminded them.

"Then two."

"You can't learn to cook in two weeks," Grant scoffed.

"I say I can. And I will."

Megan grinned at the two men trying to outdo each other. They were both determined and persistent. The two qualities she feared most in Steven.

"Is two weeks enough time?" Grant asked Megan.

"I'll do what I can." How had she gotten herself into this mess?

Steven met Megan in the kitchen the following morning. He'd already started the pot of coffee.

"You're up early." Megan glanced at her watch.

"I'm eager to begin my first lesson."

"I thought we'd start tonight."

"Nope. We're starting right now." Steven rubbed his hands together. "What's for breakfast?"

"That's up to the cook. What do you want?"

"Let's see. We should keep it simple since I'm new at this."

"How about pancakes?"

"Sounds too complicated."

"Eggs and bacon?"

"Simpler."

"Can you handle a bowl of cereal?"

Steven watched her lips twist in a silly grin. "Are you always sassy this early in the morning?"

"What if I am?" She poured coffee into a cup.

"Seeing as I have to work with you, I'd like to know what I'm up against."

"I can see that I'm up against someone who can't cook an egg." Sipping the coffee, she nearly gagged. "Or make coffee."

"That bad, huh?"

"Let's just say that I could tar the road with it." Megan dumped it down the sink. "How about we make a fresh pot together?"

Together. He liked the sound of that.

"How much coffee did you put in here anyway?"

"I filled it up."

She held up the scoop. "It only takes five of these." After starting a fresh pot, she set the skillet on the stove. "Get the eggs and bacon..."

"You're bossy too." Steven grinned.

Ignoring the remark, she went about preparing breakfast. Steven mostly watched, although he found it hard to concentrate on cooking. He watched her lips part as she explained the delicate process of frying eggs, and wondered what it would feel like to have them move under his. Deciding to stand behind her so he wouldn't be distracted by her mouth proved futile also. Even with the smell of bacon hanging heavy in the air, her flower-scented sweetness filled his senses. His focus was now drawn to her neck where he intently watched her pulse raise and lower the creamy, smooth skin. Shaking himself, he tried to focus on cooking.

She wasn't ready yet. He felt her tense up whenever he stood too close. But he was determined to win her over.

"Did you see how I did that?" Her voice brought his attention back to the frying pan, where he saw the eggs had been perfectly flipped.

"Umm. Yeah."

"Get me that plate before they overcook."

He handed it to her then dropped four slices of bread in the toaster. Steven felt a sense of pride as they carried breakfast to the dining room. He hadn't done a whole lot, but he'd enjoyed the lesson and couldn't think of a better way to start the day.

"There you are." Rosa placed her hands on her hips. "I just found out about the bet and the cooking lessons."

"Does anything go on in this house that you don't know about?"

"Not much."

"Do you have this place bugged?" Megan set a plate in the dishwasher.

"Something like that." Rosa winked. "When is his first lesson?"

"What! Something you don't know?"

"One of my spies must have slipped." She poured a cup of coffee. "What gives?"

"For your information, he had his first lesson this morning."

"How did it go?"

"All right, but, you should have tasted the coffee he made."

"Steven made *café*?"

"If that's what you want to call it. It was way too strong, with grounds floating in it."

"Sounds awful." Rosa checked her cup.

"Don't worry I already made a fresh batch."

"Good, I need this real bad."

"Late night?"

"*Sí*. My youngest boy is sick, and I was up several times with him." Taking another sip of coffee, she stated, "Steven has never spent much time in the kitchen before. I think these lessons are an excuse to be with you."

"No way," Megan denied the possibility. "It's pure testosterone. He wants to beat his dad. Besides, it wasn't even his idea. Mrs. Peterson suggested it."

"Oh, I see." Rosa grinned. "*Señora* Peterson is playing matchmaker."

"Absolutely not! There's nothing going on. Nothing at all."

"Maybe not yet. But, you don't know Steven. When he wants something, he doesn't stop until he gets it."

"Persistent." Megan echoed his words from the beach.

"*Sí*. That sums him up."

"He can't always get what he wants." Even though a part of her wanted to be close to him, it wasn't right. Distance was the answer. Keeping the physical distance would be next to impossible now. She'd have to maintain an emotional distance. If she failed people would get hurt.

"We'll see." Rosa smiled.

Steven made a beeline to the kitchen. "Starting without me?"

"Just preparing some things ahead of time."

Steven took a can of soda out of the fridge. "You like being prepared, don't you?"

"Of course." She looked bewildered. "Doesn't everyone?"

"Not me." He popped the top. "I'm a spur of the moment kind of guy." Taking a long drink, he asked, "Have you ever done anything without planning it first?"

"Once."

Steven saw something flash in her eyes. An expression he didn't recognize. "And what was that?"

"I moved here."

"You packed your things and moved to California without any thought beforehand?" He hadn't expected her act of spontaneity to be so drastic.

"That's exactly what I did." Her shoulders stiffened with firm resolve, ready to defend her actions.

"That took a lot of courage."

The tenderness in his tone melted her resolve. "It's the hardest thing I've ever done."

Steven saw the pain flash briefly in her eyes. He might have missed it under the smile she held if he hadn't been watching so closely. *What happened?* He wondered. *What could have been awful that she picked up and left hastily?* He stepped closer and Megan heard the shallow rhythm of his breathing. Her own breathing accelerated and she heard her heart slamming against her chest.

"Do you always hide your pain with a smile?" He gently rubbed his thumb across her bottom lip.

The shock, almost electric, made her jump back, her smile faded, fear replacing the sadness in her eyes.

70

His ability to see beyond the smile and recognize the pain left her feeling defenseless. The smile had always hidden the suffering. How could a total stranger see through the disguise when her own friends and family hadn't? Feeling shaky and out of control, she headed for the stove. "We need to get dinner started."

Steven stepped back, giving her room to pass.

"The potatoes need to be peeled and the chicken breaded." She hoped her voice sounded more in control than she felt.

"You're trying to change the subject."

"I'm trying to get dinner done and teach you how to cook. You only have two weeks – do you think you'll be able to learn in such a short period?"

"Megan, why don't you ever talk about yourself?

"There isn't much to tell."

"Why did you leave Illinois?"

"It doesn't matter. It's in the past."

"You left your past in Illinois and moved here to start over?"

"Exactly."

"And you don't want to talk about your past at all?"

"No!"

"Sometimes your past has a way of catching up with the present. It could ruin your future."

"If you're done analyzing me, Dr. Freud, I'd like to get dinner done sometime tonight." She handed him a potato. "Start peeling."

"How?"

She didn't know if he was kidding or not. She showed him how to use the peeler. After the potatoes were peeled and cut, she washed them, filled the pan with water then set it on the stove. "When the potatoes are cooked, we'll drain them, add some butter and milk and mash them."

"That seems like an awful lot of work."

"They taste better than instant."

"How do you make instant?"

"You bring the water to a boil, add the potato flakes and stir."

"That's more my style - simple and easy."

"The easy way isn't always the best way." Her life was proof of that. Leaving home had seemed like the easy way out, but it sure didn't feel that way now.

"Are you going to tell me why you left in such a hurry?" Steven didn't seem ready to drop the subject.

"No." The word raged through her body, hitting her heart with a thud. "Why can't you leave this alone?" She went to the sink and started filling it with soapy water.

"Because I want to know."

"It's none of your business. Quit being so nosy." She started washing the pans, scrubbing furiously as she pushed back the memories. The more she tried to hide her feelings the more intent he seemed on drawing them out. "Leave me alone!"

Steven watched her attacking the dishes and realized he'd pushed too far. She wouldn't open up. Not yet. "I'm sorry, Megan, I didn't mean to upset you."

Needing some fresh air to clear his head, he went out to the gazebo and sat on the swing. The cool breeze, lightly scented by roses and gardenias from the nearby garden calmed his jangled nerves. The scent reminded him of Megan. Unlike the overpowering perfumes worn by most of the women he dated, hers was a subdued, almost natural fragrance.

The mere thought of her turned his heart upside down and his mind inside out. He'd never felt so twisted in his life. The sound of her voice or the scent of her hair was enough to send his pulse racing. Every night he drifted to sleep with the image of bright blue eyes imprinted in his mind.

A faint smile tugged his lips when he compared Megan to all the Barbie dolls he'd dated. They were flirtatious, shallow, and materialistic. Most women practically threw themselves at him, desperately bidding for his attention. They laughed at every joke and clung to every line he handed them. Megan was different. She'd not only declined his dinner invitation, but also left him standing alone on the beach. Only, by some quirk of fate, they had met again.

Already he'd concluded that she was a complicated woman. How could one person be so many different things at the same time? She could be strong and gentle, self-reliant and dependent, sassy and genteel. She wore a smile on her face while pain obviously throbbed in her heart. She'd be serious one minute and funny the next. He found her infuriating and his serenity at the same time. She was everything that made his world go 'round.

"What's happening to me?" he asked, raking his hand through his hair.

The next day, Megan worried that Steven might still be upset. He hadn't come in for dinner, and left without breakfast this morning. "He's going to starve to death if he keeps it up," she muttered. "Listen to me, I sound like his mother. What do I care if he doesn't eat? He's not my responsibility." She slammed the dishwasher door and turned the machine on. "Oh, great. Now I'm talking to myself."

"Then stop it."

Megan spun around to see Rosa with her coat on. "Sorry, didn't hear you come in."

"Of course not, you were too busy talking to yourself."

"I wanted an intelligent conversation."

"*Sí*. Carry on, I won't disturb you anymore. I'm going to the store and Mrs. Peterson is out. Can you answer the phone while I'm gone?"

"Sure, no problem."

"*Gracias*, I shouldn't be long."

"Do you ever leave the kitchen?" Steven joked when he came home for lunch.

"When I'm not cooking."

"It seems like you're always cooking." Steven took a carrot off the cutting board.

"It's my job." Megan looked at him. "Are you hungry?

"Starving."

"That's what you get for missing dinner and breakfast."

"Why, Megan, if I didn't know better, I'd think you cared." He winked.

"Don't read too much into it."

"What's that mess you're making?"

"Strawberry shortcake dough." Sprinkling flour on the counter, she dumped the dough out. A puff of flour flew up, landing on her shirt.

"Oh!" She looked at her pink sweater spotted with flour. "You'd think I'd remember to put my apron on before my hands are yucky."

"Where is it?" Steven said with a grin.

"Hanging on a hook in the pantry."

He got it, slipping the loop over her head, standing close enough to feel the warmth of her body. Closing his eyes, he deeply inhaled the flowery fragrance, letting it fill his senses and flow to his soul. "You smell good," he whispered as his hands gingerly wrapped the strings around her slim waist, slowly, seductively crisscrossing them in front of her stomach before sliding his hands around to her back.

Shivers vibrated up her spine from the sensual motion. The heat from his body seemed to engulf her completely, she feared she might incinerate in front of him, falling to a pile of ashes at his feet. "I think you smell the quiche," she whispered. Her mind felt more scrambled than the eggs she'd used for the dish.

"No, it's you." His breath felt warm, skimming across her neck. "You smell like flowers." He slowly tied the apron strings into a bow, resting his hand on the small of her back, waiting, *wishing*. When she didn't voice any objections, he slid his hands over the curve of her hips.

The seductive movement ignited her repressed passions, sending her world wheeling. She felt his lips press against the tip of her ear, then kiss a trail down the side of her slender neck.

"Oh, Megan," he whispered as he nibbled the spot he'd been dreaming about.

His lips gliding along her skin caused conflicting sensations. Her breathing became irregular, and the beating of her heart accelerated, pounding so hard she could hear it. The pounding grew louder and louder until it sounded like a... buzzer. Megan's eyes flew open

"The quiche." She grabbed the pot holders off the counter, flinging dough everywhere and ran to the oven.

Steven moaned as he threw his hands up in the air. Needing time to cool down, he stalked out of the room.

"Talk about being saved by the bell," she muttered. "Things are getting out of control." Frustration boiled. She'd better find a way to turn down the flame before someone got burned.

Chapter 5

"Mom, where are you?" Tiffany entered the room juggling a chubby little girl on her hip, with a diaper bag and purse on the opposite shoulder. She stopped short at the sight of Megan, causing a little boy who'd been following close behind to run into her. He wrapped his arms around Tiffany's legs and poked his blond head out like a turtle, curiously watching to see what would happen.

Tiffany looked ready to topple over in her spiked heels, but quickly regained her balance and her poise. She managed to look sophisticated in a white pants suit, even with a baby in her arms and a toddler tugging at her legs. The sight astonished Megan, who hadn't pictured Tiffany as mom material.

"Where's my mom?"

"She went out."

"Oh great! She's supposed to watch the kids for me." She ran a finely manicured hand through her dark shoulder-length hair. "Where's Rosa? Maybe she can watch them?"

"She's shopping."

"Shopping! I can't believe mom forgot about my meeting." Not talking to anyone in particular, she asked, "What am I going to do now?" Searching for an answer and not finding one she sighed, "Guess I'll have to cancel the meeting." Dropping the bags, she set the baby on the floor and squatted beside the little boy. "Billy, Mommy has to go make a phone call. Can you stay here and watch your sister for me?" Her tone instantly warmed as she spoke to him.

"Okay, mama." Billy nodded.

Tiffany stood and looked at Megan. "I hate to miss this meeting, but it's too late to find a sitter now."

Megan smiled at Billy, who looked up at her with big blue eyes. "Hi. My name is Megan."

"I'm Billy." He beamed.

"And this must be Crystal." Megan bent down and tickled the little girl's stomach, making her squeal with delight. Her dark curls bobbed up and down and her blue eyes sparkled.

"She's my sissy."

Megan felt a twinge of compassion for Tiffany. Watching her with the children made her seem less obnoxious and more human. Maybe she had a heart after all.

"Tiffany, I'd be more than happy to watch the children until Rosa gets back."

"What?" She was stunned. "You hardly know me or the children."

"I know. But you're in a jam, and I can help, if you want me to. It's just a thought."

"I hate leaving the children with someone they don't know. Then again, this is an important meeting."

"I understand your concern but I'm sure Rosa will be back any minute."

"I don't know." Tiffany pondered the situation. "Billy, would you like to stay here with Megan until grandma or Rosa get home?" He nodded his head vigorously. "All right, Mommy will be back in a couple of hours." She kissed him on the cheek. "Be a good boy and help Megan with your sister, okay?"

"Okay."

Tiffany rattled off some instructions about Crystal's bottles and diapers, wrote down her cell phone number, and then hurried on her way.

Megan watched Crystal struggle to her feet and take a few shaky steps before tumbling to the floor. The little girl's frustrated wail cut through Megan's soul. Tears glistened in her eyes. She listened to the crying for a few tormented moments before pushing the pain away.

"Are you all right?" Megan scooped up the baby. "Did you fall down?" Her heart wrenched as she cuddled the little bundle. Oh, how she wanted a child. *If only....if ...*Megan shook her head. "Not now," she scolded herself. "I have a job to do."

Crystal rubbed her eyes with a chubby fist. "It's time for your nap, isn't it?" Megan checked her watch. "Billy, do you know where your sister sleeps?"

"Upstairs. I show you." Megan grabbed the diaper bag and followed his short legged waddle up the steps and into the nursery.

"Thanks. That was quite a climb for you." Megan set Crystal in the crib. "Let's go put a movie in for you." She followed Billy back downstairs. Rosa walked in just as Megan put the movie in the DVD player.

"'Osa." Billy yelled, running into the familiar open arms.

"Billy. I didn't know you were coming today." Rosa looked at Megan. "Is Tiffany here?" "She had a meeting and apparently, Mrs. Peterson forgot she was supposed to babysit. I offered to stand in until you got back." The movie started playing and Billy ran to the couch, jumping up and down. "Doggies." He pointed to the Dalmatians on the screen. "Yay!"

"Billy, no shoes on the furniture. Sit down," Megan gently coaxed. After getting Billy settled she said, "I'm going upstairs to put Crystal down for her nap."

"All right. I'll keep an eye on him." Rosa ruffled his hair.

"Stop dat." He pushed her hand away.

Megan found Crystal playing with a stuffed animal. "Hey, what do you have there?" She picked her up. "Shall we check your diaper before you go down?" Crystal cooed and made a small string of sounds in response.

After changing the diaper, Megan sat in the rocking chair. It had been a long time since she held a baby. She kissed the top of Crystal's head, inhaling the scent of baby shampoo. It was amazing how the simplest sound or scent made the empty void in her life expand. She fought against the overwhelming feeling of loss.

Closing her eyes to regain some composure, she softly hummed a familiar lullaby while fighting the memories that threatened to emerge. Determined to stay in control, she continued to sing, "Rock-a-bye baby."

Steven heard her singing as he passed by and stopped to listen. Her voice was soft, low, and slightly off key, but mesmerizing all the same. Propping his arm against the doorjamb, he flung his suit jacket over his shoulder. A warm sensation filled him as he watched the scene unfolding in front of him. The safest place a child can be is cradled in loving arms. *I wouldn't mind being in those arms myself,* he mused.

As the melody continued drifting through the air, she whispered the name, "Laura," in a raspy tone. A few tears glistened on her cheeks. Steven attentively watched as the pained expression crossed her face. *What had she been through? And who is Laura?* He wanted to help and intended to find out what was wrong. One way or another.

Megan laid Crystal in the crib, gently pulling the blanket over her tiny body. "Sweet dreams, little one."

Steven ducked into another bedroom and went undetected as she walked down the hall.

Megan went downstairs and found Billy in front of the television. "Do you want to help bake some cookies?"

"Oh, yes." He jumped off the couch, taking the hand she offered him. They went into the kitchen and got all the ingredients. Billy stood on a chair so he could reach the counter.

"What's this?" he asked as he dumped white stuff into the bowl.

"It's flour."

Billy sniffed. "It doesn't smell like flowers."

"Not like the flowers in a garden. This is special flour just for cookies."

"What's this?"

"Sugar. It makes the cookies taste sweet."

"Why is it brown?"

"It's brown sugar."

They finished mixing and scooped the dough onto cookie sheets.

"Megan?"

"What."

"How comez these don't look like cookies?"

"They will after we bake them." She slid the trays in the oven, flipped on the oven light and set the timer. Billy peered into the window to watch them bake. Megan bent down and watched with him. He slipped onto her lap and put an arm around her neck.

"Know what?" he asked.

"What?"

"I like you."

"I like you too."

"Know sumping else?"

"What else?"

"I tink you're pretty."

"I think so, too," Steven agreed.

"Unca Seeven." Billy jumped into his arms.

"Hey, sport."

"We made cookies."

"I thought I smelled something good."

"I go get 'Osa." Billy wiggled and Steven put him down. He bounded out of the kitchen.

"Pretty smart kid." Steven smiled at her.

"Yeah," Megan agreed.

"He's four and already knows a pretty woman when he sees one."

"I wonder who taught him that?"

"Are you implying that *I* would teach my nephew how to pick up women?" he arched an eyebrow in mock annoyance.

"I'm not implying anything. I'm flat out saying it."

The timer buzzed and Megan jumped. Would she ever be able to hear that sound without thinking about Steven? As she put the cookies on a wire rack to cool, she noticed Steven watching her. "Why are you home so early?"

"Dad said I needed all the extra time in the kitchen I could get."

"He did not." Megan laughed. "Did he?" She wouldn't put it past Mr. Peterson, the way he'd been needling his son.

Steven grinned. "Not in those exact words, but that was the gist of it."

"The two of you are really something." She laughed.

Steven bypassed the smile. Studying her eyes, he noticed the sadness. She couldn't hide her pain. Not from him. He wanted to ask her about Laura, but Delores, Rosa and Billy came into the kitchen.

"Grandma, they look like cookies now." Billy spotted them on the counter.

"They sure do look good," Delores said.

"And taste even better." Steven stole one and took a bite.

"Steven, they're hot." Megan scolded. "Can't you wait?"

"I'm with Steven." Rosa grabbed a cookie too. "Oh, he's right. These are delicious."

"Me want one too." Billy pouted.

"All right, but be careful, they're hot," Delores warned.

Megan went to the refrigerator, got the milk, and started pouring for everyone.

"The woman knows what I like." Steven winked.

After taking the glass she offered, he asked, "How did you become such a good cook?"

"Lots of experience."

An abrupt sound of gurgling noises, and a whimper drew everyone's attention to the baby monitor sitting on the counter. "I'll go get her," Megan quickly offered, wanting a few minutes alone. Her emotions were too tightly wrapped to keep under control. She needed to unwind for a few minutes.

"That's all right, dear. I want to spend some time with my granddaughter." Delores left and a few minutes later her voice came through the tiny box. Megan flipped it off.

"Hey. What'd you do that for?" Steven asked.

"It's not polite to eavesdrop," Megan answered.

Delores reappeared, holding Crystal, and Tiffany followed her.

"Mommy." Billy ran to give her a hug.

"Hi, sweetheart." The term of endearment struck Megan as odd. She would never have thought Tiffany capable of using such language. "How were they?" she asked Megan.

"Good as gold. Crystal took her nap and Billy helped make chocolate chip cookies."

"Chocolate chip...my favorite." Tiffany smiled.

"Aren't you afraid there's too much of something in them and you'll get fat?"

"Steven, shut up!"

"Good comeback, Sis."

"Don't you have some little tart waiting to go out or something?" A crooked smile touched her dark red lips.

"No. All your friends are married now."

Daggers shot out of her ice-blue eyes, before she could reply, Grant entered the kitchen. "I see the party is in here."

"Granpa."

"Hey, squirt. Do I smell cookies?"

"Yeah. With flowers and sugar, it wasn't white it turned brown. Then we put them in the oven."

"Can I have one?" Grant asked.

"You haf ta say pease," Billy reminded him.

"Peeease."

Billy grinned.

Grant gave Tiffany a kiss. "Are you staying for dinner?"

"No. I just came to pick up the kids."

"Why don't you stay? William can meet you here." Delores suggested.

"Mom, I'd love to, but I'm beat and William is probably tired too." Tiffany glanced at Grant. "You know how hard Dad works him." She gave her mom a quick kiss on the cheek. "How about that cookie?"

Steven grinned and handed her one. Tiffany took a bite. "All right, Billy, we have to go."

"Can we take some cookies home for Daddy?"

"Sure, honey."

Megan wrapped the cookies up and handed them to Billy. He gave her a hug.

"Thanks again for helping out today, Megan." Tiffany reluctantly acknowledged her before she left. Although, she'd been grateful for Megan's help, she still didn't seem to trust her.

"These cookies are wonderful," Grant said, one in each hand. "No wonder everyone is congregating in here."

"I need to get dinner started." Megan informed them.

"Yes, *we* do," Steven said.

Megan silently groaned. Would she ever get any downtime? Her jangled nerves were stretched so tight they might snap.

"I guess that's our cue to leave," Rosa said.

"Guess so." Grant snagged a few more cookies before leaving.

"What do you want me to do?" Steven asked.

Leave! She secretly wished, but out loud said, "I don't care."

"Megan, what's wrong?"

"Nothing," she snapped. *Everything*.

"Don't tell me that," he said, exasperated.

"I don't want to talk about it."

Steven raked his hand through his hair, making it stand up in blond spikes. He swore he felt gray hairs popping up. "Look, I don't want to fight with you."

"Then don't!" Her eyes warned him not to continue. But he couldn't let it go. *Could he?* "Are you upset over what happened at lunch?" He had to know. "Because you felt the attraction just as much as I did."

"Don't be absurd!"

"If I overstepped, then I'm sorry."

"Stop. Just stop. It's not what happened earlier, although it *won't* happen again," she assured him. "I have other things on my mind right now." She rubbed her temples, where a throbbing pain had formed. Her heart shattered into tiny pieces like broken glass. Steven's invitation to let it all out sounded tempting, but better judgment told her that wasn't a good idea. One second in his arms, she'd lose it completely. If he penetrated her shield, who knows what would happen? She could fall apart later when she was alone.

"Why won't you open up to me? If it's not about me, then what is it?"

"Please, leave me alone."

Steven saw her resistance dissolving. "I won't hurt you, Megan. I want to help."

"I'm not afraid of you, but there is nothing you can do."

"Does it have anything to do with your leaving Illinois?"

"Yes." Megan squared her shoulders. "I really need to get dinner started. If you want to stay and help, fine, but stop badgering me." She went to the refrigerator and took out two eggs.

"Who is Laura?"

"Laura!" Megan gasped and dropped the eggs, jumping back as they splattered on the floor. "How did you hear that name?" Her voice trembled.

"You said it when you were singing to Crystal."

"How dare you!" Her temper flared. "You have no right, eavesdropping on me."

"I didn't eavesdrop." He defended. "I walked pass the nursery and heard you singing."

"It's none of your business. Do you hear me? None of your business." She screamed. "Why don't you leave me alone?"

"What's going on?" Grant asked, entering the room.

"Nothing." Steven sighed.

"Megan, are you all right?" Delores asked, following her husband.

"I...I'm fine," she lied. Tears glistened in her eyes and she quivered like a stalk of wheat caught in a tornado.

"Megan, take the rest of the night off," Grant gently urged her.

"But dinner..."

"We'll go out."

She couldn't hold it together anymore. "I'll clean up this mess first."

"I'll get it, dear," Delores offered. "You go home and get some rest."

"Steven, we want to talk to you in the study," Grant said sternly. "Honey," he said to his wife, "meet us in there when you're done here," he added in a more subdued tone.

When Delores got to the study a few minutes later, Grant was seated behind the oak desk while Steven sat in one of the chairs positioned in front of it. Delores chose to sit on the black leather couch.

"Now, Steven, what is going on?" Grant demanded. "Every time I turn around the two of you are fighting."

"Dad, I just..."

Grant held up a hand to halt his protest. "I can't have this again. Stay away from Megan. Is that clear?"

"No. I was only trying..."

"Is that clear?" Grant's voice boomed. "We can't afford another harassment charge. I know your weakness for pretty women, but if you can't keep your hands off Megan, then we may have to let her go."

"That isn't fair," Steven protested. "You never hear me out. You wouldn't listen to me about April, and you're not giving me a chance to explain now. I'm not harassing Megan. I'm trying to help her."

"Help her with what? You seem to be doing nothing but upset her." Grant ran a hand through his thinning hair and inhaled deeply. "Steven, listen, you said you didn't harass that maid, and I believe you. I just think sometimes you come on too strong, and women take it the wrong way. I don't want another misunderstanding like the last one."

"Dad, if you would listen instead of accusing me all the time."

"I'm not accusing you of anything."

"It's not what you think. April purposely set me up on that bogus harassment charge so you would pay her off. And you did." Steven raked his hand through his hair. "Megan has been upset over something all night, and I wanted to find out what was wrong. I never touched her, not without her permission."

"Have you touched her at all?" Grant sat up straight.

Steven exhaled. "Yes, but..."

"Steven!" Grant bellowed, his face turning red. "When? Where? Did you have sex?"

"No!" Steven yelled back. "It's really none of your business, anyway."

"None of my business? She is my employee and you're my son. I won't be able to keep it out of court next time."

"It wouldn't have gone to court last time because it never happened, but you wouldn't believe me."

"Grant, Steven, please settle down. You're yelling loud enough to wake the dead." Delores walked over and put a hand on Grant's shoulder. "Let's stop rehashing the past, it's over and done. Now both of you, calm down."

Grant leaned back in his chair, covering his face with his hands. "What happened between the two of you?" His voice strained to stay in control.

Steven remained silent.

"Well?"

"Nothing."

"You said you touched her. Did you kiss her?"

"Not exactly."

"What do you mean, not exactly? Either you kissed or you didn't." Grant's voice rose in pitch and volume.

"We got interrupted, and I don't want to give you the details."

"Steven, if April schemed to set you up, I would think you'd be careful not to fall into that trap again." Grant advised.

"Megan isn't setting a trap for me. If anything, she's avoiding me," Steven sighed. "Do you really believe she would do something like that? She is the most honest person I know."

"Steven's right, dear. Megan would never do that. As a matter of fact, she defended Steven the other day when I asked her if he was bothering her."

"What?" Steven jumped to his feet. "How dare you talk to her about me! Did you tell her what happened with April?"

"That's enough, Steven," Grant said firmly. "You don't speak to your mother that way."

Steven inhaled and exhaled slowly. "Look, I'm thirty-six years old. I don't need Mommy and Daddy watching over me."

"You do when you're in *our* house, and it concerns us," Grant countered.

"All right. Look, I'm sorry." Steven felt his muscles tightening and shifted his head from side to side until he heard his neck crack. "Can we please get off this subject?"

"Steven, it's not that we don't trust you. We do." Delores assured him.

"It doesn't feel like it."

"I'm sorry if you think I overstepped, but your father is right. The two of you are always arguing, and I wanted to find out why. I just wanted to avoid another situation like the last one."

"The last situation happened sixteen years ago," Steven reminded them. "When is it going to be forgotten?"

"I'm sorry, Steven, but I wanted to help." Delores told him.

He paced around the room. "Mom. Dad. I know you're trying to help, and I'm sorry I blew up." His parents had always had his best interests in mind. They had supported him through his rebellious teenage years and loved him unconditionally, even though he got into plenty of trouble. They were tough when they had to be, but overall were loving, understanding, and protective parents. Steven knew they were only trying to protect him.

"I'm worried about Megan." Steven admitted.

"Why?" Delores questioned.

"I can see the sadness in her eyes when she thinks no one is watching. Something awful must have happened to make her leave Illinois."

"I saw the same thing when I Interviewed her," Delores added. "I've tried to talk to her a couple of times myself, but she doesn't want to talk about it."

"How do I get her to open up to me?"

"You can't make her trust you. She'll come to you when she's ready," Grant said.

"I feel so helpless." Steven sighed.

"Your father is right, honey. When Megan wants your help, she will ask for it. If you keep pressing, you'll only push her away."

"I found that out tonight."

"Whatever that poor child is going through, she's not ready to face it yet." Delores shook her head sadly. "My heart goes out for her."

"Mine, too, Mom."

Grant and Delores shared a glance across the room, both realizing that their son, for once in his life, had become serious about a girl.

"Just be patient, son. That's all you can do," Grant said.

"Let her know that you're there for her, when *she* is ready," Delores added.

"In other words, back off?"

"Just try to be a good friend," Delores encouraged.

"Sometimes being a friend means giving a person space," Grant added.

Steven thought about his parents' marriage and how they always backed each other up. They could count on the other for support. Even now they simultaneously gave him the same advice. He wanted that in his own life. He wanted someone to come home to. Someone to stand behind him, the way his mom always stood behind his dad.

"I know you're right," he sighed. "It's just so hard to do...nothing." He walked over to the window, staring out into the black night. It didn't matter that he couldn't see anything. In his mind, he saw Megan sitting on the beach with her feet buried in the sand, the setting sun casting a golden halo around her.

His pulse quickened at the mere thought of her. He'd never felt this way before. Women had always been objects to him, someone to go out with and have a romantic night or two. They were a decoration on his arm for special events, and then they were gone. Although most of them had wanted the relationship to continue, he had severed the ties before any emotional attachments began. He'd never trusted another woman after April. Something about Megan seemed different, even trustworthy.

"Has Megan ever mentioned the name Laura?" Steven inquired.

"Not that I recall," Delores wrinkled her brows. "Why?"

"I happened to overhear the name, when I asked her about it - she dropped the eggs and started screaming at me." He looked at Grant. "That's what the yelling was about."

"I'm sorry I jumped all over you, but I do hope you understand my position."

"Yes, Dad. I do understand." He had made a mistake as a kid, a big one, but it still ruled his life, even after all these years. "Next time give me a chance to explain."

"Deal." Grant stuck out his hand and Steven grasped it.

Megan pulled the covers over her head, closed her eyes and wished she could hide forever. Hide from the past, from the world, and most importantly from Steven and his probing questions.

Hiding, she was good at it. After all, that's why she'd moved to California. But hiding from the past wasn't good enough anymore - she wanted to bury it. And for some reason Steven seemed intent on making her dig it up.

Why can't he leave me alone? She groaned. It had taken a whole year to entomb the memories, and no matter hard she tried to forget, they always found a way to be exhumed. The unforgiving ghosts of her past were always lurking under the surface. She'd have to face them someday. Just not today.

Gathering some mental strength, she dragged her aching body out of bed and into the shower. The soothing water revived her, now if only something could revive her broken spirit. Baby-sitting had made her feelings of resentment stronger, which made her guilt and grief flare up.

What was I thinking, offering to baby-sit? Why did she always try to do the right thing, even when it hurt? Because she'd always lived her life by the golden rule - 'do unto others as you'd want them to do unto you.' But sometimes she went too far.

Chapter 6

The smell of coffee greeted Megan when she walked into the kitchen. Pouring a cup, she figured Mrs. Peterson must be up.

"I guess you get to be the guinea pig this morning."

Megan spun around to find Steven standing in the doorway, his wet hair slicked back. The damp robe clung snugly to his chest and biceps.

"Did you make this?"

"Just the way you showed me."

The smell of soap and musk filled her senses as he approached. The oxygen seemed to dissipate when he stood so close. Moving to the cupboard, she took a few deep breaths.

He smiled, looking pleased with himself. "Pretty good for my first time?"

"Actually, it's your second time. The first attempt was a disaster, remember." She handed him an empty mug.

He seemed to have deflated a tad as he sampled it and said, "Whatever. This is my first pot that actually tastes like coffee."

"I'll give you that," she laughed. "You did a good job."

"I had a good teacher." He held up his mug and Megan clanged her cup against his. After an awkward silence, Megan took the eggs out of the refrigerator.

"Megan, can we talk?"

She stiffened in preparation of the bombardment of questions he'd undoubtedly fire at her.

"I don't want you to drop the eggs again." He took the carton out of her hands. "Why don't we have a seat?" He motioned toward the small table in the corner of the kitchen.

"Steven, I don't want to...."

"Please, listen." He held his hand up to halt her. "I want to say that I'm sorry for upsetting you last night. I shouldn't have pushed so hard. I only want to help. I want to protect you and..."

"But there's nothing you can do."

"Shah." He touched his finger to her lips. "You keep saying that, but I think I can do something."

"What?"

"I can be your friend."

"My friend?"

"Yes. Don't misconstrue this as a pass or anything else. I'm offering you a shoulder to cry on whenever you need one."

"I don't know what to say."

"Just say we can be friends."

"Only friends?" she asked suspiciously

"That's it. Unless, of course, *you* want more." He quirked an eyebrow. His sense of humor came out even when he was being serious.

"No. Friendship is enough." She laughed. "Does that mean you'll stop harassing me?"

"It means I'm here whenever you're ready to talk."

"I'll take that as a yes."

"Friends?" Steven held out his hand. He knew touching her would be dangerous, but he wanted to feel her soft skin, if only for a moment.

"Friends." She shook his hand. "Now, we better get breakfast made."

Megan listened to the music on her player as she cleaned. It helped to pass the time and made the chores more fun. The gentle melodies always soothed her soul, especially when her life was full of chaos. Filling a glass with water, she wistfully stared out the window as the sad love song continued playing.

A hand on Megan's shoulder made her jump, dropping the glass.

"Sorry. I didn't mean to startle you," Steven said.

She pulled the ear buds out and hung them around her neck. "What?"

"I called your name but you didn't hear me. You seemed pretty absorbed in that song."

"Yeah, it's one of my favorites."

"What are you listening to?"

"Country?" She wiped up the mess. "What kind of music do you like?"

"I'm more of a rock and roll guy."

"I think country has more soul. I like songs that reach out and grab you."

"I like songs you can move and groove to." He wiggled his hips.

"We definitely have different tastes in music."

"Maybe you can teach me more about your music as you teach me to cook." Steven wanted to learn everything about her. There was something about her he couldn't resist. He'd do anything and give up everything to be near her.

"That won't be necessary. You can learn to cook with rock and roll as well as country."

"I wasn't thinking of changing my music. I've never really given country a chance. I might like it."

"I'm sure it will be too slow for you." Everything in his life seemed to be fast paced, including the women he dated. She'd never fit in. *Never!*

"Despite what you think, I do like some things slow." He dropped his tone to a sultry whisper. "Slow isn't always bad."

"You don't seem the type who likes anything slow." Warm sensations shuddered through her body as his sexy tone hit her heart.

"I can change, Megan."

"I'm not asking you to." She hesitantly looked into his dark eyes, filled with desire. "Are you going to help me with lunch?"

"Lunch?" Her question broke the spell. "Umm, yes, lunch." He reminded himself to keep his feelings in control.

"Here chop this up." She handed him an onion.

"How?"

"Like this." She sliced the onion and showed him the size she wanted.

He took over the chopping and watched her preparing the rest of the meal. "Do you like cooking?"

"I guess. It's not something I think about. I get hungry, I cook something to eat."

"But cooking seems to come from your heart. You always take so much care and the extra time instead of the easy way. Your food is really great because of it."

"Thanks. I cook the way my mother taught me. She used to tell me 'the way to a man's heart is through his stomach.'"

"Then why don't you have a man?"

"What makes you think I don't?"

He gently touched her third finger. "No ring."

"That doesn't mean I don't have a man," she said defensively.

"True," he agreed. "But that would explain things."

"Like what?"

"Why you haven't cooked me dinner yet?"

"I cook you dinner every night."

"No, I mean a romantic dinner with soft music and candlelight. Someplace secluded and quiet...like my place."

"You live here."

"The addition does have its privacy."

"Yeah, it's really secluded with your parents hanging around."

"It's more like an apartment."

Megan twirled her eyes in skepticism.

"Then we could have dinner at your place."

"I don't have a kitchen."

"Now that is the most original rejection I've ever heard." He tried to make the statement lightly, but Megan heard the tone of resentment in his voice.

"I'm not lying. I'm staying at a hotel."

"Why are you in a hotel?"

"I don't have enough money saved for an apartment yet."

"How long have you been living there?"

"Since I moved here." Megan tried to hide her teary eyes, as memories pushed to the surface.

Steven gently put his hand under her chin and tilted her head up until she looked him square in the face. "I'm here for you, Megan," he whispered. "I'd move heaven and earth to help you."

"I believe you would." She smiled through the tears.

"I wish I could stop your pain." He encased her in his arms.

The warmth of his arms felt so comforting that she cuddled deeper until her resolve started slipping. Realizing she'd fall apart in another second or two, she mustered enough strength and backed away. "You can't take the pain away."

He gently blotted a tear off her cheek, and mulled over a possible solution to one of her problems. He'd talk to his parents later, but their help was guaranteed. They wanted to help her as much as he did.

Megan locked the hotel room door, leaning against it for support, feeling unable to take another a step. The bag of groceries felt more like cinder bricks instead of the junk food she'd just purchased, although she liked to think of it as comfort food. Forcing her legs to move, she deposited the bag on the night stand then sat down on the edge of the bed and waited. She waited for the pain, for the guilt, and most of all, for the tears.

The battle had come to an end. She no longer had the strength to keep fighting. The anguish and grief had chipped away at her heart until there was nothing left. Suppressing her emotions and ignoring the feelings for so long only magnified the sorrow now.

She felt her sanity slipping away as the heartache reared its ugly head. The hurt and sorrow propelled themselves forward with such vigor and vitality that Megan lost all self-control.

Tears rampaged like a raging river, spilling down her ghostly white checks. Trembling hands muffled the sobs escaping from her tormented soul. She fell across the bed, burying her face into the pillow, crying uncontrollably for what felt like hours.

Feeling faint as the room dizzily spun around, she moved on wobbly legs to the window, unlocked it and pushed with all her might, but it didn't budge. Using the heels of both palms she pounded against the stubborn frame until a last-ditch heave forced it open. Megan gratefully inhaled gulps of the cool, crisp air. Pressing her hot, wet forehead against the cool glass she looked out into the dark, eerie night. How had her life turned so bleak?

"Why me?" she cried in agony. "What have I ever done to deserve this?" *How could a loving God do something so cruel?*

As if in answer, a jagged bolt of lightning pierced the dark sky, and a low rumble of thunder sounded. Then a few raindrops blew in. It seemed like Mother Nature also felt her loss. Did God really care, or understand her devastation? *I lost a son once too,* came the gentle reply. *I understand.*

"Then why did you make me go through this?" She screamed into the storm. "Why?" Fighting harder against the overwhelming loneliness and pain, she desperately tried to make the panic flee. Avoidance had been her best weapon against the sorrow, but tonight she'd have to do the one thing she'd been dreading. Tonight, she'd have to face her demons, and unleash the grief that had been locked away. It was the one thing she didn't want to do. The one thing she *couldn't* do.

A knock on the door startled her. "Who could that be?" A quick glance at the clock said it was eight-thirty." Probably the desk clerk. She wiped her eyes and opened the door.

"Steven," she gasped. "What are you doing here?"

"I need to talk to you."

"How did you find me?"

"Ralph. He remembered the hotel from when he drove you here to collect your clothes."

"When I washed them at your parents' place. I forgot about that."

Steven waited a moment. "May I come in?" Fat drops of rain danced all around his tall frame.

"Oh, yes, of course."

He stepped inside, running a hand through his damp hair. "Are you okay?"

"What makes you think something's wrong?" She closed the door.

"You've been crying."

"My allergies are acting up."

"Your eyes aren't swollen and red from allergies," he protested. "Besides, how do you explain this pile of tissues and the drenched pillow?"

She crossed her arms and said nothing.

He pointed to the opened bag of cookies. "If I'm not mistaken, Mom munches on junk food whenever she's upset too."

"Are you Sherlock Holmes?"

"I'm a friend who wants to help."

"And I've told you countless times, you can't do anything."

"Maybe not, but keeping everything bottled up inside won't help. You need to talk to someone."

Megan almost felt like giving in to his request, but she couldn't risk the flood of emotions that engulfed her. "I can't." She shook her head. She'd decided a long time ago to push everything out of her mind. She wanted to forget. "I've had a strenuous day and I can't handle this right now."

He took her hands. "You don't have to go through this alone."

"Yes, I do." She let the warmth and strength of his hands sink into her heart.

"Why?" Steven asked. "Why do you insist on going through this all by yourself when there are people who care about you?"

"Because you can't do anything. I keep telling you that, but you won't listen."

"How do you know I can't do anything?"

Megan felt her legs growing even weaker and her resolution disintegrate. She moved to the bed, wearily sitting down. She'd have the breakdown in front of Steven if she didn't get a rein on her emotions. She'd always taken pride in not showing her emotions to anyone. But her stamina had dwindled, and exhaustion had zapped her emotional strength, leaving her only one option - she started crying again.

"Can you bring back the dead? Can you give me back my daughter?"

Her sobs grew louder and the anguish mounted until she screamed out in agony.

The ear-shattering, heart-wrenching scream snatched the life out of Steven for a second or two.

"Daughter?" He cautiously sat down beside her, unsure of what to say next. He searched for sympathetic words, or something profound to say, but what could be comforting when you've lost a child?

He wrapped his arms around her, softly whispering, "I'm sorry." He held her close, feeling her shoulders heave with each fervent sob. "Was her name Laura?"

Megan nodded, hiccupping as a couple of breaths caught in her throat.

"What happened?"

The anguish in her eyes mixed with confusion. She wanted to confide in him, to talk about it, but didn't know how. She'd kept the truth locked away so deep and for so long that she was afraid to let anyone know her secrets. Yet, she was tired of dealing with pain all by herself.

"I carried her for nine months and everything was normal," she began. "I even felt her kick the night before I went into labor. When my contractions started the next morning I... I thought everything was fine. But when I arrived at the hospital my baby was... she was...dead."

"Oh. Sweetheart, I'm sorry."

Megan buried her face in the crook of his neck and let out all the pent up sorrow and anger she'd been holding in. He handed her the box of tissues along with her bottle of water.

The liquid felt good against her parched throat. He seemed to know what she needed without being asked. She was grateful he'd come. She'd never be able to face the truth without his support.

"Feeling better?"

"A little."

"Is that why you left Illinois?"

"Yes." Her long hair fell over her shoulder when she nodded. "I couldn't live with the memories any longer." She took a shaky breath. "I thought if... if I left, the pain would go away ... but ... but ..."

"The pain didn't go away?"

"No." The tears came down her cheeks in cascades.

Steven wondered how someone so small could have shouldered this oversized load all by herself. *Where is the father*? he wondered. *Why had she been facing this alone*? He had lots of questions but didn't dare ask them, not wanting to put more strain on her. Being on the verge of a breakdown, any added pressure might push her over the edge.

Her shoulders stopped moving and she slumped against him. Steven saw her eyes were closed. He brushed some strands of hair away from her wet face, and then lightly dropped a kiss on the top of her head. Protectively holding her close, he gently laid her down and pulled the covers up.

With the back of his hand he delicately wiped some lingering tears off her check. "You don't have to face this alone anymore," he whispered.

After sending Ralph home and calling his dad to inform him of the situation, he decided to take a quick shower. While standing under the spray of water his thoughts automatically drifted to Megan. He had no idea how to keep his mind off her.

He wrapped a towel around his waist and went to check on her. She was thrashing and crying in her sleep. He jumped when she suddenly sat up.

Megan began screaming.

"Megan, it's me."

"Steven?"

"It's all right. You had a bad dream." He sat down on the bed, putting an arm around her.

"More like a nightmare." Her breaths came in short, raspy gasps.

"About Laura?"

"Yes, the night she... she died." Megan drew in a deep, shaky breath, praying that the panic attack would stay away.

"What happened?"

"It was awful," she cried. "I can't bear to remember that horrible day."

"I know, sweetheart, but it will take you longer to heal if you don't deal with the pain."

"I don't care. I want to forget it!" She beat his chest in frustration. "Why did she die? Why weren't things normal?"

"I don't know."

Finally opening up to him, she explained how she arrived at the hospital thinking everything was fine. It wasn't until the nurse hooked up the fetal monitor that they suspected something was wrong.

"When they couldn't hear the baby's heartbeat, the doctor ordered a sonogram. When he flipped the machine on, I could see the gray outline of her body, but her heart wasn't beating. I could see where her heart should have been, but nothing was there. I knew she was gone before the doctor said anything, but I waited anxiously, praying that my baby would be all right –that the doctor would say there had been a problem with the machine, or that the heartbeat was just too faint to see, but that it was there." The memories cut through her soul, leaving behind the wounds of loneliness and grief. "After a long time, the doctor finally said, 'I'm sorry the baby isn't moving...

and there's no heartbeat.' I keep hearing those words over and over again until I want to scream."

"It's all right." Steven held her.

"It's not all right." She cried. "My baby is dead. After all the pain I went through, I left the hospital with empty arms. I spent ten hours in the worst pain of my life for nothing. Nothing! Do you have any idea how it feels knowing you'll give birth to a dead baby?"

"No." He didn't even know what it felt like to give birth to a live baby. "Why don't you try and get some sleep?" The hysteria in her tone made him uncomfortable.

"No. I'll have the dream again."

"Then we'll sit here for a while."

Megan finally noticed his state of undress. "Why are you in a towel?"

"I took a shower."

Observing the beads of water glistening on his bronzed skin she replied, "I can see that. But why?"

"Because I'm staying the night."

"Oh, no, you're not!" She jumped off the bed.

"Megan, I just..."

"And where do you plan to sleep?"

"There is only one place." He shifted his eyes to the other side of the bed.

"In your dreams."

"There's no couch, not even a chair."

"You're not sleeping in my bed and taking advantage of me."

"I'd never do that and you know it," Steven snapped. "I've never taken advantage of any woman."

"I didn't ask you to stay the night."

"I don't think you should be alone. You're too upset."

"I can handle myself, thank you very much."

"Yes, I can see you've done a great job so far."

His words hit her like a slap in the face. She'd done her best over the past year. She may have made some mistakes, but she was dealing with them now. Her lower lip trembled and any semblance of composure disappeared.

Steven suddenly felt like a brute. "Look...I thought you could use a friend, that's all." He gently touched her cheek. "I have no ulterior motives."

"Yeah, right."

Raking his hand through his wet hair he looked at Megan with such intensity, she thought she'd melt. "Megan, nothing is going to happen. If it will make you feel better I'll sleep on the floor, but I'm not leaving you alone." His defensive posture told her he was hurt; however, his persistence would keep him there.

Her emotions were jumbled and she took her frustrations out on him. She seemed to do that a lot lately. "I'm confused and I need some space."

"What you need is rest." He held the covers up until she obediently slipped in between. "Now, lie down and get some sleep."

"You're good at this tucking in business," Megan commented. She found it hard to keep up her brave front when he was around. All she'd wanted in the past year was someone to hold her. Someone to understand the pain. Someone to give her the strength to face the heartache. Steven now offered that.

"I had good teachers." He smiled.

"No doubt your mom tucked you in every night."

"Mom and Dad both."

"You're lucky to have two loving parents."

"I know." Steven's eyes reflected the memory of his parents' love. "Didn't your parents tuck you in at night?"

"No. There wasn't much time for things like that."

"It doesn't sound like you grew up with a lot of love."

"They did the best they could."

He looked down at her, frowning softly. "Get some sleep, Megan." He went into the bathroom and pulled on his jeans before returning to the bed. He tossed a pillow on the floor.

"You don't have to sleep on the floor. The bed is big enough for both of us."

"Are you sure?"

"Yeah, just stay on your side and don't hog the covers."

"I'll try not to." Steven picked up the pillow and sat on the edge of the bed "It means a lot that you trust me."

"I didn't say I trusted you." She felt the wall around her heart cracking, and feared it would crumble down soon. *Trusting* is always the first crack.

The morning light filtering through the window bore into Steven's eyes. Flinging an arm up, he squinted against the brightness.

"I love you," a soft voice mumbled.

Steven's eyes flew open. He shook his head chasing away the fogginess and looked at Megan. Had she said what he thought, or had he been dreaming? Was she dreaming about him or someone else? His heart wrenched at that thought. She had never mentioned being involved with anyone. But then again, she never talked about herself. If she had been involved in Illinois it must be over now. And she hadn't been in California long enough to meet anyone.

Was he jealous at the possibility of someone else? Why was he so fascinated by her? She'd been the first woman to seem uninterested in him. At first that intrigued him. He'd once thought she was playing hard to get. But, after last night, he knew she wasn't playing games. He watched Megan roll onto her back and stretch, her blond hair tumbling around her shoulders and face. He'd pictured this scene many times, only not after a platonic night.

Chapter 7

Slowly opening her eyes and wiping the sleep from them, surprise flashed for a moment before remembering the events of the previous night.

"Good morning, sleepy head," Steven teased.

"How did you sleep?"

"I've had better nights." He yawned and sat up.

"I'm sorry I kept you up."

"It's all right."

"It's seven-thirty," Megan gasped. "I'm late." She threw the covers back and started to jump.

He stopped her. "You don't have to make breakfast today."

"Why not?"

"I called dad last night. He's going to have breakfast with some guys from the office, and mom can fend for herself."

"Why did you do that? There wasn't any reason to call your dad."

"I didn't want them to worry when I didn't come home. And you need some rest."

"What did you tell them?"

"I didn't say why I stayed. I only said that I didn't want to leave you alone. I know my parents will understand."

"They probably think we slept together."

"Technically, we did." He grinned.

"You know what I mean."

"Yeah, I know. This isn't exactly how I pictured our first morning together."

"What do you mean by first? You planned on more than one night?"

I'd like a lifetime of mornings with you, he silently wished. "Mom and Dad are worried about you too."

"Look who's changing the subject now."

"I learned from the best." He winked.

"I've never talked about it because I was afraid." Megan settled back against the headboard. It did feel good to finally let her emotions out.

"What are you scared of?"

"To face the pain." Her voice quivered. "I never felt strong enough to deal with the emotions. I just shut them off."

"We all want to help you through this." Steven held her close.

She heard his heart beating loud and strong as she laid her cheek against his bare chest. For a second or two she entertained the idea that it might be beating for her, but quickly pushed that notion out of her mind. Thoughts like that would get her into trouble. She sat up, wiping her eyes dry. "Steven, I want to thank you for being here." She mustered a small smile. "It really helped."

"I won't pretend I know what you're going through because, I don't." He placed his hand over hers. "I'll be your sounding board. That's all I can do."

"That's enough."

The warmth of Steven's hand made her increase-ingly aware of his presence. Blushing beet-red, she quickly withdrew her hand and jumped off the bed. At first, she'd been appreciative of his presence. His friendship had been a godsend during those long, tormented hours. But now his touch produced feelings beyond that of a supportive friend.

"I... umm....I need to get dressed. Don't you have to get to work?"

"Not today." Steven smiled, showing his straight teeth. "I'm all yours for the whole day. One of the perks of being the boss's son, I get time off whenever I want, although dad gets furious if I take too many days off." Steven chuckled at the memory of getting chewed out.

She crossed her arms. "I don't need you to watch over me every second. You're not my guardian."

"I'm not trying to be," Steven defended. "Besides I thought you might want help packing."

"Why would I need to pack?"

"That's why I came over last night." Steven took a deep breath. "You see, my parents wanted me to talk to you." Sure, he'd blame them so she couldn't be mad at him. It was their idea, of course - he'd just brought it to their attention.

"If they have something to say, why don't they tell me?"

"I offered to deliver their message."

The knot forming in her stomach tightened and it became hard to breathe. "What message?" She sat on the end of the bed trying to prepare for the terrible news. *Have I been fired*? All his talk of offering help seemed hollow now.

"My parents want you to move into the estate until your position is finished."

"What?" Her sigh of relief quickly turned into confusion. "Move in with them? Why?"

"Mom said if she'd known you were living in a hotel she would have made this arrangement from the beginning. Since your job is only temporary, you can save money by staying with them."

"Why would they care where I'm living?"

"They want to help."

"No." She shook her head. "I couldn't possibly move in there."

"Why not?"

"I don't want to impose."

"You're not imposing."

"But people will think I am."

"You don't know my mom." Steven laughed. "I remember one Christmas Eve. I must have been around eight, and mom brought home a family whose house had burnt down. They had planned on staying in a shelter, but she insisted that they stay with us. 'A shelter is no place to be at Christmas,' she said. Tiffany and I shared some of our presents with the kids, and mom and dad gave all their gifts to the adults, including the things Tiffany and I had bought them. Later, I asked why she didn't keep anything for herself. She said, 'I have more than enough things. All I need is your dad and you kids.'" A faint smile touched his lips.

"Your parents really are amazing people."

"Mom has always had a giving heart." After a pause, he added, "They want to help."

"I know." She considered his compassionate eyes. "You were right."

"Of course, I'm always right." He flashed that hard-to-resist smile. "Right about what?"

"I have shut everyone and everything out of my life for too long. I wanted to pretend that it never happened. I thought if I didn't talk about Laura I could forget, but I only suppressed the pain and it caught up with me last night."

"You need a place to heal. You've been carrying this burden by yourself for too long. Move in and let us help."

"It's just...well... I feel like a failure and I need to prove that I can take care of myself."

"Prove to whom?"

"Myself."

"Why would you feel like a failure? Laura's death wasn't your fault."

"Yes, it was!" She buried her face in her hands. "I killed my baby."

"What would make you think that?"

Megan tried to answer but the words caught in her throat. The guilt squeezed around her heart like a python.

"Oh... sweetheart. It's not your fault. You have to quit blaming yourself." He sat down beside her.

"But...it is... my fault," she said between sobs. "It's all my fault. My baby was alive then she was dead. Just like that." She snapped her fingers.

"Do the doctors know what happened?"

"There were no conclusive answers. With stillborn babies, most of the time they never find out what happens."

"Then why do you insist it's your fault?"

"Because babies don't just die! I must have done something wrong. Or not done something I should have. There has to be a reason."

"Life doesn't always make sense," he reasoned. She not only had to deal with the death of her daughter but with this guilt as well. Steven gave her a gentle shake. "Listen to me," he tilted her face up. "It's not your fault." He said it slowly, deliberately pronouncing each word. "Do you understand me?"

"But it is," she insisted. Megan hadn't told anyone about the feelings of guilt. What would people think when they found out she had killed her baby? How could she explain that her carelessness had caused the death? "It's awful." She stood, anxiously pacing a few steps.

"Megan. Don't bury the guilt." He felt her shutting him out. "I'm here to help."

"Some help you are," she retorted. "A friend wouldn't have gone behind my back the way you did, telling your parents about my living conditions. You could have at least given me the common courtesy of talking to me first." She needed to change the subject. She couldn't face the guilt yet.

"I didn't sneak behind your back. I thought my parents were aware of your living conditions. I didn't know they hired you without an address or phone number."

"Why were you talking about me at all?" She defiantly crossed her arms. "You know I won't be able to say no to them. This is all your fault."

"Whoa! Wait a minute. Why are you mad at me?" He raked his hand through his hair. "We only want to help. I don't understand why you're getting defensive?"

"Because this is *my* life and you don't have the right to interfere. I didn't ask for your help." She threw her arms up, becoming increasingly irate.

"Will you calm down? Let's go talk this over with my parents."

"There you go again; giving orders like you're in charge."

"I'm not giving orders," he defended. "I still don't see why you're so upset."

"And I don't see why you're so insistent on me living there. Do you think you'll get something out of it?"

"Exactly what do you mean by that?" He definitely didn't like her innuendo.

"Only that you'll think you are entitled to some kind of compensation for all your help."

"Now, that's not fair!" He jumped up, almost knocking her over. "Are you saying I might rape you?" His jaw tensed with anger.

Ashamed at suggesting such a thing she quietly said, "Not rape. But we need to keep distance between us and that will be too hard living in the same house."

Steven's jaw loosened, compassion slowly replacing his anger. She was so beautiful, and had been through so much. "I'd never do anything to hurt you," he said. "And I'd certainly never force myself on you or any woman."

"I know." A few tears slid from her long lashes. "That's not what I meant," she said sheepishly. "I meant that... well...you seem to have a way of being...very persistent."

"I like to think of myself as assertive."

"Assertive, persistent... it means the same thing. You're used to getting what you want."

"Yes, I am," Steven admitted. "But I always win fairly. I've never forced *any* situation, in business or pleasure."

"I'm not saying that you'd force me. More like you'd wear me down." Megan looked Steven fully in the face. "I only want to be friends. That's all I have to offer. I'm afraid you want more."

You're right about that, he thought. *I want a lot more.* He wanted her to love him in a way that no other woman ever had. He wanted her to be his one and only. These words and feelings were foreign to him and he didn't know how to handle them. He didn't know how to handle her. "If I wanted to take advantage of you I could have done it last night. But I was here as a friend, nothing else."

"I'm not sure what your definition of a friend is."

"A lot better than yours, it seems."

Megan felt the sharp jab of seriousness in that remark, and reasoned he every right to be angry. He'd been a good friend, staying up most of the night, holding her while she sobbed her heart out. He'd even taken the day off work to watch over her. And how did she return his kindness? By accusing him of not being a gentleman. She hadn't meant it. She often blurted things out in anger. He was - by all accounts - one of the best friends she'd ever had. It was easy to open up to him, a little too easy at times. Maybe that's why she was always on the defense with him. "Steven, I'm sorry. I didn't mean it." She smiled prettily. "Do you think you can find it in your heart to forgive me?"

"Maybe... but on one condition."

"What might that be?"

"You move in to my parents' house."

"I don't want to put anybody out," she sighed.

"And who would you be putting out? It's not like they don't have the room. Besides, you'll be closer to work. You can sleep in and even make breakfast in your pajamas."

"But..."

"You have no excuses. I promise to give you all the space you need." Steven held up his right hand. "Scout's honor."

"You don't strike me as the Boy Scout type."

"I've never actually been in the Boy Scouts."

"Then you can't use their honor code."

"Why not?"

"Because it doesn't mean anything to you. It's like swearing by your mother's grave when she's not dead."

"Then what do you want me to swear by?"

"Nothing." She gently shook her head. "Your word is good enough for me." She believed he'd keep his promise. *He's better at keeping promises than I am,* she thought.

"Why don't you go shower and get ready. I'll call Ralph to come pick us up. Are you hungry?"

"Yes, I'm starving."

"I'll see if he'll bring some breakfast too."

"It won't take me long." She headed to the bathroom. Steven was good at taking charge of situations. Not that it really bothered her. She felt safe and secure having someone taking care of her.

Steven hung up the phone and stretched out on the bed. He grabbed the pillow Megan had slept on and inhaled her faint scent. It filled his mind, his heart and his soul. *Friends,* he sighed, and drifted off to sleep.

A repeated tapping awakened him. He opened his eyes and saw Megan greeting Ralph.

"Good morning, Miss Black."

"Why be so formal? Please call me Megan."

"Very good, Megan."

Steven sat up in the bed, stretched, and yawned. "Hey, Ralph."

"Good morning, sir."

"We'll eat before we leave." He looked at Megan, "Is that okay with you?"

"Yes. That's fine." She wondered what Ralph thought. They didn't present the most wholesome sight. If he was shocked, he covered his feelings well. No expression showed on his face.

"I'll bring the food in." Ralph walked back to the limousine.

"I'll help bring in the table." Steven slid off the bed.

"Table?"

"I had him bring a card table and chairs so we have a place to sit."

"For a man who doesn't like being prepared you sure are detail-oriented."

"I never said I didn't like being prepared. I just like doing things on the spur of the moment. I can be very prepared when I have too." Steven ran out the door in his bare feet. "Be right back."

"You're going to catch a cold." Megan yelled after him. Folding her arms and leaning against the doorjamb she noticed the cool breeze had been freshened by the recent rainfall. The sun played peek-a-boo with the large, fluffy clouds. The bright, cheery morning made her believe anything was possible.

'Things that are impossible with man are possible with God.'

The Bible verse made her feel as though she would be strong enough to handle the situation. And she wasn't alone either. She had Steven, his parents, and God.

She held the door open as Steven carried in a square table and two chairs. Ralph followed with two silver domed-covered platters and a basket on his arm containing a linen tablecloth, dishes, and two sets of wrapped silverware.

Ralph placed everything on the table Steven had set up and said, "I'll be right back with the drinks."

Megan lifted one of the lids on the warm platter. "Oh, my goodness." She licked her lips at the stacks of pancakes and French toast. Eggs Benedict were artfully arranged on a plate with sides of sausage and bacon. A small bowl held an assortment of fruit, and a toasted bagel.

"I'm hungry, but I don't think I can eat all this."

"I didn't know what you wanted, so I ordered an assortment of everything." He walked around the table and pulled out her chair.

"Thank you." Her smile made Steven's heart skip a beat.

Ralph returned with a container of coffee and juice. "Will that be all, sir?"

"Yes. Thank you," Steven replied.

"I'll be waiting in the car." With a nod to Steven and Megan he said, "Enjoy your breakfast."

"We will," Steven assured him.

"Ralph, this is the most elegant breakfast I've ever had," Megan beamed.

"I merely carried out my orders." He took his leave.

When Steven looked across the table he saw tears in her eyes. "What's wrong?"

"It's just that…" She spread her hands to indicate the table. "You shouldn't have gone to so much trouble.

When you said 'breakfast', I was expecting McDonald's in a paper bag."

"This is breakfast, Peterson style." He winked. "Besides, all I did was make a couple of phone calls. It's not like I cooked it myself."

"Thank goodness for that."

"All right, quit picking on my cooking." Steven pointed his fork. "Start eating."

"Yes, sir." Megan saluted. Then looking at Steven with serious eyes said, "I don't know how I can ever repay your kindness."

"Your beautiful smile is more than enough payment."

Megan looked down and started rearranging the food on her plate, hoping he wouldn't notice her face turning red. For some unknown reason, she felt radiant in his presence. He had a way of making her body feel like a woman. A single touch, a smile, even a mere word caused her heart to flutter.

Steven chuckled to himself after noticing her blush. He didn't know many women who blushed when they received a compliment. Megan seemed so innocent, and it was refreshing to see that some women were still actually ladies.

The long black limousine stopped in front of the estate. Megan sat in the back seat, nervously playing with her hands, fretting about this decision. *What am I doing?* She would now be sharing living quarters with the one man that she needed to be far away from. Trouble was the only thing she could see looming in her future.

"Megan."

She looked up to see Steven watching her. "What?"

"You haven't heard anything I've said, have you?"

"No. I guess not." She looked back down at her hands. "What were you saying?"

"It wasn't important. Why do you look so nervous?"

"I feel like I'm going into the lion's den."

Steven chuckled. "Come on, it's not that bad."

"I don't mean to imply that it will be bad. It's just... I don't know." She couldn't tell him that the idea of living under the same roof with him felt danger-ous. She didn't want him to know that she thought about him at all. *No ties, s*he reminded herself.

"Megan, things will work out, wait and see."

"I hope you're right."

"I'm always right." Steven covered her hand with his and gave her a wink.

The touch felt warm and gentle. His devilish smile made her laugh. "You're not only persistent but conceited too."

"I like to think of it as confident."

"Persistent and confident - sounds like a deadly combination."

"I don't know about deadly. I've survived this long."

"What about the women you date. Do they survive?"

Steven stiffened. "Are you ready to go in?"

The temperature dropped a few degrees. Megan got the impression she'd treaded on untouchable territory. "So, talking about the women you date is off limits?"

"Megan..."

"I don't want to talk about it." She finished the sentence for him.

Brown eyes clashed with blue and for a long moment they held each other's gaze. Steven looked away first. "All right, I see what you're doing, putting the shoe on the other foot." Raking a hand through his hair, he sighed. "I don't want my past to scare you away."

Finely tapered brows arched over surprised eyes. "Why would it?"

"You aren't the only one running from ghosts. I have a few chasing me as well."

"And you don't want to share."

"Maybe later." His eyes bore into her. "Right now, I want to concentrate on you." He smiled. "We need to get you settled in." Stepping out he extended his hand.

Megan took a deep breath. *Here I go.*

Rosa directed Ralph and Steven upstairs with the luggage, while Delores coaxed Megan into having a cup of coffee in the dining room. Rosa joined them a few minutes later. "I have the room all ready, *Señora* Peterson."

"Thank you, Rosa."

"I'll show you to your room when you're ready, Megan."

"I'm ready now." She looked troubled.

"What's wrong, dear?" Delores asked.

"What if I get lost? This place is huge. I think I need a map."

"*Sí*, I know the feeling." Rosa chuckled. "When I first started working here I was scared too, but now I know this house like the back of my hand."

"That's why you're the head maid. This house would fall apart if it weren't for Rosa."

"*Señora* Peterson, you're too kind." Her dark skin seemed to brighten. "Megan, if it will help, I'll take you on a tour later."

"I'm afraid I'll need a couple of tours to remember where everything is."

"Do you remember how nervous you were when you first walked into the kitchen?" Delores asked. "It only took you a couple of days to find your way around. Now you know where everything is. Soon you will know this house without any problems." She patted Megan's hand. "Dear, I want you to think of this as your home. You do what you want and come and go as you please."

"Thanks, Mrs. Peterson."

"Now go get settled into your room."

"Shouldn't I get lunch started?" She glanced at her watch.

"We're going out to lunch today. I told Grant we'd meet him at the restaurant."

"Is Steven going with you?"

"Yes, and you, too."

"Me?"

"You deserve a break. You haven't had any free time since you moved here."

"But, Mrs. Peters...."

"Go get unpacked and be ready by twelve," Delores ordered.

Megan followed Rosa up the stairs and down the long hallway that led to her room.

"Wow!" Megan gasped.

The room had been elegantly done in shades of pink and white. Large white flowers trimmed in gold were pasted on the soft pink background of the wallpaper. A large white framed canopy bed stood in the center of the room. Pink satin and chiffon loosely covered the top and hung down the sides, securely fastened to the bedposts with gold braids. A pink satin quilt adorned the bed, while a large group of satin ruffled pillows sat artfully arranged on top. Gold ropes also tied back the pink satin curtains on the windows. Two matching white dressers with gold knobs stood against opposite walls. A gold vase of silk white magnolias sat on the night table next to the bed.

Megan looked through the French doors and watched the palm tree branches sway slightly in the late morning breeze.

"It's beautiful, sí?"

"Yes. The view is as magnificent as the room."

Rosa opened the doors to the adjoining bath and walk in closet.

"This closet could be another room." Megan stated in disbelief.

"You like it?"

"I love it." Megan touched the satin on the bed. "It's like the room I always wanted as a kid. Only even in my dreams the room was never this elaborate."

"The Petersons wanted you to have the best."

"Why?"

"So you'll be comfortable."

"I don't understand why they are so insistent that I stay here."

"It's just the way they are. They like helping people."

"Rosa, what do you think about me moving in here?"

"What does it matter what I think?"

"I'm worried that people will think I'm using them."

"You worry too much." Rosa patted her arm. "Now put your mind at ease. If the Petersons didn't trust you they would never have made the offer. It doesn't matter what anyone else thinks, does it?"

"No, I guess not. Thanks, Rosa."

"*De nada*."

Rosa left Megan feeling much better about moving in. She unpacked, then turned and jumped when she saw Steven standing in the doorway.

"Oh, hi." She laughed. "I didn't know you were there."

"Sorry, I startled you." He'd been watching her tiny frame flit around the room like a humming bird. Watching her do the simplest task made his gut churn.

"How long have you been standing there?"

"I just got here," he lied. He didn't want her to accuse him of stalking. Her uneasiness about moving in was mostly because of him. "Are you ready to go?"

"As ready as I'll ever be."

They drove to a charming Victorian house on Chapala Street, which had been renovated into a small restaurant. A lone palm tree waved its branches, welcoming guests into the bright red building trimmed in white.

Megan's apprehension softened in the romantic and casual atmosphere. She ordered pasta while

Steven devoured his stuffed pork chop. Grant ate a steak, and Delores enjoyed some blackened seafood. Megan didn't do much talking, but she enjoyed the view offered by the large bay window until a young lady pushing a baby stroller walked by. The knife twisted in her heart. *That should be me.* She tried to fend off the injustice.

She thought about the brand new stroller she'd been given as a shower gift. It sat untouched. Just like the clothes, bottles, crib and dresser. All her plans and dreams had died with Laura. *It's not fair!* She silently screamed.

Steven found Megan searching through the fridge.

"You're hungry already? How do you keep that tiny figure?"

"I'm planning dinner, not eating, and my figure is none of your business."

"Ouch, touchy, aren't we?" Steven grinned. "Dinner is hours away. I thought we could do something."

"Rosa is going to give me a tour of the house."

"I can do that." He held out his hand.

Megan hesitated. "But Rosa..."

"Won't mind if I take you instead, now what's the real reason you don't want to go with me? Don't you trust me?"

"Of course, I trust you." How could she go into all the complications that would transpire if she gave into this attraction? Staying strong and unattached was becoming harder to do. Letting down her guard enough to enjoy the security he offered could be a tremendous mistake. Then again, it was nice having someone to lean on. Someone who truly cared. "All right, let's go." She took his hand.

They re-entered the kitchen a few hours later, Megan laughing at something Steven had said. He laid his hand on the small of her back, guiding her through the doorway.

"You two look like you had fun." Rosa smiled, pleased to see them looking cozy.

"Yes, we had a nice time," Steven said. "But Megan still thinks she needs a map."

"I don't see how anyone can find their way around here. I'll get lost looking for the kitchen."

"You'll find your way around in no time," Rosa reassured her. "By the way, Tiffany and William are coming for dinner tomorrow."

"Speaking of dinner," Megan looked at her watch. "We better get something started."

"I have to finish upstairs, and then I'll be going home. I'll see you both tomorrow. *Adios*."

"'Bye, Rosa," Megan and Steven said in unison.

"Do you think you're ready for the cook off with your dad?" Megan asked, watching Steven fumbled with the can opener. "Maybe you should cancel?"

"Cancel? Never." He grabbed a spatula, holding it like a sword. "A Peterson never gives up. We fight to the death."

"Since your mom and I are judges, we'll be the ones dying if you don't master these lessons."

"I know how to cook," he protested.

"You know how to brew coffee, mash potatoes, and make toast."

"I can chop vegetables too."

"Wow!" Megan teased. "Maybe you should do more than chop vegetables tonight."

"What's this?" Grant asked as Megan brought out dessert.

"Cherry cobbler. Steven made it."

"Is it safe to eat?" Grant asked, patting his stomach.

"I only read the recipe and measured some ingredients. Megan did most of the work," Steven confessed.

After dishing out a helping for everyone and putting a scoop of vanilla ice cream on top, Megan sat down to enjoy her dessert.

"This is wonderful," Delores said. "Honey, if Megan keeps teaching Steven, he's going to beat you."

"Never."

"Come on, Pops, you sound worried." Steven snickered.

"I'm not worried one bit."

"Whatever."

On the way to her bedroom Megan passed the nursery and noticed a light shining under the door. Pushing the door open and looking around suddenly made her heart fill with anguish. The baby crib and the colorful teddy bears dancing on the curtains only served to mock her memories. Her chest constricted, producing a sharp pain that made it hard to breathe. The lingering sent of baby powder brought back memories too overwhelming to ignore.

The memories swirled around like a whirlwind. One by one, she relived each awful detail. The remorse wouldn't be pushed away. Grief and guilt battled back against her will, struggling to be released from the depths of her heart.

She remembered coming home from the hospital and walking into the nursery, which she'd decorated in the latest trend with clouds, moon and stars. She stood in the middle of the room with nothing but emptiness and despair to hold on to.

I should be bringing my baby home, she cried. *Why had fate been so cruel? Why give me a baby, only to snatch her away?* Hurt quickly swelled into rage. "It's not fair!" she screamed, knocking the baby items off the top of the dresser. In a crazed panic, she overturned every piece of furniture and emptied the dresser drawers. After practically disassembling the crib with her bare hands and ripping the curtains down, she curled up in a corner. Wrapping her arms around her knees, she rocked back and forth as white baby powder settled over the room like fine snow. "It's not fair," she repeated. "It's not fair."

She tried to pull back from the memory but it was too late. "Nooo!" She felt her knees buckle.

Chapter 8

Strong arms caught her before she hit the floor and carried her to her room.

"Megan, I'm here." The voice sounded familiar. But she couldn't decipher if it was real or her memory.

"My baby!" she cried. "I want my baby."

She lay back against the pillows sobbing, as the intensity became uncontrollable. Muffled voices swirled around her fuzzy mind. The past blended flawlessly into the present leaving her confused.

"Steven, how is she?" Delores sounded worried.

"I don't know, Mom. She was like this last night."

"I wasn't happy when you stayed the night," Grant admitted. "But after seeing her now, I know you did the right thing."

"Thanks, Dad." He held her hand. "I don't know what to do."

"Stay with her till she calms down," Delores said. "I'll go make some tea."

Megan's disoriented state lasted for several long minutes. As her senses started to return, the blurry image of Steven sitting on the edge of the bed came into focus.

"Are you feeling better?" he asked.

"What happened?"

"Something in the nursery must have triggered another memory."

Brushing her hair back, she struggled to sit up. "Baby powder."

"Baby powder?"

"The smell of it brought back the memory of…" Tears stung her eyes.

"It's okay, you're safe now." Steven brushed a light kiss on the back of her hand. "You're not alone, either."

"That's right. We're all here for you, dear." Delores brought in a tray with a flowered teapot. "Here, this will settle your nerves." She handed her a matching cup.

"Thanks." She took a sip. "It's delicious."

"Just what the doctor ordered." Delores poured herself a cup, too. "Perhaps I should give Dr. Brent a call."

"Oh, no, I'm fine. Really there's no need for that."

"We want to help you, dear."

"The tea is enough."

"You two better go. I'll help Megan get ready for bed," Delores ordered.

"You don't have to do that, I'm capable of…"

"Megan, let us help. That's all we want." Grant kissed the top of her head. "Get some rest."

"Good night, Mr. Peterson."

"I'm going to stay in my old room," Steven said. "If you need anything, just holler."

"You don't have to rearrange your life for me."

"But I want to." She got the feeling that he'd re-arrange the planet to be close to her. "Isn't that what friends are for?"

Megan nodded. She felt safe enough and strong enough to finally face the memories head on. "Thank you all."

The men left and Delores helped Megan into her nightgown.

"Goodnight, dear."

"Goodnight, Mrs. Peterson." The lights went out and Megan snuggled under the covers.

Steven paced across the floor in the next room. He hadn't used this room in more than a decade, but wanted to be close by for the next few nights, at least until Megan felt better. A light rapping on the door stopped his pacing. "Come in."

"Do you have everything you need?" Delores asked. "Are there clean sheets on the bed?"

"Since when doesn't Rosa have clean sheets on every bed?"

"It's been a long time since you've slept in here."

"I know. It feels strange, like I'm a kid again."

"You're definitely not my little boy any more. You've grown into a fine young man, and I'm proud of you."

"Proud of what? All I've ever done is mess up my life." He habitually ran his hand through his hair. "I still live at home. I bounced from one college to the next before dropping out completely. I'm not married. I go from one girl to another. What exactly are you proud of, Mom?"

"I'm not saying there haven't been some bumps in the road, but when you were heading down the wrong path you were smart enough to turn around and head in the right direction. I'm proud of you because you've opened your heart to help someone."

"The only problem is I can't do anything. I can't fix it."

"That's the problem with men. You always want to fix everything. Sometimes in life there are things that humans can't fix. We need to leave our broken hearts in God's hands."

"So, what do I do for Megan?"

"The same thing you're doing now. Just be her friend. You can't fix her heart, but you can listen when she needs to talk. And praying would help."

"I feel so helpless."

"Try and imagine what she's going through and how helpless she must feel."

"I don't understand why she blames herself."

"Sometimes we need someone to blame, even if no one is at fault. It looks like Megan is taking that blame on herself."

"She is beating herself up and she won't listen to me." He looked at his mom, "I know you can convince her it's not her fault. Will you talk to her?"

"Of course, although I'm not sure I'll make any headway, either. This is something she must work out for herself."

"If you can't do it, no one can."

"Thanks for the vote of confidence." Delores smiled. "Now you'd better get some sleep."

The dim sunlight slowly seeping into the room cast shadows on the wall and floor. Megan looked at the clock and snuggled against the pillows, letting the warmth engulf her. It did feel good to sleep in, however she had to get up sometime.

Slipping into her robe and slippers, she walked out into the hall. The door next to her room stood open, and she peeked in to see Steven still sleeping. She turned to leave.

"How did you sleep?" Steven's asked, sleep heavy in his voice, still sleepy and heavy, surprised her.

She spun back around to see Steven propped up on his elbow. He looked like a little boy with his blond hair disheveled and a half-asleep look clouding his face. "Fine. What about you?"

"Okay." He yawned. "But I've outgrown this bed." He stretched and tossed the blanket back, jumping up, forgetting he was only in his underwear.

Megan blushed and turned around.

"Sorry." He tried not to laugh as he donned his robe.

They headed downstairs in silence. Steven helped with breakfast, then got dressed and left for work, leaving Megan and Delores alone.

"I want you to take some time off today," Delores insisted.

"No," Megan argued. "I have a lot of work to do. Besides, I had most of yesterday off."

"I think I'll call Tiffany and ask her to come over another night."

"No, you've been looking forward to this dinner, and I'm really feeling better. I know I looked fragile last night, but I have been dealing with this for a long time."

"No, you haven't dealt with it, you've been suppressing it."

"I'm not going to let it affect my job."

Delores took a sip of her coffee. "Is that why you left home?"

"Yes." Megan nodded. "I thought if I didn't talk about Laura the pain would go away. But it only built up pressure and then exploded. I feel like such a fool."

"You're not a fool." Delores gave her a hug. "You didn't know how to handle something so difficult. You thought that by leaving you could forget."

"But it didn't work, and now on top of grieving, I'm homesick, too. I seem to keep multiplying my problems." Megan wiped the tears away. "I wish I could be strong."

"Tears don't mean you're weak. I once heard it said that 'every teardrop is a piece of ice that melts from your heart.' You have a whole lot of ice built up. Now it's time you have a good cry and let some of that pain melt away. You'll feel better in the end."

"I don't want to feel better. I don't deserve to feel better. I don't deserve anything."

"Just let it all out." She held Megan while she cried. "It's not your fault Laura died. Sometimes things happen in life and we have no explanations. It's no one's fault."

"It was my fault." Megan insisted. "I killed her."

"Stillbirths aren't anyone's fault."

"But I fell asleep on my back that night. The doctor told me to sleep on my side. But I was tired that I drifted off to sleep on my back."

"I don't think falling asleep on your back would kill the baby."

"It cuts off the circulation. What else would have caused it? I felt her kick before I went to sleep. She was fine. Then I woke up the next morning and she was dead. Don't you see - it had to be my fault!"

"Even if sleeping on your back did cause the death, it was an accident, a...mistake. Quit blaming yourself."

"I can't," Megan cried. "I killed my baby. How am I supposed to live with that?" Despair etched itself so deep that guilt was all she could see.

Delores talked her into taking a shower. Soon she returned refreshed and dressed in a white knit sweater and faded jeans.

"You look better." Delores said.

"I feel better."

"Good. Why don't you take a walk or lounge by the inside pool? You need some time to yourself."

"I don't feel like being alone."

"Because you don't want to face the pain."

"I'd rather be working."

"It's time to give your hands a rest. Let's go do something fun. How about shopping?"

Megan wanted to go shopping about as much as she wanted to jump off the top of Willis Tower. But how could she say no to this kind woman? "Let me go throw on some makeup so I won't look as bad as I feel."

"That's the spirit."

Twenty minutes later they were in the back of the limousine heading to downtown Santa Barbara. They turned onto Lower State Street and drove along the historic district.

"There are a lot of people out for a weekday," Megan commented.

"It's always busy downtown." Delores laughed.

"Back home it would be almost dead this time of day. Everyone is out in the fields or at work."

"We have a lot of retired people living in Santa Barbara."

Megan watched the suntanned surfers whiz by on their inline skates. "They seem pretty young to be retired."

"Those are students, probably skipping class, or playing hooky from work." As if that comment sparked a thought, Delores added, "Do you mind if we stop by and see Grant in his office?"

"No. Of course not." Megan was a little excited to see the Peterson Corporation. Her expectations were not disappointed when they pulled in front of the white stucco building. The tinted glass windows almost looked black in the glare of the sun.

"It's beautiful," Megan commented as they started up the steps. The white walls were accented with large, vivid paintings, and plants softened the corners of the hallways and rooms. The elegance of the building was exactly what Megan had pictured.

"Grant and I helped design the building."

"Did you design your house too?"

"Yes, we did." Delores laughed. "Almost everybody thought we were crazy. Everyone else just hired people to draw up the plans. But we had a vision and knew what we wanted, so we did it ourselves."

"You two could go into construction."

"Don't mention it to Grant. I'm sure the thought has been in the back of his mind for twenty some years."

They got off the elevator and walked down a long corridor with a row of office doors on each side. Some of them stood open, revealing desks, chairs, copying machines, computers and coffee makers. Other doors were closed, warning employees to stay out. As they entered a large office at the end of the building, A pretty redhead was typing and talking on the phone.

She hung up the phone and smiled at Megan and Delores as they entered. "Mrs. Peterson, how nice to see you."

"Good to see you too, Betty. Is Grant in?"

"Yes. He's meeting with a client now, but I can buzz him and let him know you're here."

"Oh, I don't want to bother him if he's busy."

"It's not a very important meeting. He's with one of our regular clients. They are probably just shooting the breeze by now." She pushed her black-framed glasses up the bridge of her nose. Then pushed a button and informed Grant his wife was here.

The door opened to another office and Grant, Steven, and another man came out. Megan didn't pay much attention to the group, as she looked out the window, viewing the city. She heard Steven talking with the secretary. A booming laugh made her turn around. The cadence sparking recognition.

The laughter ceased abruptly, and surprised blue eyes regarded her carefully. "Why I'll be, if it ain't pretty, little Megan from Illinois."

"Tex." Although she'd met him only four weeks ago, and they had chatted on the plane for a few hours, he felt like an old friend. It seemed only natural to cross the room and give him a friendly hug. "I thought you would be back home by now."

"I was home but had to make one more trip back to close the deal." Picking up his Stetson from the table in the back of the room, he asked. "Are you here on business?"

"No. I work for the Petersons."

"You're working here, now?" His eyes brightened.

"Not here." She shook her head. "I work at their residence as their cook."

"How long is this vacation of yours going to last?"

"I've decided to move here."

Steven didn't like the easy conversation or the hug. "How do you know each other?" His tone seemed more than causal.

"We bumped into each other at the airport," Megan explained.

"Literally," Tex laughed.

"So why are you here, Megan?" Steven was abrupt, almost rude.

"Your mom and I were going shopping and she wanted to see your dad." She felt small, worthless, like she had no business being there. Not the usual feelings Steven provoked in her.

"I see." His face grew hard as his eyes darted between her and Tex.

"Come on, Steve, lighten up," Tex said. "You should know better than to be rude to pretty women."

"What I should know, and what I do is none of your business."

"Whoa. Easy, buddy." Tex held up his large hands as if trying to stop a team of horses. "What's gotten into you?"

"Nothing."

Grant and Delores joined them. "Do you have any plans for lunch, Tex?" Grant asked.

"No, sir."

"Why don't you join us?" Delores offered.

"I'm sure he has a flight home." Steven disliked the idea of him and Megan spending any more time together.

"Nope. I have a red-eye home tonight. The rates are cheaper the later you fly."

"Great. Then we'll see you later. That gives us a few hours to shop." Delores kissed Grant good-bye. "Don't be late," she called out to him as she and Megan walked out the door.

They shopped at several small boutiques, old family businesses that had been around for years. The whole district had a quaint feel about it.

Megan fell in love with every article of clothing she tried on, but had a heart attack when she looked at the price tags.

"Why do they want so much for a swimsuit? There isn't much material to it."

"You pay for the name, dear."

"I don't have a problem with the name Wal-Mart."

"Don't worry about the price, now go try this on." She handed Megan a black dress and hustled her off to the dressing room. The sales clerk helped pick out other outfits that would enhance her small frame. Later, they let Megan have a rest as she enjoyed a cup of tea and some pastries.

Delores purchased some packages and put them in the limousine. Then they were off to another store, where she went through the same exhausting routine, trying on one outfit after another.

Finally, it was lunchtime. They met the three men at a small seaside restaurant. Megan talked them into sitting out on the patio, where they could enjoy the warm, sunny day while listening to the sounds of the ocean.

"It's such a beautiful day," Megan commented. "I can't believe it is November when it's so warm."

"It feels a bit chilly to me," Delores said. "Maybe you should put your jacket on."

"No, I'm perfect." Megan closed her eyes and tilted her face toward the sun.

"You should see her home state," Tex teased. "I froze just going outside for a cigarette."

"I wonder if we have snow on the ground yet?" Memories of home unfolded in her mind's eye.

"Snow?" Delores made a face. "Yuck."

"Have you ever seen snow?" Megan asked with a laugh.

"Only in pictures, dear."

"That doesn't count. You have to experience it in person. The way the snow covers the fields like a white blanket, making everything look pure and un-touched. It sparkles like diamonds when the sun shimmers off it. And when the rain freezes on the tree branches it hangs down like nature's crystal. It's the most breathtaking scene."

"Sounds like you miss home," Delores noted.

"Sometimes," Megan sighed.

"Heck, when you use words like that I wouldn't mind seeing the snow myself," Tex chuckled. "Although I think you left out a few details, like the freezing cold wind, below zero temperatures, and slick, icy roads." Tex opened his menu.

"You have a point there," Megan laughed. "Although I miss home, I'm excited about starting my life here, and I love the beach. It's so soothing."

"They say water is good for the soul." Delores put her hand on top of Megan's.

"It feels peaceful." Megan hid her face behind the menu, trying to avoid Steven's glare, and to hide the pain that briefly crossed her eyes.

It was strange that she could feel both sadness and peacefulness at the same time. She also had hope that the future would be as bright as the day. She had a few loose ends that needed to be dealt with. Then she could truly start her life anew.

Megan devoured her cheeseburger and fries, then ate some of Delores's fried shrimp. Grant offered her his coleslaw.

"You can give me a run for the money," Tex teased, and patted his stomach, which was stuffed with the platter of assorted seafood.

"I don't know why I'm so hungry." Megan ate a fry. "I swear shopping is more strenuous than climbing a mountain."

"Climbed a lot of mountains, have you?" Tex laughed.

"I've always said that I had to start my own business to make enough money to support her shopping habit." Grant gave Delores a nudge with his elbow.

"I only bought a few things," she insisted.

"The trunk of the limousine is full." Megan laughed.

Steven was unusually quiet, sulking and glaring throughout the lunch. When Megan dared to glance in his direction, he looked away.

Tex tried bringing him into the conversation. "So, Steven, how is that new Koenigsegg CCX handling?"

"Fine."

"Picking up a lot of women with it?" Tex winked.

Steven bit back his snide comment, knowing his father would never approve of rude behavior to a client. "I'm not in the market for a new girlfriend." His crisp tone was chillier than the air. His brown eyes bored a hole, first into Tex, then into Megan. "What about you? Married yet?"

"Nope." Tex chewed on a toothpick.

"The last thing I heard you were pretty serious about some chick." Steven wanted to show him as a playboy, or, at least off the market.

"Naw. She decided she wanted to be Miss Louisiana instead."

"I'm sorry." Megan noted the hurt that passed across his face. "That must have been hard on you."

Tex shrugged his wide shoulders. "Nothing I won't get over." He looked at Steven. "So why don't you have a girl?" He could play this game too. "You always have a new girl."

"I do not." Steven stood, throwing his napkin down on his untouched plate. "I'm going for a walk."

His attempt at making Tex look bad seemed to have backfired. Now Megan felt sympathy for Tex, and he'd been painted as a playboy. Why did Tex have to show up today? Why did nothing he do convince Megan to like him?

"I don't think he's too happy," Tex commented.

"I've never seen him act like that before." Megan watched Steven move further down the seashore.

"Jealousy can make people act crazy." Tex blew out a puff of smoke, making him look like a dragon.

"He's not jealous," she denied. "Where did Mr. and Mrs. Peterson go?"

"To pay the bill." Tex snuffed out his cigarette in the ashtray. "Why don't you go talk to him?" He nodded his head in Steven's direction, not ready to drop the subject.

"There's nothing to talk about."

"Megan, I don't know you very well, but I sensed there was more to the story than just a vacation on the plane." His dark blue eyes stared at her from under his Stetson. "I was right."

Feeling the weight of his stare, she looked away. "We're only friends."

His deep, booming laugh drowned out the sounds of the ocean. "Now I've heard it all." He leaned forward, crossing his arms on the table. "I've known Steven for a number of years. He'd give me a girl he was dating quicker than my granny can whip up a sweet potato pie."

"What would a guy like Steven see in a simple girl like me?"

"Honey, you don't give yourself enough credit. It's not just your incredible looks. You have a goodness...a ..." he searched for the right words. "A wholesome quality about you that really gets to a man." He winked. "You're as innocent as a lamb being led to the slaughterhouse. It makes us men want to protect you."

"Is that what you're doing now?"

"Maybe." He sat back in his chair. "Or, maybe I'm trying to help a friend."

"Would that friend be me or Steven?" She arched a tapered, blond brow above her blue eyes.

"Both."

When Megan came into the kitchen the next morning, Steven was attempting breakfast.

"Good morning." She yawned, pouring a cup of coffee.

"'Morning." His reply was curt.

"What are you making other than a mess?"

"Pancakes - and I can't help it if this flour flies all over the place."

"You need a gentle hand when cooking."

"I don't have that, yet." He noticed how drained she looked. Worry replaced his anger. "Are you still tired?"

"I'm beat."

"Too much excitement yesterday." Although his mood seemed lighter, he still wasn't acting like his usual, jovial self.

"I wouldn't think shopping and lunch would be considered overly exciting." Megan wasn't exactly in the best of moods either. "Maybe it was putting up with your bad attitude that stressed me out."

"My attitude?" Steven pointed to her. "How about you?"

"I didn't do anything." Her eyes glazed over with confusion.

"Right." Steven went back to mixing the batter, stirring with more vigor than necessary.

"I have no idea what is eating you, but don't take it out on me."

"Do you want to know what's bothering me?" The muscles ticked in his jaw. "I've spent weeks wooing you to no avail. Then I have to watch you flirting with Tex."

"I wasn't flirting," she denied. "And if your idea of wooing is treating me like dirt then you did a terrific job yesterday. Who was that little performance for, Tex or the secretary?"

"What performance?"

"The little act in the office with you treating me like an employee." Tears filled her eyes. "You made me feel invisible. Not even Tiffany makes me feel that worthless."

"And how do you think I felt watching you fawn all over another man?"

"You're being unreasonable." She wiped the tears away, stiffening her back.

"You're the one being unreasonable," he countered.

Megan watched as he poured the pancakes on the griddle. "Don't make them so big or they'll be hard to flip over."

The tension was awkward for a while. But tempers settled down by the time the pancakes were done.

"Look, Megan, I'm sorry I acted like such a jerk." He didn't like being the one causing her tears. "I was jealous," he confessed.

"Tex is a friend, if you can even call him that. I barely know the guy."

"It was still hard watching the two of you."

"I didn't like thinking about you and the secretary, either."

"There is nothing between me and Betty." He laughed. "She's practically engaged."

"I didn't know that." She looked him in the eyes. "I also resented your behavior towards me in front of her."

"I'm sorry. I don't want to ever hurt you. I want to protect you. That includes my sister." His tone was softer now. "Are you prepared for tonight?"

"Yes. I'm making spaghetti and meatballs."

"That isn't what I meant. Tiffany isn't exactly the easiest person to get along with. I don't want her upsetting you."

"You don't have to fight my battles. You're not responsible for me. I'm not your possession."

"I'm not treating you like a possession."

"Yes, you are."

"I just want to protect you."

"But I'm not yours to protect."

"I know," he sighed. *But I want you to be mine.*

"What happened in here? It looks like World War Three broke out," Rosa said.

"Steven made breakfast this morning." Megan wiped the flour off the counter.

"My goodness! What is this world coming to?"

"A mess," Megan laughed. However, her life felt as messed up as the kitchen. She needed to do some cleaning to straighten it out.

"How did your day off go?"

"I had a lot of fun. I went shopping with Mrs. Peterson."

"*Sí.* I got my sweater this morning."

"She loves to shop, doesn't she?"

"Giving gifts is her way of showing how much she cares."

"Mrs. Peterson has the biggest heart of anyone I've ever met."

"When I first started working here, I was around twenty-one or twenty-two. My family ran into some trouble in México and I needed a large sum of money to get them out. The Petersons loaned me the money and I told them to take a little bit out of each paycheck until I had it paid back."

"How long did it take you to pay them back?"

"I never did." Rosa smiled. "Every paycheck came in the full amount. I would go to them and tell them they forgot to take their share out. Mrs. Peterson would smile and say, 'I didn't forget. You need the money for your family more than I need it.' She has been saying that for over twenty years now. To this day, she has never taken a dime out of my checks."

"So, you understand how I feel. I'm uncertain that I can ever pay them back."

"Trust me on this, they don't want to be paid back. They do things out of the goodness of their hearts and for no other reason."

"Okay, I hear what you're saying."

Rosa eyed Megan for a long moment. "You know, we all want to help. That is the bottom line."

"I know."

"Guess I better get back to work." Rosa left Megan to chew over her advice.

"Megan, can we go over the plans for Thanksgiving dinner tomorrow?" Delores asked.

"We can go over them later tonight, if you want."

"Just because you are living here doesn't mean you're going to work twenty-four hours a day. I know Thanksgiving is approaching fast, but I'm sure you will handle it fine. The plans can wait until tomorrow."

"Sure, tomorrow is fine."

"Is that cake batter?"

"Yes. I thought the kids would enjoy it."

"Oh, they will, although William isn't big on chocolate."

"I can make something else."

"Don't trouble yourself, he doesn't eat many sweets. Tiffany isn't much of a baker. She's always watching her weight." Delores cocked her head and asked, "Did Steven really make the pancakes for breakfast?"

"Yes. He had a little trouble at first flipping them. The first couple of pancakes didn't land on the griddle, but he had it down by the end."

"I can't believe he's actually learning to cook."

"Steven's doing great. Either you guys are exaggerating how little he'd been in the kitchen or he's a fast learner."

"We're not exaggerating. He never came into the kitchen unless he smelled something baking. He's never been interested in cooking before."

"Then he must be a natural. I think he really enjoys it too."

"That doesn't sound like Steven. Then again, you seem to have a positive influence on him."

Megan wanted to deny the statement but couldn't. Of course, it was true, but she had too much on her plate to worry about falling in love right now. *He isn't serious, anyway*, she thought. *He went through women as often as people change their socks. If I mean anything to him at all, it's a passing fancy and nothing more.*

Chapter 9

"Do I smell cake?" Grant sniffed.

"It could be." Megan lifted one blond brow.

"Chocolate?"

"Yes."

"With chocolate icing?"

"Do you want chocolate icing?"

"I'll pay extra for it." Grant's hearty laugh resounded through the dining room.

"It might break the bank."

"I think I can manage." He winked.

"No desserts until you finish your supper though." Megan shook her finger at him playfully.

"Of course. I wouldn't want to set a bad example for the grandchildren."

Megan had almost finished setting the table when the gang walked in.

"Here she is," Delores cheerfully announced. "Megan, this is William." Delores introduced her to a tall, handsome man in his mid-forties. His sandy-blond hair had been cut and layered to fall in straight lines above his ears. His square jaw was set in a tight line and his gray eyes were serious but gentle.

"It's nice to meet you." He shook Megan's hand and smiled stiffly.

Tiffany walked in carrying the baby. "There, Crystal is all dry now." She patted the baby's bottom.

"Megan!" Billy bounded into the room, jumping into her arms and almost knocking her over.

"Hi, Billy." She gave him a tight hug and looked up to see daggers shooting out of Tiffany's eyes. "Dinner will be ready in about half an hour. If you'll excuse me, I need to check on it."

Steven followed Megan into the kitchen. "What is up with Tiffany? I can almost feel the tension."

"I don't know what I did to her."

"It's not you, sweetheart. She's always been this way. You have to stand up to her."

"I don't want to cause trouble."

"It won't cause trouble. Once she knows she can't push you around, she'll leave you alone."

"Steven, it doesn't matter what she thinks or does."

"But she'll be like this every time if you let her."

"I don't care. I have...what? A little over a month here and I'm done. I won't be working or living here anymore."

Reality smacked him like a rock. He hadn't thought about her leaving. He wanted her to stay and be part of his family. Part of his life. "I don't want you to go," he mumbled.

"What?"

He cleared his throat and said, "Do you need help or should I go?"

"I've got everything under control. You go spend time with your family."

Megan brought the food out and everyone took their places at the table.

"I like sketti," Billy announced.

"I thought you would. And if you eat all your dinner I made a special dessert just for you."

"Dessert, yay! What is it?"

"It's a surprise. You'll have to wait until after dinner to find out."

"Aw! I want to know now."

"I know it's hard," Megan ruffled his hair, "but it'll be worth the wait."

She made another trip into the kitchen and returned with the garlic bread and salad.

"Is this homemade bread again?" Delores questioned.

"Yes."

"You're too much," Grant said.

"I'll say," Tiffany quipped.

"Megan, where is your place setting?" Delores asked.

"I thought you'd want some privacy."

"Sit yourself down at this table, young lady." Delores's note of authority took Megan by surprise.

"Since when do we fraternize with the help?" Tiffany asked.

"Not now, Tiffany." Grant sternly stared at his daughter.

"Mrs. Peterson, really I think it would be better if I ate in the kitchen." Megan wrung her hands while her eyes pleaded with Delores not to make her sit with Tiffany.

"Nonsense," Grant added. "Now sit down."

"Come on, Megan, I'm hungry. Sit down so we can eat." Steven joined in.

"Sit by me, Megan. Pleeeez!" Billy begged.

Megan looked into his big excited eyes. How could she say no to such a request? "Looks like I'm outnumbered." She took a plate from the hutch and sat down.

Grant said the blessing.

"Great, now let's dig in." Steven helped himself to the spaghetti, and then passed the bowl to William, who took a small helping.

"William, I know you're used to eating my sister's cooking, but unlike hers, this food actually tastes good."

That remark earned him a kick under the table.

"Ouch!" Steven scowled at Tiffany.

"Spaghetti is one of my favorite dishes," Grant remarked.

"Everything is your favorite dish," Delores teased.

"Hey, Dad. We could make spaghetti for the contest," Steven suggested.

"Setting your sights a little high, aren't you, son?"

"Are you afraid you can't handle spaghetti, or is it the meatballs that give you a problem?"

"I'm not afraid of anything." Grant smiled. "Except eating your cooking."

"What on earth are you two talking about?" Tiffany questioned.

"Your dad and brother are having a contest," Delores explained.

"Another one?" Tiffany rolled her eyes.

"The contest is about cooking?" William asked surprised.

"Yes. Megan and I are the judges," Delores said proudly.

"You poor souls," William said.

"I'm going to whip dad."

"That's what you think," Grant grunted.

"That's what I know."

"What are the rules of the contest?" William asked.

"Whoever makes the best tasting dish wins?" Steven shrugged.

"Are you going to cook the same dish, or do you each make something different?" William's mind always worked over the small details. That's why he was CEO of the Peterson Corporation.

"We haven't discussed that yet," Steven said.

Megan felt like a scared mouse trapped in a room, trying to scurry out of the way before getting stepped on. Of course, Tiffany was the only person she wanted to get away from. She didn't dare say a word, for fear of being on the receiving end of those frosty eyes.

"Megan, I hear you're new to town. What state are you from?" William asked.

"Illinois."

"I've been there on business, around the Chicago area."

"I lived west of Chicago. In the country."

"Sounds nice. I bet you don't miss the cold weather."

"No, not really, but I do miss the snow."

"How could anyone miss that awful stuff?" Tiffany wrinkled her nose.

"What is snow, Mommy?" Billy asked.

"It's cold white stuff," she answered in her condescending tone. It was clear she didn't want to talk about Megan. William scowled at her and she glanced away.

"What brought you to California?" he asked her again.

Megan's gaze dropped, and it seemed that William felt he'd asked the wrong question. She cleared her throat and gave her rehearsed answer. "I needed a change."

Tiffany, however picked up on the vibe and wasn't about to let the subject drop. "How did you manage to find your way here?"

"I saw the ad in the paper and came for an interview."

"Tiffany, that's enough." Delores said gently, but her eyes grew sharp.

"How did you get roped into this contest?" William tried changing to a safer subject.

"I'm not involved directly."

"She's giving me cooking lessons." Steven said.

"Lessons. I bet!" Tiffany snorted.

"Tiffany, I'm warning you." Steven kept his tone even but struggled with his temper.

"Oh, come on, Steven. You're not in that kitchen trying to cook. Well, you're cooking up something, I'm sure but it's not food."

"For your information, Sis. I made pancakes for breakfast and I helped with dinner tonight."

"Yeah, right."

"What is your problem?" Steven asked.

"My problem is this little twit steps off an airplane from some forsaken state, then blows in here and has everyone under a spell because she can cook."

"That's enough, Tiffany," Steven growled. "Watch what you say."

"Why, because you're sleeping with her?"

"Stop it, both of you!" Grant ordered loudly. "Tiffany, as long as Megan is staying in this house, you will treat her with respect."

"Staying here? In this house? Have you all gone insane?" Tiffany stood up. "You hire her without any references because of mom's instincts. She puts the moves on Steven and now she's camped out here. What are you thinking? You're inviting trouble!"

"Mommy, stop yelling, you're hurting my ears." Billy covered his ears with his hands. "Why are you mad at Megan?"

Not my own son, she thought. This woman had taken over everything in her life. Tiffany ran from the room, crying.

William went after her. An eerie silence settled on the occupants around the table. Only Crystal's crying broke it. Delores took her out of the high chair and tried to calm her down.

"I think I'll go get dessert." Megan's voice quivered as she hurried off to the kitchen with tears in her eyes.

She started slicing the cake then heard voices drifting in form another room.

"Tiffany, you're being unreasonable." William said gently but firmly. "You don't have any reasons to dislike her. She seems very nice and held together pretty good, considering the way you attacked her."

"That seems to be the unanimous opinion around here. Megan is a saint."

"Why are you so against her?"

"I don't trust her. We don't know anything about her and my parents are losing their minds."

"Your parents are the smartest people I know. Maybe you should trust their judgment."

"It's not that easy. You know what happened with April."

"Honey, that was years ago. Leave the past in the past."

"I witnessed the destruction she caused my family. She lied and got Steven in trouble and threatened to take my parents to court. Steven and my parents fought for years, and he has never trusted a woman since. And what did April get? A large sum of money."

"I know it was a hard time for everyone, but Steven has his life back on track. He and your parents are closer than ever, and if you ask me, he seems pretty smitten with Megan."

"That's the problem. He's not using his head. He's falling for another pretty face, and is too infatuated to see he's being used again."

"Would you think that if Megan were ugly?"

"What?"

"Why do you think she's using him?"

"Because she weaseled her way into staying here."

"Did you bother to find out why she is staying here?"

"No."

"Then don't jump to conclusions. Go have a talk with your parents and find out the facts before losing your temper."

"Why are you always so diplomatic?"

"Because you are too emotional and need me to calm you down."

"I don't keep you around because you're diplomatic, you know."

"You don't?"

"No, I keep you around because you're cute."

"Well, I keep you around because you're emotional."

"Why?"

"Let's just say, I like making up after a fight."

They were quiet for a long pause and Megan could only guess they were kissing.

"Let's go back and try not to upset anyone. You really should give Megan an apology too."

"I'm not sorry for trying to protect my family," Tiffany defended.

"Megan seems harmless."

"April seemed harmless too."

"All I'm saying is give her a chance."

"Why?"

"Because I think Steven is falling for her."

"What makes you think that? Sure, she's pretty, but he's been with lots of pretty woman."

"Maybe, but has he ever learned to cook for them? Can you see Steven making meatballs for someone he doesn't care about? He also has never defended a girl like he did in there."

"I hate it when you're right."

"You love it when I'm right."

Steven can't be falling for me, Megan fought the idea. William simply read more into his actions. They were only friends and that would be as far as they could ever get. At least until she totally dissolved her past.

"Do you need help?" Steven asked.

Megan jumped.

"Sorry. I didn't mean to startle you."

"My nerves are a little rattled."

"Tiffany was pretty brutal."

"She's only trying to protect you."

"From what? You?"

"She feels I'm a threat. From her point of view, I can see..."

"Megan, you are too forgiving. She had no right to say those things."

"Forget it." She held up the cake. "Here take this to the table."

Steven wondered how anyone could have such a big heart. "She owes you an apology." He turned to go.

"Who is April?" She blurted out.

He made an about-face. "Where did you hear that name?"

"I...umm...overheard Tiffany talking." She couldn't quite read his expression. "Look, I don't mean to pry. It's none of my business. But whatever happened, your sister thinks I might do the same thing."

"Never!"

"I want you to see her point of view."

"Her point of view is judging people without any cause. She has always been judgmental."

She digested that for a moment. "I think she'll behave now."

"What makes you say that?"

"William talked to her."

"Aren't you becoming quite the little eaves-dropper?" Steven grinned.

"I wasn't eavesdropping. I...I just happened to hear the conversation."

"That's what all good snoops say."

"Snoop!" One blond brow shot up in defense. "I wasn't snooping."

Steven laughed as he walked out of the room.

"Of all the nerve," Megan sputtered, picking up the pie and following Steven.

"Cake," Billy exclaimed. "Is that da surprise?"

"It sure is." Megan smiled.

He fidgeted in his chair. "Is it chocolate?"

"Yes."

"That's my favorite."

"I know. Your grandma told me."

"Yay!"

"I also made apple pie."

"Now, Megan, how am I supposed to choose between my two favorite desserts?" Grant rubbed his chin.

"I don't know about you, Dad, but I plan on having a piece of both," Steven suggested.

"That solves the dilemma for me." Grant patted his stomach.

"I think I'll have the pie," William stated. "It looks delicious."

"It's the best," Grant assured him.

Megan dished out the desserts and when she got to Tiffany, hesitantly asked, "Do you want something?"

"I'm not a big dessert person." Tiffany crossed her arms and sat back in the chair. "But I will try a small slice of pie. I keep hearing so much about it."

Megan gave her a plate.

Grant and Delores smiled at each other then turned their smiles toward Tiffany. Steven glared at her, deciding he'd talk to Tiffany later. He wasn't as forgiving as the rest of his family.

Megan felt more relaxed, less nervous with Tiffany and her better manners. She could understand why Tiffany was protective of her family. If this were her family, she'd feel the same way.

After dinner Megan served coffee in the living room, chatting with Steven and William while Tiffany talked with her parents in the study.

The guys discussed work and she learned that Grant had started The Peterson Corporation thirty years ago, as an advertising agency. It had grown into a multi-billion dollar commercial conglomerate and poured hundreds of thousands of dollars back in the community every year. The bus driver wasn't kidding when he said that the Petersons had done a lot for the community. They gave money to charities for children, cancer, housing the poor, and hospitals.

She was glad when the night finally ended. Her muscles groaned in protest as she slowly made her way up the long winding staircase. Her entire body ached - it had been a rough night--a rough couple of days, a rough year all together. How she'd gotten through the worst year of her life wasn't clear, but she'd made it and things were looking up. Being surrounded by this loving family uplifted her spirits. Their love and compassion would help her to heal. Maybe God's hand had directed her here for that very reason. 'Be of good courage, and he shall strengthen your heart, all ye that hope in the Lord.' Psalm 31: 24 ran through her head. Did God plan on using this family to strengthen her heart? Would she find the hope she needed? The forgiveness her soul longed for?

Opening the door to her room, she stared in bewilderment at the boxes and packages on the bed. Her first thought was she'd entered the wrong room; however, she noticed her robe hanging on the bathroom door.

"What is all this?" Perhaps, someone accidentally left them in the wrong room. Sneaking a peek inside one of the bags she gasped and pulled out the black dress she'd tried on in the shop. An envelope slipped to the floor. Tears sprang to her eyes as she read the card, "Dear Megan, I bought you a few things from our shopping trip. I hope you enjoy them. Love, Delores."

"A few things." She laughed. Going through the packages she found several pants outfits and a couple more dresses with matching shoes for each outfit. She even found things like nightgowns and undergarments.

Megan carefully put everything back in the bags and boxes. She couldn't possibly accept all these things. Tiffany would definitely think she was using her family for their money. Yet, it meant a lot to Mrs. Peterson to boost her spirits, which in a small way it did. The day had been fun and the clothes were beautiful. She'd never felt so pampered in her life. Nor had anyone ever done anything that wonderful for her. Still, she felt uncomfortable excepting such extravagant and expensive gifts. She'd talk with them first thing in the morning.

She found Delores and Grant sitting at the table drinking their morning coffee. Delores was making a list while Grant read the paper. She wanted to broach the subject of giving back the clothes, but was unsure how.

"Mrs. Peterson, may I talk to you for a minute?"

"Of course, dear." Delores winked at Grant. "But it's a little early to go over the Thanksgiving plans, don't you think?"

"It's not about Thanksgiving."

"Oh?" Grant looked up from the newspaper. "What's wrong?"

"It's about all the things that were left in my room."

"What things?" He looked puzzled.

"I told you, I bought her a few essentials while we were shopping yesterday." Delores smiled.

"A few essentials!" Megan exclaimed. "You bought the whole store."

The paper wiggled as Grant chuckled. "I told you she wasn't going to accept the gifts without a fight." He looked over the top of the paper at his wife.

"I really appreciate the gesture, but I can't accept all those things. They're too expensive."

"Megan, we want you to have them. I bought gifts for a lot of people and they aren't returning them," Delores said.

"Most of those were for your family but..."

"No, buts. I bought the clothes as a gift."

"What about the new iPod and speaker?" Megan asked. "I don't even remember going to an electronics store."

"Oh, well that gift came from Steven. He wants you to download your song lists onto It."

Megan took a deep breath and rubbed her temples. "Why would he do that?"

"He said you have an old, beat up little box, forget the name." Delores drew her brows together. "Anyway, he wants you to download your song list on to the iPod so he can hear the songs too."

"This is crazy," Megan muttered under her breath. "Look, how about a compromise?

"A compromise?" Grant looked intrigued.

"What if I keep one outfit and you return the others? And I don't need the iPod."

"Absolutely not. Everything belongs to you. Besides, I can't take them back." Delores informed her. As for the iPod, Steven would be crushed. He's starting to like that country music and wants a better quality sound. He's very technical, you know?"

"I don't want to hurt your feelings or sound ungrateful, but you two have already done so much for me, and it's not right to take anymore."

"I know it seems like a lot of money to you, but it's nothing to us," Grant added. "A few articles of clothing aren't going to break the bank."

"I know you have money, but that doesn't make it right for someone to sponge off you."

"Sponge?" Delores protested. "You earn your keep. We couldn't get through the holidays without you. You're staying here as part of your wages and you haven't asked for one thing. I wanted to do something nice for you. Stop worrying about what other people think. Tiffany was out of line last night and we told her so."

Megan wondered how people who were virtually strangers could feel such compassion. Then again, they were always helping people. "There is one other problem," Megan stated. "I have no place to wear such fancy outfits. I can't wear them while I'm cooking."

"You can wear them when you go out," Delores said.

"I don't go out anywhere."

"Well, we'll have to do something about that." Delores winked. "Besides, Thanksgiving and Christmas are coming. You need to be dressed appropriately. Consider them on-the-job clothing."

She couldn't win. They had an answer for every-thing.

The next few days passed quickly and un-eventfully. Steven came into the kitchen every spare moment, absorbing everything Megan taught him.

"You really want to beat your dad, don't you?"

"It started out being about the contest, but now I like it. I enjoy cooking. It's amazing how you can take one thing and turn it into something else. Meatballs for example, you start out with hamburger, add other ingredients, and presto, you now have something totally new, something different."

"You really are getting into this, aren't you?"

"I can't explain it. It's like power at your finger-tips. You control the ingredients and turn it into whatever you want."

"You men go on power trips over everything," Megan laughed.

"You don't feel the same way?"

"Not really."

"Don't you like it when things turn out perfectly and get upset if they don't?"

"Of course. Cooking is a passion. There's a big difference."

"Making something into whatever you want is power not passion."

"But the emotion behind cooking is passion. The way I see it, if you have a raw egg or a cooked egg it's still an egg,"

"But there is a lot you can do with one egg. It can be fried, scrambled, boiled, poached, or made into an omelet. If you add it to other ingredients you can make a cake, pancakes, or a meatloaf. You don't feel power over creating whatever your heart desires?" Steven stared so earnestly into her eyes that he touched her soul. "That is power, Megan, sheer power."

"Maybe so, but looking at you right now, I see passion. The thrill and excitement of creating, all the energy and emotions you put into it - that is passion. You must have the vision before you can create anything."

"Women! Everything is about emotions," he snorted. "What about creativity?"

"It falls under passion."

"That's only because you want to win the argument." Steven grinned. "A friend of mine once stumped us with some trivia questions. You know those tall, white hats that chefs wear?"

"Yes."

"How many pleats are in them?"

"I haven't the foggiest idea."

"One hundred and one," he answered proudly. "Know why?"

"I don't suppose it has anything to do with Dalmatians?"

"No." Steven laughed. "It's because a chef should know one hundred and one ways to cook an egg."

"That's a lot of egg dishes."

"The point is there is power in knowledge. And creativity takes knowledge."

"I guess when it comes to cooking you have to have both passion and power," Megan suggested.

"I couldn't have said it better myself. And now that we have that settled, why don't we take a break and go swimming."

"Swimming?" She drew her eyebrows together. "I don't really feel like getting wet."

"Come on, Megan. You need to have some fun. I'll meet you at the pool." He started running from the room.

"All right, but I'm not going in," she yelled after him.

Twenty minutes later she entered the pool house wearing her new swimsuit and a short white terry cloth robe.

"I was getting ready to come look for you. I thought you might have gotten lost." Steven grinned.

"No. I couldn't find my book." She arranged a lounge chair, laid her book down, and untied the belt.

"Why do you come to a pool to read? You can read any..." He stopped in mid-sentence as Megan slipped the robe off. The white fabric of the suit hugged her figure, showing every curve, while the back plunged down daringly with gold cords criss-crossing.

"I already told you, I don't want to get wet. I thought I'd read for a while."

Steven had to drag his eyes away from her. What had he been thinking? Seeing her in a swimsuit wasn't his best idea. How was he supposed to handle being *just a friend* when desire overtook him at the mere sight of her? *Stop!* He scolded himself, and dove in with a big splash.

Megan had just settled into a chair and opened her book when the splash hit her. "Steven Peterson!" She jumped out of the chair.

"What's the matter? Did you get a little wet?"

"You did that on purpose."

"I just dove in the water."

"You dove in about as gracefully as a cow."

"Are you calling me a cow?" Steven got out of the pool, striding over to stand in front of her. His overpowering presence made it hard to breathe. She took a step back, setting the book on a table.

"No, I didn't mean you are a cow." She saw the amusement twinkling in his eyes. "I simply said you jumped like one."

Steven wanted to be as close as possible. She was beautiful, even in a swimsuit she looked like an angel. He took a few more steps forward. "I'm shocked that a farmer would have such an aversion to cows." He could feel her warmth. "Didn't you raise cows on your farm?

"Ye...Yes." Her mind fumbled for words. "But we mostly worked in the fields, wheat, corn and soybeans." She stepped back again trying to clear her head.

"Megan, why are you afraid of me?"

"What makes you think I'm afraid?"

"You keep moving away every time I come near you."

"You're dripping on me," she said, backing up one more step. She'd never compare him to a cow again; he seemed more like a lion ready to devour his prey.

"You don't want to get wet?" he teased as he stepped closer, knowing the pool would block any further retreat. "Why?"

"I told you I don't feel like getting wet."

"Since I jump like a cow maybe you could show me how to be more graceful. Swans are graceful, don't you think?"

"S...swan?" Her throat felt dry.

"That's the animal I'd compare you to." He touched her shoulder with one finger, slowly running it down the length of her arm, leaving a trail of fire behind.

Megan retreated another step and suddenly found the fire from his touch extinguished by the cold water. She gasped for air but only cold liquid filled her lungs. Surrounded by blue, she frantically flung her arms trying to get back to the surface. Back into the air.

Powerful arms grasped her waist, pulling her up to the surface. She spat out the offending liquid, gulping in fresh air as she clung to her lifeline. Choking and coughing, she tried to catch her breath.

"Just breathe normally, sweetheart."

"You saved me," she cried and hugged him even tighter.

"Are you all right?"

"Yes." Blue eyes met brown ones, and for an instant, the eyes' owners clung to each other. Her body pressed so tight against his chest that she could feel his heart beating rapidly.

"I suggest we put some space between us."

Stunned back into realization, she let go and swam to the edge where Steven hoisted her up out of the water. While she sat on the edge with her feet dangling in the water, Steven opted to work off some of his energy doing laps.

His body ached and his blood felt hot as it pumped through his veins. No matter how many laps he did, he couldn't forget about the blonde goddess sitting on the other side of the pool. He wanted her more than any woman he'd ever known, but she wasn't ready. Any doubts about that disappeared when she took a tumble into the pool trying to avoid his touch.

Megan watched Steven swim back and forth across the pool. Lately, it seemed he was always there to rescue her. *Of course, I wouldn't have fallen in the pool in the first place, if it hadn't been for him,* she thought ironically. But then again, he'd only touched her, one touch and she'd completely forgotten the pool was behind her. *He must think I'm a ninny.* Did it really matter how he viewed her? After all, when the holidays were over she'd never see him again.

Her heart tugged slightly at that concept. She'd developed feelings for him, even though it wasn't appropriate, and it certainly wasn't convenient. She couldn't afford to lead Steven on, but she wasn't ready to let him into her life yet.

Chapter 10

The big day arrived, and Steven and Grant took over the kitchen trying to prepare dinner. They had finally agreed that the main course would be steak, but the side dish could be anything. They went all out, even including dessert.

Delores and Megan decided to go out for lunch and leave the men to the chaos in the kitchen. They strolled around the bustling Stearns Wharf looking in different souvenir shops. They had lunch at a beach side café afterwards, working off some calories with a long walk by the seashore.

The relaxing sound of the waves rolling up on shore soothed Megan's soul. The talk between them was relaxed and comfortable. Delores felt more like an old family friend than a stranger who'd hired her for a job.

"Thank you for a wonderful lunch," Megan said.

Delores smiled, slipping her arm through Megan's. "Thank you for accepting the invitation. I figured we may have to fill up at lunch since we don't know how dinner is going to turn out."

"Those two are something else." Megan laughed. "They're always competitive. Steven's determined to win."

"And so is Grant." Delores laughed. "Like father like son."

"How can you judge between the two? Do you pick your husband or your son?"

"I pick the best tasting dish, it's that simple. These two are always having contests but only in the spirit of fun. They've never gotten angry over a decision. If they had I would have put a stop to it years ago."

Megan looked out across the ocean, deep in thought.

"Is something troubling you, dear?"

"No. Well, I've been thinking about Laura," she admitted. "I miss her."

"I know you do." Delores put her arm around Megan's shoulders. "It's hard right now, but time will ease your heartache."

"My heart aches so hard that it actually hurts. Sometimes the pain is strong enough that I can't breathe." She listened to the sad rhythm of the waves. Even the wind seemed to blow across her life, bringing the memories back. "I can't imagine this pain ever going away."

"The pain is intense right now, but it will lessen in time. I'm not saying it will be easy, and I'm not saying you'll forget Laura, because you won't. But the emptiness you feel will decrease as time goes by. The trick is learning how to deal with it and not hide from it."

"I didn't want to feel anything." Megan felt a sob stick in her throat. "It hurts too much."

"That's why it's called pain. You are strong enough to get through it." Delores patted her arm. "I know you are."

"I'm not!" Megan shook her head. "I'm not strong at all. I've always depended on everyone else to take care of me."

"The problem is you're depending on the wrong people. You need to trust and depend on God. Only He can give you the strength you need to overcome this trial."

"That's the problem. I'm too angry with God to ask for help. I can't figure out why He is punishing me."

"Not everything in life is a punishment. Sometimes God gives us tests. We don't always understand why, but you must believe that it is for a reason."

"If it's a test, then I flunked."

"You are a lot stronger than you give yourself credit for."

"If I were strong, I wouldn't have left the way I did. I would have stayed and fought, instead of messing up my life, and everyone else's."

"Why did you leave so suddenly?"

Megan picked up a seashell. The top felt smooth while the sides were jagged and sharp, worn away from being tossed about in the ocean. She'd been tossed about in an ocean too, the ocean of life. "I was tired of fighting the pain." She shrugged. "And tired of my life, it had become automatic. I got up and did the same routine day after day. I hoped that by starting a new life in a different place I could put the past behind me." Her eyes glistened. "Now I'm afraid that by leaving, I only hurt more people."

"You can't think about anyone else right now. You have to concentrate on yourself. You!" Delores pointed to her. "You're what's important now."

"But I'm responsible! Not only is she gone, but I'm the one who killed her, and that's what I can't forget or forgive."

"If you don't forgive yourself, you can never carry on. Forgiving doesn't mean you're going to forget her."

"Forget her!" Megan said, enraged. "I never knew her. I was cheated twice. Not only is my baby dead, but I never even got the chance to know her. I never got to see her eyes open or feel her heart beat. I never got to sing to her, or dress her in any of the outfits I'd bought. All of my plans died with her." Megan threw the shell as hard as she could into the sea. A small part of her wished she was there at the bottom of the sea as well. She was weary, and death seemed like it would be an end to the pain. But somehow, even in the darkest of days, she had found the strength to carry on. God always managed to bring someone or something into her life, giving her the strength to hold on.

"Megan." Delores' gentle voice drew her from her reflections. "I know you won't stop blaming yourself until you're ready. I can stand here and tell you it's not your fault, but until you're ready to accept it, you won't believe it. However, I can tell you this - your baby is gone because God wanted her. He is the only one who can give life and only God can take it. I know it's not fair, but life is a roller coaster full of ups and downs. This is the worst time of your life, but I promise you there will be more ups."

Megan sighed. "I have to take the good with the bad, but I haven't felt any good for a long time."

"That's because you've been too busy burying your feelings. Now that you're working through them, you will see the light, and it will happen soon, I'm sure." After a long pause, Delores added, "Maybe you should call your family. Including them in your pain will help you heal."

"No." Megan shook her head. "I've burnt all my bridges there."

Megan woke up from her nap and went downstairs, she found Delores sitting in an oversized stuffed chair in front of the living room fireplace. "Did you have a nice nap, dear?"

"Yes. I can't believe I slept so long." Megan stretched, trying to shake the groggy feeling.

"You need your rest." Delores wished she could do something, but this was a battle only Megan could fight.

"Hey, Sleeping Beauty awakens," Steven greeted her with a smile. "And I wanted to give you a kiss to wake you up."

"I don't see a crown on your head. Only a prince can wake Sleeping Beauty."

"I see the nap not only made you more beautiful but sharp as a tack." Grant gave her a fatherly kiss on top of her head.

"We came to escort the two most beautiful ladies in the world to dinner." Steven held out his arm for Megan. Grant did the same for his wife.

"Flattery won't get you a thing." Delores teased as they headed to the dining room.

"I wasn't trying to score points," Steven defended. "It's the truth."

"Wow, this is beautiful." Megan stared at the transformation of the dining room. A lace cloth covered the table and an antique candelabrum sat in the center. The flickering flames were reflected in the crystal glasses, and dimmed lights gave a romantic ambiance to the room.

"Everything looks wonderful," Delores agreed.

"Thank you, my dear." Grant smiled triumphantly.

"She didn't say you won, Dad."

Grant laughed and winked at Megan.

"Don't try and butter them up. They're too smart for that," Steven said.

"I don't have to butter them up," Grant stated. "We'll let the food speak for itself."

"Well, what are you waiting for?" Steven pulled out a chair. "Have a seat."

The sound of the doorbell echoed through the house, stopping the commotion around the table.

"Who could that be?" Grant asked.

"I'll see." Delores left and returned with Tiffany and William.

"Grandpa, we're here." Billy announced, loudly.

"I see that." Grant picked him up and set him on his lap.

"We can hear you too, squirt." Steven put his finger in his ear and wiggled it. "Although I might be deaf now."

Tiffany noticing the candles and fancy place settings said, "I'm sorry, Mom, I should have called first. I see you're busy."

"Nonsense. We're just sitting down to dinner." Delores gave her a hug. "Since when do you have to call?"

"You're welcome here any time." Grant added. He stood up with Billy in one arm and shook William's hand. "Good to see you, son."

"You too, sir."

"Sir." Grant laughed. "You and Tiffany have been married for eight years, when are you going to stop calling me sir?"

"Sorry, force of habit."

"Did I forget a special occasion?" Tiffany noted the fancy table.

"No, dear. This is your dad and brother's handiwork."

"Sit down. You can help judge for the contest," Grant suggested.

"The contest is tonight." Tiffany looked amused. "Maybe we'll come back another time."

"Nonsense. Have a seat." Grant pulled out a chair. "Steven, get some more plates."

"I don't know," Tiffany said, skeptically.

"Oh, sit down, the food's getting cold." Steven's irritation at the unwelcome intrusion was evident in his crisp tone. But he obediently got the extra plates, glasses and silverware.

Everyone got seated and passed the food around. Grant's grilled steak was done to perfection, and he'd served it with mashed potatoes and salad. Steven chose to broil his steak, after it had been sitting in a lemon and garlic marinade. He also made a side dish of cheesy potatoes, and steamed green beans with a lemon sauce.

"Honey, your steak is good, but I do have to admit that Steven's is better," Delores said.

"I agree," Tiffany grudgingly offered. "What did you put on it?"

"Just some spices." Steven looked at Megan, hoping she would say something, but she seemed to clam up whenever Tiffany came around. Who could blame her, the way Tiffany kept attacking her? He wanted her to stick up for herself and tell Tiffany to take a flying leap, but Megan was too polite, too shy. However, he intended to let Tiffany have a piece of his mind. "What do think, Megan?"

"Very good, Steven. Your steak is tender and delicious. I don't know where you got the recipe for the potatoes, but I'd like to have it."

"Look at Billy eating them." William said. "He's even eating the green beans and he never eats vegetables."

"Well, son, looks like it's unanimous. I guess you win." Grant winked. "It really is good, Steven." Looking at Megan he added, "I can't believe you taught him how to cook in two short weeks."

Megan smiled at Steven. "He was a fast learner."

"I think you've found a hidden talent," Delores said proudly.

After the women were done cleaning the messy kitchen, Tiffany and Delores joined the men, while Megan made an excuse to stay in the kitchen a little longer, wanting the family to have a chance to talk privately. While piddling with some chores, she heard Steven's voice carry in from the foyer.

"There you are." His usual easy-going tone was replaced with an angry one. "I want to talk with you."

"Not now, Steven," Tiffany said. "I have to get..."

"Now!" Steven seemed to be straining to keep control of himself. "I'm only going to tell you this once. Leave Megan alone. Is that understood?"

"Steven, I..."

"I don't want to hear your excuses. You're mean and rude to everyone. Trying to pass your attitude off as protecting your family isn't going to fly. I have news for you, little sister. I don't need you watching out for me. I'm a grown man and able to make my own choices."

"Protecting my family isn't an excuse, it's the truth. And someone needs to have a level head around here," Tiffany defended.

"And you're the only one with a level head?"

"Sometimes. Yes. You get suckered by every pretty female that passes by, while mom and dad are so generous they never stop to think someone could take advantage of them."

"I got suckered once, and that was a long time ago. And you're telling me that you have more sense than a man who started a small business and turned it into a billion-dollar company. You really think you're smarter than Dad?" Steven sounded disgusted. "Gall is the only thing you have more of, and this time you've overstepped."

Megan had heard enough and decided to go talk to them. "Steven," Megan interrupted, "I can hear you in the kitchen." Looking at Tiffany she said, "I'm sorry, Tiffany, but last week I overheard you and William talking. I didn't mean to eavesdrop but..."

"You heard us and didn't bother to acknowledge your presence?" Tiffany asked.

"I was going to, but you were done before I got the chance."

"Megan, you don't owe her an apology." Steven glared at his sister. "She owes you one."

"I'm not apologizing for watching out for my family. No one knows anything about her."

Steven blew up. "You don't know her either. You have no right judging someone you know nothing about."

"Steven, I told you to let this go," Megan said. "She has a valid reason for wanting to protect her family. I can't fault her for that." Megan didn't like being the cause of tension. It would only give Tiffany more ammunition against her.

"You're too polite to say what you think, so I'll tell her for you," Steven said.

"Exactly what do I think?" Megan crossed her arms defiantly. "How dare you presume something that isn't true? I told you how I feel and you're ignoring it." She grew irritated. "You don't want your sister fighting your battles, and I don't want you fighting mine."

Tiffany's lips curved in amusement. She couldn't think of a time when any woman had spoken to Steven like that. Most of them were too busy plotting how to marry him, or at least keep hold of him to argue. Even more surprising was the way Steven's expression softened when he looked at Megan. *William might be right,* she thought, *Steven is falling for her.*

There was an awkward growing silence. Steven was angry with Tiffany, because she was angry at Megan, who was now angry with Steven. Someone had to break this vicious circle.

Megan spoke. "Look, Tiffany, I understand how you feel. I can assure you that I'm not out to trap your brother or to steal from your parents. They gave me a job, and they're trying to help me out. They've been kind and wonderful; I'd never hurt them. Never!"

"Well, I might have been too hard on you, but only time will tell. I'll take you at your word for now." Tiffany turned and went up the stairs.

Megan looked at Steven. "Will you leave her alone?"

"You're too much, you know that?" He smiled. "You defend everyone even when they're wrong. You're like a magnet for goodness."

"Well, this magnet needs some fresh air. I think I'll go for a walk."

"Do you want some company?"

"No. Stay with your family."

"I'd rather take a walk."

"Well, if you're going my way." She smiled.

As they strolled around the grounds, Megan was glad Steven had joined her. She'd only been in the gardens during the day and could easily get lost in the dark.

"Did you really like the dinner tonight?" Steven asked.

"Yes. I'm very proud of you. I really didn't think you could pull it off, but you worked hard and did a wonderful job."

"I had a good teacher."

"Your dinner wasn't only cooked to perfection, but was very creative too. That came from your heart It wasn't anything I taught you."

"Is that the passion you were talking about the other day?"

Megan's light laugh drifted on the breeze. "Exactly, although your dad's food was good, it lacked the creativity yours had."

They came to a gazebo and sat on the swing that hung there. They listened to the crickets chirping along with the creaking of the swing. The dim light from the moon bathed the rose bushes encircling the gazebo in a silvery light, turning the pink, peach, and yellow buds almost white.

"What are you thinking about?" Megan quietly asked.

You, he silently thought, but out loud said, "This has always been my favorite place."

"I thought the beach was your favorite place."

"No, I said that was the most beautiful spot in the whole world," he corrected. "The beach can be crowded. This has always been my private sanctuary."

"I know what you mean. We had a small pond on our property and I always went there to be alone or to think. It was peaceful and I loved hearing nature: the frogs croaking or the birds singing, even the buzz of dragonflies sounded soothing."

"Everyone has a special location that is all their own, a place where they can go and hide."

"Especially in my case," Megan sighed. "I had six siblings and it was hard to find quiet times in our house. The pond was always soothing and quiet. It was the only time I could reflect on life without someone bothering me."

"Do you ever go back and visit?"

"Sometimes, but it's been a long time."

"Have you been there since Laura died?"

"No. That was the last place I wanted to be." Sadness washed over her. "I stayed away from quiet places so I wouldn't have to think about what happened."

"I'm sorry. I didn't mean to bring that up." Steven put his arm around her shoulders.

"I've cried more in the past week than I have in the past year," Megan sniffed.

He wanted to say something profound that would stop her hurting, but nothing came to mind. So, he simply said, "It's okay to cry, sweetheart."

"I thought you were going to quit calling me that." She changed the subject. "Remember we had a deal. You wouldn't call me sweetheart and I wouldn't pick on your girlfriends."

"All right, you can take a shot at any girl you please, and we'll call it even." After a pause, he added, "But, if I remember correctly, we never sealed it." He winked. "However, we could seal it now."

"You want to kiss me?" She wiped a few tears away. "I'm a mess."

"You're beautiful," he whispered.

"I look awful. I've been crying all day."

"You're always beautiful to me." He laid his head on her shoulder, inhaling the sweet fragrance of her hair. "I like your hair down," he whispered, pushing a soft curl behind her ear. His breath felt warm as it skimmed across her skin. A shuddered vibrated through her like a tornado, scattering her senses, and her resolve. She fought to collect her thoughts, but ended up closing her eyes, revealing in the delicious sensations of his kisses.

However, a small voice somewhere deep inside said, *no.* It grew stronger and louder, forcing her vocal cords to utter it out loud. "No." She abruptly stood up, taking Steven by surprise. "I'm...I'm sorry, Steven. I just need some..." *air,* that's what she needed.

"Space." He sounded distraught. "I know." Noticing a tear slip down her cheek, he stood, hugging her tightly. "Oh, Megan, I'm sorry. I didn't mean to upset you."

"I shouldn't have...have led you on."

"It's my fault." Holding her protectively made him never want to let her go. "You didn't lead me on, sweetheart. You didn't. I just can't help myself."

When Megan pulled away, he realized how empty his life felt without her.

"I'm really sorry, Megan. I don't know what to say."

"It's not your fault." She wouldn't look him in the eyes.

"I'm trying to take it slow, but I want you so much. I want you in my life for the rest..."

"Stop! Steven, please, stop." She held up her hand. "I can't handle this right now."

"I know, I'm pushing you. But can't we at least go out to dinner or something?" He jammed his hands in his pockets. "I promise not to touch you."

"Steven, I'm not afraid of you." She felt better in control of her emotions. "It's not that I don't want to go out with you. I *can't!* Not right now."

"Why?"

"I'm not ready to get into all that. My life is in shambles and I'm trying to rebuild it. A new relationship is not what I need. At least not right now."

"How about tomorrow?" Steven joked.

Megan couldn't help but laugh. "What am I going to do with you, Steven Peterson?"

"I could tell you, but you'd probably blush to the roots of your hair." He gave her that devilish grin. "Let's go back to the house." She followed him down the path towards home.

⁓ ⁓ ⁓

Megan awoke with a start, her heart pounding and hands clammy, reminders of the recurring dream that kept her awake most nights. She groaned and wondered if she'd ever be rid of the haunting nightmares.

Hoping a homemade remedy of warm milk might help ease the jitters, she went downstairs. The earlier conversation with Steven played in her mind. She couldn't keep fighting this attraction. Her resolve kept deteriorating. *Steven isn't up for any kind of commitment*, she reminded herself. He was a free and wild spirit, wanting dinner and some fun. Yet, when he held her, she felt safe. *Am I fool enough to believe that a man like Steven Peterson would be interested in me?*

Entering the kitchen, she put a pan of milk on the stove, and then got a mug from the cupboard. "Ahhhhhhhhhh!" she shrieked as a figure from the shadows rushed towards her.

"Shhh, Megan, you're going to wake the whole house." He put his arms around her, holding her close.

"Steven!" She shrugged out of his grip. "Are you trying to give me a heart attack?"

"I didn't mean to scare you." He gave her a sheepish grin. "Why are you so jumpy anyway?"

"You're always sneaking up on me." She got the pan from the stove. "Why are you up?"

"I thought I'd come down and check on you."

"My knight in shining armor, to the rescue again." Megan poured the milk into her mug. "I'd say you're doing a poor job of protecting me. First, you almost drown me. And now you give me a heart attack."

Steven felt her shutting him out. "If you don't want to talk just say so. Don't make me the bad guy." He turned to leave.

"Steven, wait." She marveled at how well he understood her. "I'm sorry. I didn't mean to pick a fight."

"I only wanted to see if you were okay."

"I'm just having trouble sleeping."

"I've had a restless night myself." Although his insomnia was caused by her, he found it harder and harder to sleep when she walked through his dreams.

"Do you want some?" She held up her mug.

"What is it?"

"Warm milk."

"Only if you add some cocoa. Do we have marshmallows?"

"Check in the pantry." She made his cocoa. "I thought only kids liked marshmallows in their hot chocolate."

"I'm a big kid."

"That's for sure." She sat down at the table.

He put a handful of marshmallows in his mug of cocoa and joined her. They sat in silence. There was no need for words just then.

"Can I ask you something?" Megan approached the subject she'd been curious about.

"Sure, my life's an open book." He leaned back in his chair, placing his hands behind his head.

"You seemed reluctant to discuss this before." She ran a finger around the rim of her mug.

"April?"

She looked at him surprised. "How did you know that was on my mind?"

"Sweetheart, I can read you like yesterday's newspaper." He smiled. "Plus, it's been on my mind lately."

"Is she the one who broke your heart?"

"Who said anything about a broken heart?"

"Rosa told me you'd been in love once. But your heart was broken and you've never had a serious relationship since."

"Rosa talks too much," he said dryly. "But she knew what April was up to from the start. She tried to warn me. I didn't listen. I thought I knew everything."

"You were in love?"

Steven set his mug on the table. "Yeah. I guess so."

"Who is this woman who captivated your heart?"

"I'd hardly call her a woman." He cleared his throat. "She was a mere girl, nineteen. I'd just turned twenty. My parents hired her as an upstairs maid. She was beautiful. I followed her around like a puppy." He paused. "She used to leave little notes in my room after cleaning it. Sometimes we'd sneak off for long walks. We even went out a few times."

"Was she in love with you too?"

"At the time, I thought so." He stared into his mug, watching the marshmallows bobbing. "But you know that old saying 'love is blind?'"

Megan nodded. "What happened?"

"Rosa caught us kissing one time. She tried to tell me that April was only using me. But I didn't believe her. My parents tried keeping us apart too. They said it was inappropriate to have a relationship with an employee. Mom never had a good feeling about April. But I was young and stubborn. Our relationship finally progressed to the point that we made love."

"Was she your first?" Megan asked hesitantly.

"My first love, or my first sexual encounter?" Steven stifled a laugh as her cheeks turned red. "I like it when you blush."

"We're not talking about me." She didn't want her questions getting sidetracked. "What did she do?"

"Besides pulling the rug out from under my life and ..."

"Breaking your heart," Megan finished gently.

"My heart was the least of the damage." His mouth twisted into a snarl at the memory of the betrayal. "After our encounter, she said she loved me. But I soon found out that money was the only thing she loved." Hatred and pain were etched in his tone.

"Did your parents pay her off to leave you alone?"

"No. They didn't like April any more than Rosa did, but they would have never interfered like that. No, April claimed I forced her to have sex and threatened a sexual harassment suit if they didn't pay her off."

"Oh, Steven, how awful!" No wonder he'd never trusted anyone again. That certainly explained why Tiffany felt so protective. "If it was consensual how could she claim rape?"

"It was her word against mine."

"What about the letters she'd written you? Wouldn't that be evidence on your side of the story?"

"I kept them in the drawer of the dresser in my room. She'd taken every last one, along with any other trace of her."

"She had every detail planned out, didn't she?" Megan said astonished. "But what about Rosa? She had seen the two of you kissing. Wouldn't that have been proof of a relationship?"

"Our lawyer felt that the word of another maid, especially one who didn't get along with April, would be dismissed as a grudge and not taken seriously."

"Your parents paid her off?"

"To the tune of five hundred thousand dollars."

"Half a million dollars for a lie! You've got to be kidding."

"I wish I were. My parents decided it would be better to keep it out of the courts. They gave her the money and she went quietly away."

"Leaving a path of destruction behind." She now had a better understanding of this man.

"She definitely caused a lot pain, that's for sure. What hurt more than her betrayal was losing my parent's trust - they could never look at me again without wondering if I was a rapist." Bitterness pinched a line between his eyes, his lips drew tight.

"Oh, Steven." Megan stood, wrapping her arms around him in an effort to comfort him. "I'm sure they believed you. No, I'm positive they did. They were looking out for your best interests, not wanting to drag your name through court."

"I felt like such a fool, Megan. Why didn't I listen to everyone?" Burying his head in her waist, he let all the pent-up anger and hurt flow out.

"Because you were in love, when you're in love all you can see is that person. How could you have known she had a cold calculated plan for getting rich and you were just a pawn in her cruel game?"

Steven lifted his head, looking into her blue eyes, finding understanding and compassion. "I've never talked to anyone about April. What is about you that makes me open up?"

"I'm in the right place at the right time." Megan smiled, locking her hands behind his neck. "You've been holding this in for so long. It's time to let it out." She repeated his advice.

They stared at each other for what seemed like an eternity, until a voice broke the silence.

"Steven."

Surprised, they both looked toward the door and saw Grant tying the loop of his belt. Horror filled Megan as she realized the picture they presented. "Mr. Peterson. She pulled out of Steven's embrace and fidgeted with her robe. "This isn't what it looks like."

"I know, Megan. I've been standing here long enough to know what's going on." His voice sounded gentle, no traces of anger. "Thank you for sticking up for me."

"Oh... I... Umm," She couldn't find any words.

"Do you mind if I talk to my son alone? It seems we have some business that needs cleared up."

"Of course." She was grateful for an excuse to leave.

"I want her to stay." Steven's statement caught her off guard.

"You'll be fine. Just talk to him like you did me." Touching his shoulder in a vote of confidence, she walked out of the kitchen and headed upstairs.

Chapter 11

The sun rose filling Megan's room with the light of a new day and new expectations. Hopefully, unresolved hurts and misunderstandings would be brought out of the dark and cleared up. She hoped Steven and his dad could make amends.

"Morning, sunshine." Steven sauntered into the kitchen.

"You certainly are chipper this morning, especially since you didn't get much sleep last night."

"Yeah...Dad and I were up pretty late talking. He repeated the same words he'd said back then, but the interpretation was different this time."

"You've matured, and things always look different when you're older."

"Hey, are you calling me old?"

"No, I said more mature."

"Ouch! Two words you never want to hear linked together."

Megan smiled. "Did you guys patch things up?"

"I'd say we put the whole issue behind us once and for all." He took a sip of coffee. "I was hurt. I thought dad paid her off because he believed her. I wanted to fight it, and being young I didn't understand what he was trying to do. But now, I understand that he wanted to protect me. Even though he told me that before, I hadn't believed it."

"Do you believe it now?"

"With all my heart." Steven wondered why he spoke and felt things differently around her. He'd never used words like *love* and *heart*. "I could kick myself for all the years I wasted being angry. I became rebellious afterwards, and I got into a lot of trouble. I caused fights and got kicked out of college, eventually quitting altogether. I only wanted to party and have fun. Mom and Dad threw me out, forcing me to get a job. Even then, I went from job to job. I felt aimless - my life had no direction. It took me a long time, but I finally came to my senses and went back to college. That's when Mom and Dad let me move into the addition, the only condition being that I kept out of trouble and studied hard."

"You look like you're doing a good job," Megan offered.

"I get teased, because I'm thirty-six and live at home."

"Does that bother you?"

"Not really. I don't have to stay here. I moved in so I could devote time to my studies. After graduation, I went to work with Dad. I just haven't felt the need to move out again." After a pause, he added, "The only reason Dad hired me was so he could keep an eye on me."

"Hired you!" Megan repeated, shocked. "Aren't you partners or something?"

"No, I started out working in the mailroom."

"The mailroom." She couldn't envision this strong, intelligent, incredibly handsome son of a billionaire working in a mailroom.

"Yeah, I know. Doesn't it sound like something right out of a TV show?"

"Wouldn't you inherit the company if something happened to him?" She immediately wanted to retract that. "I'm sorry, that's none of my business."

"It's okay. To be honest, if something had happened back then, I don't think Dad would have trusted me enough to handle the business. It would more than likely have gone to William. He's CEO of the company."

"What about now?"

"I don't know. I have moved up through the ranks in the last five years, but I still have a lot to learn."

"I can name one thing you don't have to earn. His respect." They paused, gazing at one another, before he smiled softly and said, "Thanks." There was another soft, expectant pause. He looked around, cleared his throat and finally asked, "Do you need any help?"

"Nope. The blueberry waffles are almost done."

"My favorite." Steven smacked his lips.

"I know." She smiled. "I figured since you didn't get much sleep, you should have a big breakfast to keep your energy up."

"Good morning, everyone." Delores seemed to bounce into the room.

"Good morning, Mom."

Delores gave Steven a hug. "I didn't think I'd find you in the kitchen, since your lessons are over."

"I'm not cooking." He kissed her cheek. "If you ladies will excuse me, I need to get dressed."

Delores squeezed Megan hard, nearly taking her breath away. "I want to thank you for helping get through to Steven."

Megan smiled, glad that in some small way she could contribute something to this wonderful family who'd given her so much.

"*Buenos días,*" Rosa greeted her with enthusiasm.

"You certainly are in a good mood. Something must be in the air."

"*Señora* Peterson just told me I have a vacation day. I'm taking the day off."

"Then why are you standing around here?"

"I wanted to see if you want to go out, maybe to the mall."

"I'm afraid I don't have any vacation days. I'm stuck working."

"She said you had the day off, too."

"Oh. She didn't mention it to me."

"Maybe she wanted to surprise you." Rosa shrugged. "Sorry if I spoiled the surprise."

"It's not a big deal. I guess the mall would be fun, although I'm tired of shopping."

"I don't shop," Rosa explained. "I like watching the people."

"All right. Joe told me about the malls around here."

"Who's Joe?" Rosa raised a dubious brow.

"The bus driver - he was always giving me interesting facts about the city."

"Sounds like he would know the city best." Rosa checked her watch. "I'll go home and change, then swing by and pick you up."

"Okay." Although she hadn't felt like sightseeing much when first arriving - she was beginning to get a taste of this city, and wanted to see more.

Forty minutes later they turned into the Loreto Plaza. After getting some cappuccinos and doughnuts from a small coffee shop, they sat on a bench in the middle of the huge building. Talking and joking, they laughed and had a good time watching the crazy hairdos and outfits walk by.

"There." Rosa pointed out a young man dressed in black leather. "He's a seven, no?"

"Seven?" Megan's forehead wrinkled.

"*Sí.* On a scale of one to ten I rate him a seven. What do you think?"

"Rosa!" She scolded. "Aren't we a little old to be rating men?"

"No. Besides, you can learn a lot about a woman from the men they like."

Megan leaned closer and whispered, "Well, I don't think he's a seven, maybe a two. What's that tell you?"

"That you have bad taste in men."

"I'm not the one with bad taste," she defended, and pointed to a dark headed man in a pin striped suit. "There, he's a seven."

"Too stuffy. You like that business look, don't you?"

"I like a well-dressed man. Don't you?"

"Sometimes. But I'm more of a free spirit. I like outfits that scream for attention."

"Like yours." Her bright colored, striped outfit was a cross between something from Mexico and a trend from the seventies.

"You don't like it?"

"Let's just say that your spirit couldn't get any freer or scream any louder."

Rosa laughed. "I think *Señora* Peterson agrees with you. That's why she makes me wear the uniform."

They browsed around some of the stores before going to lunch.

"I know a great Mexican place," Rosa offered.

They entered the El Paseo restaurant and Megan immediately liked the decor. The red tables and cherrywood chairs added the right touch to the festive atmosphere.

"This place is great."

"I told you." Rosa led the way to a table in the corner.

While they waited for their lunch Rosa filled her in on the history of the place. "This place was built by one of Santa Barbara's founding fathers, Don Antonio de la Guerra, in 1826, although it wasn't turned into a restaurant until 1922."

"Santa Barbara is filled with so much history. Is Mexico like that?"

"*Sí.* History is all around you. There is no history in Illinois?"

"I suppose there's some, but none of it is exciting."

"That's because you grew up there. This place is new. That always makes it more interesting."

"I guess."

"I'm glad we had this time together." Rosa smiled, sincerely. "I'm sorry for all the trouble you've had, but I'm glad it brought you here."

"I never thought about it like that." Megan looked into the deep, dark eyes of her friend. "If I hadn't lost Laura, I'd never have ended up here. I'd never have met you or the Petersons. I guess something good came out of all the pain."

"*Sí*." Rosa reached across the table, taking Megan's hand. "Life always has lessons to teach us. If we learn these lessons and go on, we become stronger. I think you've learned yours well."

"I don't know," Megan sighed, still feeling like she was being punished.

Megan stood in the kitchen preparing lunch and singing along to the songs on her new iPod and speaker. Steven crept up behind her, sliding his arms around her waist.

"I've missed you," he sighed.

"Missed me?" She wriggled out of his grasp. "You see me every day."

"But not like I used to. Dad gave me all that time off for cooking lessons, now he has me working overtime to make up for it."

"I think you'll survive the jungles of the work-place."

"I'm not complaining about the hours. I just miss working in the kitchen with you." This was dangerous territory but he had to see if she felt the same way about him. Slow had never been his style.

She couldn't tell him what he wanted to hear, not yet. She knew he wouldn't wait forever, he'd grow impatience and move on to the next girl soon. However, she wasn't ready to take the risk and couldn't tell him that she missed him too. "You know, I'm busy with Thanksgiving preparations; it's probably best you're not around. Thanksgiving is only a couple of days away and things are pretty hectic."

Steven felt the disappointment settle into his heart, but he didn't say anything. Pushing her too hard now would only result in disaster. He felt the beating of his heart increase as he watched her move around the kitchen. Mentally counting, he tried to slow the beat to a normal pace, tried to push those blue eyes and haunting smile from his mind. Instead he let the words of the song fill the long silence that ensued. "Who's singing?"

"Tim McGraw - isn't he great? He's one of my favorite artists."

"Loneliness, dancing with the devil and being a better man! I can identify with the lyrics," Steven sighed.

"What?"

"Nothing." He'd made his move and she rejected him again. What was it going to take to get a date with her? Then, he had an idea, gallantly bowing, he asked, "May I have this dance?"

Megan stopped wiping down the counter and looked at him. His lopsided smile and rich chocolate eyes shimmered with a dare. She tried convincing herself that one dance wouldn't hurt. She'd already disappointed him and didn't have the heart to do it again. "Why yes, sir," she said in her best southern accent. She curtsied and pushed the warning thoughts away.

Steven slipped his left arm around her tiny waist, slowly waltzing her around the kitchen. The song ended but another tune by Lady Antebellum started. The soft, gentle, and somewhat sad melody reminded him of Megan. The words *"dancin' away with my heart*" fit his mood. If only he could find some way to keep her close to him.

"You dance quite well," he commented. "Much better than your Southern accent."

"Your accent wasn't any better." Megan laughed. "My high school boyfriend taught me how to waltz for our senior prom."

"He must have been a good teacher."

"Yes, his mother was a dance instructor."

Steven wondered if this guy was the father of her baby. But, he wasn't about to ask the question and risk upsetting the relaxed mood settling on them. Megan finally seemed at ease in his arms as she talked about her hometown.

As one song led into another their steps slowed considerably until they gently swayed to the music and they gradually melted together. Steven found Megan was now pressed tight against his chest and he tightened his embrace so she couldn't escape - in case she tried. He'd dreamt about holding her since the first moment they'd met. Now that his dreams were coming true and he wasn't about to let go. The music faded into the background and the rest of the world disappeared. Time seemed suspended. The attraction building was undeniable. Laying her head on his chest, Megan wrapped her arms around his neck, enjoying the serenity of his protective embrace. Submerging herself in the sensations of his soft caress, Megan felt her defensive wall crumbling brick by brick. Soon she'd be defenseless with no strength left to fight. But at this moment she didn't care.

Steven softly brushed his lips against her temple, causing shock waves to spark through her body. His strong, yet tender arms allowed her to contemplate giving in to the temptation of feeling his lips pressed against hers. *Would it be wrong to kiss him, just this once?*

Steven's heart thundered faster as he considered her mesmerizing eyes, searching for objections, but not finding any. Her soft, pink lips were slightly parted and very inviting. Lowering his head, he slowly kissed a trail to her earlobe, nibbling on the appetizer before going to the main course. His body was on fire and only her gentle kiss could quench it.

The warmth of his body left her feeling dizzy and disoriented. She'd forgotten everything else - her past, her sorrow, she couldn't even recall her own name. The only thing that mattered was how she felt in his arms. His kisses left her weak while igniting buried passions. Closing her eyes, she tilted her head up slightly, giving his hungry lips easier access. Steven devoured the sweetness like a starving man eating a four-course meal.

A soft moan escaped her lips, as a swirl of emotions swept through Megan. She barely had time to enjoy the moment when the scent of smoke and the hideous shriek of an electronic alarm broke the mood. Abruptly stopping the kiss, she pulled back from Steven's embrace, noticing the thick, black smoke billowing out of the oven.

"Oh, no! The pies." Grabbing the potholders, she dashed to the oven, coughing as she shooed away the smoke. She set both pies on top of the stove, while Steven wrestled with the smoke alarm until the deafening noise ceased.

"My goodness, what happened?" Delores asked as she entered the kitchen.

"I forgot about the pies in the oven," Megan said, truthfully, without going into details about what had distracted her. "I'm sorry, Mrs. Peterson."

"No harm done." Delores noticed her flushed expression." Are you feeling okay?"

"Yes, I'm fine, but the pies are ruined."

"*Sí,* those pies are burnt to a crisp." Rosa laughed. "We need to open a window and let the smoke out." She tried the window but it was stuck. "Steven, can you give me a hand?" Silence answered her. "Steven?" Her dark brows arched as she looked at the doorway. "Where did he go?"

"I don't know." Delores looked puzzled. "He slipped out of here quickly."

Both women looked at Megan. She shrugged her shoulders. "Let me help you with that window."

Steven took a long walk, allowing the cool air to chill his fevered body. Megan was his destiny; he felt that to the very core of his being. Why did fate constantly keep interrupting them? She'd been ready to give in to the attraction. He knew she felt it, just as deep as he did, but something always made her hold back.

After raking a hand through his wind-tousled hair, he shoved his fists into his pockets. "So close," he muttered aloud. "I was so close to getting her to let her guard down." He had to convince her to go out with him. *But how?*

Megan set the breakfast table, and greeted Delores when she walked in. "Good morning, Mrs. Peterson."

"Good morning, dear." She stretched and yawned. "I'm tired - I feel like I've run out of gas."

"The holidays take a lot out of you. I've been really tired lately, too. I thought, I'd have to call the SWAT team to get me out of bed a couple of times," Megan confessed.

"I suppose you're right. We have been busy the past few weeks. You know I love the holidays, but I'm getting too old to enjoy them anymore."

"I know the feeling," she sighed.

"You're not old." Delores declared.

"I know," Megan agreed, "but I don't enjoy the holidays anymore. I can't find anything to be thankful for, and Christmas is just too depressing."

"It's hard to see things clearly when you're in the middle of despair. But you have many blessings and they will only multiply."

"Maybe someday I will look back and be thankful for everything in my life, including the pain I'm going through. Eight now it's too hard."

"You'll find the strength you need." Delores smiled. "God only gives us what we can handle."

"There was a time I would have believed that, but not now." She still struggled with her faith. Even though she'd witnessed God's provision, she still couldn't get over her anger. "I don't have the strength to handle this."

"That's when you have to lean on God. He shows us his strength through our weakness."

"It's a lesson I could have missed," she said bitterly. "Where is Steven, anyway?"

"He left already. He had something to do this morning."

"I guess I can put his plate away." Megan wondered if he was trying to avoid her. Divine intervention had stopped that kiss. It wouldn't be smart to start anything with him, but she found herself powerless whenever he came around.

"Good morning, ladies." Grant gave Delores a peek on her cheek. "Can you believe Thanksgiving is tomorrow? It's seems like time goes by faster every year."

"It certainly does," Delores agreed. "I just told Megan that I'm getting too old to enjoy the holidays."

"Sweetheart, you're not too old to enjoy anything." Grant took in his wife's attire. The purple, cotton robe accentuated her slender body. And, her eyes were still as bright a blue as years ago. In his mind, she looked the same as when they were young. "You're still as beautiful and energetic as the day I met you." He gave her a kiss.

"You're such a liar," Delores teased. "But it's one of the reasons I married you."

Megan got up at four the next morning and put the turkey in the oven. She toyed with the idea of going back to bed, but opted for a walk instead - hoping the morning air would clear her head. As usual, she wound up thinking about Steven. This man had somehow connected with her at a time when no one else could. Not even her family and closest friends had been able to pull her from the grip of grief. He made everything seem possible.

The air felt crisp and Megan could faintly see her breath, but enjoyed the solitude of the early morning hours. Contentment filled her as the sun slowly crept up in the sky, waking the sleeping world with a mere touch of its golden hand. She watched the sun climb higher in the sky until her coffee and fingers turned cold. Back in the house she found Grant sitting at the table reading the morning paper.

"Good morning, Mr. Peterson." She dumped out her cold coffee, refilling it. Wrapping her hands around the mug for warmth sent a chill through her body, making her teeth chatter.

"It's a bit cold for a morning stroll." Grant peered over the top of his glasses, resting on the end of his nose.

"Just a little, but I like watching the sun come up." She took a sip of her coffee and let the hot liquid warm her within. "Isn't it funny how the same sun looks different in various places?"

"The sunrise is different in Illinois?" Grant questioned.

"Yes, the colors vary in shades."

"Guess I've never paid much attention to the sunrise." He turned the page of the paper, "Or the sunset for that matter."

"Dawn is my favorite time of the day. The colors are the brightest in the morning."

"I like sleeping," Grant grunted.

❧   ❧   ❧

Megan spent most of the morning in the kitchen with Steven helping. He couldn't wait to learn how to make a Thanksgiving meal. Although Megan had most things already chopped and ready to go, she managed to keep him busy, showing him how to baste the turkey, make stuffing, corn bread, and croissants.

After lunch Megan started to feel queasy and light-headed.

"Megan, what's wrong?" Steven asked. "You're white as a ghost."

"I don't feel so good."

"Mom, come here!" Steven shouted.

Delores walked in, and one look at Megan told her why she'd been summoned. "Child, what's wrong?"

"Nothing. I'm just hot." She fought the wave of nausea overcoming her.

"No fever." Grant touched her head with the palm of his hand. "I think she over-exerted herself."

"Steven, take her up to bed," Delores demanded.

As Steven hoisted her up into his arms, she felt the urge to vomit. Wanting to protest but feeling too sick, she quietly let Steven take her upstairs.

Megan woke up feeling more refreshed but with a start remembered Thanksgiving dinner. She rushed downstairs to the dining room where Rosa and Mrs. Peterson were setting the table.

"Are you feeling better?" Rosa asked.

"Yes, why are you here so early?"

"I told Mrs. Peterson, I'd come and help you set up for the meal."

"Thanks."

"Well, the color has come back to your cheeks," Delores noted. "Everything is under control, but I'm sure you'll want to check for yourself. So, go in the kitchen and get a briefing from Steven. Then carry yourself back upstairs and get ready."

"Do you want me to wear my uniform?"

"No. I want you to wear one of your new outfits - that's what I bought them for." Delores ushered Megan off to the kitchen where Steven had everything running right on schedule.

She looked like a movie star with her long hair softly flowing past her shoulders. The elegant black and white pants suit enhanced her dainty figure. A hush fell over the room and every eye watched her move down the stairs. Steven proudly waited at the bottom of the steps to escort her. After reaching him, she put her small hand into his and nervously smiled.

"Why is everyone staring at me?"

"You look so beautiful that no-one can keep their eyes off you."

"I think you're exaggerating."

"Am I?"

Steven gently guided her through the crowd of people who smiled and nodded in her direction. She bashfully smiled back.

"You look beautiful, dear." Delores gave her a hug.

"Thanks. You look wonderful yourself." The simple blue dress brought out her eyes.

"I must say, Delores certainly knows how to shop. You look like a million dollars." Grant brushed a fatherly kiss on her forehead.

"It probably cost that much," Megan teased. "You look very handsome too." His double-breasted navy suit matched Delores's dress.

"Megan, this is my husband, Antonio," Rosa said to introduce them.

"This is the Megan I hear so much about." He smiled underneath his dark handlebar mustache. "It's a pleasure to meet you." His dark eyes sparkled.

"It's nice to meet you too, Antonio."

Rosa also introduced her oldest son, who was almost twenty, and her seventeen-year old daughter, who resembled Rosa. The youngest boy was eight, but he'd disappeared, playing with Billy somewhere.

"My, my, don't you two look nice," Tiffany re-marked as she and William approached the crowd.

Megan couldn't read her tone and didn't know if she was being sarcastic or not. "You look nice too," she hesitantly offered. Tiffany's dark hair had been artistic-ally styled in an up do, while her purple pants outfit sparkled like the diamonds she wore on her ears.

"Thank you. This is a new outflt."

"Every outfit you wear is new. You need a warehouse to keep your clothes in," Steven scoffed.

"I wouldn't talk if I were you, big brother; I've never seen this suit before." Tiffany smiled triumphantly.

Megan's eyes roamed across the expanse of his chest, admiring the cut of the black suit, which accentuated his tall frame and muscular build. "You do look dashing tonight." She stroked the lapel of his jacket, brushing off an almost invisible mote of dust, and looked right into his smoldering eyes.

"My goodness, where are my manners?" Delores asked. "Would you like something to drink, Megan?"

"No, thank you. I'd better get in the kitchen and get dinner ready." It wasn't long before Steven joined her.

"What are you doing in here?"

"I came to help."

"You're the host. Get out there and mingle."

"I'm not the host, my parents are. Now what can I do?"

"Putting the turkey on the platter would be a big help."

"Can I do anything?" Rosa bustled in.

"Sure, check the croissants in the oven." Steven put her to work and soon all three were busy getting the last-minute preparations done.

They brought the food to the table and the guests began to take their seats. Everyone clapped when Steven brought out the turkey.

"This turkey looks like it came off the cover of a magazine," Delores cooed.

"I didn't do it by myself," Megan commented. "I don't think dinner would be ready at all if Steven hadn't taken over." Looking at Rosa, she added, "The table looks beautiful."

"*Gracias*. It was nothing."

William whispered to Tiffany, "I told you she would be good for Steven."

"I do have to admit I've never seen him look so happy. And I have definitely never seen him do so much work in the kitchen." Tiffany gave William a sideways glance, "Does that mean I'm going to hear 'I told you so?'"

"Not now. I'll collect later."

Grant gently tapped his fork against the side of his crystal glass, causing a hush to fall over the room. "First of all, I'd like to thank you all for coming and sharing this special day with us. I'd especially like to thank Megan for all her hard work in preparing this feast. Now, if we could all bow our heads I'd like to thank God before we eat." He closed his eyes, bowing his head.

"Dear Lord, we are gathered today in your presence to give thanks for the wonderful blessings you have bestowed on us all year. I pray that you would be with every one of us through the coming year and give us strength to face our trials, wisdom to know how to handle life, and above all, I pray for happiness and love to be found in abundance. Thank you. Amen."

Megan's food got rave reviews from everyone, including Tiffany. After dinner, the guests retired to the living room, while Megan stayed behind to clear the table. She busied herself with taking the food back to the kitchen and putting it away.

"What are you doing in here?" Steven asked.

"Cleaning up." She put some containers in the refrigerator.

"Come join the party."

"I have to put the food away before it spoils."

Steven gently spun her around to face him. "Megan, what's wrong?"

"Nothing."

"You wouldn't be keeping yourself busy unless you were trying to bury your feelings."

"I don't know," she said exasperated. "I just feel so...I can't explain it. I've been down lately."

"Oh, sweetheart, you've been through a great deal. It's a heavy burden to bear alone." He put his arms around her.

She tried not to cry, but in his arms, she was starting to feel safe enough to let go of the pain. "I'm messing up your jacket." She wiped at the tear stain.

"Don't worry about it. I think your make-up is messed up more than my jacket."

"I probably look like a raccoon." She dabbed at her eyes.

"You look beautiful, no matter what." He brushed a light kiss on her forehead. "Now go fix yourself up. We're playing charades."

"Charades? I haven't played that since I was a kid." Her mind drifted back through the years to a time when she played games with her brothers and sisters. The memories of those times brought a pang of guilt. She had never been away from her family on any holiday. "This is my first Thanksgiving by myself."

"You're not alone. There's a whole house full of people who care about you."

"You and your family have been great. I just miss my family, that's all."

"Why don't you call them? It will help ease the homesickness."

"Maybe later. We better get in there before they start without us." She quickly walked away.

Steven realized that she'd shut everyone out of her life including her family. He'd hoped that after facing the past, she would be free to open up completely. But it was obvious she still held on to the fears.

He felt helpless knowing he couldn't do anything. It was all up to Megan now.

Steven wiped the steam off the mirror, generously lathering his face he carefully shaved, while planning his next move with Megan. He had to formulate a judicious strategy to woo her without scaring her away.

Dressed in a pair of blue jeans and a white sweat-shirt, he went to find Megan. No doubt he'd find her in the kitchen, where she seemed to spend most of her life. But today he hoped to lure her away.

"Hey, good looking, what ya got cooking?" Steven sang the words of the old song.

"Pancakes." Her voice was soft and barely audible.

"Are you all right?" He noticed the dark circles under her eyes.

"Just tired." Megan yawned.

"Didn't sleep well?"

"I don't know why I'm so tired all the time."

"Know what I think?"

"No, but you're going to tell me, whether I want to know or not."

"Right about that." He chuckled. "I think you need to get out of the house for a while."

"And where should I go?" She flipped the pancakes.

"We could go to the beach."

"The beach?" She would enjoy seeing the ocean again, but it felt too much like a date. "I better not."

"Come on, it'll be fun. I'm meeting my friends and we're having a game of volleyball." He figured she couldn't object to a group outing.

"I don't like the game very much."

"Don't like volleyball?" He hadn't anticipated that. He hoped a group session would lessen her anxiety about being alone with him. "Why not?"

"I'm not very good."

"You don't have to be a pro. It's only some of my friends."

"I'm too short and the ball hurts my arms." She wasn't sure she wanted to meet any of his friends.

"That's a copout."

"No, it's not. Besides, I have a lot of work to do."

"That's the problem, you're always working. You need to get out and have some fun, get some fresh air. It will do you good."

The idea of getting out for a while did sound inviting. She'd been feeling poorly lately, and fresh air and sun sounded like a cure. "I was planning on getting some of the Christmas decorations done today."

"Christmas is a month away. You have plenty of time to decorate. Isn't Saturday your day off?" Steven watched her mull over the idea. "I'll even help you with the decorations if you want."

"Why can't I say no to you?"

"Because I'm so adorable." He grinned.

"Because you don't take no for an answer." She stacked the pancakes on a platter and handed them to Steven, then picked up the plate of bacon.

"Whatever the reason, it works." Steven winked and grabbed a slice of bacon.

Chapter 12

"Ready?" Steven asked as she descended the stairs.

"I guess." They would be in broad daylight, surrounded by a group of people. *It's not like it's a date,* she tried convincing herself.

"You look cute in pink." Steven winked. Her pink turtleneck sweater over pink leggings reminded him of cotton candy.

Steven pulled the red Koenigsegg CCX Spyder into the parking lot of the Carpentaria State Beach. The sun brightened the sky and warmed the sand. A large group of people crowded the beach, enjoying the

They headed towards the pavilions and picnic tables.

"Hey, Peterson, you made it." A guy in his mid-thirties slapped Steven on the back. His shoulder-length brown hair whipped around his face. "So, you finally decided to roll out of bed and join us." His eyes roamed over Megan approvingly. "I can see why you're late."

"Knock it off, Don." The tension in Steven's voice was unmistakable.

"Easy, buddy." A tall, well-built man with short dark hair approached, equipped for battle. "Are you two ever going to quit fighting?" His presence eased the tension. "Hi, I'm Andrew," he shook Megan's hand, "and this is my wife, Catherine." He put his arm around a small blonde with green eyes.

"Wife!" Megan repeated, a little surprised.

"Just because I'm not married doesn't mean all my friends are single," Steven laughed.

"I'm sorry, I...it just took me by surprise." Megan blushed.

"None of us can believe they were fool enough to get hitched either." Don's muscles tightened around his mouth, as if he were a bit envious.

"If you met someone as wonderful as Catherine, you would understand." Andrew playfully squeezed his wife's waist.

"It's nice to meet you - I'm Megan."

"Don't mind the guys, Megan. They act crazy but they're harmless." Catherine had a gentle quietness about her that seemed out of place among the rowdy brood of men.

"Since no one has bothered to introduce me," he cleared his throat, "I'm Don." Shaking her hand, he drawled, "It's *very* nice to meet you. And I'm single if you're interested."

"Nice to meet you too." Megan withdrew her hand, looking at Steven anxiously.

"Take it easy Don, this one is mine." Steven possessively placed his arm around her shoulders.

"Really? I don't see a ring on her finger."

Megan flinched as if she'd been hit in the gut.

"Okay, Don, that's enough. We don't want to scare Megan off on her first outing." Andrew smiled warmly, and turned to Megan. "You'll have to forgive these two - they have had a rivalry going since college."

"You have all been friends since college?"

"I've known Steven longer. We've been getting into trouble together since eighth grade." Andrew slapped Steven on the back. "He was best man at our wedding."

"Yeah, always the groomsman, never the groom, hey, Stevey?" An attractive brunette slipped her arms around his waist, seductively rubbing her breasts against his back, completely ignoring Megan.

"All right, Amy, that's enough." Steven peeled her arms off his body. "This is Megan." He waved his hand toward her.

"Hello, Amy." Megan smiled cordially, but her expression was met with cold hazel eyes, narrowing at the sight of competition.

"Yeah, whatever," Amy said with disdain. The tension in the air seemed thick enough to suffocate the small group. The intrusion of two more men was a welcome relief.

"We got the net up." One of the men who'd just joined them, Jack, walked over to the cooler and grabbed a beer. "Hey, Steven, you want one?"

"No, thanks," Steven gave Megan a wink. "I think we should get the game started."

"Sounds good to me," Don replied.

"Steven and Megan can be with us, and you four can play together," Andrew suggested.

"I don't think the teams would be fair." Catherine looked at her husband. "Why don't I play on the other team and let one of the better players be with you and Steven?"

"Honey, you're always worried about being fair. This is just a game and I want you by my side whether you're good or not." He laid a gentle kiss on her lips.

"I wouldn't worry about it being fair. Jack is probably too drunk to hit the ball anyway." Steven smirked.

"Hey, this is only my second beer," Jack protested.

"You mean, second twelve-pack." Don laughed.

"All right, quit picking on me. Let's play ball and I'll show you a thing or two." He pushed his red hair away from his face. "Drunk or not."

"Great, both Barbies on the same team. This should be fun." A venomous smile crossed Amy's face.

"Why don't you go back to bed and get up on the right side?" Andrew suggested.

"Shut up. Let's play ball." Grabbing the volley-ball, she stalked off towards the net.

"The couples are challenging us singles." Don laughed with resentment. Stripping off his sweatshirt he, too, headed to the net.

"Have you ever thought that Don and Amy should get together?" Andrew said. "I mean, such warm personalities should have a lot in common."

"Are you kidding? They'd kill each other," Steven said.

The game ended up being a lot of fun, even though Amy occasional directed rude remarks at Megan or Catherine. At one point, Amy intentionally spiked the ball toward Megan, and she jumped to get out of the way, falling down landing on her arm.

"Amy, that's enough." Steven yelled as he helped Megan up.

"What? That's part of the game," Amy defended herself. But after Steven's angry look, she decided to cool it.

After the game, Megan sat listening to the roll of the waves and watching the seagulls dive for their lunch.

"Are you feeling okay?" Steven joined her. "You look a little pale."

"I'm fine. Just a little light-headed."

"Are you sure my friends aren't upsetting you?"

"No, they're great."

"Not all of them. I have some problems with a few members of the group, but we all met in college and no-one wants to break the group up now." Shrugging, he added, "Don and I have been fighting since the day we met."

"What about Amy?"

"Not much to tell. We went out a few times and it didn't work out."

"She's very pretty." The statement was safer then asking why it hadn't worked out, or if he was still involved with her.

"Yeah, but that's as far as it goes." He looked out across the ocean. "There's no warmth to her, no... substance. We went out a few times but it didn't feel right, to me, at least, so we decided to stay friends. It was better to be amicable, since we have mutual friends, and neither one of us wanted to give them up."

"Does she still love you?" It slipped out accidently.

"I don't think it ever amounted to love."

"She sounds hurt."

"Hurt? No, that's her personality. She's mean and grumpy to everyone. And we're her friends. I'd hate to be her enemy."

"I know what you mean." Megan rubbed her elbow. "Catherine and I got the brunt of her fury."

"I'm sorry about that. Amy has never forgiven Catherine for marrying Andrew. She feels like Catherine stole Andrew away."

"Did she?"

"Not really. It never felt right to Andrew but he didn't want to hurt her feelings. Unlike me he doesn't know how to break up quickly. Anyway, Amy took their relationship a lot more seriously than he ever did. Once he met Catherine, it was the end of Amy... and any other woman."

"First you, then Andrew - sounds like she's had a hard time with love." Megan understood more than any one the heartache of loss and what it could do to a person's soul. "No wonder she's angry."

"She brings it on herself." His voice was cold

Was this the same man who held her through the night? The same man who gave her the security she needed to face her demons? Could he really be indifferent to someone else's pain when he vibrated warmth to her? He seemed to be two different men. Megan didn't know which one was the real Steven.

"Do you want to get some lunch?"

"Yes. I'm starved." She stood, brushing the sand off.

"Zookers isn't far. We can walk if you feel up to it."

"Sure. I'd enjoy a walk."

As they neared the water Megan felt the sand move under her feet.

"What's that?" She stopped and watched the little creatures burrow under the sand.

"Crabs and sea anemones - they wash up on shore with the tide."

Megan giggled as the small crabs tickled her feet while burrowing under the sand.

Afterwards, they entered the small restaurant, choosing to sit at one of the tables outside and enjoy the sound of the sea while they ate their fish and shrimp.

"Stay here. I'll be right back." Steven slipped away with a mischievous grin. He returned a few minutes later with a bottle of wine and two crystal champagne flutes.

"Where did you get that?" Megan laughed.

"I have my ways." He winked and popped the cork.

"It's a nice thought Steven, but I don't drink."

"It's non-alcoholic." He turned the bottle so she could read the label.

"Sparkling apple juice. You think of everything."

"I try to." He loved the way her eyes sparkled in the sunlight. "Shall we make a toast?"

She held up the glass. "What to?"

"Friendship. What else?"

"To friendship." The crystal chinked over the sound of seagulls squawking. "I have something to show you."

"What?"

"I want to show you, not tell you."

They cleared away the mess and headed back to the beach.

"There." Steven pointed toward the ocean.

Megan's eyes followed his finger, her mouth dropping slightly at the sight of seals and sea lions playing on the huge rocks that sat a ways off shore.

"Oh, Steven! How adorable!"

"They migrate here this time of year."

They stood watching the sea creatures play for a long time. "I wish I had some binoculars. They're too far away," Megan commented.

"I didn't think to bring them."

"You said you thought of everything."

"I said I try," he corrected. "Besides, I know a better way to view the rookery."

"What's a rookery?"

"That's what they call the seals' nesting spot." He took her hand. "Come on. Let's go say goodbye to the others and take off."

"I told you he was in love," Catherine whispered to her husband, after watching the couple holding hands as they walked to the parking lot.

"She seems nice. A quiet girl and a good cook from what I hear," Andrew commented.

"It would be nice to see him settle down. Who knows, maybe you'll be best man at his wedding before too long."

"I wouldn't start any plans just yet, honey. Steven's had lots of girlfriends." Andrew knew his best friend better than anyone else. "They don't hold his attention for long."

"True, but it's been ages since anyone has had his attention at all."

Steven and Megan went to the car and drove to the Carpentaria Seal Preserve where Steven asked to see the seals. It was crowded but they managed to find a spot overlooking the rookery. Megan excitedly watched the seals and pups play. Some sunned themselves on the large rocks while others dove for fish.

"We have a much better view from here," she smiled.

"They built this so people could enjoy watching the seals without endangering the babies."

"Look." Megan pointed at two seals fighting over a fish.

"They look like us," Steven teased.

"We wouldn't fight so much if you weren't such a buffoon." She jabbed him in the ribs.

"Ouch!" He put his arm around her. "Are you ready?"

"Do we have to leave? The seals are cute."

"There's an artisans' fair going on. I think you'll enjoy it."

"That does sound fun."

After driving back downtown and securing a parking space, they walked among the tall palm trees of Cabrillo Boulevard, fighting the throngs of people and enjoying the artwork and trinkets made by local artist. Steven bought her a seashell necklace.

"I can't accept this," she protested. "It's too expensive."

"Nonsense. Besides the money will help this talented lady."

"Oh, yes." The plump artist with stringy strawberry blond hair eagerly sided with Steven. "Your young man has fine taste."

"He's not my young man." Megan quickly corrected him.

"It's a gift from one friend to another." Steven placed the shells around her neck. "Friends are allowed to buy each other gifts, aren't they?"

She rolled her eyes. "Then I must buy you something," she stated as they walked to the next stand.

"I don't need anything. Besides, your smile is enough."

"I hardly think my smile is worth the price of this necklace."

"No. It's triple the price of a few shells."

"You can save your sweet talking," Megan teased. "Look." She pointed to a man sketching pictures. "That's what I'm going to buy you." She pulled Steven toward the booth.

They laughed at the caricature portraits on display.

"What am I going to do with a drawing like this?"

"Hang it on the wall."

"No. Someone will see it."

"Is the great Steven Peterson scared someone will make fun of him?"

"No." he defended. "I'm not scared. I'm... reluctant."

"You aren't so vain that you can't laugh at yourself, are you?" She challenged.

He didn't answer.

"Come on. It'll be fun. I'll pose with you."

"Oh, all right." He'd do anything for the chance to be close to her.

They laughed at the exaggerated features. Steven had a wide forehead while Megan had been drawn with a long nose and chin.

"I think he captured you." Megan laughed.

"I look like Mr. Potato Head."

"You look great." She paid the man.

"Where to next?" Steven asked.

"Aren't you leading this expedition?"

"Your wish is my command." He bowed.

"Well, then, let's see what's going on over there." She pointed to a group of people dancing.

"That's the conga drum circle."

After watching the dancing and listening to the drums beating over the noise of the crowd, Megan started to get a headache.

"Why don't we grab something to eat?" Steven suggested.

After dinner, he took her for a ride in a krazy kart. She laughed as he zoomed them around in the neon green kart. Between the laughing and the motion of the car she soon started to feel dinner churning.

"I think we better get home," she stated. "The Cajun must have been a little too spicy."

"Yeah, but worth it." Steven helped her out of the kart and held her hand as they walked to his sports car. They rode home in a friendly silence.

"Thank you for a wonderful day," Megan said when they reached home. "You were right. The fresh air was good for me. But you kept me too busy for it to be relaxing."

"Sorry about that. I just wanted you to have a good time."

"I did have a good time. It was nice to see some of the local sights."

"You need to get out more often. Santa Barbara has a lot to offer."

"I'm sure it does. I just haven't been in a sightseeing mood." Fun had seemed impossible with the pain and sadness lurking below the surface.

"I'm glad you're putting the past behind you and moving on."

"I wouldn't have, if you weren't here to help." She had more to tell him, but felt too drained to get into the story. There would be plenty time later. "I better get to bed." She stifled a yawn. "Good night."

"Good night, sweetheart."

"Megan, there's a delivery for you." Rosa popped her head into the kitchen.

"I haven't ordered anything." Megan wiped her hands on a towel and followed Rosa to the front door in bewilderment.

A tall man wearing a dark blue cap with a label that read, "Flowers for You," was waiting impatiently. "Sign here, please." He handed her the clipboard.

As Megan scrawled her name, another man started up the walk with a bunch of balloons so big, she half expected him to fly away. "Oh, my!" Megan exclaimed.

The man handed her the balloons. "Have a nice day."

"Thank you."

"Who are they from?" Rosa asked excitedly.

"I don't know." Megan set the balloons down on the table in the entranceway and started looking for a card. "Wow! There are flowers under all these balloons." She moved the assortment of balloons to reveal a breathtaking collection of roses, in every color imaginable. She found the card nestled between the buds. She laughed and read the card aloud, "This is a small token to thank you for brightening my life. You'd brighten my day even more if you'd accept my dinner invitation. All my love, Steven."

"How *rómantico*," Rosa said.

Megan inhaled the scent of the flowers. "There must be two dozen here."

"Actually, three." Megan and Rosa wheeled around to find Steven standing there. "Do you like them?"

"Are you kidding?" She pretended to smell the flowers again, hoping he wouldn't notice her tears. "I love them."

"I think I'm going to go ah...clean something." Rosa scooted off.

"I'm prepared to beg if I have to." Steven bent down on one knee.

"You certainly are persistent, aren't you?" Megan smiled.

The sound of his laughter filled her heart. "As I said before it's my middle name. However, I'm hoping to get you to change yours."

What will one dinner hurt? she mused. After all, she needed to move on with her life. "Okay, I'll go out with you."

Steven jumped up. "Oh, sweetheart, I promise you're going to have the best time." Picking her up he twirled her around, bumping her into the table and almost knocking the flowers and balloons to the floor.

"Steven, be careful. You're going to knock the flowers over."

"Then I'll buy you new ones. I'll buy you a whole florist if you want!" He set her down. "It's hard to believe some flowers and a few balloons could melt the ice queen's heart." Steven winked.

"A few? I've seen fewer balloons at a hot air balloon show." He hadn't won her over with gifts. His caring and compassion had melted her heart.

Steven paced impatiently at the bottom of the stairs. He started to run his hand through his hair but decided against it. He'd spent half an hour combing it to perfection and plastering it with hair spray. He nervously shoved his hands into the pockets of his well-tailored pants.

"You look a little nervous, son." Grant smiled.

"I am." Steven had never felt this way before. He'd dated a lot of women, but none that he wanted to impress as much as this one. "I have to make sure the night is perfect. It took me forever to get a date. I don't want to blow it."

"You'll do fine, Steven." Grant laid a reassuring hand on his son's shoulder. "Don't worry about impressing her. She has her own reasons for taking things slow. It has nothing to do with you."

"I know. I just can't help feeling like something will go wrong." Steven paced again. He'd had a strange feeling in the pit of his stomach all day.

"You've inherited your mother's intuition, huh?"

"I don't know about that. I'm sure it's just a case of the jitters. It's probably..." His words fell silent as Megan appeared.

The sheer sheath snugly fit every curve while elegantly floating around her knees. She'd styled her hair into a French twist with lots of ringlet curls delicately framing her face.

Steven found it hard to breathe as she descended the stairs. He felt like a teenager with clammy hands and beads of perspiration on his forehead. "You look stunning." His voice was barely a whisper.

"So do you." Her eyes devoured his attire. The silver satin shirt shimmered against the black suit. He wore a blue and silver tie, artfully blending the blue into his ensemble by wearing a blue handkerchief in the breast pocket of his jacket.

"The limousine is out front," Steven said.

"Oh, we're taking the limousine?" Megan sounded a bit nervous herself. She didn't know where they were going and the thought of being seen with someone rich and influential terrified her.

"I thought you'd like that." Women always loved riding in it and somehow came to expect it.

"My idea of a perfect ride would be a horse-drawn carriage. Just like Cinderella."

He should have known she'd be different. Everything about her was different. "Maybe next time, sweetheart."

"So where are we going?" Megan asked as the limousine pulled out of the driveway.

"It's a surprise."

"You've been saying that for days," she complained. "I didn't even know what to wear."

"If it's any consolation, you look great."

"It's not." Cocking her head, she curiously eyed him. "Why is everything such a big mystery?"

"Women like mysterious men."

"Have you been reading romance novels?"

A mischievous smile spread across his face. "Where do you think I get all my remarkable lines?"

"I wasn't aware you had any," she teased. "At least none I've heard."

"Ouch! You can cut a man to shreds with that tongue."

"What's wrong? You don't like getting a dose of your own medicine."

"You sure are sassy tonight," he said, shifting uncomfortably.

"It must be the company."

Steven's good-natured laughter filled the back seat, warming her heart. "Our reservations aren't until seven. We're going someplace special first."

"And let me guess - you're not telling me."

"Since this is our first date I feel there's something you need to know." He leaned closer, his brown eyes dancing with mischief. "I'm a secret agent and if I told you my plans I'd have to kill you. A matter of government security, you understand?"

"Too many spy novels also." She laughed, rolling her eyes. "Funny, I didn't stake you as a reader."

"I'm not. But I love James Bond movies."

"Romantic comedies are my thing." Megan settled back into the cushioned seat.

"That's what I would have guessed."

The limousine turned onto Mission Ridge Road.

"We're almost there."

"Franceschi Park?" Megan read the sign as they pulled into the parking lot.

"You can't find a more breathtaking view of the city than from here." They got out of the limo, and he heard her take a sharp breath.

"Oh, Steven, you weren't kidding." Her eyes widened in amazement. "This is the most beautiful view I've ever seen." She turned around in a circle. The panoramic view offered a majestic sight in every direction. She could see the city, mountains, and the ocean without taking a step. After walking up a path they stood on a ledge overlooking the lush green lawns of the park.

"I can see the whole city from here," Megan breathed. She found it hard to imagine that the creator of this world had made her too. And not just her, but her baby as well. Although sadness filled her heart, she felt peace surrounding her. *God is in control.*

"On a clear day, you can see all the way to Channel Island." He pointed in the direction. They watched the big orange sun sink over the city. Emerging shadows enveloped the tall buildings and hovered over the ocean. The dark background served to lighten the half ball as it slipped further down. Megan intently watched the color display in the sky while Steven watched her. She captivated his full attention.

Feeling the weight of his stare she turned and asked, "What are you thinking about?"

"I was remembering the first sunset we watched together."

"We didn't watch it together," she corrected. "I was enjoying the show when you interrupted."

Her wit always made him laugh. "You were just playing hard to get."

"I was not!" She stated in mock outrage. "At least, not back then."

"Then you do admit to playing hard to get at some point?" Steven's thick, blond brows curved up. So did the corners of his mouth.

"No. That's not what I meant." She looked him squarely in the eye. "I have reasons for not getting too close." Although the mood was playful she had a note of seriousness in her tone.

"I know you do, sweetheart. I'm only teasing. You don't have to explain your reasons to me. I understand what a horrible ordeal you've been through. But I want you to forget about the pain and have fun tonight."

"If only it were that easy." She looked back to the sky, trying to formulate her thoughts and words but lacking the courage to speak them out loud. She had to tell him sometime, but now didn't feel right. She just wanted to enjoy this night. *Maybe later*, she sighed.

"We better get going."

She gave him a questioning glance when they pulled into the parking lot of the El Encanto Hotel.

"This hotel has the most romantic restaurant in town," he reassured her. "The Dining Room is very quiet and upscale."

He was as good as his word. Megan found herself in the most romantic setting she'd ever seen. The square tables and white tablecloths were set in a dimly lit room. Candles and vases of flowers adorned the tables. Soft music added more romantic ambience to the scene.

She felt a bit nervous at first, but soon relaxed under the cheerful and fun-loving conduct of her date.

They went out on the terrace where more tables were set up.

"I thought we'd eat out here, under the stars," Steven said.

"This place has another wonderful view of the city," Megan commented. Although darkness had descended she could make out the outline of the housetops, and see the lights from skyscrapers. Her curiosity was roused by the sound of scuffling feet, laughing, and noises below. Megan looked down, noticing all the people.

"That's State Street." He informed her.

"It looks pretty busy."

"Santa Barbara is just getting started. There's a lot of night life."

"Can we go for a walk after dinner?"

"Yes. But I have a special place I want to take you."

"You're just full of surprises tonight."

"I just want everything to be perfect."

"It is, Steven."

The waitress brought menus and took their drink order.

"These prices are extravagant," Megan said.

"But the food is worth every bit of it." Steven opened his menu. "Why don't we start with an appetizer?"

"Eww. Grilled octopus." Megan wrinkled her nose.

Steven laughed. "Have you ever had octopus?"

"No."

"You should try something before deciding you don't like it."

"I'm not that adventurous."

"How about oysters?"

Megan shook her head.

"Tell you what. We'll order two appetizers, oysters and something you want, but you have to try one oyster."

She wrinkled her nose again.

"Come on, Megan, be adventurous."

"I'm sure I'm going to regret this, but I will try one oyster." She held up one finger.

They chatted until the oysters and cheese and fruit plate arrived. Megan picked up a piece of the toasted bread, put a small chunk of cheese on it and was about to take a bite when Steven stopped her.

"Why don't you taste the oyster first?"

She sighed and looked at the six oysters in their shells, sitting on a bed of crushed ice. She watched Steven pick up a shell and a slice of lemon. He squirted a little juice on the oyster, then picked up the silver pitcher of sauce and drizzled a little over the top. He slurped it into his mouth, after swallowing, he said, "See it's easy."

"What is the stuff in the pitcher?"

A mignonette sauce. It's made with shallots, cracked black pepper and vinegar."

"And you put that on top of the oyster." She looked at her cheese plate. "The oysters are sounding worse and worse."

"You don't have to use the mignonette sauce. I typically only use a little lemon, but I like the sauce they make here."

He picked up another shell, carefully reaching across the table, waiting for her to take it. She reluctantly took it.

"Careful, you don't want to spill the liquor. "

"Her brows furrowed. "There's alcohol in here?"

"No." Steven laughed. "That is what they call the liquid that is naturally in the oyster."

She brought the oyster close to her mouth and sniffed. "It smells salty."

"It is. You will first taste the saltiness from the brine. Chew two or three times then swallow. The brine will be followed by cucumber taste."

"Cucumber?"

"Yes, these are fanny bay oysters and they have a smooth taste with a cucumber finish. I wish they had Kumamotos or Olympias, they have a sweeter finish,"

"I had no idea there were different kinds of oysters or a certain way to eat them."

"Oh, yes, they are many different types. And eating an oyster is an art." He held up a lemon slice. Want some?"

"No thanks, I think I'm going to eat it plain." Megan took a deep breath. "Here goes."

Steven watched her slurp it into her mouth, and now understood why some people thought of them as an aphrodisiac. He smiled as she made a face and shook her head. "Well?"

"Yuck!"

"They are an acquired taste. The more you eat them the more you like them."

"I'm just going to stick with my cheese."

Next ordered salads. Steven had the kale salad while Megan stuck with the only salad she recognized, a Caesar salad. For the main course, Megan ordered short ribs on a bed of mashed potatoes. Steven ordered the mushroom and truffle risotto.

Megan eyes widened when the waitress placed her food on the table. "This plate is beautiful." The rib was placed over the bed of mashed potatoes with a sauce circling the plate. "But the portion is quite small for the price."

"You pay for the artistic plating and the quality of food."

Megan dug into the rib, closed her eyes and sighed in contentment.

"Like it?"

"I love it." She took another bite. "I've never had anything so moist and tender."

"The best part of smaller portions, there is always room for dessert."

Her blue eyes brightened. "You're right. I hardly ever room for dessert because I'm full from the meal."

After finishing their meal, they lingered over coffee and dessert, neither in a hurry to leave. It had been a wonderful dinner and she was finally starting to relax. When they got around to paying the bill and leaving Steven said, "We're going to Goleta Beach."

"Is the beach open this late?"

"Don't worry - they rarely enforce the time limits."

"You better not get me into trouble." She wagged her finger at him.

They walked along the sandy beach in the dark. The full moon gave enough light to watch the white caps of the wave crash onto the beach.

"Look at all those stars." She pointed upward. "They seem bigger and brighter when reflecting off the ocean."

"I've been to all the beaches around here, and for some unexplained reason the night sky is magnified best at this beach."

"This must be a special spot in the world." She snuggled into the crook of his arm.

"My sentiments exactly." He'd never felt closer to anyone than he felt to her right now.

Megan pointed to a cluster of stars. "See that open cluster of stars? That's Hydes and Pleiades. And over there is Cassiopeia."

"Who is that?"

"You've never heard of Cassiopeia, the Queen?"

"No."

"What about Orion?"

"Of course, I know the mighty hunter." Steven pointed to the three stars in a row. "That's his belt, but I've never figured out the rest of him."

"See those stars? They make up his bow." Megan pointed out the shapes. "There are his legs and his body."

"How do you know so much about constellations?"

"I took an astronomy class in college."

"I didn't realize you went to college."

"Only for two years. I had to drop out."

"Didn't you like it?"

"Oh, no. I loved it. But my scholarship ran out and I couldn't afford to continue. I always wanted to go back, but things happened and it never worked out." She tried summoning the courage again to tell him about her past, but once she met his dark eyes she lost the words. Their eyes met, holding the gaze for a long timeless moment, each searching deep into the other's soul, finding something they could hold on to for the rest of their lives.

Seemingly unable to resist any longer, Steven lowered his head, brushing her lips ever so slightly with his own. The mere touch sparked passion, triggering her knees to go weak, and almost causing her to fall had it not been for Steven's arms supporting her. He always seemed to be there giving her assistance, not only physically but emotionally. She'd leaned on him many times during the past six weeks. He was her strength, her rock, and her future.

Leaning closer he kissed her more passionately. Her arms went around his neck as they melted together. They suddenly broke apart, as a cold jolt struck them. Staring down at the tide as it washed over their feet, soaking them to about mid calf, they both laughed.

"This water is fre...freezing," Megan stammered.

"Let's get going before we catch our deaths," Steven said. He needed more than wet feet to squash the jolt of desire surging through his body. He couldn't wait to kiss her without something interrupting them. They ran to the limo and had Ralph turn the heat on. Steven's wet pants clung to his ankles, causing his teeth to chatter the whole way home.

He took her in his arms at the front door. "I need to change out of these wet pants. Will you wait for me? We can have a nightcap."

"Sure." She didn't want this night to end either. "I'll be in the living room," Megan suggested as they entered the foyer.

"Good, and if my parents don't have a fire going already, I'll start one." He smiled as an image of them sprawled out in front of the fire, talking through the night, entered his head.

"Well, isn't this cozy?" A deep, gruff voice startled them.

Megan spun around, her eyes filling with horror and disbelief as a familiar voice rang through the air, smacking her in the face. "John!"

She desperately tried to inhale but the room seemed to run out of oxygen.

Steven eyed the tall stranger, noting his wide shoulders and large arms tensed with fury. His hands were clenched into tight fists, and he looked angry enough to explode. Clearing his throat, Steven calmly asked, "Can I help you, sir?"

"I think you've done quite enough." The stranger growled through gritted teeth and adjusted his cowboy hat.

Megan trembled under his glare.

"Look. I don't know who you are, but you should leave. You're upsetting Megan."

"I'm upsetting her?" His deep voiced boomed through the house. "That's funny." But his face held no humor. His lips were pressed tightly together under his thick, black mustache, and his pale blue eyes were hard as stones. "As for leaving, I'm not going anywhere without my *wife.*"

"Wife!" Steven's gut twisted as if he'd been punched.

Megan felt the room spin out of control. Her legs grew weak, and she felt her body falling before a sharp pain exploded in her head. Then the world went dark.

Chapter 13

"Megan." Steven started towards her, but stopped short at a low growl from the stranger.

"Stay away from my wife!"

Delores and Grant rushed in from the living room, Delores going to Megan and bending down, feeling her forehead for a fever. The two men stared each other down, - neither one daring to make the first move.

"Will someone help her up to her room?" Worry lines developed between Delores' brows. "Grant, call the doctor."

"You're not taking her anywhere. I'm taking her home," the stranger insisted.

"To Illinois?" Delores gasped. "Mister Black, I don't know what's going on here, but I do know that she's hit her head on a marble floor. She may well have a concussion and traveling would not be advised."

"And I'm not letting you take her anywhere," Steven challenged. "How do I know who you are? Megan never mentioned a husband. You could be any nutcase off the street."

"How dare you!" He took several steps forward. "First, you steal my wife, and now you're calling me a liar."

Delores stood between the two men. "Look, this isn't helping Megan." Looking at Steven, she said, "Take Megan to her room." Looking at the stranger, she added, "Mr. Black, why don't you come back tomorrow when she's awake and we can get this settled. We all need to calm down."

Steven scooped up Megan, cradling her as he moved to the stairs.

Delores put her hand on John Black's chest, stopping him from moving towards Steven. "I mean it, Mr. Black. You are welcome to come back in the morning, but if you don't leave right now, I'll call the police."

"I will be back," he snarled from under his old, brown hat. "You can count on that." He stormed out of the door, slamming it behind him.

Megan woke up with a bright light boring into her brain. Squinting, she tried to swat the intrusive light away.

"I'm Dr. Brent." An elderly man with gray hair smiled at her.

Megan started to sit up, but a throbbing pain shot through her head. Closing her eyes, she tried to remember what happened.

"Lie down. You hit your head pretty hard, little girl. I want you to stay in bed and rest for the next couple of days." He looked at the Petersons. "Her pupils aren't dilated, so she doesn't have a concussion. She might have some disorientation for a while, and her head is going to be sore for the next couple of days. Make sure she rests and give her some ibuprofen for the pain. She'll be fine."

"Thank you, Dr. Brent." Grant shook his hand.

"I'll call and check on her tomorrow."

"I'll walk you to the door," Delores offered.

"No need, I know the way out. Good night."

Steven sat by the bed holding her hand. He saw the swelling and redness and knew there'd be a big, ugly bruise. He had many questions, but she'd drifted off to sleep and couldn't answer them.

"Mom, do you think that man really is her husband?" He wanted this to be a bad dream. She belonged to him, not someone else. "Maybe he's lying."

"I don't know, Steven. But I don't see why he'd make up a story like that." Delores knew he really cared for Megan. He'd be hurt if she left.

"If she is married, why didn't she tell me? Why didn't she tell anyone?"

"I can't answer your questions, honey." Delores looked at the slumbering girl. "Only Megan can."

"I know. I'm just thinking out loud." After a pause, he added, "You know it's possible they are divorced and he doesn't want to accept it. That would explain why she left Illinois so quickly. She was probably trying to get away from him."

"We can't speculate on what is happening," Delores chided gently.

"You saw how angry he was. He looked like he wanted to tear me to pieces."

"If Megan is his wife, I think her being out on a date with you would prompt any man to be angry. Imagine how you would feel if the same thing happened." Delores didn't want to hurt her son, but she couldn't let him build false hopes.

"I can't wait to talk to her." He rubbed his hand up and down her slender arm.

"You'll have to wait until tomorrow. Why don't you get some sleep?"

"No, I want to stay with her. Besides, I'm not tired."

"Try and get some rest, at least. I need to get her ready for bed."

"Okay." He finally relented. "I'll come back in a little bit." He gave Megan a gentle kiss on the cheek before leaving.

"Mrs. Peterson?" Megan noticed the older lady rummaging through the dresser. She tried to sit up and the pounding returned. "Ouch." She grabbed her head.

"Lie down again, Megan." Delores walked to the bed, trying to restrain her from sitting up.

"I just had the worst dream ever, but it felt so... real." She tried to figure out what happened. "Why does my head hurt so much?"

"It wasn't a dream, Megan. Your husband showed up. You fainted and hit your head. Now take it easy."

"John...was here?" She tried to recall the events, but each thought brought a new wave of pain. She felt like she was lost in a thick fog. "Steven?"

"He's in bed and John will be back tomorrow morning." She wanted some answers just as much as Steven, but knew this wasn't the time. Eventually all the pieces to the puzzle would be put in place and the mystery solved.

Megan gulped.

"Let's get your nightgown on." Delores didn't want to be upset until she knew the whole story.

However, the mother in her felt protective, and didn't want to see Steven get hurt.

"How did he find me?" Megan asked as she slipped the garment over her head.

"I don't know, Megan." Delores wondered if Steven might be right. Maybe she had been trying to get away from him. Delores looked at the pale fragile girl and felt protective of her too. *How can I be mad at her?* "We'll talk tomorrow. For now, try to get some sleep." She flipped the light off.

Steven couldn't sleep. Pacing around the small living room of his apartment, he tried to make sense out of what had happened.

"Talk about a bad ending to a date," he muttered out loud. He felt cheated again. Every time he made a little progress, something interrupted them; timers going off, pies burning, waves crashing on them, and now...a husband showing up.

"A husband!" He flung both hands up in the air. What rotten luck! He'd waited a lifetime for a someone like her. Only to find out she was already married. Was there any hope of a future with her?

John Black checked into the Pike Hotel. Lying in bed with his hands folded behind his head, he stared into the darkness. Had she finally lost her mind? Had she gone over the edge of reality? What was she doing in that fancy house? And why had she gone on a date with someone else? Was that guy the reason she left? She'd met some rich geek and now a simple farmer wasn't good enough for her? But how could she have met someone like him in Illinois? Especially since she rarely went anywhere after the baby's death. "So many questions and no answers," he mumbled in the dark. He wanted to rip that guy's head off and drag her back home. *Have I been a fool all these years?* This just didn't sound like his wife. His Megan. *What went wrong?*

His mind drifted back to when the baby died. His heart ached at the memory of that day and he knew it had been worse for Megan - it almost destroyed her. She never cried and wouldn't talk about it. But she'd started changing from that moment. She shut herself off from the world and wouldn't let anyone near her. Not him. Not friends. Not even her family. Did her actions now have something to do with Laura? Had he failed her in some way? Why did she leave without a word? Why California?"

The sun spread its bright, rays over the mansion, warming the air outside but none of the occupants noticed. It had been a restless night for them all, and they all hoped to get some answers today. However, the only person who could ease their minds and calm their fears still lay in a state of confusion. Megan had developed a slight temperature during the night and wasn't very responsive.

"How's she doing?" Steven asked.

"Dr. Brent said that a slight fever isn't anything to worry about." Delores put a cool washcloth on her forehead. "We have to give her lots of liquids and keep her comfortable."

"It doesn't look like I'm going to get any answers today." Steven looked haggard and worn.

"I'm afraid not, honey."

"I think I'll go for a walk."

"The fresh air will do you good."

The doorbell rang, and Delores told Rosa that she'd get it. She answered the door, hoping that the cowboy had calmed down. "Good morning, Mr. Black," she said with as much cheerfulness as she could muster.

"Can I see my wi...Megan?"

"She isn't up yet. She started running a fever and..."

"A fever?" he interrupted.

"Yes. The doctor said it's nothing, but I'm afraid she hasn't been awake much." She saw the concern in his face. "If you want to come back later, Mr. Black, maybe she'll be awake then."

"My name is John." He didn't know if they were trying to stall, or if Megan really was sick, but losing his temper wouldn't get him anywhere. "Please, can I see her? I won't wake her if she's sleeping. I just want to make sure she's all right."

"I guess that's acceptable as long as you promise not to disturb her." It went against her better judgment. She had no idea what was going on and she didn't know if she could trust this stranger. But he seemed genuinely concerned.

"Would you like a cup of coffee, John?" She figured she could be polite, at least.

"Yes, I would, thank you." He'd showered and dressed before coming straight over, not even stopping for coffee.

"What do you take in it?"

"Just black, ma'am."

"Call me Delores."

"Yes, ma'am." He extended his hand. "Thank you, Delores."

"I know the circumstances are unusual but I hope we'll have the whole situation straightened out soon." She shook his hand, noticing their size, huge and callused, the hands of a working man.

"I hope so."

Delores brought him a mug of coffee and he followed her up the stairs to the bedroom. Megan was still sleeping soundly. He slipped into the chair next to the bed, staring at her for a long time. It had been a long time since he'd looked at her face. He carefully caressed her cheek with his thumb, relishing the feel of her skin. She always felt so soft and feminine compared to his callused, leathery hands. He noticed the swollen purple bruise on her temple and forehead.

"Are you sure she's okay? Maybe we should take her to a hospital?"

"Dr. Brent is stopping by later. You can talk to him if it would make you feel better." Delores noted the lines and tension on his face relax and a look of rugged tenderness replaced them.

"I would like that. Thank you," he said. He stared at Megan sleeping and muttered to himself, "I love her so much. I can't lose her now."

Deloris overheard the words and reasonably satisfied that he wouldn't disturb Megan, she made an excuse and left the room.

John watched her sleeping in the oversized, over-priced bedroom. After stirring and mumbling some incoherent words, her eyes fluttered open. But the light was too bright and she squeezed them closed again, covering her eyes with her hand.

John walked over to the window and drew the curtains shut.

"Steven, is that you?" she asked, groggily.

John immediately tensed. All the tender feelings left, leaving behind the hurt and betrayal. "Sorry to disappoint you, but it's me - your *husband!*"

"John?" She still felt dazed. The pain in her head flared up every time she moved. "What are you doing here?" She fought back the tears forming from the pain.

"I travel two thousand miles looking for you, and that is your first question to me?" His mouth twisted under his mustache. "I should be asking you that."

"Oh, John." She struggled to sit up.

John quietly sat and watched her. His heart wrenched at the pained expression on her face. He didn't like watching her suffer. Yet he felt she deserved it for all the distress she'd put him through.

Steven walked in and saw Megan crying. "Get away from her!" he yelled. "Leave her alone."

John locked eyes with Steven, the animosity filling the air. "I'm not going anywhere." He strained to keep his voice under control.

"Megan doesn't need you upsetting her any more." Steven said, protectively. He wouldn't believe this stranger was her husband.

"I'm not doing anything to upset her."

"Then why is she crying?" Steven asked. "So help me...if you touch her I'll..."

"You'll what?" John sneered, standing and drawing himself up to his full height. He tried to control his temper, but he wasn't about to let this little pipsqueak threaten him.

"Please, stop!" Megan grabbed her head. "The yelling hurts my head."

Both men stopped and looked at her; frail, small, and helpless.

"I'm sorry, Megan." Steven wanted nothing more than to gather her in his arms.

"I'm not crying because of anything John did. I tried sitting up and the pain overwhelmed me." She sounded weak.

His eyes raked over John. "Are you that heartless? You can sit there, watching her writhe in pain."

"And what should I do? I can't ease the pain. Are you a witchdoctor who can cast a spell and heal her?" He smirked at the image of this rich spoiled brat dabbling in voodoo.

"No, I'm not a witchdoctor, but I can get some aspirin or offer her a drink. It's called compassion."

"Steven, please." She felt like the prize at a county fair the two were battling over. "Can you get the ibuprofen?"

Steven went into the bathroom and came back with the bottle of pills and a glass of water. She took the pills and washed them down. "Thanks."

"Now lie down and rest," Steven urged.

"Isn't that nice? You have her all tucked in. Now her pain has magically disappeared just because you care," John sneered.

"At least I do care!" He'd never cared so much.

"And I don't? She's my wife." John's voice vibrated through the bedroom. Megan covered her ears and cowered under the quilt.

"No wonder she left you. You have a heart of stone."

"Why, you little rat! I ought to rip you into pieces." John clenched his teeth.

"Go ahead, take your best shot."

Neither heard Megan's pleas to stop and both were oblivious to Grant and Delores running into the room. Each only saw his anger, and his enemy.

"You homewrecker!" John bellowed as he advanced towards Steven, planting a fist into his eye.

Steven stumbled back, but caught his balance and came at John swinging. He might not win the fight but he'd get a few punches in before he went down. One punch landed right in John's gut and doubled him over. The second slug connected with John's jaw. John rocked back, but his right uppercut connected, while his left fist jabbed into Steven's stomach almost simultaneously. The move sent him flying across the room.

Steven didn't seem to be done yet, fighting for something important to him. He staggered toward John once more, but Delores blocked his path, while Grant stood in John's path, blocking him.

"You need to leave before I call the police." Grant informed him.

"What is it with you guys and the cops? I bet you have them in your back pocket. All you rich folks do." He wiped the trickle of blood off his mouth. "I'll be back later." Looking at Megan he added, "You can count on that. I don't care how many cops you have here." He stormed out of the room.

Steven leaned against the dresser, gasping for air, while Megan cried in agony. Each sob brought a new rush of pain. She had caused this whole nightmare. "What have I done?" she cried. "What have I done?"

Delores carefully attended to Steven's cut lip while Grant tried to calm Megan down, having returned from escorting John to the front door. "Megan, this isn't doing you any good. You need to settle down."

"It's all my fault!" She held her head and trembled. "All my fault."

"Megan, please try to rest. We can talk about this later when you feeling better," Grant said soothingly.

"No! No!" she cried. She'd made a mess of her life. No matter how hard she tried, she always managed to muddle things up. "It's all my fault."

Grant finally got her to relax and covered her with the quilt. She surrendered to the warmth and softness that aided her overwhelming need for peace. The only reprieve from the intense pain would be sleep.

Grant looked tired and frustrated when he entered the kitchen. "I don't think this is what Dr. Brent meant when he prescribed rest for her."

"No." Delores smiled wearily. "There's been too much excitement for me. I can't imagine how she feels."

"I think the emotional strain is taking a toll." Grant looked helplessly at his wife. "There's not much we can do for her."

"There's not much we can do for Steven either. He's going to have a doozy of a black eye. I gave him an ice pack, but I think his heartache is going to hurt more than his eye."

"Uh huh." Grant took a sip of coffee and felt his head clearing.

"I just don't understand it." Delores shook her head "Why didn't Megan tell us she was married?"

"Only she can answer that, honey - and right now she's in no condition to talk."

"I know. I'm baffled." She went to the refrigerator. "Do you want a sandwich?"

"That sounds great."

She fixed the sandwiches. "What if Steven is right? John does seem like a dangerous guy. Maybe he was abusive and she is trying to get away from him."

"You're speculating. And what makes you think that he's dangerous?"

"He beat up our son! And yet, he was so nice to me. It's like he just exploded. Does that sound normal to you?"

"It sounds like a grown man who feels scorned. Steven is as much to blame for the fight as John," he reminded her, gently. "I think they both feel betrayed."

"So, they beat each other's brains in?"

"It's a man thing." He shrugged his shoulders and picked up the sandwich. "Men don't talk issues out like women do. They fight them out."

"Thank goodness, I'm not a man!" Delores said exasperated.

"Yes, thank goodness, or we wouldn't have been married for forty wonderful years." He winked.

Steven lay on his couch with an ice pack on his swollen eye. It hurt, but nothing compared to the pain he would suffer if Megan left him. He was still assuming Megan had left her husband, or was about to. He didn't want to think about losing her. He couldn't, not now. Not when he'd finally found the perfect woman and opened his heart to her. *Fate couldn't be this cruel. Could it?*

His phone vibrated in his back pocket, interrupting his thoughts. He let the call go to voice mail. He didn't feel like talking to anyone and wasn't even sure if he could speak clearly with his lip all puffed up and numb.

Andrew's name came up on the screen. Steven punched the voice mail button. "Hey, buddy just wanted to see what you were up to? Give me a call when you get in."

Steven knew talking to his best friend would help him sort out the whole mess, so he pushed the call back button.

"Steven,"

"Yeah, it's me." He grimaced with pain.

"What's wrong?"

"It's a long story."

"I have time."

"I'm not ready to talk about it right now." Steven wanted to forget about everything and turn everything back to a time when Megan seemed to belong to him.

"I'm here for you, buddy."

"I know." There was a long pause then Steven asked, "Can I call you back later? I'm really tired."

"Sure, but why don't you come over for dinner, and bring Megan?"

"Now isn't a good time." Steven ran his hand through his hair. He yelped with the resulting pain that shot through his wrist.

"Steven, what's going on?" Andrew's tone demanded an answer. "Does this have something to do with Megan? Don't tell me you've broken up with her already."

Steven didn't want to lie, but he wasn't yet ready to admit the truth. "No, I didn't break up with her."

"Then what is it?"

"I need to go, Andy. Talk to you later." He hung up the phone.

John went back to the hotel, but felt too agitated to do anything but pace awkwardly around the tiny room, which felt smaller than ever, because of his size. "The little twit has either lost her mind, or she has been playing me for a fool all this time."

The Megan he had known had too much integrity to go running off with some spoiled brat. He'd married a warm, loving, sensitive, and caring woman. *His* Megan - *his* wife - stood behind her promises and would never betray the people she loved. It wasn't the same woman, lounging in the plush bed of an expensive mansion, with a rich boyfriend attending to her every need. The woman who had packed up her things and moved two thousand miles across the country without so much as one word to him. She had not only left him and their life behind, but she'd left her entire family without one goodbye.

Feeling antsy, and hungry, he decided to grab a bite to eat. Maybe a full stomach would settle his nerves and help him sort things out. He drove to a tiny restaurant and sat down in a booth, staring out of the window.

"Do you want to order now or would you like a few minutes?" The waitress asked.

"I want two cheeseburgers, fries and a coke."

"Okay, I'll be right back with your drink." The waitress had a warm smile. She was the first person to not be disturbed by his presence here in California.

Rubbing his hand over his rough face, he felt stiff whiskers. He hadn't bothered to shave this morning. Then again, he was used to a scruffy face. You don't have to look pretty when working in the fields. The farm hands didn't care what he looked like. But for some reason, looks suddenly seemed to have become important, and he realized that he must look awful. How could he compete with that pretty boy when he looked like a grizzly bear?

The waitress brought his drink and set it down in front of him.

"Thanks." He mustered a smile.

"No problem, that's what I get paid for." She winked and hustled off to another table.

Sure. She's getting paid to be nice. "What a welcoming party," he mumbled out loud. He thought about the Petersons and wondered what kind of welcome he'd get when he returned to the estate. They'd probably called the cops by now, having them camped out on the front doorstep, but he didn't care. He would go back to get some answers. He *needed* answers, and had every right to get them. *After all,*

I'm still her husband, which should count for some-thing.

Steven lay stretched out on the couch in the addition which served as his apartment. He didn't move when the doorbell rang. His whole body ached and he wasn't in the mood for company. For all he knew, it could be John coming back to finish the job. He pretended not to be home.

"Steven?" Andrew's voice called from the kitchen. "Are you home?"

"Yes." Steven sat up slowly.

"Man! What's happened to you? I haven't seen you this beat up since college. Remember the time you went out with the football player's girlfriend?"

"Yeah, how can I forget that? But, she told me they'd broken up."

"I know, but you still got the brunt of her boy-friend's fists. What happened this time?"

"I really don't want to talk about it. Didn't I say that on the phone?"

"You did. That's exactly why I came over. You can't hang up on me now." Andrew smiled. "Why don't you tell me the whole story? It will help to talk about it."

"You should have become a shrink instead of a lawyer," Steven teased. Deep down, he was glad Andrew was here. It always helped to talk things out with him.

"I thought about it, but lawyers make more money." He looked at Steven's black eye, "How does the other guy look?"

"Not as bad as I do, although I did see a trickle of blood on his mouth." Steven held up his swollen hand, "But I'm paying the price for that too."

"I see you're a little rusty at this fighting business." He checked Steven's hand.

"I may be rusty, but he was big."

"Why are you picking fights with someone bigger than you?" He moved Steven's hand back and forth.

"Ouch," Steven yelled. "You're hurting me."

"I don't think anything is broken, you big baby, but you might want to have it checked out anyway." He shrugged his shoulders. "After all, I'm not a doctor."

"I hear they make good money." Steven grinned.

"Quit trying to change the subject," Andrew scolded. "Who is this guy and why were you fighting?"

"He says he's Megan's husband." The distasteful words sounded even worse when spoken out loud.

"What?" Andrew stood up, shocked. "Why are you dating a married woman?" He knew Steven was capable of a lot of things, but he never figured him for the sort of snake who broke up marriages.

"I didn't know she was married. She never said anything about it." The hurt inside flared up. He hadn't let himself feel the pain because he'd been too busy trying to deny the situation.

"Oh, Steven." Andrew sat down again, noticing the torment in Steven's eyes. "I'm sorry."

"Don't be sorry yet. I think I still have a chance. I don't know why she left him, but he's a brute... they may be getting divorced." Steven sounded hopeful. He wanted to believe it.

"Did she tell you that?"

"No. She hasn't been able to explain anything." He filled Andrew in on the details leading up to the fight. "He's a maniac. Look what he did to me."

"Steven, I hate to say this, but you really don't know what is going on." Steven wanted to hide behind the false scenarios he was inventing, so he wouldn't have to face the truth. "And in defense of her husband, if you walked in and saw your wife with another man, wouldn't you lose your temper?"

Steven knew he was right, but didn't say anything.

"All I know is, if I caught Catherine with some other guy, I'd want to tear him apart." Andrew put a hand on his friend's shoulder. "It's something to think about."

"I don't want to think about it," he said, stubbornly.

"I'm here for you if you need to talk."

"I know." Andrew started to walk away. "Hey! Andy, thanks."

"It's Andrew." he smiled. "And no problem."

Chapter 14

Megan rolled over, causing a sharp pain to explode in her head. She quickly rolled onto her back until the pain subsided. Groggily opening her eyes and analyzing the sun streaming through the window, she guessed it was around late afternoon.

She remained motionless for a long time, and listened to the silence of the house. It was so quiet that she wondered if everyone had gone out. Then again, the size of the house made it hard to hear noises, unlike her small farmhouse where every little noise was magnified. She slowly sat up.

"I see you're awake." Delores walked in. "How are you feeling?"

"Better. My head doesn't hurt as much, but my stomach feels like I've been bungee jumping."

"Not surprising. You haven't eaten all day."

"What time is it, anyway?"

"Almost four."

"I've slept all day!" she exclaimed. "I have to make dinner."

"You are in no condition to work," Delores said. "We'll order takeout. Do you like Chinese?"

"Yes." Her memory slowly replayed the events of the morning as if in a haze. Visions of John and Steven fighting filled her head. Horrified, she recalled seeing Steven fly across the room like a rag doll. "Steven!" she gasped. "Is he okay?"

"He's bruised and sore, but he'll be fine." She patted Megan's hand. "The doctor will be by soon to check on you."

"Why are you being so nice to me?" she asked, choking back a sob. "Why don't you kick me out? That's what I deserve after all I've done." Tears burned her eyes.

"Megan, I don't understand why you didn't tell us you were married, but I'm reserving my judgment until I hear the whole story."

"It doesn't get any better."

"Do you want to tell me about it?"

Not really. But she knew everyone had questions, and they deserved answers. The only problem was that she had no idea why she'd done any of these things. How could she explain it to them when she didn't understand herself? "Oh, Mrs. Peterson, I don't know why I didn't tell anyone."

"Why don't you start from the beginning?" Delores sat in the chair next to her." Why did you leave?"

"I told you before that when Laura's birthday came I felt overwhelmed. I packed up and left." Megan sniffled.

"Yes, but you neglected to tell us that you had left a husband behind." Delores reprimanded. She got a few tissues and handed them to Megan.

"John and I had grown so far apart, and I just figured he would file for divorce. Dealing with my grief consumed all of my energy and I wasn't ready to talk about my failed marriage." She dabbed at her eyes, and looked at Delores, silently pleading for her to understand. "I was going to tell you. I tried to tell Steven a few times but could never muster the courage. I'd planned on explaining everything to him last night, but..." her voice trailed off. Delores knew what had happened that night. "Mrs. Peterson, I'm so sorry. I didn't want to hurt anyone. I just wanted to forget about Laura and everything else in my past."

"The past has caught up with you, my dear. You can't keep running from your problems. You have to face them."

"I don't know what to do or say." She wasn't sure why John had come. He must be pretty angry to track her all the way to California.

"You need to answer some difficult questions. Just tell the truth, no matter how much it hurts." It was the best advice she could give. "I better go order some dinner."

"Mrs. Peterson. I'm really sorry. I can't tell you how sorry I am."

"I know, Megan." Her sympathetic tone eased Megan's tension.

Making good on his promise, John walked up the front steps and rang the doorbell, surprised that the cops weren't there to arrest him. The door swung open, revealing Grant – appearing as a soldier ready to defend his family. His arms were crossed at his chest, and he gazed down sternly.

"I'd like to see my wife." John's tone had mellowed from his last words spoken in the house, but was still insistent.

"We've been expecting you, Mr. Black." He opened the door, allowing John to enter the foyer. "Come in, but I'm warning you, no more fighting. You must keep your temper when you're in my house. I realize you want answers and so do we, but not at the risk of Megan's health," Grant said.

"I know, and I'm sorry. The last thing I want to do is hurt Megan."

"As long as we're clear on that. I'll go see if she's awake."

"Yes, she is." Delores came down the stairs to join them.

"How's she doing?" John asked.

"She's feeling better, but still in pain. The doctor should be here any minute to check on her."

"Can I see her?"

"Yes."

He followed Delores up the wide staircase and pass a few doors before stopping at Megan's room.

"Thank you," he said.

"No problem, but take it easy." She warned.

Megan sat in bed, thinking over her situation. She had a lot of explaining to do and didn't know how to clarify anything. A light rapping on the door made her jump.

"Megan, can I come in?"

"Yes." She felt her heart beat faster at the sound of John's voice. She swallowed hard, fighting a wave of nausea, steeling her nerves for the battle.

John sat down in the chair, his blue eyes penetrating her soul. He sat for a long time in silence, waiting for her to speak, with the ominous awkward tension growing between them.

"John, I'm really sorry," she finally blurted.

John held his hand up to stop her apologies. "I don't want to hear apologies. I want to know why you left." Right to the point. A matter-of-fact fellow, he never wasted words.

"I honestly don't know why I left..." That seemed to be the question of the day and she had no answer to it. "I just did," she whispered quietly.

"Come on, Megan." John stood and paced a-round the foot of the bed. "You can do better than that." He obviously wasn't satisfied with her answer.

"What do you want me to say? I snapped. I went to Laura's grave. I stood there not knowing what to do, or how to feel. The loss and pain overwhelmed me and I... I just lost it. I went home, and packed and left. There are no easy explanations."

"Give me more credit than that, will ya?" He shoved his hands into his pockets. "I may only be a simple farmer but I'm not stupid!"

"I never said you were." Megan looked down at the floor. His tone of voice told her how angry he was."

"No, you left because you found yourself a rich boyfriend."

"That's not true!" Megan's eyes widened. "How dare you make such an accusation?"

"Really?" John stared at her, venom in his narrowed eyes. "Look at you, in this fancy bedroom." He swept his hand around to indicate the room. "In a mansion, coming home all dolled up, with that rich brat panting after you."

"That's not fair! You don't -"

"Fair!" he yelled. "You walk out on five years of marriage with no explanation." He forced his voice into a hushed growl. "Five years of busting my butt to give you everything I could. Then I come here and find you put up in a mansion by some rich scoundrel. Does that sound fair?" He pounded his fist into his hand. "I guess I'd never be able to keep you satisfied, if this is the lifestyle you want." He suddenly sounded defeated. He'd never be able to compete with Steven. He'd never have this kind of money, no matter how well the farm did.

"It's not what it looks like," she defended herself.

"Oh! And I guess you're not lying here, in this fancy bed, being pampered. I'm imagining all this?"

"You're not giving me a chance to explain. You come in here demanding answers then you don't let me talk. You keep interrupting, yelling, and jumping to wrong conclusions."

"What am I supposed to think? When I ask you for an explanation all you say is, 'I don't know'," he mimicked.

"I have trouble putting my feelings into words. You don't understand how devastated I was when Laura died."

"No, I don't," he admitted, "because you never let me in."

"You're right." She looked through tear-filled eyes. "I shut myself off. I didn't want to feel anything, least of all the pain. Talking about Laura forced me to remember, and all I wanted to do was forget. Everyone seemed intent on making me relive that awful day. All of you kept talking about her over and over again, pushing me into the nightmare I was trying to ignore. I eventually withdrew from everyone so you'd all leave me alone."

John walked over and sat in the chair. She had never talked about Laura before. He had tried getting her to open up several times, but she would never do it. She barely talked to anyone after the baby died. He understood the heart-wrenching pain all too well. "Why did you go to Laura's grave?"

"I took some balloons for her birthday." The heartache was evident in her voice. "But I'd spent so much time and energy trying to forget what happened. Pretending that Laura wasn't real, that it was all a dream." Tears streamed down her cheeks. "Suddenly, I was standing at her grave and everything became real." She shook her head. "I just couldn't handle it."

"So how did you end up here?" he asked quietly.

"I wanted to see the ocean."

"How did you end up in this mansion?"

"I answered an ad in the paper for a cooking job."

"You're trying to tell me you work here?"

"Yes."

"Then why do you have a room?"

"It's a long story." She didn't want to get into anything involving Steven.

"I see," he drawled "You don't want to tell me how you became a kept woman."

"I'm not a kept woman!"

"Really?" He jumped to his feet as his anger overpowered all his other emotions. "What else would you call it? You're living in this palace, with people waiting on you hand and foot, and your boyfriend in the - where does he sleep, Megan?"

"How dare you!" She sounded outraged. "You have no right calling me a prostitute."

"I have no right?" he repeated. "I have every right. You're my wife, and I find you shacking up with some pretty boy, trying to feed me a line about being a cook. Well, I don't think your little rich boy is interested in your cooking, at least not anything made in the kitchen."

"It's not a line," she yelled back. "See? You never listen." She cringed in pain. Her head ached but she wasn't backing down from him. "You want to know why I left?" She stared him down. "I left, because I didn't think you'd even notice I was gone." She let him see her loneliness and pain. "You were never there."

"What do you mean I was never there?"

"You were always in the fields or with the animals." His abandoning her had only added to her grief at Laura's loss.

"I'm trying to earn a living, trying to get ahead. It takes a lot of time to run a farm."

"It's always been the farm with you." After the loss of the baby she'd wanted him by her side, to hold her and tell her everything would be all right. She wanted to hear it wasn't her fault. But there were no comforting words to ease her broken heart. "After Laura died, you were never around and I needed you."

John couldn't argue - she was right. He hadn't been able to deal with his own pain and he certainly didn't know how to deal with hers, so he'd thrown himself into his work. "You didn't seem like you needed me," he said quietly.

"I was going through a lot." She had never found the courage to tell him it had been her fault that Laura died. She carried the burden of guilt alone because she was frightened of facing his fury.

"So was I, Megan," he said softly. His anger had now been replaced by sadness. "So was I." His eyes filled with tears.

"I know." She hated being the person who'd caused him so much pain. "That's why I couldn't talk to you." They had both tried to deal with their loss separately, instead of facing it together. John went to work in the fields, day in and day out, while Megan shut herself up inside the house.

"So, you ran off?" His anger now seemed to have almost completely subsided, and she heard the hurt in his voice.

"I didn't know what else to do. I only wanted to stop the pain. I'm sorry, John."

"Sure, you are," he sneered. "You look like you're doing fine to me." He still wasn't ready to let go of all the hurt and anger. She'd left him for another man.

"Will you stop it? I didn't leave you for Steven," she said, exasperated. "I'm staying here until my job ends. That's the truth whether you want to believe it or not."

"I don't believe it," he snapped. "And to think of all the weeks I sat at home, worrying about you. No one knew where you were or why you left. You didn't even say goodbye to your parents. We called all over trying to find you. Every hospital, every hotel - we even had the police involved for a couple of weeks. And here you were the whole time, living like some princess in a fairytale."

He hadn't eaten or slept properly in weeks. He'd barely gotten any work done. If it weren't for his brother-in-law and the field hands the farm would have collapsed. He looked haggard and felt exhausted, and there she sat looking as beautiful as ever. Her long hair, though crumpled and tangled, fell loosely over her shoulders. She looked prim and proper. If he hadn't been so angry, he'd have taken her in his arms and made love to her all night long.

But she'd betrayed him, and his anger ran deeper than his desire.

"I didn't mean to worry everyone." Her gentle eyes glazed over with an expression he couldn't read. "How did you find me, anyway?"

"It wasn't easy. I got the credit card bill with a purchase of a ticket to Santa Barbara. Then I was able to track the hotel down through the bank, using the check. Imagine my surprise when the clerk said you'd checked out weeks ago with Steven Peterson." His lips formed the name with disdain. "Luckily, the lady knew where they lived and gave me directions. Here I am."

Megan sat quietly pondering what he said. He'd gone through a lot of trouble to find her, but why? Her mind swam with questions but she never had a chance to ask them. Delores knocked on the door.

"Can I come in?"

"Of course, Mrs. Peterson." Megan answered.

"I'm sorry to interrupt, but Dr. Brent is here." She looked at John who paced angrily across the floor. "Do you want to stay and talk with the doctor, John?"

Although agitated and angry with Megan he was still concerned about the bruise on her head. It had swollen so much it looked like it might burst. He forced his tone to be calm before replying, "Yes. Thank you."

"How are you feeling?" Dr. Brent asked, shining a light into her eyes.

"All right, but my head hurts."

"How many fingers am I holding up?"

"Three."

"No double vision, that's good. Any signs of blurry vision or trouble focusing?"

Megan shook her head. The movement caused some pain, visible to everyone in the room. "Just my head and I feel sick to my stomach."

"Most head injuries don't usually cause nausea, but it can happen. Sometimes related to stress. I want you in bed for another day or two."

"Another day? I can't stay in bed all day again. I have to get to work."

"Megan, if the doctor says to stay in bed, that's where you'll be," Delores said firmly. "We can fend for ourselves for another day or so."

"Are you sure she shouldn't be in a hospital?" John asked.

"I can admit her if it will make you feel better, but there isn't anything they can do. She doesn't have a concussion and, other than a headache, she seems to be in good health."

"You're sure she's all right?" John seemed to want to double-check.

"She's fine. All she needs is rest."

"And some food," Delores chimed in. "She hasn't eaten all day."

"No wonder your stomach hurts, little girl." The doctor smiled kindly. "You better get something inside you."

"We have food coming," Delores said.

"Good. I guess I'm all done here."

"Thank you, Dr. Brent." Grant shook his hand.

"Since you're already here, doctor, could you check on Steven before you leave?" Delores asked. "He was in a fight today and..."

"I know the routine." The doctor laughed. He'd patched Steven up many times. That's when he started making house calls. The Petersons received too much publicity if they went to the ER, so he came to their house to protect their privacy, although it had been years since he'd made a house call.

"Thank you, again, doctor." Delores smiled.

"I'll show you the way," Grant offered.

The two men walked out of the room. Delores gave Megan some ibuprofen. "You look tired."

"I'm fine."

"Do you want to eat in here or join us down-stairs?"

"I think I can manage getting out of bed. I'd like to stretch my legs."

"John, do you want to stay and eat? We ordered Chinese. There's more than enough." Delores was courteous, but still had her doubts about him. She didn't know if his temper or the mere size of him brought on these feelings of mistrust. He was big enough to make a grown man cower in fear. However, she'd noticed when the anger subsided, he did have a tender side. She had to give him a chance to prove himself, even if his intrusion into their lives destroyed any hope of Steven and Megan getting together.

Megan's little laugh startled them both. "He doesn't like Chinese food."

"I don't eat anything I can't pronounce. Besides, I grabbed a bite before I came over."

The doorbell interrupted the conversation. "That must be the food. Please excuse me." Delores left the two of them alone.

"Can you hand me my robe?" Megan pointed to the bathroom door.

"This isn't your robe," he stated, as he took the garment off the hook. He remembered that she had a white, cloth robe, not a satin floral print. The material felt very expensive.

"Mrs. Peterson bought it for me, along with some other outfits." Megan got out of bed and took a few steps, grabbing the bedpost when she got dizzy.

Probably gifts from pretty boy, he fumed. Noticing her wobble, he squelched his accusations and rushed to help her. "Are you all right?" He put his arm around her waist to steady her.

"I'm just a little dizzy."

It felt good to be near her again. He'd grown accustomed to holding her after a hard day's work. When he had felt tired and his body ached, one hug from her had made the pain and worries disappear. He wanted to hold her like that now more than anything, but he still couldn't let go of his rage. He still loved and wanted her. However, the thought of another man touching her sent him on a roaring angry rampage. His arm tightened around her waist with each vivid image that flashed through his mind.

"John, I can't breathe," she gasped.

"Sorry." He loosened his grip. He had to get out of there before he hurt someone. "I sometimes forget my own strength."

"Yeah." She could feel his body tensing and knew his anger was about to explode again. John helped her downstairs, put his hat on and left.

Deloris helped Megan to the dining room table.

Megan helped herself to the contents of the different boxes scattered on the table, not realizing how hungry she was until she started eating. She was taking second helpings of food, when Steven joined them. Their eyes met briefly, but he looked away, obviously disturbed by her presence.

"Steven, I'm so sorry." Tears sprang to her eyes when she saw his right eye swollen shut with shades of blue and purple. His lip was also enlarged and split open and a brace on his right hand revealed he'd suffered a sprain.

"You didn't beat me up." The fight only furthered his speculation of her leaving John because he was abusive. He wasn't ready to give up the idea yet.

"I might as well have done it." She dropped her fork and buried her head in her hands. "This all happened because of me."

"Megan, no one can fault you for leaving a brute like that. You had to protect yourself. I understand that. What I don't understand is why you didn't tell me about him." Steven wanted to comfort her, but his sore ribs and black eye made him think twice about touching her.

Megan's eyes narrowed at his statement. "Steven, that's absurd." Almost as absurd as John thinking she left him for Steven. "I didn't leave John because he abused me. He's never laid a hand on me."

"Then why did you leave?" He couldn't get rid of the sinking feeling. He was about to hear the truth and wasn't going to like it.

"I already told you why I left. My reasons for leaving haven't changed. I left because I couldn't face the pain of Laura's death. John and I had grown far apart, I felt alone and overwhelmed."

"So, you left because of your baby and not because of him?" Steven wasn't letting go. "Then again, women who are abused never admit it."

"Steven." Her tone was soft and gentle but her words hit him like a ton of bricks. "I love my husband, that hasn't changed. I left because I couldn't cope with my grief, nothing more."

"Let me get this straight. You left a perfectly *wonderful* marriage because you couldn't cope." He still didn't believe her.

"I didn't say it was perfect. We were having problems, but not abuse like you're suggesting."

He had a ray of hope. They were having troubles. But, was it severe enough to get a divorce? "Laura's death couldn't be the only reason you left."

"Yes, it was," she said, aggravated. *What is up with these men? Can't they hear?* She'd already faced John and couldn't deal with Steven at the moment.

"You can only use Laura's death for so much. You can't hide behind your grief forever." Angry at the situation and at fate, he stormed out of the room.

Megan suddenly lost her appetite. Folding her hands, she laid them in her lap, staring down at them. Confusion, hurt, and anger swirled inside her heart. Both men felt the same way. She'd caused all this turmoil. *How have I gotten into such a mess?* She'd only wanted to stop the pain. The problems multiplied, intensifying, leaving her feeling like she was inside a pressure cooker about to blow any minute. *How can I stop the pain?* Her chest constricted. *I've got to get away! Away!*

"Megan, do you want to go back up to bed now?" Grant asked as he laid his chop sticks down. She continued staring at her hands, thinking about all the lives she'd destroyed, starting with her little girl.

"Megan, dear. What's wrong?" Delores asked.

Megan unblinkingly stared ahead of her, as if in a trance. "It's all my fault," she finally muttered.

"What's your fault?" Grant asked confused.

She didn't respond to his question, but only mumbled, "It's all my fault. It's all my fault."

"Megan." Deloris reached over, covering Megan's hands with hers. She shook her lightly. "Megan." Worried eyes looked to Grant when there was no response.

Grant came over to Megan, putting a hand to her brow. "Her eyes aren't moving."

"And she's getting so pale." Deloris, covered her mouth with a shaky hand. "What's wrong?"

"I'm not sure but she appears to be in some kind of a trance." Grant lifted her tiny frame. "Go call the doctor, I'm taking her to bed."

Megan felt disoriented and heard a commotion of hushed voices floating around her like a dream. She tried to understand what they said, but her connection to reality was severed. Her body was floating in the air. It felt like a feather rising higher and higher until it settled down on the softest, fluffiest cloud. She felt warm and safe as the pain subsided, and a soothing peaceful sensation washed over her as she drifted off to sleep.

Grant came downstairs as Delores hung up the telephone. "How is she?"

"She's sleeping now, but she wasn't responding to anything." He looked troubled. "What did Dr. Brent say?"

"He'll come by tomorrow morning."

"Does he think this episode has anything to do with her injury?"

"No. But he can't be positive until he checks her out."

"It's probably stress-related?"

"More than likely," Delores agreed. "That poor child has been through so much and all this fighting isn't helping." Delores looked frantic. "I've heard of people slipping over the edge and never returning. What if that happens?"

"That's not going to happen." Grant put his arms around her. "Megan is going to pull through. She's a fighter."

"What if she feels she doesn't have anything left to fight for?"

"She has plenty to fight for. We'll make her see that." He tried reassuring his wife, but deep down he wondered the same thing. What if she decided that holding on wasn't worth the pain?

"Should we tell Steven?" Delores asked.

"No. He's had enough to deal with today. Besides there isn't anything he can do."

"You're probably right." Delores wiped her eyes. "I'm going to go check on Megan, then go to bed."

"Me too."

Steven was awake most of the night, rehashing the events of the past weeks. His memory drifted back to the first day he'd seen Megan, sitting on the beach and the fight they'd had. He marveled at how fate had brought them together again. He'd been smitten with her from that moment on. His heart had broken the night he held her, as she wept and grieved for her child. Her life for the last year had been devastated by that incident, and all her decisions were based on the one moment.

He didn't want to be angry, but couldn't help it. Life had played a cruel trick on him again. He'd thought he'd found love once, but his lover had turned out a traitor. Then along came Megan, but now it turns out she's already married. *Why doesn't love ever work out for me*? he wondered angrily.

He clung to a thin thread of hope. They had to have been brought together for a reason. Was there a possibility Megan would leave her husband? Maybe this would be his turn for love after all.

It was late and he needed to get to sleep, or he'd never get up in time for work. He dreaded going into the office. Everyone would surely want to know what happened. What could he say? "My girlfriend's husband beat me up"? Yeah, that sounded real good, and "I got into a fight over a girl," made him sound like he was back in high school.

He finally drifted off to sleep dreaming about Megan. He dreamt of kissing her soft lips, touching her creamy skin, and running his fingers through her silky hair. He dreamt of their wedding day, the honeymoon, and the lifetime of love they would give to their children.

Suddenly sitting up with a start, he felt his heart beating faster, and his palms sweating. "It was only a dream," he told himself, or was it? He searched his memory for the elusive pieces of the dream that had somehow turned into a nightmare.

He had been standing at the altar, watching Megan walk down the aisle in a beautiful wedding gown. Her long, train flowing behind her as she walked cautiously, ever so tentatively, down the aisle. Her steps had slowed until she seemed to not move at all. When she'd finally reached his side, he had held her small hand in his as they recited their vows, never taking his eyes off their clasped hands. However, when the preacher had come to the words, "I pronounce you husband and wife," Steven looked up and discovered John standing beside Megan, her hand now clutched in his. The sound of their laughter had grown louder and louder.

Was this a cruel joke on Megan's part? Had she used him all along like April?

The dream had started out beautiful but ended in a cruel twist of fate. Was his dream of them being together an impossible one?

"Only fate knows," he said to himself. "If Megan is my destiny, it will all work out."

Chapter 15

John showered and shaved, wanting to look his best when he saw Megan. He felt better since getting some sleep. He'd also had time to mull things over. Megan had accused him of not listening and she was right. He'd only vented his anger. If he didn't start listening, he'd never get any answers.

He stopped in front of the iron gate and pushed the buzzer. When the gate opened, he drove up the long driveway, parked in the circular area in front of the house, and then bounded up the steps two at a time.

"Oh, John, it's you," Delores said when she came into the foyer. "I was hoping you were Dr. Brent."

"He's coming again?"

"Yes. Please come in."

"Can I see Megan?"

"John, we need to talk about that," Grant's voice boomed from the dining room. "Why don't you come have some breakfast?"

"I don't want breakfast. I want to see my wife."

"Something has developed."

"What's happened? Is it Megan?"

"Please, come and sit down, we'll talk over breakfast." Grant insisted. "I have to get to the office."

John's hunger got the better of his curiosity, and he realized he wasn't going to get any immediate answers, so he followed them into the dining room.

278

"I'm afraid it's not much." Delores handed him a plate of scrambled eggs. "Megan has spoiled us with her cooking."

"Yeah, she's always been a good cook." Maybe she wasn't lying about being the cook after all.

"We were fortunate to get her." Delores cringed at the dejected look that crossed his face. Their good fortune had been his misfortune. "Oh, I'm sorry, John. I didn't mean to sound so selfish. I only meant that she helped us out of a real jam. No one else would take the position temporarily."

"This is temporary?"

"Yes. Our cook will be back in January, but we couldn't get through the holidays without Megan's help."

"How long has she worked here?" He wanted to trust his wife, but still felt skeptical.

"Since the end of October," Delores said.

The dates checked out.

Steven walked into the room and abruptly stopped, nearly spilling coffee on his khaki suit. "What's he doing here?" he ground out from between swollen lips.

"Good morning, honey. John came to see Megan, and since we were sitting down to eat, we asked him to join us." Delores smiled brightly.

"I don't want him here! I don't want him any-where near Megan."

"What do you mean you don't want me near her? She is *my* wife!" John stood and his chair flew back. "I want *you* to stay away from her."

"Both of you sit down," Grant said, not looking up from the table.

"We don't need any more fighting, it isn't helping anyone, especially Megan," Delores said helplessly. She prayed they would listen and not start swinging.

John and Steven's eyes locked for a long, awkward minute, neither one willing to back down.

"Please, sit down," Delores pleaded. "We have to talk about Megan."

John pulled his chair closer and sat back down. Steven set his coffee on the table, before jerking his chair out and plopping down. He took a sip and winced as the hot liquid touched his split lip.

"Coffee hot?" Grant subdued a smile.

"No, my lip is sore." How can my own parents have breakfast with the lug that beat me up? Steven glared at John.

John tried suppressing his laughter but a tiny smile escaped, enraging Steven even more. He felt a twinge of guilt looking at Steven, but it quickly passed. Maybe the kid would think twice before trying to steal another man's wife. Even so, John had to admit that his ribs were still a bit tender, and he couldn't remember the last time someone had punched him hard enough to draw blood.

"Now that we have your attention, there is something we need to discuss." Grant cleared his throat. "I know how anxious everyone is to get answers from Megan, but right now her health is in a delicate state, and I don't want either one of you bothering her for the next couple of days."

"What!" John gasped. "I want to see my wife."

"I know, but I don't think that's the best thing for her right now," Grant said. "Talking to both of you yesterday put too much strain on her."

"Megan seemed fine at dinner," Steven stated.

"She had a relapse after you left," Delores explained.

"I knew we should have taken her to the hospital," John said. "The doctor said she'd be fine."

"Her condition may not have anything to do with her injury. We won't know anything for sure until the doctor sees her again," Grant offered.

"Dad, you're not making any sense."

"What is wrong with Megan?" John felt agitated too.

"Her condition is more of a ...well...a mental one, I guess." Delores nervously explained.

"A mental condition?" John's forehead wrinkled in confusion. "She has never been mentally unbalanced."

"I wouldn't call it mentally unbalanced," Grant clarified. "She has been dealing with an enormous emotional strain lately, and it has finally worn her out. Confronting the pain and loss of her child has taken a toll on her stability. Then you show up, John, taking her totally off guard. Next, the two of you start fighting like raging bulls in heat. And, if that isn't enough to send a fragile girl over the edge, you both start ranting and raving, giving her the third degree." Holding his hand up to curtail John's protest, he continued. "I'm not saying that you don't have a right to be angry, or that you don't deserve some answers. All I'm saying is everything is happening too fast for her. She already blames herself, and your accusations and anger aren't helping. Has either one of you thought about what *she* is going through?"

Both men looked at each other, ashamed that he was right. Neither one had looked past their own hurt and anger to notice the pain Megan suffered.

"What exactly happened last night?" John wanted to know "And why can't I see her?"

Grant filled in the details for him.

"We feel it is in Megan's best interest right now to keep things calm, so we don't want anyone seeing her until Dr. Brent checks on her. Then, we'll wait and see what he has to say," Delores added.

"Sure, and since you're paying his bill he'll automatically side with you," John said. "I don't care who you pay off, you're not keeping me from my wife. You may have the doctor in your pocket, but you don't own me or my wife."

"John, I will not tolerate such behavior. This is my house and you will abide by my rules," Grant demanded. "Just so you know, our pockets aren't big enough to have the whole town stuffed in them."

Isn't that just like rich folk? They want to control everything, John silently fumed. Then again, he'd demand the same respect of anyone in his house.

"It's not only you, John. Steven won't be seeing her either."

"Why?"

"We don't want any trouble." Delores shot a firm look towards Steven.

"Why are you looking at me like that? I'm not starting any trouble. He's the troublemaker." He glared at John.

"I'm not going to make any trouble either," said John.

Steven's protest was silenced by the ringing of the doorbell.

"That must be Dr. Brent," Delores announced.

John and Steven stood up at the same time.

"Sit down and finish your breakfast, boys. I'll see if he's here." Delores left them.

"You guys heard her," Grant said, "Sit down and finish eating." They reluctantly sat down again.

Steven idly played with the food on his plate.

"Steven, you need to eat," Grant said.

"I'm not hungry," he snapped. "If I can't see Megan, I'm going to work."

"Wait a minute," Grant objected. "You need to take the next couple of days off."

"Why? I'm fine."

"Maybe you are, but the clients don't want to see you looking like a punching bag." Grant's tone softened. "Besides, I think you could use the rest."

"I'm a big boy, Dad. I can take care of myself."

"Then maybe you better start acting like one." Grant stood, throwing his napkin on the table. "If you will excuse me, I want to see the doctor."

He left the two fuming men to finish their breakfast by themselves. The silence stretched like a thick, murky fog, cut only by the sound of clanging silverware against the china plates.

Grant returned a few minutes later. "Okay, I've spoken with the doctor and there isn't much he can do for her right now."

"What happens next?" John asked.

"I don't know." Grant sighed. "Dr. Brent said he could give her a sedative but since she seems to be resting comfortably, we'll wait until later. It's going to be up to Megan if she pulls out of this. There isn't much we can do."

"Are we allowed to see her?" Steven asked impatiently.

"Yes, but just one person at time, and to reduce the stress level, only for fifteen minutes at one visit." He looked at John "Dr. Brent said that the more support she has, the better chance there is of her pulling through. I've talked with Delores, and we agree that the best thing for Megan is for you to stay here."

"What?" Steven jumped up. "No way!"

"Steven, I know this is hard, but you two must find a way to get along. Megan needs all of us right now."

"But I..."

Grant held up is hand to fend off any protests. "This is my house, and I will decide who comes and who goes. John, we have more than enough room." Grant glanced at his watch "I have to get to work, so why don't you get your things from the hotel, and Rosa will make up your room." He turned on his heel and left before anyone could say another word.

Grant had taken command of the situation and executed his plan efficiently and effectively. John was clearly dumbfounded, seemingly unused to taking orders.

Steven stormed off, muttering to himself and flinging his arms in the air. Even though he'd been annoyed with his dad for treating him like a child, he was glad he didn't have to go into work. *There's no way I'm leaving that man alone in this house with Megan.* "No way!"

Looking around and not seeing anyone, John cautiously crept up the stairs, into Megan's room, and took a seat next to the bed. He took her small hand, he fought back the tears as he looked at her. The only color on her pale face was the black and blue mark of the bruise.

"Megan, can you hear?" he asked softly. "I need you to come back to me. Please fight, baby-doll." That had been his nickname for her. "Do you remember our first date? I said that you looked like a baby-doll next to me. I've called you that ever since." Well, except for the last year. She hadn't wanted to hear the word "baby", or anything associated with it after Laura's death.

He absently rubbed his thumb over the back of her hand. He'd missed everything about her - the feel of her skin, the sound of her voice, the smell of her hair. He couldn't lose her. Not now, not after all they'd been through.

"John, I didn't know you were still here." Delores walked in, with Rosa following close behind. "When I didn't see you downstairs, I assumed you'd gone to get your things."

"I wanted to check on Megan first." He put her hand up to his lips and pressed a gentle kiss against it.

"It's hard seeing her like this." Delores looked as helpless as John felt.

"I've missed her so much."

"I know." She saw it in his eyes. Although she'd had doubts about him when he first showed up, she now saw his love for Megan. She also had to admit that a part of her had wanted Megan to be with Steven, and that part had searched for faults in this stranger, but on reflection, she realized that any man in his right mind would have reacted just as angrily if his wife had taken off one day. As a matter of fact, if he hadn't come looking for Megan, she would have doubted that he even loved her. But he had managed to find her, and now sat by her side where he belonged. "You can stay for a few more minutes, but then we have to let her rest for a while."

John nodded. She did need rest, but he wanted her awake. He fought back the urge to shake her awake. He watched the maid deposit a bouquet of flowers on the dresser. "Where did those come from?"

"The garden," Rosa responded. "I thought Megan might like the scent. She loves the garden."

"Yeah, she has a flower garden back home."

"I don't think anything would cheer her up faster than a room full of flowers," Delores said cheerfully. "I'll bet she'll be up before you know it."

"I hope so." Standing, he added, "I think I'll go get my things now."

"Rosa will show you to your room when you get back."

"Sure thing."

Steven watched the small blue car drive away. Once it was out of sight, he ran through his apartment, into the main house and dashed up the stairs to Megan's room. "Mom, you're still here?" he said breathlessly.

"Yes." She rearranged the flowers in the vase.

"I saw John leave." He walked over to the bed. "I thought I might be able to spend some time alone with Megan."

"He went to get his things. He'll be back soon," she warned.

"No wonder, the way you and dad are treating him. Are you going to roll out the red carpet?"

"Steven, I know this is hard on you. It's hard on everybody. But it's the best thing for that poor child." She pointed to Megan. "So, whatever your problems are right now, you will have to put them aside until she gets well."

"My problem is John," he said. "Why did you have to invite him to stay here?"

"Because the doctor said that surrounding Megan with people who love her, and talking to her might bring her out of this, sometimes hearing familiar voices can help."

"He could have done that from the hotel by phone."

"I know, but your father and I both felt it would be better to have him here. I believe Megan would want that."

Steven scowled but said nothing out loud. He still hoped that when Megan woke up she would choose him over John. He didn't care what anyone else thought. He couldn't let her get away.

John packed his suitcase and settled his bill at the front desk, then drove the rental car back to the shop. Delores had insisted that he didn't need to waste money on a rental car, when they had extra cars sitting around that he could use. Being a very practical man, he saw the reasoning in that and accepted the offer.

The limousine however, had not been so practical. But Delores insisted on it too. Even though he argued with her, she somehow managed to win the argument. His second defeat in one day. He'd grown accustomed to winning most debates. However, there was something strange about the way both Petersons manipulated any disagreement and took control. They could talk you into anything, and had an answer for everything. He wondered who won the fights when they argued with each other. *That would be something to see,* he smiled to himself.

Steven sat on the seat of the bay window, staring blankly across the yard. The pouring rain blocked the view, but he didn't notice the scenery. His thoughts were on Megan. It had been three days since she'd entered her own little world. He'd never feltas helpless or alone.

He'd been avoiding John, and, though it was easy enough in a house this large, he hadn't seen much of his family either.

Using his little kitchen meant he could avoid joining the others in the dining room. Avoiding his parents when visiting Megan had become effortless. However, trying to punish them by being absent hurt only him. Even though he was engulfed by loneliness, he wasn't ready to forgive his parents yet. They were siding with the enemy. *Is John the real enemy?* The real problem stemmed from his anger at life in general. Destiny had let him down again.

He paced around the room for a while, biding his time until he could see Megan. Anxiously looking at his watch, deciding to wait a few more minutes until the coast was clear. Finally making his way up the stairs and down the hall, he ran into his mom. *My timing wasn't as good as I thought*, he mused.

"I caught you." She smiled.

"I'm not running," Steven defended.

"No, but you've been hiding."

"You and Dad are the ones who invited him to stay here," he reminded her. "I'm just trying to stay out of his way."

"I don't think the two of you can avoid each other for ever."

"I can try."

"And what about us? Are you going to avoid me and your father forever?"

"I guess that depends on how long I stay mad." The muscles in his face tightened.

"We aren't doing anything to hurt you. We are trying to help Megan, and nothing more. Why can't you see that?" Delores asked exasperated.

"Why can't you ever take my side?" He pointed to his chest. "Just once, I'd like to know that my parents are on my side."

"We're always on your side, Steven. We always have been, and always will be."

"You weren't on my side with April and now you are taking sides with John."

"No one is taking sides, and why are you rehashing history?" She crossed her arms. "As your parents, it is our job to protect you. That is what we did with April and it's what we're doing now."

"What are you protecting me from?"

"From yourself. You don't want to accept the truth and it will end up hurting you more in the end." She looked her son in the eye and said as gently as she could, "I know this is hard for you, but that man in there is her husband, whether you want to face it or not, and he loves her."

"I love her too," he exclaimed.

"The sooner you accept the truth, the better off you will be." She took his hand, trying to soothe his heartache away.

Steven looked past his mother at the door she blocked. "Mom, I really don't want to get into all of this right now. I want to see Megan." He wanted any excuse not to face the truth his mother was pushing towards him.

"John is in there right now."

"What! Why is he in there?" Every time he turned around he found John there. He felt like John integrated himself into every aspect of his life. "This is my time slot."

"I know, but John missed his sitting, so I said he could make it up."

"Of course, cut into my time because he's the husband."

"Steven, I don't know how to get through to you. I'm trying hard to understand how you feel, but it's no excuse for your rude behavior."

"Sure. Blame my behavior. Isn't everything my fault?" His tone dripped anger.

"No, not everything. Only the trouble you create for yourself. You know, if you would take a little advice now and then, you wouldn't suffer so much adversity."

"What's that supposed to mean?"

"If you had listened to us about April, she never would have had the opportunity to use you the way she did. Your father and I tried to warn you. Even Rosa told you she was bad news. But you wouldn't listen to anyone. You have no one to blame except yourself."

"Megan is nothing like April." Steven resented the implication.

"That's not what I'm saying. I'm suggesting that you look at the situation and do what's right."

"You're telling me to follow your advice and back off. To just let her go without a fight."

"Yes. Holding on is only going to complicate things. I don't want to see anyone get hurt, especially you."

"Thanks, but I don't need Mommy watching over me anymore."

"If you're such a big boy, then why don't you quit acting like a spoiled child?" Delores stomped away.

Staring after his mother, he realized she had spoken the truth. He just couldn't face it yet. and couldn't bear it. He still clung to hope, though.

The door to her room opened and John stepped out. "Steven." John nodded politely.

"How is she doing?" Steven didn't feel like being cordial, but he was interested in Megan's condition.

"The same." John sounded hopeless.

Steven nodded, making his way past John and into the room, breathing a sigh of relief after closing the door. *Alone with her at last.* He walked to the chair, but felt too agitated to sit. Standing by the window, he peered through the slowing rain, watching the sun slip behind a row of trees, casting shadows over the wet ground. The light quietly faded as the day came to a close. Another day ended, without any signs that Megan would wake up. She'd hidden herself in some secluded world that no one could penetrate. He felt helpless doing nothing, and felt guilty that his temper had partly been to blame.

A soft moan penetrated his thoughts. Looking towards the bed, he saw her move, and rushed to her side. "Megan, can you hear me?"

She softly moaned again and mumbled something incoherent. Although she'd been murmuring and whimpering for the past three days, the broken sentences he had heard didn't make any sense. He wasn't sure if she was waking up or still dreaming, but nothing prepared him when she screamed out, "Laura!"

Her cries cut through his heart like a shard of glass. Her devastation of losing her daughter went deeper than he imagined. Although he'd helped to give her courage to face the pain, he couldn't understand the loss and hopelessness she felt. He wanted to do something, but could only stand by and watch her struggle with the grief and guilt.

Kneeling by the bed, he took her hand. "Megan, listen to me. It's not your fault." She'd never be free from the pain if she didn't let go of the guilt. "Wake up, sweetheart."

The minutes slowly ticked by, the stillness making it feel more like hours. Eventually, she moved again. "Megan," he whispered softly. "Please, wake up."

Her blond lashes slowly fluttered open. At first, he thought he'd imagined it, but then she weakly spoke his name, "Steven?"

"Megan!" He couldn't believe he actually heard her speak. It seemed like years since he'd heard her soft, tranquil voice. "Oh, Megan you're awake! You woke up!" He kissed her hand. "I'm looking into your gorgeous blue eyes and it's not a dream."

"No, it's not a dream." She licked her parched lips. "I'm thirsty."

"You should be. You've been out for three days."

"Three days!" she repeated, shocked.

Steven nodded. "We've all been worried about you." He filled a glass with water and handed it to her. She drank most of it at once.

"Take it easy," Steven said.

"I didn't mean to cause so much trouble," she said and finished the water.

"Oh, sweetheart, you didn't cause any trouble." His kissed her hand again. "I'm the one who's sorry."

"For what?"

"For getting angry with you. I didn't give you a chance to explain. I should never have put so much pressure on you."

"I'm the one who lied." She felt bad about not telling him the truth. She'd developed strong feelings for him and didn't want to hurt him. Why did she end up hurting everyone she cared about?

"I don't want to get into it right now." He smoothed her hair back.

She winced as she tried sitting up.

"Are you in pain?" He helped her.

"A little." She looked around the room, noticing all the flowers and cards. "What's all this?"

"You've had a lot of people praying for you. Mom picked those flowers from the garden." He pointed to the vase. "I bought you the roses over there, and Andrew and Catherine sent you these." He pointed to the flowers next to the bed. "Even Tiffany stopped by with a card that the kids made for you." Walking over to the dresser he picked up the construction paper card with a small hand on the front of it. "Billy made it." He handed it to her.

"That's so sweet."

"You have a lot of people who care about you."

"I know." She brushed a few tears away. "What does someone have to do to get some food around here?"

He smiled with relief. "I'll be right back with something." Kissing her on the forehead, he dashed out. Flying down the stairs, jumping the last two steps and landing at the bottom, he yelled. "She's up. Megan is awake."

The other three rushed out of the dining room. "What?" Delores asked, "Megan is up?"

"Yes."

"Is she all right?" John asked anxiously.

"She seems fine, just hungry. I'm going to get her something to eat."

"Hungry, that sounds like a good sign, doesn't it?" John looked to Grant for affirmation.

"It sounds like a great sign." He slapped John on the back. "Why don't we go see for ourselves?"

"Yeah." John took every other step to the second floor. Running down the hall, he almost skidded past the door.

"Megan." He rushed to give her a huge hug. "You're awake."

"John," she said a bit surprised, "you're crushing me."

"Sorry." He let go. "I didn't mean to hurt you."

"I'm fine," she assured him. "I'm just shocked you're here this late."

"He's staying here," Grant said as he walked into the room, "Across the hall."

Delores gave her a hug, "How are you feeling, dear?"

"Tired, although Steven told me I've been sleeping for a few days."

"Your body needed some rest. You're going to be fine, now." She patted Megan's hand tenderly.

"I'm glad you decided to rejoin us, Megan." Grant kissed the top of her head.

"What happened? I don't remember anything."

"You seem to have slipped into your own little world for a while," Delores told her. "The doctor looked at you, but there wasn't anything he could do. No one could do anything except pray."

"We were all here, talking to you. Could you hear us at all?" John asked.

"No. I mean I don't think so. I had some strange dreams, but they're very vague."

"Well, you're back now and going to be fine," Delores said optimistically.

"I second that." Steven brought a tray of food to her bed. "All you need is some good home cooking and you'll be good as new." He set a dish of chicken and rice in front of her.

"This looks wonderful." Megan took a bite. "It's delicious."

"I learned from the best." Steven bowed.

"You made that?" Grant asked, astonished.

"Yes. It's almond chicken with rice pilaf."

"I love it." Megan devoured the rest of the meal and washed it down with three glasses of water. "I guess I'm pretty thirsty too."

"I think everyone should leave and let you get some rest," Delores suggested.

"I've been sleeping for days. I want to get up," Megan insisted.

"I know you're anxious, but you need to take it easy." John looked at her tenderly. "You already admitted that you still feel tired."

"I did, but the food hit the spot and now I feel much better."

"I agree with John," Grant said "You have to take it easy." He leaned over and kissed the top of her head again. "Goodnight, Megan."

Delores tucked her in bed. "I'll see you in the morning."

"Good night, Mr. and Mrs. Peterson."

"I'll take this downstairs." Steven picked up the tray.

"Thanks, Steven."

Everyone left, and Megan found herself alone with her husband. The tension grew uncomfortable as neither seemed to want to break the silence.

"I guess I should go too." Leaning over, he gave her a kiss on the forehead, "Goodnight."

"Goodnight, John."

He turned out the light and closed the door. There was a lot he wanted to say, but wasn't going to push her. His questions could wait.

Megan snuggled down in the softness of her bed and looked around the room. All the signs of love and support overwhelmed her. She didn't have to face life alone and realized that she didn't even have to be strong. God surrounded this family, if she could only trust in His love, she'd be able to find peace and rest.

Chapter 16

John lay in his bed staring at the ceiling, relieved that Megan was all right, but still wondering if he'd lost her. He'd overheard the conversation between Steven and Delores. Steven admitting that he loved Megan played over and over inside, twisting his heart into a pretzel. He wanted to get the conversation out of his head, but couldn't find the eject button. *Steven loved Megan, but did she return those feelings?* The uncertainty of the whole situation made him feel uneasy.

Deciding to grab a snack from the fridge, and try to formulate a plan, he headed downstairs. "What is my next step?" he asked himself as he entered the kitchen.

"Couldn't sleep either?" Grant was sitting at the table.

"Nope."

"Want some hot cocoa?"

"You drink that stuff?"

"It's good." Noticing the anxiety lines around John's eyes he added, "And soothing."

John doubted cocoa could soothe his jangled nerves, but filled a mug anyway. He joined Grant at the table and sat staring into the mug for a long time.

"You have to actually put it to your lips and take a sip to decide if you like it or not," Grant said quietly. He was looking at a glossy magazine pullout - cars or something, John couldn't see from here. He didn't look up, just continued sipping.

John came out of his trance, "Oh... umm. Yeah." He took a swig. "Not bad." He reached for a cookie. "I guess I never took you for a cocoa and cookies kind of fellow." "I wasn't until Delores kept trying to get me to drink warm milk whenever I couldn't sleep. I didn't like it so she starting adding chocolate."

"Warm milk must be a woman thing." John laughed softly. "Megan's always offering it to me. But I prefer it ice cold."

"I know what you mean."

John took another sip. "The chocolate does kind of kill the taste of the warm milk."

"Exactly." Grant laughed. "Do you have a lot of sleepless nights?"

"Not until recently. Farm work tuckers me out. I'm usually out as soon as my head hits the pillow."

"You've had a turbulent couple of days." Grant said, sympathetically. "No wonder you're restless."

"It's been a turbulent year." He took another swig, trying to wash the lump in his throat down.

"I can't imagine the pain you've suffered. Losing your baby must have been hard."

"The hardest thing I've ever lived through. But as bad as it was for me, it hit Megan even harder." John blinked back the tears. "And now I've lost my wife, too."

"I know you've been worried about her, but she'll be good as new."

"I lost her long before this."

"I don't think you've lost her yet."

"Really? She left me without a word. Leaving a stupid note on the kitchen table with her wedding rings."

"I'm not saying that you don't have some problems to work out," Grant admitted, "but you need to figure out how to solve the problems."

That's rich, John mused. Considering his son was one of the problems. "I think it's too late."

"It's never too late. The question is if you still want it."

"It's not a question of what I want anymore." He jabbed his thumb toward the ceiling. "I don't know what she wants."

"I suggest you find out," Grant advised. "It would appear the major problem is communication."

"Your son filling her head with all kinds of crazy dreams is the real problem." He blurted out. "Me and Megan do talk."

"Steven isn't the problem. You're using him as a scapegoat so you don't have to face the real problem."

"All right, then, Mr. Expert," John said. "What is the real problem?"

"I already told you, but you're not listening."

"Gees, now you sound just like Megan."

"I think that's enough to prove my point. If you want to keep her, you better start listening, and showing how much you care."

"How do I do that?"

"You seem to be a very practical man, which is a good thing. You have a good head on your shoulders, but that leads to the problem. You think too much with your head and not enough with your heart. Women - on the other hand - think with their hearts, not their heads. Megan is looking for romance."

"That ain't me. My head isn't filled with pretty words."

"I'm not saying you have to become a poet. I'm suggesting that you look for the little things, anything to prove you care. Think about what she likes and try to plan something around that."

"I don't understand." John felt frustrated and Grant had confused him more.

"Let's take an inventory. Megan is romantic. She loves flowers, reads romance stories, and notices the different colors in the sunrise. These are all little things that make up her personality."

"You're saying I should buy her some flowers?"

"That is one thing you could do, but don't just buy her things. Tell her what's in your heart."

"We've been married for years. She knows how I feel without me saying anything."

"Really? Then why did she leave?" Grant posed the question as gently as he could. "I've been married for forty years and not a day goes by that I don't remind Delores how beautiful she is. Or tell her how special she is to me."

"But I do tell her that I love her."

"Sometimes that isn't enough. Sometimes you have to show her in other ways."

"I think I'm starting to see what you mean." He'd come down here to figure out a game plan and this was it.

"Well, I better get some sleep. I have work tomorrow."

"Thanks, Grant."

Grant patted John's shoulder. "You're welcome, my friend."

Megan woke up early feeling more relaxed and much more alert. She threw the covers back and gently slid out of bed, slowly making her way into the bathroom.

Looking in the mirror she cringed at the reflection starring back. The dark circles under her eyes, and the remaining traces of the black and blue mark were the only hints of color on her pale face. Her long blond mane was tangled and snarled. She tried to run a brush through it but flinched at the pain. Turning on the shower and stepping into the stream of warm, soothing water, she let it beat down on her back and shoulders, loosening the stiff, sore muscles.

After dressing in a pair of blue jeans and a purple sweater, she brushed through her hair effortlessly this time, due to the extra conditioner. Partially blowing her hair dry and securing it in a ponytail, she then lightly applied some makeup, trying to add color to her washed-out appearance.

Looking in the mirror a second time, she still didn't recognize the image of the girl starring back. For the image wasn't a girl at all. Instead she saw a full-grown woman. Where had the small, carefree child gone? The little girl who relied on everyone else had disappeared, leaving in her place an adult who was responsible for her choices.

She'd borne the guilt of killing her baby all by herself. No one had been there to sustain her. She'd faced the fierce reality of life all on her own. That feeling of loneliness and isolation had driven her away from home, and her husband. She'd even been angry with God for abandoning her.

She now realized that the cruel twist of fate had helped her start to transform. Having faced the demons of her past, she now must face the consequences of her actions. She had to find the strength to stand on her own two feet, and stop relying on everyone else. "It's time to start acting like an adult," she said into the mirror.

Walking into her room and looking at the bouquets of flowers, she leaned over to inhale the fragrance of the beautiful blossoms. She didn't find any from John. Then again, it wasn't like him to buy flowers. In the five years they'd been married he had only bought her flowers once.

She stepped into the hall, almost getting knocked over by John coming out of his room at the same time.

"Sorry." He grabbed her shoulders to steady her.

"Yes." Megan laughed. "You weren't kidding about being right across the hall."

"Nope. I wanted to be as close as possible, to keep an eye on you." He also wanted to protect her like he'd always done. "What are you doing upthis early?"

"I think I slept enough the past few days. It's time to start living again."

"You promised to take it easy and not overdo it."

"I don't think making a pot of coffee is going to kill me," she stated irritably.

"Look, it's too early in the morning for fighting. Why don't we go downstairs and have some coffee before we get into a brawl?"

"I'm sorry, John, I shouldn't have snapped at you like that. I don't want to fight either." That's all they seemed to have done in the last year.

"Good, because I wanted us to watch the sunrise together." Her skin glistened from the recent scrubbing and she smelled sweet. He wanted to take her in his arms and... it'd been too long since he held her.

"Since when do you care about stuff like that?"

"I've always enjoyed the sunrise, but I'm usually in the barn or the fields when it comes up." He'd put the first step of his plan in action. He was determined to win her back.

"Watching the sunrise sounds like a wonderful idea." Megan studied her husband for a second.

"What's wrong?"

"I'm trying to figure out what's different."

"Well, I shaved." He ran his fingers over his chin.

"That's not it." Giving him a wifely once-over she noted how his favorite blue jeans hugged his hips and thighs like a second skin. The gray flannel shirt stretched taut under his wide shoulders, threatening to tear at the seams. He'd cuffed the long sleeves to the bottom of his elbows, leaving the top couple buttons undone, giving him a casual appearance. He was a handsome man, in a rough rugged kind of way. He didn't have Steven's polished features, but the cowboy look was attractive on him. "I know what it is," she exclaimed at last. "You're not wearing your hat."

"I don't need it here. But I can't go without these." He held up a foot to show his old worn out cowboy boot.

"I should have known." Megan laughed. "You never leave home without them."

"Not true," he said. "I didn't wear them to our wedding."

"I beg to differ. You wore them at the reception, remember?"

He paused a moment, then laughed. "That's right. I couldn't dance in those confounded things that came with the tux. Besides, I seem to recall you putting on tennis shoes."

"Yes, but no one could see them under my dress." John's softer attitude made her feel more at ease. "I guess you could say we were both comfortable."

"Yep, you could say that."

They walked down the stairs reflecting on their early years of marriage. Those days had been carefree, filled with promises of bright tomorrows that would end happily ever after. But their storybook life had been shattered by the brutal reality of life. And five years later they found themselves not only coping with their daughter's death, but barely holding on to the marriage.

Megan poured two cups of coffee and handed one to John. She led the way out to the garden where they settled into the swing. They watched the sky turn a dramatic shade of pink as the sun peeked its head over the horizon.

"Isn't the sunrise sensational this morning?" Megan smiled, enthusiastically.

"Yep, it's real pretty." He'd never paid attention to it before. Never looking at it as being something beautiful or wonderful. To him, it signaled the start of another day's work.

Megan took a sip of her coffee and set the cup down on the table beside the swing. They sat there quietly, enjoying the peace and tranquility of the morning. It was the start of a brand new day and they were sharing it together.

The cool, crisp air caused her to shiver.

"Are you cold?" John put his arm around her shoulders, offering some warmth.

"Just a little." She snuggled against him.

"Do you want to go in?"

"Not yet. I feel like I've been cooped up for months instead of days."

The last few days had been long, endless days of worry. Wondering what he'd do if she never woke up. And worst of all, what if she woke up and didn't want him anymore. He wished he could tell her all the things in his heart. But his experience with speaking his heart was limited. He didn't know how to put into words what he thought or felt. He simply settled for, "I'm glad you're okay."

"I wasn't thinking, John. I only wanted the pain to go away." Her tears began to fall. "I didn't mean to hurt you. I didn't want to hurt anyone."

"I want to believe that. But I don't understand. Why did you leave?"

Megan shook her head. "I can't explain it. I tried to be strong and get on with life." She took a deep breath and tried once again to make him understand. "But as I stood by her grave, all the feelings I'd been trying to forget pushed to the surface. All the progress of the past year faded and I relived the whole nightmare over again. The pain and fears overwhelmed me and I felt like a rubber band being pulled tight. Then something just snapped. All I could think about was getting away from the pain."

"Why didn't you say something to me?" He tried not to show his anger but the hurt was too strong to ignore. "I deserved more than coming home to an empty house, with a note and your rings on the table."

She swallowed hard. "How was I supposed to say anything when you were never around?"

He wanted to remind her that he had to work, but it was a weak excuse. He hadn't been able to cope with Laura's death either. "You didn't seem like you wanted me around. I thought you wanted space, so I left you alone."

"What!" Megan straightened up. "Why would you think that?"

"Because you never talked to me. I tried getting you to open up but you wouldn't even mention Laura's name. And, except for the night when you ripped up the nursery and I found you crying in the corner, you never showed any emotion towards our daughter. I started to wonder if you even cared."

"Of course, I cared! I loved her." Shaking her head Megan said, "I can't believe you thought that."

"What was I supposed to think? You wouldn't talk to me about anything concerning her. And everything I said and did was wrong. You shut yourself up in the house and didn't seem to need me."

"I did need you," she softly admitted. "I just didn't know how to deal with the pain." Putting her hands over her face she wept uncontrollably. "I miss her so much!"

"I do too." John could no longer keep his emotions in check. Holding her close, they grieved together for the first time.

The tears eventually stopped, and they sat holding each other for a long time while a strange calm enveloped them. The peaceful, quiet morning seeped into their souls, uniting their hearts.

"We should go in. I have to get breakfast made." She hated breaking the contentment she felt, but she had a job to do.

"Yeah. I need some fresh coffee." He wrinkled his nose at the distasteful chill, the bitterness. "This stuff is cold."

Megan stepped into the kitchen, and saw Steven. "You're up already?"

"What time did you get up?" He took a sip of coffee. "And what are you doing out there this time of the morning?"

"We decided to watch the sunrise."

It seemed he was about to ask what she meant by "we", when John came into the house. His heart dropped and his stomach tightened. "I see," he said, trying to keep his tone level through gritted teeth.

"What do you want for breakfast?" Megan quickly tried to lessen the tension in the room.

"I don't care." John responded first.

"Anything is fine with me," Steven added.

"That's a big help." Megan went to the refrigerator and gathered the ingredients she needed.

"How are you feeling?" Steven asked.

"Much better." She set the milk and eggs on the counter.

"I'll make breakfast. You should be resting," Steven mildly reprimanded her.

"I'm fine. I've had enough rest."

"I'm only concerned about you," Steven replied.

"I know." Megan glanced at him, but quickly averted her attention to the task at hand, not wanting to give John any reason to feel jealous. After all, Steven still wore the bruises from John's last burst of temper. "I'm really feeling much better. I'm quite capable of getting breakfast made." Reaching up in the cupboard for a bowl made her slightly light-headed - she lost her balance, stumbling against Steven.

"Are you sure you're up to this?" Steven asked as he steadied her.

"I just lost my balance," she lied. "However, it would be much easier for me to finish if you two are out of the kitchen." She needed some breathing room, and had caught John's glare towards Steven.

"I want to help." Steven didn't like the way she ignored him when John was around. He missed their days of working side by side in the kitchen - their carefree talks, and her soft laughter when he teased her. He didn't like the indifferent attitude she now had towards him now. The distance between them seemed even wider and deeper than it ever had. He didn't know if unrelenting persistence could bridge the gap this time.

"No, I can manage." She smiled to reassure him.

Grunting, he reluctantly walked out of the kitchen.

John poured another cup of coffee, then stood there as if ready to say something, but decided against it and left too.

Finally breathing a sigh of relief, she set about fixing breakfast.

"Should the two of them be left alone?" she asked herself, suddenly horrified. Putting the sausage in the skillet, she went to look for the men. She found them in the dining room, sitting at opposite ends of the table, glaring at each other while an invisible whirlwind of intense tension swirled around. Each looked ready to attack if the other should cross the invisible boundary line.

"Steven, can you check the sausage for me, while I set the table?"

"Sure." He smiled, glad to be finally included.

Megan went to the hutch and got the plates.

"You didn't have to do that," John said.

"Do what?"

"Run interference between us."

"I'm not. I need to set the table."

"You don't have to worry about me beating up pretty boy again. We have an understanding."

"An understanding?" Megan arched her brows.

"Yep. No more fighting." A mussed smile crossed his lips. "Unless warranted."

"And what would warrant smashing in someone's face?" She set the plates around the table.

"Stealing another man's wife."

"How many times do I have to tell you that Steven had nothing to do with my leaving." She tossed the handful of silverware down on the table with a loud clang. "When are you going to start listening?"

"You said he had nothing to do with your leaving in the first place, but what about now, Megan?" The question was finally out.

"Steven is a friend," she stated.

"Come on, Megan," he exploded. "How am I supposed to believe anything you say when you won't tell me the truth?"

"I'm not lying."

"And you're not telling the truth either. You keep avoiding the issue."

"He's a friend." She insisted again.

"And what else?"

"John, what do you want me to say?"

"I want to know if the two of you are lovers?"

"No!" Her shocked response burst forth. "How could you think such a thing?" Didn't he know her better than that? She may have dealt badly with her emotions surrounding Laura's death, but she still had her integrity. She was still the same small-town girl with the same small-town morals and values.

"Maybe because I follow you all the way across the state, and find you coming home from a date?"

"That was the first time we'd gone out."

"Oh, I see; you just didn't have time to sleep with him."

"I'm not going to stand here and be degraded by you." She started to walk away; he grabbed her arm, twirling her around.

"I'm trying really hard to understand what's going on in that pretty little head of yours, but I need to know where I stand." When he felt sure she wouldn't leave, he let go of her arm.

She rubbed the red spot left by his grip and glared at him. "I told you we are just friends. Steven was there when I needed him. He helped me to face my fears."

"So now, he's your best friend." John narrowed his eyes. "He was there for you when I wasn't, is that it?"

"I don't know what you're talking about."

"You leave me while I'm out in the fields earning a living, claiming that I wasn't there for you. All the while you're wrapped up in another man's arms, letting him console you." He pointed to himself. "I'm your husband, Megan. You should have turned to me." He'd wanted to be the one to comfort her, but something had always stopped her from opening up to him.

"How can I turn to you when you're never around?" she responded. "You use the farm as your crutch whenever you don't want to face something. I've spent most of our married years alone. You've always taken me for granted, and I've never complained before, but when my baby died I needed you." Tears spilled down her cheeks. "I needed you," she repeated, softly.

"You turn to another man instead of me, and then try to pin the blame on me."

"I'm not blaming anyone, I'm trying to explain my feelings, and as usual you don't understand."

"I guess that's the one thing we agree on." He skewered her with his stare. "I don't understand any of this."

"Nothing happened. It's the truth."

"I saw the way he looked at you in the kitchen. I know he wants to be more than friends."

"I told Steven from the beginning that all we could ever be is friends."

"Then what was the date all about?"

"We went out to have some fun."

"You go out gallivanting around with another man while your husband sits at home. Then you act all hurt when I want to know what's going on. Now, you tell me something. What's wrong with that picture?"

"What do you except from me?" she yelled. "Yes, I made a mistake and I left home, but it had nothing to do with Steven." She took a few deep breaths trying to calm her jangled nerves. "I figured our marriage was over. Am I supposed to stop living?"

Her words struck him hard; he could barely breathe. "So, you do want a divorce?" He had his answer. She'd throw everything away like it didn't matter.

"Isn't that why you're here?" She tried to disguise the hurt. "Do you have the papers for me to sign? Were you so furious that you had to watch me sign with your own eyes? You couldn't trust a lawyer to do the paperwork?" Tears stung her eyes. It seemed unfair to be discussing this after such a tender moment in the garden. She'd allowed herself to entertain thoughts of reconciling, but now, here he stood, accusing her of adultery and demanding a divorce.

"Obviously, you can't get rid of me fast enough," John fumed. "Is this the life you want? Being married to a farmer isn't good enough anymore." His throat constricted and he could barely get the words out. "Maybe Steven isn't the reason you left, but can you deny he's the reason we're apart now?" He walked away with his head hung down. She'd ripped the heart out from his chest.

She watched him leave, trying to understand what had happened. *If he wanted the divorce, why did he look hurt and wounded*? "That man is so confusing," she sighed. Wishing she could read his mind, or at least get a clue as to what he wanted.

***

"Megan," Rosa exclaimed. "It is good to see you up and about." She gave her a hug.

"It's good to see you too."

"How are you feeling?"

"Fine, I guess."

"Why do you sound down?"

"I have some things I need to deal with."

"The same things that laid you up in the first place?" Rosa sounded concerned for her friend. "Megan, don't make the situation more complicated, just let things play out slowly."

"I don't think I can. I made this mess and now I have to clean it up."

"Life always has a way of working out."

"But I'm responsible."

"That's the problem. You're too hard on yourself."

"I made decisions and now everyone is caught up in the aftermath. I made choices that led to my baby's death, and because I wasn't strong enough to handle the pain I left my husband. Then, I moved here and met Steven, and now there's so much anger and hurt going around." Megan pressed her fingers against her temples. "I don't know what to do."

"You have already made the choices and you can't change them now. You can't change the hand of fate."

"Why not? I started it."

"You can't worry about what anyone else is feeling. You need to follow your own instincts," Rosa said.

"I did that once, and look what happened."

"You didn't listen to your heart at all, that's what landed you here." Rosa put a reassuring arm around Megan's shoulders. "If you follow your instincts they won't let you down."

"Can you look into your crystal ball and tell me what to do?"

"I see you helping me put up Christmas decorations." Rosa winked.

"Thanks a lot, Madam Rosa."

John sat in the same spot that he and Megan occupied earlier that morning, feeling lonely as he stared off into the distance. His mind was thousands of miles away, on a small farm - his farm. These memories felt as though they were from another lifetime. A life that he and Megan had once shared, but now it seemed as if that life was over. *What am I going to do without her?* He'd built his whole world around her. Nothing had ever mattered to him until she came into his life. She was his ray of sunshine in a dark world.

His heart ached and he felt his chest squeeze as he thought about facing the days alone without his baby-doll. He'd sufferedenough loss already and he didn't know how much more he could handle. "What's the point?" Looking up to the sky, he yelled, "Can you tell me, Lord, what is the point?"

He knew that everything happened for a reason. God was in control. He desperately wanted some answers, to understand why all of this was happening. *How do I get my life back, Lord?* No longer able to fight the pain that swelled inside him, he put his head in his hands and wept bitterly.

Chapter 17

Steven looked out the window of his office, idly clicking a pen. His thoughts were so filled by Megan that he found it hard to concentrate on anything else, especially work.

"Steven." His thoughts were interrupted by a familiar voice.

"William?" Steven looked at his brother-in-law somewhat startled. "Come in. I didn't hear you knock."

"I can see that." William closed the door. "Where were your thoughts?"

"Not here." Steven avoided answering the question.

"Yes, and Grant's been complaining all morning. He said you should have stayed home, for all the work you've done today."

"Dad sent you to talk to me?"

"I brought the reports for the Anderson case." He tossed a manila folder on Steven's desk.

"You're always prepared, William." Steven managed a slight smile. "That's a good excuse."

"That's why I'm CEO." William sat in a chair in front of the desk, "But more importantly, I'm a friend."

"You're married to my sister. That makes you more than friends." Steven tossed the pen down. That makes you family."

"Does that mean you want to talk?"

"No. Since you're family, I can brush you off." Steven grinned.

"I don't want to pry. However, I'm guessing it has something to do with a woman. Since I know you're attracted to that new cook... umm... what's her name?"

"Megan."

"Right. I'd venture to say it has something to do with her."

"And I'd venture to say that you already know what's going on." Steven leaned forward. "So, why are you pretending you don't?"

William shrugged. "I don't know the whole story."

"You want me to fill in the missing pieces?" He knew his brother-in-law better than that. "Or, is this fishing expedition organized by Tiffany?"

William's brows shot up in surprise, "How did you know that?"

Steven gave a hearty laugh. "I know my sister."

"She's worried about you. And, after seeing you today, so am I."

"I'm not sure I want Tiffany to know what's going on."

"She's going to find out one way or another." William pointed out. "After all, you just said that you know your sister."

"I'm surprised Mom hasn't said anything to her already."

"We know Megan wasn't feeling well, but that's all Delores would say. It's been driving Tiffany nuts."

"I don't even know where to start." Steven sighed.

"The beginning is always a good place."

"You're right about one thing, I do care for her. As a matter of fact, I think I might be in love."

"In love!" William laughed. "That's great! I never thought it would happen to you."

"I didn't either. However, there's a complication."

"What kind?"

"She has a husband."

"A husband?" William's mouth dropped open. "How on earth did you fall for a married woman?" William paused for a second. "Is he the one who beat you up?"

"Yes. And, I didn't know she was married. By the time I found out, I'd already fallen in love."

They sat in silence for a few minutes while William considered the implications. "Steven, she's married. She has a commitment to another man."

"I know that," he snapped "Why does everyone keep reminding me of it?"

"Maybe because you're not listening."

"She left him in Illinois. I don't think the marriage is very solid," Steven explained. "They could get divorced."

William waited a minute before responding. "I know you've waited a long time for the right woman," he said at last.

"My whole life," Steven corrected him. "So why do I feel a 'but' coming?"

"Because it's wishful thinking on your part. Besides, if they do get divorced, would you want someone who'd been unfaithful to her first husband?"

"Unfaithful!" Steven shouted. "She's married to a brute. Look at my face. She'd be better off without him. And just for the record, I'll take her any way I can get her."

"Has he abused her?"

"She claims he never touched her."

"But you think she's lying?"

"Abused women always protect the abuser."

"Sometimes, not always."

"I don't care what you think!" Steven sounded frustrated that no-one seemed to want to take his side.

"I'm sorry," William said. "I only wanted to point out some facts."

"Well, keep your facts to yourself." Steven glared at him. "What do you know about all this, anyway?"

"I know you're in a lot of pain. I wish I could do something to help." William walked to the door. "Just remember, I'm here if you need to talk." He shut the door behind him quietly.

"What does he know?" Steven grumbled to himself. "He doesn't know anything!"

William had no idea how Megan made him feel. She'd opened his eyes to a new world, and opened his heart to possibilities that he'd never dreamt of before. She was the missing link in his life. The one spot that needed to be filled John's hunger got the better of his curiosity, and he realized he wasn't going to get any immediate answers, so he followed, and she'd fit it perfectly.

Megan helped Rosa put the finishing touches on the Christmas tree that stood in the foyer. They'd heard shuffling behind them and turned to see Delores dragging a large box.

"Mrs. Peterson." Megan made their presence known before Delores ran them over. "What are you doing?"

"Oh, girls, I didn't see you there." Delores stretched her back. "I'm trying to take this into the living room."

"Let us help you with that." Rosa picked up the box and it started to slip out of her hands. "What's in here? Dumbbells?"

"Just some Christmas decorations the kids made when they were younger." Delores tried to help steady the box but they ended up setting it back down.

"Let me help you with that?" said John, who had just walked in.

"Thank you, John." Delores said a little breathless.

He hoisted up the box as if it weighed nothing, his brawny arms bulging only slightly as he carried the heavy load. Megan smelled the familiar outdoorsy scent. The wind had tousled his black hair and colored his cheeks a ruddy red. She felt the coolness of the air emanating from his body, and fought the desire to wrap her arms around him to warm him up. It seemed inappropriate under the current circumstances.

Megan watched as John followed Delores into the living room, her eyes devouring the sight of him.

"He's a looker," Rosa winked.

"Oh, yes." Megan blushed slightly.

Megan was mixing the meatloaf when Steven walked in. It was like many times before, except this time felt different. So much had changed between them in the last week.

"Megan, we need to talk." He still felt a little edgy from his talk with William.

"I'm busy right now." She held up her gooey hands. "Can this wait until later?"

"I'm tired of waiting, Megan."

"I know, Steven but..."

"I need answers." His tone softened and his eyes pleaded with her.

Megan went to the sink and washed her hands. Steven stood behind her, placing his hand on the small of her back. He needed to feel her body close to his.

"Steven, please...I can't." She grabbed the towel off the counter and moved out of his reach.

Steven impatiently ran his hand through his hair. "That's it! I can't take any more. I need to know who you're going to choose."

"Who I'm going to choose?" Her eyes clouded with confusion.

"Don't play dumb with me." Although he didn't explode with outbursts like John did, Megan could see the muscles ticking in his jaw. "Is it going to be me or him?"

"That him, as you just referred to, is my husband and he has a name," Megan defended. She put the meatloaf in the oven.

"I guess from that remark you're choosing him."

Megan slammed the door shut. "This isn't a game, Steven. This is my life. Am I supposed to say, 'Eeny, meeny, miney, moe' and choose someone? I don't know what's going on. My life has been turned upside-down, and so has everyone else's. I don't have an answer for anyone. I don't know what John wants, I don't know what you want, and I most definitely don't know what I want."

Steven stood directly in front of her. "I can help you with one of those dilemmas. I know what I want - you." His brown eyes bored into hers and she felt the rhythm of her heart speed up.

These feelings she felt for Steven were so different from those she felt for John. These were new, exciting and dangerous. Steven was romantic and told her all the things she wanted to hear. He made her feel special and needed. He was easy to talk to, and fun to be around.

But John was her husband, and good or bad, she'd made a lifelong commitment to him. Their current troubles didn't erase the promises she'd already made. "Steven, please don't do this. I can't handle it right now," she begged him.

"I don't want to push you, Megan." His eyes filled with tenderness. "I want you to know that I'm not giving up on us. I'm going to fight because I know we were meant to be together."

"Steven," she whispered. "John is my husband and if he wants me, I have to stay with him."

"Sweetheart, you don't *have* to do anything. Look around you. I can offer youa lot more. You'll never have to work again. In fact, there will be people working for you. You'll have everything you've ever dreamed of. I'll buy you the world, Megan."

"Do you think I care about money?" Her eyes narrowed into blue slits. "Well I don't! I married John because I loved him. That is the only reason I would ever marry anyone." She brushed past him, feeling hurt. He'd just made her feel cheap and inferior. "You can take your money and shove it." She crossed her arms.

Throwing his hands up in the air, he left. Still getting no answers and managing to upset her even more. This day just went from bad to worst. He knew Megan didn't care about money. That's what attracted him in the first place. Why had he said such a stupid thing? He only wanted to offer her the best life possible, to help her see the potential of a life with him. Destiny had brought them together, how could he convince her of that? He'd say or do anything to keep her in his life.

***

Megan set a place for everyone, but only she and Mr. and Mrs. Peterson ate dinner that night. Steven had stormed off after their argument, and no-one had seen John since he had carried the box into the living-room. The tension loomed like a dark cloud over the room. Grant and Delores exchanged small talk about work and about the activities of the house, but Megan didn't contribute much to the conversation, being too caught up in her own thoughts.

"Megan, dear, are you feeling all right?" Delores asked. "You look a bit pale."

"I'm just tired."

"You're over-exerting yourself," Grant said. "I wanted to ask you to do something, but considering the state of your health right now, maybe I should forget it."

"No, I'm fine, what is it?" She welcomed a distraction.

"I don't want you to tire yourself out, and you don't have to do it, if it's too stressful." He hesitated.

"Mr. Peterson, I can't tell you if I can handle it until you tell me what you're talking about."

"Would you consider cooking a business lunch next week? You did such a marvelous job for Delores. And Thanksgiving was s huge success." Noting her shocked face, he added, "I know it's short notice and close to Christmas. Please don't feel you have to accept."

"I think I can handle it."

"Great. I figure treating my clients to your home cooking will give me a leg up on getting the account." Grant winked.

"I'll do my best."

"Megan, you're a lifesaver." Noticing how she played with her food and barely eating, he said, "Why don't you go up to bed? I'll take care of the dishes."

"You?"

"Yes. I know how to clear a table and load the dishwasher."

"Isn't that what you pay me for?"

"Yes, but since I threw a curveball at you just now, I figure you're going to need your rest. Now scoot." He nodded his head toward the door.

"I'd normally argue with you, but I am tired."

"You wouldn't win anyway."

"I know."

She bid them goodnight, then went upstairs. Pausing in front of John's door and noticing the light shining underneath, she raised her hand to knock, but hesitated. There were still many unanswered questions. She wanted to give him time to sort out his feelings, and she'd wait until he came to her, if he ever did.

Deciding not to disturb him, she went into her room, flopped down on the bed and gazed at the material covering the canopy. She'd spent so much time in bed over the past week that she didn't relish the idea of going to bed early. Not wanting to waste any more time lying around, she turned on the radio, then ran water for a bath.

John had been sitting in a chair looking out of the window when he sensed Megan's presence. He sat up straight, holding his breath, hoping she'd knock. He wanted to hear her say she still loved him. Still wanted him. Or at least give him a chance to convince her to stay with him. However, she chose to walk away. Again!

He paced the room anxiously, trying to loosen the knot forming in his gut, and wondering whether he should just leave. After all, Megan had made her choice. She'd walked out of his life twice. He wasn't so dense that he didn't understand that. However, quitting had never been his style.

Besides, he still had some hopes. She could change her mind. He wanted to change her mind for her. He wanted to bust down the door and force her to choose him. But strong-arm tactics would only drive her further away, or more likely, right into the waiting arms of Steven. No, it was safer if he was patient, giving her some time and space. But not too much, otherwise Steven could sneak right in and steal her away, just like a fox stealing a chicken from the hen-house.

His rumbling stomach reminded him that he'd skipped dinner. He didn't want to create another scene, and felt his temper was too raw to handle, so he'd retreated into his room until the coast was clear. But he should be able to grab a bite to eat now.

Pausing outside Megan's room, he listened to the radio playing the country hits that she loved. He wondered whether she was waiting for him to make the first move. After all, she was from the old school, believing that men made the first move. Or was that just wishful thinking? This would be a test of his patience. Normally he wasn't a patient man.

"She'll come to me when she's ready."

Megan opened the doors to the balcony and stepped out into the evening air. A slight breeze chilled her freshly bathed body, making her feel alive and invigorated. Her mind always seemed sharper when outdoors. The brilliant sky offered a reprieve from the current predicament. The shimmering stars twinkled in the darkness, calming in her heart. She sat down and studied the constellations, remembering the day she had met John.

It had been the first semester of her sophomore year in college. She'd been running across the campus lawn, not paying attention as she dug around in her backpack for a notebook. Suddenly, she bumped into someone – or more accurately ran into him – she'd toppled to the ground, scattering her books.

"Are you all right, miss?"

"Yes, I think so." She felt like she'd run into a brick wall. Looking up she found the tallest man in the world looking down at her. Of course, only being five feet four inches made everyone seem tall. "I'm sorry. I wasn't paying attention to where I was going." She started collecting the books.

"It's okay." His blue eyes twinkled when he smiled. "Where are you off to in such a hurry, anyway?"

"I'm late for my astronomy class."

He bent down, picking up one of her books.

"Thanks." She stuffed it into her bag.

He helped her up. "Are you sure you're all right?" he asked again, feeling her hands tremble.

"Ye...yes," she stammered. "I'm worried about being late." His touch had turned her knees into jelly. Her heartbeat quickened and she felt a strange tingly sensation as they talked. "It's me who should be asking you if you're okay."

"Never better." He chuckled "It would take more than a mite like you to dent me."

"I guess sometimes it's better to be small." She smiled, nervously.

"I guess so. By the way, my name is John. John Black." He shook her hand lightly before letting go.

"I'm Megan Garver." She looked at him curiously. "I don't believe I've seen you around campus before. Did you transfer here?" He couldn't be a freshman, he looked several years older.

"No, I'm taking a few business classes." He winked. "I'm a little old to be a student."

"You could be a senior," she suggested. "Besides, age doesn't have anything to do with education."

"You think I'm a late bloomer?" He raised one dark eyebrow and she detected a faint smile under his bushy mustache.

"Could be."

"I'm more of a hands-on kind of fellow. I'd rather be working in the fields than wasting time in a classroom."

"To each his own. I love learning."

"Don't get me wrong I like learning too. I just do it in a different way."

"Oh, I didn't mean to...to...imply you're...umm...dumb or anything. That came out wrong. I only meant that I like being here."

"I'm not offended. Don't fret about it, Megan." She liked the sound of her name coming out in his deep, gruff tone.

The chapel bells rang out across the campus, reminding her that it was now ten o'clock. "I have to go." She started running but called out over her shoulder, "'Bye, and I'm sorry."

She'd felt like such an idiot for acting like a schoolgirl with a crush instead of a nineteen-year-old college student. *I must have come across as being a clumsy air-head.* It wasn't until after class that a friend pointed out a big grass stain on the backside of her white shorts. *I bet that made an impression!* She silently groaned.

However, two days later, she found a book on constellations sitting by her dorm door. She smiled as she read the note. "Hope you enjoy this book. John."

"Guess I didn't make too bad of an impression after all." She smiled to herself.

It hadn't been flowers, candy, or any of the usual gifts that guys use to try to impress girls. John's was a practical present and in its own way, the most special gift she'd ever received. She'd never been able to look at the stars since without thinking about him.

Even now as she gazed up at the clusters of celestial bodies her thoughts were about him. They had shared many star-filled nights together, and now she wondered if he could ever forgive her. Or was the marriage over?

***

Megan hadn't seen John or Steven for the next several days, and wondered if everyone else was also using the time to reflect. She certainly valued the time alone to sort things out.

"Megan, why don't you plan the menu for Grant's lunch with him before dinner?" Delores suggested.

"Sure." Megan took the papers off the counter and walked into the study. "You're home early," she said, sitting down in the chair.

"I've been working late for the past few weeks and decided to treat myself to an early day." Grant smiled. "To what do I owe the pleasure of your company?"

"I wanted to go over some ideas for your business lunch."

"Good, because I have a couple of suggestions."

"You do?" Delores hadn't had any suggestions at all. She'd left everything in Megan's hands, which had added to the pressure. "I'm all ears."

"I'm thinking about your sausage gravy for the main course, and apple pie for dessert."

"Your two favorites."

"Of course, I'm sure it will be a hit with my clients."

"That's not a problem. Do you want mashed potatoes and biscuits?"

"Of course."

"I'll also fix another pie just in case someone doesn't like apple."

"Who doesn't like apple?" Grant teased. "Every hot blooded man likes apple pie. It goes with America."

"Not everyone is as red blooded as you." She winked. "Now what about drinks?"

"Coffee and soft drinks. No tea for us men."

"I could make iced tea. That's manly enough for the rough and rugged."

"Umm, maybe."

Grant liked hearing her laugh, and saw the spark in her eyes.

Megan walked into the dining-room and noticed John sitting at the table.

"Good, fried chicken. My favorite." He grabbed a chicken leg.

"John, you need to wait," she scolded.

"Oh, let the man eat." Grant slapped John on the back. "I can't wait myself." He helped himself to a piece of chicken.

"Men have no manners, Megan," Delores complained as she sat down.

"It's not bad manners, it's good food." Grant laughed.

"I'll second that," John said with a mouthful of chicken.

Megan smiled as she took her seat. It lifted her spirits to see John in such a good mood.

Steven walked in. "Did you save me some food?"

"No, we don't want to share," Grant said.

"Sit down, dear, and help yourself," Delores offered.

"Don't mind if I do." He took his seat, and spooned some broccoli and rice casserole unto his plate. Steven's easy-going mood appeared to evaporate when he looked at John. Both men stiffened but remained civil. However, the tension in the room went up a few notches.

Megan wondered what had brought them both to the table tonight. They had both been absent over the last few evenings. Was it coincidence that they showed up now? Were they up to something? Or did they just think alike. She couldn't imagine them thinking alike when their personalities were so different.

Steven was easy-going, and his light-hearted, flamboyant ways made him fun to be around. He could be romantic and knew how to make you feel special. That compensated for his sometimes childish and insensitive ways. He depended on his good looks and his family name to get him what he wanted.

John, on the other hand, had always underplayed his good looks and worked hard for everything he had. Being a practical man he seemed more reserved with an understated sense of humor. He was passionate and explosive with a temper to match. Conversations with John always revolved around the farming. The farm wasn't just a job to him, it was his life. Those fields were as much a part of him as the blood running thorough his veins. He never had fancy words or said things from his heart but he'd always been loyal and dependable.

Right now she couldn't say the same.

"What are you doing?" John asked Megan as he followed her into the kitchen after the meal.

"Cleaning up."

"It looks clean to me." He looked around the spotless room.

"Almost, I need to put the food away and load the dishwasher." So far, the conversation had been friendly. "I was surprised to see you at dinner tonight."

"I know." He looked away for a second, as if trying to collect his thoughts, then looked back at her. "I'm not very good at this, Megan. I don't know what you want me to say."

"I don't know what to say to you, either."

"I don't want to get into another fight."

"Neither do I."

"But we have to clear things up. The last time we talked we both lost our tempers and said some horrible things. Now, I've tried to give you time to sort things out, but I need to know where I stand. Are you really going to throw away our marriage like a dirty rag? Does it mean that little to you?"

"What do you mean I'm throwing away our marriage? You're the one who wants a divorce."

"No, I don't! Why do you think that?"

"You were so angry and I thought...you ha...hated me... for leaving." Her lower lip trembled.

"I can't deny being angry. I was mad as a hornet when you took off. And I got even madder when I saw you with Steven. But divorce never entered my mind. I promised to love you until death." Pinning her with his blue eyes, he stated, "I intend to keep that promise."

"So, you didn't follow me here because you want a divorce?"

"No. I want you to come back home."

"You don't hate me?" Tears fell from her eyes.

"Of course, not." The crucial point had arrived. He had only this one chance to persuade her to come back to him, but he didn't know what to say. He'd never been good with words.

"Megan, I love you. My life revolves around you." His eyes bored into hers. He desperately wanted to make her see his heart, for all the words he wanted to say were locked up in there. "I don't know what to say to make you see and believe that."

"You just said it." Megan smiled. She knew his life didn't revolve around her. It revolved around the farm, but she liked the idea of him putting her first for once.

John wiped a tear from her cheek. "Do I mean anything to you?"

"Yes, of course. You mean everything." She felt a pang of guilt. Although it was the truth, she also felt something for Steven and those feelings ran deeper than she'd thought.

"Does that mean that you'll come back home with me?"

"I can't, not yet," she whispered.

John's smile quickly faded and Megan saw the muscles tighten in his jaw. "Why not?

"Because there is a lot going on, and a lot of people to consider."

"Like Steven." His teeth were clenched together so tight that Megan thought his jaw would break.

"Yes, he's one," she confessed. "The Petersons are counting on my help through Christmas. I can't take off and leave them stranded. That wouldn't be fair after all they've done for me."

John inhaled deeply before asking, "Are you saying that you can't come home with me right now?"

"I'm saying that things are complicated."

"Oh, and let me guess what one of those complications are." John threw his hands up in the air. "Steven, right?"

"John, please." Megan looked down at the floor. "I thought you wanted a divorce. I thought it was over between us and I..."

"So, you got yourself a rich boyfriend."

"He's not my boyfriend," she yelled. "I believed our marriage was over and I was trying to move on with my life. Steven helped me do that. He's been a good friend and I don't want to hurt him."

"Oh, yeah, I forgot he is *just* a friend," John mocked her. "And such a good one that you won't leave him and come back home with your husband."

"I need time to sort my feelings out."

"Time?" he shouted, "I've been here over a week. How much more time do you need?" He paced across the floor.

"Until tonight, I've been operating under the assumption that we were getting divorced. Now you're telling me you don't want that. I need to reevaluate the situation."

"What are you reevaluating? Calculating what you'll miss out on if you move back into our tiny farmhouse?"

"I'm sick and tired of everyone talking about money around here. You should know me better than that."

John stepped closer, towering over her. She backed up against the counter. John slammed his palms down, caging her in with his large arms. Bending down he harshly whispered, "Let me tell you something about my *wife*. My *wife* would never have left me without a word. My *wife* wouldn't be living in a mansion refusing to come home where she belongs. Now, I've accepted your reason for leaving, because no one knows better than me the pain you suffered. I can also accept your excuse for staying here because of your job. But something I cannot and *will not* accept are your feelings for another man."

"John... I..."

He pressed a finger against her mouth lightly. "I'm not done yet." The feel of her soft lips sent a jolt through him, and he quickly withdrew his finger. He stepped back to give himself breathing room, he then forced his mind back onto the subject at hand. "You say I should know you, but you aren't acting like the woman I used to know. You need more time to sort out your feelings and to figure out who it is that you love." He began to pace again. "I'll give you the time, but don't think I'm backing down without a fight. We have something real, something special between us, and I know you feel it too. Be prepared for the battle of your life." He turned on his heel and left.

Megan stood there trying to absorb what he'd just said. His references to "fight" and "battle" were troublesome. John was a very accurate man. When he talked about doing something he meant it literally. She fretted about what that might mean for Steven.

Her first instinct was to curl up in a ball so as not to face this horrible nightmare, but hiding wouldn't solve anything. Finding some inner determination, she squared her shoulders, vowing she would be strong this time. No more running, hiding, or trying to avoid reality. She would face her problem like an adult and make a choice. The situation didn't apply to her life only anymore. There were two strong capable men awaiting her decision. The longer she took to make up her mind, the more hurt one of them would suffer.

Chapter 18

John tried working off his excess energy with a long walk. He maneuvered along the paths until he came to the large white gazebo, slightly illuminated by the crescent moon. He sat down on the top step, thinking of Megan. He felt like a warrior who'd just lost the battle – defeated, and shot through the heart.

He'd tried doing something romantic, watching the sun rise together. He thought they'd connected on an emotional level, but somehow, they'd ended up fighting. Going for the direct approach and telling her what was in his heart hadn't persuaded her either. Every plan he'd tried seemed to fail. What else could he say or do? He had to think of something. He couldn't give up.

"Nice night we're having."

The voice from the shadows startled John. "Who's there?" He turned and saw someone sitting there.

Steven emerged, and took a seat next to John. "It's only me. I didn't want you to think I was spying, so I thought I'd make my presence known."

"Oh, you've made your presence known all right." The words came out in a half-sneer, half-sigh. Here sat the enemy. The man responsible for everything that was wrong in his life. "I'm glad to see that you're an honest thief. I can cross peeping Tom off your list of sins."

"I'm not a thief," Steven defended.

"You stole my wife."

"I didn't know she was married."

"You do now. Are you backing down and letting her go? Or are you fighting for her?"

Steven thought for a long time before responding. "I won't lie to you, even if it means getting punched again. I owe you the truth." Intense brown eyes stared into John's blue eyes. "No, I'm not backing down, and I have already told Megan that. I may know she's married, but it's too late now for me to walk away. She's worth fighting for." Steven couldn't read John's reaction in the darkness.

"I know she is," John sighed. "And just for the record...I'm not going to punch you." It wasn't that he didn't want to, but he respected him for telling the truth.

Steven mentally breathed a sigh of relief. "Good. The black and blue marks from our last fight are only just now fading."

"Well, I don't feel guilty. That's the consequence of trying to take a man's wife."

"Even though I didn't know she was your wife at the time. And just for the record, nothing happened."

"Because I showed up and spoiled your date." John remembered what the clerk at the hotel had said. "What happened when you spent the night in her room at the motel?"

"How did you find out about that?" Steven knew Megan wouldn't have divulged that information.

"You aren't denying it." John felt the fury building up inside. This was too much honesty. He repeated his question.

"I did stay with her, but it's not what you're thinking. I never touched her."

"You expect me to believe that you spent the whole night and nothing happened?"

"Ask Megan if you don't believe me. I stayed the night to help her through a rough time. She was close to an emotional breakdown and I didn't think she should be alone." Looking John squarely in the face he added, "She told me about Laura that night. She was too overwhelmed and in so much pain to think about anything else."

"And exactly what did you do to help her?" His tone hovered between sarcasm and sincerity.

"We talked. She told me everything she'd kept locked inside. Once she started to let it out, and face it, she started to regain control of her life."

"You really expect me to believe you spent all night with my wife and you never touched her?"

"Look, John, I'm not saying I didn't want to. I'm no saint and she is beautiful, but she was in no condition to think about anything romantically. You saw her last week."

"So, while she's pouring her heart out to you, she never mentioned me. Not even once?" He sounded more hurt than angry.

"No. She was grieving for her child. Laura was the only person on her mind."

"At least she talked to you about Laura. I tried and failed."

"I'm sorry about all the things that have happened to you." The genuine compassion in Steven's voice was obvious. "I know it had to be hard losing your child and now you're..."

"Don't say I've lost Megan because I haven't. I'm going to fight for her with everything I have. We've been married for five years. We have a history together and we have shared more than you can compete with. You've known her for what... two months?"

"I haven't known her long. But I feel like I've known her my entire life."

"Well, you can't have her. She's mine. Why don't you go find your own woman?"

"I can't let Megan go that easily."

"Then I guess we have a full-fledged war going."

"It looks that way," Steven agreed.

The two men sat in silence for a long time.

"Guess I better head on in." John stood.

"Going to plan your attack?"

"Something like that." He walked away a few steps, then turned and asked, "Should we set some rules of combat?" John liked to win, but he'd always won his battles fairly.

"No. Anything goes." Steven hated being constricted by rules. "May the best man win."

John nodded his head. "I plan to."

"Good morning." John yawned, heading for the coffeepot.

"You never sleep in this late unless you're sick.".

"I'm fine." He stifled another yawn. "I was up late, that's all."

"Do you want something to eat?"

"No. Coffee's good." He took a swig and watched her add a few more things to the shopping list. "I was hoping we could go sightseeing or something."

"I really have a lot to do. I've got to go to the store and pick up a few things for Mr. Peterson's business lunch."

"What about tomorrow?"

"I have the lunch tomorrow. I doubt I'll have much free time."

"You're too busy to spend a day with me. Is that what you're saying?"

"No, John. I'm tied up for the next couple of days. Why don't we try and do something on Saturday? It's my day off."

"I wanted to spend some time alone with you sooner, but I guess Saturday will have to do."

"If you really want to spend time together you can come shopping with me. I'm leaving in half an hour."

"Shopping?" He wrinkled his nose. "Nah, I'll pass."

"Thought so."

Steven called Andrew and told him all about the conversion with John the night before.

"He actually said 'this is war'?" Andrew laughed.

"His exact words."

"What did you say?"

"I told him may the best man win."

"Steven, you didn't!"

"By the end of the conversation, I think we had a mutual understanding."

"Hey buddy, I hope things work out for you. But keep in mind they have a strong bond that will be hard to break."

"John said pretty much the same thing. You still think I don't have a chance?"

"I'd be careful and not get your hopes too high. After all, anything can happen."

"Yeah, yeah," Steven rolled his eyes.

"You're not listening to a word I'm saying, are you?"

"I've heard it from just about everybody."

"Then, how about some better news?" Andrew sounded as though he was ready to burst with excitement.

"What's up?"

"I wanted to know if you'd be a godfather to our child?"

Steven laughed. "Aren't you jumping ahead of yourself? You two need to have children before worrying about godparents."

"Yes, I know."

Steven sat up on the couch as the meaning of Andrew's words slowly dawned on him. "You're having a baby? Catherine is pregnant?"

"Yes. You're going to be an honoree uncle."

"I can't believe this. That's great! Congratulations, buddy."

"Can you imagine a little me running around?"

"No, I can't. One of you is enough."

"Always the funny man." Andrew laughed.

"How is Catherine feeling?"

"She has morning sickness and getsvery pale and nauseous."

"Is she supposed to be like that?"

"Yeah, the doctor said it's normal and there's nothing to worry about. I've been trying to do more around the house so she can get her rest."

"You're such a great guy," Steven teased. "Why, if I were a girl, I would've grabbed you up myself."

"No, you wouldn't have. If you were a girl you'd be ugly."

"I see fatherhood has given you a sarcastic side."

"You're rubbing off on me," Andrew said.

"Give Catherine my best."

"I will."

Steven hung up and went in search of Megan. It felt natural that she'd be the person to share the good news with. He found her in the dining room setting the table. She looked up when he walked in, but quickly averted her gaze, not knowing how to deal with the strange awkwardness between them.

"I have the greatest news." He smiled brightly, ignoring the distance he felt had come between them.

"Wow, it must be. You're almost glowing." Megan liked the twinkle in his eyes. That spark that made him Steven.

"I just got off the phone with Andrew. He and Catherine are going to have a baby." "Steven, that's terrific. I'm happy for them." However, a pang of sadness sounded in her voice...regret for what she'd lost.

He noticed the flicker of pain in her eyes. "Does that news bother you?"

"No. I am happy for them. Just sad for myself."

"I'm sorry, Megan, I shouldn't have mentioned it."

"Don't be silly. I'm glad you told me." She turned away.

"You don't have to hide your tears from me. I've already noticed them." Nothing got past him. Walking up behind her, he put his hands on her shoulders.

"I'm sorry. I don't want you to think that I'm not happy for them, because I'm glad they're starting a family. It just makes me think about Laura, and the void in my life because of her absence."

"No one blames you for missing your daughter. It's perfectly natural to feel that way. You're not a bad person and you don't have to hide your pain." He turned her around to face him. Placing a hand under her chin, he tilted her head back until she looked into his eyes, "At least not from me."

"I can't hide anything from you." She smiled warily.

"And you better remember that." Wrapping his arms around her, he held her tight. It felt good to be close to her again.

John stepped through the door, witnessing the tender moment. His fists clenched into balls and his teeth ground tight.

He wanted to barge over and slug Steven in the mouth – it seemed the little rat had wasted no time. But that would be the biggest mistake he could make. Not only would Megan be angry, the Petersons would kick him out. He had to play it cool. That was hard to do as he watched another man hold his wife. Well, two can play that game. he told himself.

"Rosa, you're here early."

"*Sí*" I wanted to get some things done before Mr. Peterson's lunch today. I want everything to be perfect. You don't lookvery well."

"I feel really sick," Megan confessed.

Rosa pulled out a chair. "Here sit down. I will finish setting the table."

"Thanks." She took a seat, breathing in deeply.

"Good morning, everyone." Grant smiled as he walked in. "You women are looking exceptionally beautiful this morning."

"You're in a chipper mood," Megan commented, "and looking very distinguished in that dark gray suit."

"Thank you." Grant noticed her pale complexion. "Are you feeling ill?"

"Just a little upset stomach."

"Maybe I should make plans for a restaurant."

"Nonsense." She stood up and swayed as the room spun.

"Megan." Grant slid am arm around her waist to steady her.

"I stood up too fast, that's all."

"I think there's more to it than that. I want you back in bed."

"No," she said defiantly. "I'm fine. I can handle it." She was determined not to let him down.

"I should never have asked you to do this lunch."

"It isn't too much pressure. I'm sure I'll be better by lunchtime." She met his brown eyes with a look full of confidence. "I can do this."

He smiled to himself. "Okay, if it means that much to you."

"It does."

After showering and changing into her uniform, her stomach stopped somersaulting. She went back into the kitchen and started preparing lunch.

"You look a little better," Rosa said. "Some color has come back to your cheeks." She poured a cup of coffee.

"Yeah, I feel better. It seems like I haven't felt good since I came to California."

"Maybe it's the weather. A change in climate can play havoc with your nerves, and your body."

"Whatever my problem was, I'm feeling better now."

"If you need any help let me know. I'll be dusting the foyer and the study."

"I think I have everything under control. Stop worrying and go do your chores."

"Okay. Okay. You're such a slave-driver." Rosa swatted Megan with a dishtowel then left.

Megan started peeling potatoes.

"What are you doing?" John asked as he walked in.

"What does it look like?"

"All right, *why* are you peeling potatoes at ten in the morning?"

"Because if I do it now, I won't be wasting time later."

"I see." He walked over to the coffeepot.

"No, you don't." She laughed. "Trust me, I have a system and everything will be done on time."

"I trust you," he said with sincerity. He had a system too, one that would land her back in his arms. "What are you making for this lunch thing?"

"Sausage gravy."

"Aww, that's my favorite. I'm sorry I'm going to miss it."

"Aren't you going to be eating? I have more than enough."

"I won't be here."

"Where are you going?"

"On a date." He sipped his coffee slowly, and watched her reaction over the rim of his cup.

"A date!" Her blond brows rose with surprise. "With whom?"

"I'm glad you still think I'm worth getting jealous over." He laughed.

"I'm not jealous," she defended. "Just... surprised."

"If you say so." He winked. "I'm having lunch with Delores."

"Why are you going out with Delor...umm...Mrs. Peterson?" she asked curiously.

"She asked if I'd join her. I didn't see any reason not to." He shrugged his shoulders. "Is there a problem?"

"No, not at all." She tried to sound nonchalant. "Where is she taking you?"

"She isn't taking me. I'm paying."

"Did she say that?"

"No. But the man always pays."

"Hah! Not with Mrs. Peterson."

"I will pay when they bring the check."

"Right! Good luck with that."

"Now, I'll get out of your way. I just needed a refill." He held up his cup.

"Have a nice time." She smiled.

"Thanks, I will. And good luck to you too." He kissed her on the forehead. "Not that you need any."

When Grant and his guests arrived, Megan served coffee and some bite-sized appetizers while they talked in the study.

"Thank you, Megan," Grant smiled as she poured his coffee.

"What time would you like lunch served?"

"Why don't you give us about an hour? If we finish sooner, I'll let you know."

"Very well."

"Be careful, gentlemen. You don't want to ruin your appetite," Steven warned, watching the men devour the appetizers. "Megan is the best cook in town." He winked, and noticed her blush.

"Don't worry about me. If lunch is as good as these, I'll have plenty of room." A chubby man with brown hair picked up another appetizer and popped it into his mouth. His cheeks filled out like a squirrel hoarding acorns.

"Easy, Matt." An older gentleman with a wrinkled face and gray hair laughed. "I bet there's plenty of food. You don't have to stuff your mouth."

"Sorry," he said his mouth still full of food. "It's so good."

"That's true," Grant said with pride. "But do save your appetite because Megan has not only prepared lunch, but also made some wonderful pies for dessert."

"Dessert is my favorite part." Matt licked his fingers.

"Somehow, I figured that out." Grant laughed. "Megan, could you bring us more appetizers."

"Yes, sir." She took the empty platter and headed for the kitchen.

"Excuse me, gentlemen. I'll be right back." Steven left the room.

"Your new cook is not only talented but beautiful as well. It seems she has enchanted your son."

"And from what I hear, that is quite a feat," Matt snickered.

"Yes. She's just as sweet as she is beautiful. But she's only the temporary cook," Grant explained.

"Come on Grant, what's the scoop with the two of them?"

"I hate to disappoint you, Robert, but there isn't any scoop."

"Steven didn't take his eyes off her the whole time she was in the room." Robert said.

"It's hard not to notice someone like her. Your eyes were glued as well," Grant said.

"Yes, but I didn't shoot out of here like a rocket after her." Robert smiled, triumphantly having made his point. "Do you disapprove of your son falling for the hired help?"

"I most certainly do not," Grant protested. "If she were available, I'd be the first one to congratulate him on such a rare find. I'm sorry to say that she's already married. I can only hope that Steven will find someone like her to settle down with."

"I seem to recall an incident some years back involving your son and a maid. I would think you'd be more cautious about this sort of thing." Robert's gray eyes gleamed.

"How do you know about that?" Grant's eyes narrowed and his voice deepened.

"I did my homework." Robert sat back in his chair with a smug smile. "I make it my business to find out about the people I'm getting involved with in business."

"We're not in business yet," Grant reminded him. "I kept that quiet. Only our family knew. How did you find out about April?"

"He has lots of resources." Matt smiled smugly.

"Now take it easy, buddy. I'm not digging up dirty laundry on your family so I can blackmail you into a proposition. I'm only asking on a personal level if it's wise to let him get involved with the help again?"

"I hardly know you. I don't consider us buddies," Grant said, sternly. "And I don't like people nosing into my family's private affairs."

"As I said already, I'm not bringing this up to hurt you or your family, I'm merely concerned." Robert's smile held more than concern, showing that he enjoyed having power over his business partners.

"And I've told you nothing is going on. At least, nothing you need to concern yourself with." They heard voices coming down the hall. "I'd appreciate you not mentioning this subject around Steven," Grant warned him.

"Of course. I understand." Robert nodded his head.

Megan brought in a tray with a pitcher and some glasses.

Steven set the tray of appetizers down on the desk. "Sorry I took so long, but I wanted to help Megan."

Robert sat forward and took an appetizer off the tray. "Thank you." Smiling, he glanced at Grant. "You didn't miss anything, just some small talk."

"I brought iced tea in case anyone gets thirsty." Megan smiled at Matt.

"You read my mind," he smiled back.

She handed him the glass. "If that's all, I'll let you get back to work."

"Thank you, Megan." Grant smiled, but the pleasantness usually surrounding him was gone.

The men were still busy at work an hour later when Megan knocked lightly on the door.

"Come in," Grant called.

Megan tentatively walked in. "I wanted to see if you gentlemen need anything, or whether you were ready for lunch?"

"No, nothing right now," Robert replied.

"I'm kind of getting hungry," Matt said sheepishly.

Megan looked at the empty tray. "Would you like more snacks?"

"I think we could all use a break. Why don't we pick up here after lunch?" Grant offered, casting a glance at Robert.

Robert didn't seem too delighted with the idea, but nodded reluctantly.

"Good, I'm starving." Matt beamed.

"How can you be starving?" Robert asked. "You ate most of the appetizers."

"I couldn't help it. They were good."

The men sat down at the table and Megan served. Matt almost inhaled the food, and Megan wondered if he even took time to chew it.

When Robert had finished two helpings of his sausage gravy, he wiped his mouth with his napkin and set it beside his plate. "My compliments to the chef on a most fascinating meal."

"Thank you, sir."

"This is the best meal I've had in... well since...I don't know when, probably my whole life." Matt said, enthusiastically.

"That's probably the biggest compliment I've received in my whole life." She smiled brightly making Matt's cheeks color a little.

"She's not only talented and beautiful, but witty as well." Robert noted. "I like those qualities in a woman." His gray eyes raked over her.

Not sure how to respond, Megan said nothing. She loaded up the dishes and took them to the security of the kitchen.

The men returned to the study to finish business. Megan later served the pies and a fresh pot of coffee in there. The lunch went off without a hitch. She felt more relaxed this time, although she didn't like the way Robert kept smiling at her.

***

At dinner that night everyone chatted excitedly about the activities of the day. John made them all laugh with details of the lunch he'd shared with Delores.

"So, the waiter brings the check and I reach for it, but Delores grabs it at the same time and said 'lunch is on me'. I told her that a gentleman always pays. She actually tried to wrestle the tray out of my hand. It was the funniest thing." John laughed.

"How did you get the check away from him?" Grant asked.

"He's too strong for me." Delores smiled. "He ended up with the check. Luckily, we were at a restaurant I go to often, so I told the waiter to put it on my account."

"Told him?" John laughed. "You practically screamed it."

"I told you she would end up paying." Megan gloated. "Guess I win."

"I didn't know it was a bet." John smiled. "How did the business lunch go?"

He directed the question to Megan, but Steven answered. "Lunch was great. Business, not that great. He quoted a ridiculous price, didn't he Dad?" Steven was determined to interrupt the cozy conversation between John and Megan.

"Yes, quotes were low. We had to end for the day but nothing is settled yet." Grant sighed.

"Robert and Dad kept rehashing the same old thing and no one got anywhere," Steven complained.

Grant grunted at the mention of Robert's name. Something about him didn't seem right. He particularly didn't like the snooping into his private life and not knowing what Robert intended to do with the information.

"It'll be fine, dear," Delores said reassuringly "You always manage to work these deals out."

"Yeah." He prayed he could handle this one before his family got hurt.

Chapter 19

Megan came down the stairs the next morning to find John waiting for her.

"Ready to go?" He fidgeted, shifting his weight from foot to foot.

"Where?" Her mind felt fuzzy.

"Sightseeing. It's your day off."

"Oh. Yeah." She yawned. "But I haven't even had any coffee."

"I'm taking you out for breakfast." He wanted to spend as much time alone with her as he could.

"Well, at least, let me go get ready."

"You're already dressed."

"I need to put on some makeup."

"You don't need makeup, and you never have. You're beautiful the way you are."

Megan felt her heart skip a beat. John usually didn't say things like that. "That's sweet, but I don't feel very beautiful," she complained.

"All you need is some coffee, then you'll perk right up."

"Why are you in such a hurry?"

He shoved a jacket into her hand, pulling her toward the door. "I have a full day planned and I want to fit it all in." He held up a set of keys. "Plus, we have the Mercedes-Benz."

"I see. You aren't anxious to be with me, you just want to drive the car." She pouted for a second, then smiled, mischievously.

"You got it." He grinned and held open the car door.

"Where are we going?" she asked, as she slid into the seat.

"Delores told me about some great spots. She even gave me directions." He pulled a piece of paper from his pocket. "Starting with the best place in town for breakfast."

"You have thought of everything, haven't you?"

"You bet. We're gonna have a blast."

They arrived at East Beach Grill and sat at a table outside.

"Why don't they have tables inside?" She asked.

"I guess you can't enjoy the view from inside." John had to speak loudly over the roar of the ocean.

"I can't believe we'rethis close to the water."

"Yeah. It must only be a few hundred feet or so." He flagged down a waitress and ordered. They watched as some people took an early morning swim while waiting for their breakfast. "I bet that water is freezing," he commented.

"How can they swim when it's cold?" Megan asked.

"Beats me."

"This view is wonderful." She enjoyed it, even though the salt from the ocean mixing with the smells from the kitchen made her feel a little queasy. She pointed at the seagulls. "You wouldn't see birds flying around like that back home."

"Nope. We're smart enough to have our tables indoors, especially this time of year." He winked.

John filled her in on his planned itinerary as they enjoyed their pancakes and fought off the birds that wanted to share their breakfast. They laughed together hysterically when a bird pooped on a man a few tables away. "Maybe that's why everyone is swimming," John laughed. "They have to wash off the bird poop."

"Let's hurry up before we're next."

They finished breakfast, then went to Sterns Warf. They walked along the wooden plank pier, taking in the sights of the ocean and old, weatherworn shops. The smell of seafood wafted around them from the restaurants, and the salty mist from the ocean clung to their skin. Megan inhaled deeply, loving the scent of the ocean. Thankfully her queasiness had subsided enough for her to enjoy the rest of the day.

"Look, ice cream." Megan pointed to the shack. "Can we get some?"

"It's only ten o'clock," John said. "Isn't it too early?"

"It's never too early for ice cream." Megan pulled him to The Great Pacific Ice-cream Company shack, and they ordered ice cream cones.

"What's next," she asked, licking her butter pecan ice cream.

"The Red Tile tour." He pulled the paper out of his pocket. "Or we can hit a few stores."

"You hate shopping," Megan laughed.

"Yes, but Christmas is just around the corner."

"So, you're willing to go shopping with me, even though you hate it?"

"If it makes you happy." He stopped walking and took her hand. "I'm willing to do anything to make you happy."

Megan studied him. His strength and vitality flowed through her hand and into her heart. "It wasn't that you didn't make me happy, John. I was trying to run away from my heartache." She turned away, looking out over the ocean. The vastness of the water filled her mind. "We just grew apart."

John wrapped his arms around her waist. "I want to fill that gap between us."

"Me too." Deciding that the emotions were getting too strong, she changed the subject. "Do you want to go to the Sea Center? They have touch tanks."

"Like touching fish and stuff?" I can do that when I'm fishing."

"Come on, it'll be fun."

John groaned, but followed her.

Later, they held hands and walked back to the end of the wharf, where the car was parked.

"So, what's next?" John asked.

"Shopping." Megan's eyes lit up bluer than the sky.

"I want to get the Petersons something special. What do you buy people who have everything?" Megan looked at John, hoping he'd be able to come up with some ideas.

"Beats me." He shrugged his large shoulders. "You're better at this gift buying stuff than me."

They wondered around the store until they came to the lingerie section. "What about this?" John held up a sexy nightie.

"For Mrs. Peterson?"

"I think it would be for both of them. I know Grant would thank us."

"I knew you wouldn't be any help." She elbowed him in the ribs and took the flimsy red garment from him. "I don't think Mrs. Peterson would wear this." She put it back on the rack.

"Well, how about you?"

"I don't think so." She laughed, and walked away.

Stopping to admire the collection of crystal ornaments in a glass case, she spotted an exquisite angel holding a baby. "Isn't this beautiful?"

"Yes."

"I always think about how the angels are taking care of Laura." A tear splashed on the counter. "I picture them giving her angel rides. Holding her close while they fly from one cloud to the next."

"I know she's happy." John slipped his arm around her waist. "Do you want to get it for them?"

"No, we can't afford it." She wiped away her tears and straightened up.

They went in and out of several stores but didn't find anything that looked interesting for the Petersons. However, they found a train set for Billy and a doll for Crystal.

Next on the list was the Red Tile tour, "So we can walk this tour or take the waterfront trolley," John informed her.

"Let's take the trolley. My feet are sore after all the walking we've done."

"Mine too."

After getting a seat on the trolley they followed the route with glimpses of the historic, old buildings like the County Courthouse and the Old Mission. The Spanish-Moorish architecture was quaint and beautiful, with tropical gardens and lush lawns. Megan noted several museums on the tour but didn't dare ask John to go in. He hated museums more than he hated shopping.

When the tour ended, John asked, "Are you hungry?"

"Starving." Megan looked at him. "Do you have a place in mind?"

"I'm open to change if you have some place you want to go. But Delores said The Habit has the best burgers in town."

"A cheeseburger sounds perfect."

Although the restaurant's atmosphere was causal, it offered a spectacular view of the ocean. Megan smiled as she watched the seagulls flying over the water.

John watched her smile and felt his mood drop a few degrees. If Megan loved the state so much, she may never come back home. "The ocean seems to be all over the place."

"Yeah, isn't it beautiful?"

"It's all right. But I'm more of a land man."

"Well, there are mountains here too."

"It's not the same as fields of flowers and trees."

"I know. But there's something special here. I'm not sure if it's the ocean, or the majestic views, or the excitement of people rushing around all the time, but I feel a connection to this city."

John refrained from asking if the connection was Steven. He'd vowed to have a light-hearted and fun day. Dragging the competition into the day wasn't part of his plan. "It is pretty," he said. "Better than our honeymoon."

"We didn't have a honeymoon," she reminded him. "You couldn't take time away from the farm."

"I know," he said remorsefully. "I wish we could have done something more exciting than going to the hotel for the weekend."

"The hotel was fun, especially when you got locked out of the room in a towel." Megan laughed.

"It wasn't very funny then. I about knocked the door down, pounding on it so hard."

"I was in the shower. I didn't hear you."

"By the time you opened up the whole hall was looking." John winced at the memory of his humiliation.

"They wouldn't have come out of their rooms if you hadn't been making all that noise. Besides, you looked good in that towel." Desire still struck her when she remembered the sight.

"I guess it was pretty funny," he chuckled.

I liked ordering room service too," she added.

"Good thing considering we never left the room." He smiled at the memory of their lovemaking. It had been the first time and they'd been so wrapped up in each other that the world outside hadn't existed.

"No, we didn't." She thought back over the years. "That was the happiest time in my life."

"Mine too." A long pause ensued before he spoke again. "I'm sorry, Megan."

"For what?" She should be the one apologizing.

"For not being there when you needed me. For not putting your needs first, but most of all, for taking you for granted. That's something I'll never do again."

"John, it's not all your fault. I had some problems and I needed to learn how to deal with them."

"Have you?"

"I think so. I'm not counting on other people to take care of me anymore. All my life I've always depended on someone else, and when I needed to stand on my own, I didn't know how to do it. I had to grow up, face the consequences of my actions, and find myself." She pointed to herself. "I had to find a way to cope with my pain." She looked across the table, not sure what she'd find in his face, but saw only tenderness. "I have done that."

"Are you happy here?"

"Here as in Santa Barbara? Or, here as my position in life?"

"I guess both." Although he wasn't positive what she meant.

"I'm happy with my life. I don't know if it has anything to do with being in California, or that I have successfully dealt with my heartache."

"Are you ready to come home?"

"I don't know." She didn't like the hurt in his eyes. "I'm sorry, John. I just don't know yet."

That little word "yet" gave him hope. "I'm trying to be patient, Megan, but I do have to get back to the farm sometime."

"I know. You have given me the space I needed and I respect you for that. Who's minding the farm, anyway?"

"Your brother."

"Which one?"

"Lee. Who do you think?"

"But he's only twenty-one. He can't run a farm."

"He's been helping me for years. He knows that farm better than you think. Your problem is you still think of him as your little brother and you haven't noticed that he's grown up."

"You're right. He'll always be my baby brother."

They finished their lunch while chatting about things they'd seen and some things they still wanted to do. The conversation was easy and light, and they didn't talk about anything heavy the rest of the meal.

After lunch, he whisked her off to the Santa Barbara Zoo. It was a small zoo and only took an hour to visit, but Megan laughed as she got to feed the giraffe. Its black tongue tickled her fingers as it ate the lettuce in her hand. John felt more at ease being around animals, even if they were monkeys, lions and elephants. Animals were something he knew about.

They spent the next couple of hours walking around the Botanical Garden. After an hour of walking the paths looking at flowers and plants they walked over the dam that led to the Old Mission. Megan noticed John appeared to be at ease. His arm loosely rested around her shoulder and his eyes gleamed brighter than the sun. Plants, land and animals were more his field of expertise than the beach, ocean and sea creatures.

Although she'd only been here a few months, she'd come to love the sound, smell and look of the ocean. Sea creatures were still amazing to her, and the excitement and beauty of the city hit her heart. She felt at peace here. Something she couldn't explain.

"Are you up for a walk on the beach?" John asked. He was strong and athletic but she felt tired and winded. Her legs ached, and as much as she loved the beach she couldn't walk any more.

"Can we have dinner first?" she asked.

"Sure, if you're hungry already."

"Already? It's been four hours since we had lunch."

"I'm sorry, you're getting tired." John squeezed her hand. "I forget you aren't used to physical labor."

"It's not physical labor," she answered. "But we have been walking a long time, and I'm starving."

"I didn't mean that to put you down in any way. I'm just used to working long hours, and you're not."

"So, I do nothing all day?" She stiffened and walked away from him.

John caught up, taking her arm to stop her, he forced her to meet his eyes. "That isn't what I meant. I know you work hard. You clean the house, shop for food, cook and wash clothes. You help take care of the animals and support everything I do. I couldn't do anything without you. The last few months have shown me how much I need you." His light blue eyes pierced her heart. "What I need to know is, do you still need me?"

"What kind of question is that?"

"One that needs an answer."

"John, please don't do this. You know everything and you know my feelings. Don't keep pushing me. I need time.

"I don't know what else to do, Megan. Tell me what I can do or say."

"Let's just get something to eat and finish the evening without a fight."

"I'm sorry, I don't want to fight. Let's go eat." He walked away and she followed.

They wound up back at Sterns Wharf and went to the Harbor Restaurant & LongBoards. "This is the best view of the sunset while we're eating," John said.

"It's so beautiful and romantic." Megan looked out the window, watching the sun set over the water in a vibrant array of colors.

After dinner, she felt better and less cranky. They took a walk on the beach. Megan's thoughts quickly turned to Steven, and this made her feel guilty. *What am I going to do*? No matter whom she chose someone was going to get hurt.

By the time they reached the estate Megan felt exhausted and barely made it up to her room. She fell across the bed, thinking about the events of the day. She'd spent the most pleasant day of her life with John, but Steven had been in the back of her mind. "I'm confused," she confessed to herself. How could she spend the day with one man, her husband no less, and still be thinking about someone else?

John awoke early from a sporadic and inadequate night's sleep. The intense physical needs of his body overwhelmed his sanity. His mind replayed the date with Megan. Everything had gone off without a hitch, but she'd still kept him at arm's length, especially when they returned. He'd hoped to spend the night holding her – but instead he'd endured another night alone with an aching deep in the pit of his stomach. An ache that only the love of his wife could cure.

Sitting up and rubbing a hand over the stubble on his face, he stumbled into the bathroom to shower and shave. Half an hour later as he stepped into the hall, he noticed Megan's door was ajar, and knocked lightly. Not receiving a response, he pushed it open wider, figuring she'd still be asleep. He noticed the bed was empty as he neared it, and the sound of running water caught his attention.

The ache in his body intensified as the image of her standing under the running water filtered through his mind. He couldn't get the picture out of his head, or heart. Pulling off his blue T-shirt, he walked over and closed the door, then quickly entered the bathroom. He'd be risking everything if she wasn't ready. But he'd know exactly where he stood in her life.

Megan stood under the stream of water, letting it massage her neck and shoulders, slowly rolling her head from side to side as the warmth loosened the knots. Hearing a noise, she opened her eyes and saw the curtain move. She raised her hand to strike the intruder before realizing it was her husband.

"Megan, it's me."

"What are you doing in here?" she scolded, and smacked his arm.

"I thought you might need some help." He held up the bar of soap, a mischievous grin plastered across his rugged face.

"John, we can't..."

He silenced her protest with a hard, passionate kiss. She felt warm, sweet, and he didn't want to stop. His hands slid down her back, relishing the feel of her smooth, velvet skin.

John reluctantly ended the kiss, leaving her breathless and disoriented. She fought for control of her mind, but the sensations pulsating through her body made it hard to think. "John...someone might hear us," she protested.

"I doubt if anyone's up yet." His mustache tickled the delicate skin on her neck as he placed kisses along the column of her throat.

Megan searched for some kind of protest, but none came to mind. John's strong, callused hands roamed over her body, igniting her desires. These were the hands that knew her body, the only ones that had ever touched her.

John could taste traces of soap and water as he kissed a trail up to her earlobe, tightening his embrace. When she gave no resistance, his lips claimed hers again.

Megan's body swam with fervent longing and her mind went blank, forgetting everything and everyone else. This moment in time was all that mattered.

John's muscles rippled underneath his weather-worn skin. It felt good to have her in his arms, where she belonged. "I love you, Megan," he whispered. Her name exploded from his lips, echoing through his mind and soul. She not only filled his heart, she filled his life.

Megan rested her head against his chest enjoying the warmth of his body, and the steady pulsating of the water beating down on them, until the water hit her with a cold blast.

"The water's freezing," she exclaimed.

"I guess we used up all the hot water." He turned off the stream of water.

Grabbing a towel off the counter and wrapping it around her, she went to the linen closet and tossed one to John.

"Thanks."

Megan wiped the steam off the mirror and ran the brush through her hair. John wrapped his arms around her waist and kissed the back of her neck.

"You're in my way."

"I love your neck." He pretended to bite it.

"I think you're part vampire," she smiled at him in the mirror.

"I think you taste good." Smiling wickedly, he tried undoing her towel.

Wrapping it tighter and moving out of his reach, she walked into the bedroom. However, he was by her side in a couple of long strides.

"I have to get dressed," she objected as he kissed her again.

"I want you again," he whispered, looking toward her bed.

"We just made love."

"It's been a long time, Megan." He kissed her neck again, fiddling with the knot of the towel. "We have some catching up to do."

"John, I have to get..." She fell silent as the towel slipped to the floor.

"It's Sunday, you don't work today." When his lips touched hers, she felt the hunger that remained.

"We still have to eat," she whispered, breathlessly.

"We'll be really hungry by the time we get done." His warm breath skimmed across her skin. "I'd much rather have you for breakfast anyway."

She felt a yearning from deep down grow until her body craved his touch again. "Oh, John," she murmured.

That was all the invitation he needed, swooping her up, he carried her to the bed. "I've missed you," he said kneeling beside her, drinking in every detail of her body.

Her own appetite surged strong and fierce not giving her the opportunity to mince words. Instead, she pulled his head down to her mouth and kissed him with all the desire of a wanton woman. Then she was his once again.

Megan's head rested on John's chest as he idly stroked her hair, basking in the afterglow of their lovemaking.

"Now I'm too tired to make breakfast." She laughed softly, playing with the dark curls on his chest.

"And I'm starving."

Megan propped herself up on her elbow. "Do you want me to go make breakfast?"

"I'm just kidding." His eyes sparkled. "Lie down again, I'm tired too." A contented sigh escaped him.

She gladly obliged. Closing her eyes, she quietly mumbled, "I've missed you." She drifted off to sleep.

He'd won her back. Kissing the top of her head he smiled, then closed his eyes and found the most peaceful sleep of his life.

Megan woke up alone in her bed. Stretching, she sat up and watched the shadows from the palm tree dance across the floor. She was feeling tired, but at the same time energized, and this only served to emotionally confuse her more. Worst of all, she knew that John thought their recent encounter had settled everything, and that was far from the truth. *What was I thinking?* She silently chided herself.

Pulling on a pair of black skinny jeans and a long gray sweater, she then went into the bathroom to see what could be done with her hair. Since it had been wet when she fell asleep, it had dried in a disordered untidy mass. Winding it up in a bun, she went across the hall to see if John had gone back to his room.

"He's downstairs," Steven informed her. "You slept late."

"Yeah, I was tired." She suddenly felt guilty about why she was tired.

"Must have had a busy day yesterday." Steven hadn't liked the idea of them spending the whole day together, but was relieved to see her knocking on John's door. He'd been awake all night, wondering if they might have spent the night together as well.

"Yes, we had a nice time." She felt uncomfortable talking to Steven about the day she'd spent with John. "I better get downstairs."

"Are you in that big a hurry to see him?"

"I want to get something to eat," she said. "What's wrong, anyway?"

"You spend the whole day with him, but you can't take five minutes to talk to me."

"Steven, I'm not trying to ignore you."

"Yes, you are. And you have been ever since *he* got here." He jerked his thumb in the direction of John's door.

"He's my husband, and—"

"That doesn't mean anything!" he broke in. "So you're married to him, but you also have feelings for me. I know you do, Megan. I can see it in your eyes."

"Steven, please." Her eyes begged him to understand.

"No. I'm through with sitting around while he tries to steal you away from me. Maybe technically he's your husband, but you can't deny that we have something special." He grasped her shoulders, forcing her to face him. "Can you honestly look me in the eyes and say that you don't care about me?"

Searching his chocolate eyes and seeing the pain he wrestled with left her feeling regretful. "No." Breaking eye contact, she looked down at the ground, wishing she had the strength to lie.

Steven lifted her chin, until she looked him in the eyes once again. "I'm not giving up on us." He walked away.

***

Megan found John in the kitchen, talking to Grant.

"There you are, sleepyhead. I thought you might be hungry, so I made a sandwich for you." John's smile lit up the room. His spirits were exceptionally, high and she knew why.

"Isn't it a little early for a sandwich?"

"Nonsense. I'll eat a sandwich any time of the day." John's eyes roamed approvingly over her.

"I guess I was really tired."

"You need your rest." Grant kissed the top of her head. "You work too hard. I'm glad to see you're finally taking some time for yourself. Now, if you'll excuse me, I need to find my wife or we'll be late for church."

"What were you guys talking about?" she asked John when Grant had left.

"Not much. Why?" John transferred the sandwich to a plate.

"Did you tell him about us...umm...making love?"

He stared at her a long moment before answering. "No. Why do you look nervous? It's natural for a husband and wife to make love."

"I know it's natural." She took a deep breath and tried to word her feelings as delicately as possible.

"I'm not sure that making love was the wisest decision."

"Why, wasn't it good?" Bitterness emerged.

"It confused the issue."

"The only one confused around here is you." He positioned himself directly in front of her. His massive shoulders seemed to fill the whole room. Bending down he whispered in her ear, "I know what I want." His eyes probed hers as if trying to read her heart. "The question is…what do you want?"

She looked into the handsome, rugged face and watched his well-groomed mustache twitch. This was the face she'd stared into for the past five years. The face that had shared her joys and sorrows. She'd shared her life with this man, and now she stood before him totally baffled. "I truly and honestly don't know," she whispered.

"Even though you made love to me, you still have Steven in your head." The disappointment showed in his eyes.

"John, I don't want to hurt you anymore."

"Don't." He shook his head. "You aren't going to hurt me, because I know the truth. You're the only one that doesn't see it yet."

"And what truth is that?"

"You love me. You told me that with your own lips, and you proved it to me this morning. You wanted me as much as I wanted you."

"Yes, I've missed you in that way." She couldn't deny how much she'd enjoyed their lovemaking. It had satisfied her body and soul, but her heart and mind still seemed to be in turmoil. "But that's what's so confusing. My body says one thing, and my head says something else."

"Making love wasn't just your body. You don't work that way. It involved your heart too." He watched her nervously lick her lips. "And as far as your mind goes, you always think too much."

"It's not that simple, John."

"Yes, it is. You have to make a choice, and you're confused because you're using your head and not your heart. Steven may be in your head," he touched her temple, "but I'm in your heart." He moved his finger to rest over her heart.

Megan knew he spoke the truth. How could you spend years of your life loving someone and not have them in your heart? But she felt Steven there too. Maybe not as strongly, but there nonetheless. "I need more time."

She watched the muscles jerk in his neck and knew he was fighting to control his temper. After breathing deeply several times, he finally said, "I've given you time. I can't stay away from the farm forever."

"I know," she said. "I don't have any right to ask you to wait any longer. I'll understand if you want to go back home."

"Oh, don't get me wrong, baby-doll. I don't like waiting, but I'm not leaving here without you." He'd never leave her alone while Steven circled her like a dog in heat.

"You sound certain that I'm going to pick you over Steven."

He shrugged his shoulders "It's only a matter of time." He pressed a light kiss on her lips, picked up his sandwich, and walked out the door.

Chapter 20

Megan found herself more perplexed than ever. She felt pulled in two different directions. In her own way, she loved both men, and didn't want to hurt either of them. However, she couldn't have both. She had to decide, and soon.

Tiffany and William's visit only added to her anxiety. She didn't feel like a lecture from the "Tiffanizer." She could hear Tiffany gloating over how she'd been right about Megan all along, and that Megan had been up to something, and now Steven's heart was broken because of her. It saddened her that it was at least partly true. She would be the cause of his broken heart. True or not, she didn't want to be under Tiffany's scrutiny all night.

Her plans for solitude, however, were short-lived.

"How many places are you setting, dear?" Delores placed a bouquet of flowers in the center of the table.

"I figured John and I would eat in the kitchen."

"You figured wrong." She rearranged the flowers. "You and John are our guests."

"Technically I'm your employee," Megan reminded her.

"Only for a little while, but your husband is our guest, and it would be plain rude to make our guests eat in the kitchen." Taking a step back, eyeing the arrangement. "There, that's better." Turning her attention to Megan, she smiled. "Set a place for you and John."

John entered the dining room as Delores left. "Do you need some help?"

"Sure."

"I finally get to meet the great Tiffany." He took the silverware from the velvet-cushioned box in the drawer, setting the utensils at each place setting.

"You've heard about her?"

"Grant said she can be difficult."

"That's the understatement of the year."

Their conversation was interrupted as the whole Peterson clan came into the room. Megan hoped Tiffany hadn't overheard the remarks about her.

"Megan. You're all better." Billy ran over and jumped into her arms.

"Yes, Billy, I'm all better now. And, thank you for the lovely card you made."

"Mommy helped trace my hand."

"She is a very good tracer." Megan glanced over at Tiffany and saw a slight smile pass her lips. "Thank you both."

"It's the least we could do." Tiffany walked over and took Billy out of her arms. "Come on, Billy let's go wash your hands. Then we can help Megan get dinner on the table."

"Okay." Billy ran over to Grant. "G'andpa, you come help me wash my hands?"

"Sure." He took his grandson's small hand and headed for the bathroom.

Delores took the opportunity to introduce John to everyone. Tiffany stood next to John and Megan, so she shook his hand first. "It's a pleasure to meet you." She smiled a little stiffly.

"Same here, ma'am." John suddenly felt awkward.

"It's good to meet you." William extended his hand.

"Strong grip there, William," John complimented him.

"Well, I do try and work out every chance I get."

John stepped closer to Megan hoping to draw support from her. After all, she'd met these people before and knew what to say and do. He possessively put his arm around her waist.

Steven's knee-jerk reaction was to walk over there and remove his hand. Instead he asked, "Are we ever going to eat?"

· "I'll bring out the food right away." Megan hurried off.

Steven's brown eyes smiled triumphantly at John. "I'll go help her."

"That's all right, big brother. I'll give her a hand." Tiffany headed towards the door.

"Tiffany!" Steven eyed her carefully. "I'm going to warn you one time and only one time…"

"I don't need any warnings, Steven." She held up her right hand, "I promise to be good." She disappeared into the kitchen.

Steven plopped down in his chair, snorting out loud. Tiffany had just blown his only chance to speak with Megan alone. Looking over at John he saw the amusement in his eyes.

Causally sauntering over to his chair, John turned the chair around backward and straddled it like a horse. Crossing his arms on top he leaned forward and whispered, "What's wrong with you, buckaroo?"

Steven ignored the urge to jump up and slap the smile off his face. "Nothing," he snapped. "I'm just hungry."

William overheard the exchange and felt bad for Steven. His brother-in-law was struggling with this situation.

Deep down Steven knew that the right choice was Megan's husband, but he wasn't ready to let go of his dreams yet.

"What kind of farming do you do, John?" William broke the tension.

Steven sat there stewing while the two men talked about the farm and business before the conversation turned to sports.

Tiffany was helping Megan with the last-minute prep of the meal. "How long have you and John been married?" she enquired.

"Five years." Megan knew where this conversation was going, and she didn't want another altercation.

"You know my brother has feelings for you?" Tiffany wasn't beating around the bush.

"Yes, I know." Megan mentally prepared herself for the tongue-lashing she felt she deserved.

"So why did you leave your husband and come out here?"

"Because I thought my marriage was over," Megan cried. "I lost my daughter and I felt like my marriage had died, too. I couldn't handle the pressure, so I ran as far away as I could." Megan threw a dishtowel on the counter fighting back the emotions churning inside her.

"You don't need to be defensive."

Megan looked shocked. "You've done nothing but attack me since you first saw me. Now you have all the proof you need to gloat over being right from the beginning."

"I've treated you unfairly. I tend to jump to conclusions before I have all the facts. That's why I'm asking you for the facts now."

"What kind of facts do you want?" Sarcasm edged each of Megan's words. "Do you think that I might still marry into your family and rob them blind? Or maybe you think that John somehow conspired with me. The two of us had this whole thing planned from the start? Now your brother is going to be the one to pay with his heart." Angry tears rolled down her cheeks and Megan brushed them away brusquely.

"I'm not that heartless," Tiffany informed told her. "I can understand the pain and devastation you went through when your daughter died. I'm a mother too, and I can only imagine how horrible I'd feel if anything ever happened to my children. Believe it or not, I do understand why you felt the need to run away. It's an automatic reaction when bad things happen that we have no control over."

"What's the catch? Why aren't you ripping me apart for hurting Steven?"

"I was hard on you before. I'll admit that I've never trusted new employees, after all the pain my family went through with April."

"With good reason." Megan understood the protection towards her family.

"I won't say I was wrong about you." Ice-blue eyes pinned her with a hard stare. "You've hurt my brother just in a different way. But even so, I believe you've done a world of good for Steven. He'd shut up his feelings for so long that he didn't know how to care anymore. You've helped him unlock his heart."

"What good is that going to do him if I walk out and break it again?"

"I don't think he'll isolate himself this time. Hopefully now he's older, it means he can handle rejection better. He'll cope with the pain and come out a stronger man in the end." She leaned closer. "But I'd advise you to choose very carefully."

"That sounds like a threat." Megan shivered a little at Tiffany's cold tone.

"It's friendly advice." Tiffany picked up the pan of lasagna and left for the dining room.

"It didn't sound that friendly," Megan muttered to herself. Of course, Tiffany didn't really have a friendly personality; she guessed it was the best Tiffany could manage.

Everyone went home and Megan finished cleaning the kitchen. The house felt quiet and peaceful again. Steven had disappeared right after dinner. Delores had gone to bed early and Grant had started working in the study. Megan had no idea where John had wandered off to.

She cut a slice of cake and knocked on the study door, entering when Grant answered. He was leaning back in his chair with his arms behind his head, staring at nothing.

"I thought you might like another piece of cake before I turn in for the night."

"How thoughtful of you. Thank you."

"Can I get you anything else?"

"No, I'm fine."

"Are you sure? You've seemed distant and distracted lately. Is there something I can do to help?"

"No." He shook his silvery head. "It's business related."

"I thought so. You've been acting strange ever since the business lunch. It has something to do with that older gentleman, doesn't it?"

"Robert." He supplied the name. "How did you guess that?"

"It seems like you've had something on your mind ever since he came here."

"That's very observant of you." He looked into her eyes and asked, "So what did you make of him?"

"I didn't like the creepy way he kept smiling at me," Megan confessed.

"He's sly and ruthless. Now I'm afraid he may go after my family." His tone turned grave and serious.

"You mean like a mobster?" Her eyes widened with fear.

"Not with guns or anything like that. But he does seem to have information that could damage our reputation."

"Mr. Peterson, I can't believe anything could do that."

"He knows about April." His dark eyes turned solemn.

"April?" she gasped. "But that happened so long ago."

"I know. I'm afraid if it comes out now it will look like we paid her off to cover up the crime." Grant slowly shook his head. "If this leaks to the press now it will look like an even bigger cover-up." Grant ran his hand through his thinning hair. "No one would ever believe our side of the story."

"What if you go public first and explain the events? If it's going to come out anyway, isn't it better to come out on your terms?"

"You're a smart cookie." He said. "That's what I'm debating. But it's not an easy decision."

"You seem to be between a rock and a hard spot."

"Kind of like your situation. You have a tough decision too."

"I don't know what to do, either."

"Listen to your heart."

"I don't know what it's saying."

"Most people know... they simply refuse to listen." His gentle brown eyes told her what she had to do. She just needed to find the strength to do it.

"It looks like we both have a tough decision to make this week."

"Yes, we do. Both of us," Grant agreed.

Megan had just drifted off to sleep when a soft whisper stirred her senses. Cuddling closer to the warm sensation, she sighed.

"I don't want to spend another night away from you," came the whisper.

"John?" she murmured sleepily.

"Yeah, baby-doll, it's me." He kissed her neck, burrowing his face into the soft blond tresses spreading across the pillow.

A burning sensation of desire stirred her consciousness awake. "John, what are you doing in here?" She sat up.

"You can't figure that out?" He leaned forward and gave her a kiss that vibrated all the way through her body.

"John, please." She broke away. "We can't do this again." Her body already ached for him, but it was harder to convince her mind.

"I know you want me." he smiled. "You want me as much as I want you."

The feel of his mouth and touch of his hands sent shivers through her body, weakening her defenses. Her mind quickly succumbed to the desires. "I do want you, John."

"I want to hold you in my arms." He kissed a trail down her neck. "I don't want to spend another lonely night away from you." Megan moaned in pleasure as he kissed the creamy white skin of her shoulder. "It's time to make your choice, Megan," he whispered. "It's time to choose."

"I know," she sighed. "I know."

The room was dark, but rays of light were starting to touch the sky outside. Knowing it would be morning soon, John rolled onto his side and watched the slumbering form next to him. She looked beautiful even in the dim light. His large arms wrapped around her and he prayed he'd never have to let go. She was the love of his life, and he wasn't about to lose her. He'd execute his last battle plan today.

Megan snuggled into his embrace as she stirred awake. It felt good to wake up in his presence, always feeling safe and secure in his arms. "Good morning," she softly whispered.

"It certainly is a good morning." He smiled. "And how did you sleep last night?"

"Like a baby."

"Your skin is as soft as a baby's." He rubbed his hand up her bare arm to her shoulder. "I could touch it all day long."

"No, you don't." Megan pushed him away laughing. "I have to get breakfast."

"You could be a little late," he groaned

"I have to shower."

"That's an even better idea." He grinned mischievously.

"Alone!"

"That's no fun."

"It's not supposed to be fun, that's why it's called work."

"There's no law against having some fun before work." Bending forward and kissing her again, he asked, "How about a proper good morning?"

Steven got up, and finding not finding Megan in the kitchen, made the coffee, and sat reading the morning paper.

Megan appeared in the doorway, looking as beautiful as ever, her hair still damp from the shower. When Megan finally got downstairs, she found the coffee had been made and Steven sat at the table reading the paper.

"You slept in late again," he said.

"I'm sorry." Suddenly feeling awkward. "I'll get breakfast started right away." She hurried to get the skillet and dropped it with a loud clang.

"You seem to be a ball of nerves." He eyed her curiously. When Megan met his gaze he suddenly realized the answer. His stomach twisted into a knot making him feel sick. "Never mind breakfast." He threw the paper down. "I just lost my appetite." He stormed out of the room.

Megan felt the confusion setting in again. She had to make her choice and let one of them go before the wounds got any deeper.

Grant had been right, her heart would make the right decision, but she had one piece of unfinished business to deal with. It could determine the course of her fate.

John wrapped his arms around her waist, kissing the back of her neck. "What are you making for lunch today?"

"Don't tell me you're hungry already." Megan finished rinsing the last cup and placed it in the dishwasher.

"No. I was just wondering."

"Tuna casserole."

"That's perfect."

Megan arched her blond eyebrow in surprise. "You don't usually like it."

"I know. I have other plans for lunch. With you."
He grinned.

"I can't leave," she protested.

"You can make it ahead of time and Rosa will finish off."

"But the Petersons—"

"Have already agreed to it." He grinned.

"Sounds like you have another plan in mind."

"I do. Meet me in the rose garden at noon." With a quick peck on her cheek he left her.

"Guess I have no choice," she mumbled to herself.

Megan gave Rosa some last minute instructions while questioning her friend. "Do you know what's going on?"

"*Sí.*"

"But you're not telling me?"

"Right again."

"Well, thanks for taking the time out of your busy schedule to do this."

"No *problema*. Especially when it's for love."

Megan walked out the door. The bright sun warmed everything in its path. This kind of weather made it hard to believe that Christmas was less than a week away. Gingerly strolling along the path that led to the rose garden, she wondered how John would react to the subject she had to broach. She'd made her decision, but had to tie up this last loose end.

John waved as she turned the corner. Leaning down he gave her a kiss. "This is for the pretty lady." He pulled a yellow rose from behind his back.

"It's lovely." She took it from his hand and lightly sniffed the delicate fragrance.

"Not half as lovely as you."

"That's sweet, John." She placed her hand on his cheek. "Yellow roses are my favorite."

"I know." He clasped her hand in his. "Shall we go for a walk?"

"I couldn't think of anything more delightful on such a beautiful day," Megan smiled.

Holding hands, they walked around the garden for a while, pausing to watch the birds splashing around in the birdbath. Next, he led her down a path she'd never noticed before.

"It looks like the gardener hasn't kept this section up," Megan remarked as they headed down the path blocked with large trees and thick overgrown bushes.

"I'll bet it's an old part of the garden that no one uses anymore."

"That's a shame. It looks like it was very beautiful once."

"Yeah. But just wait until you see where it leads." He pushed some bushes out of the way and led her through the thick mass of dead trees and overgrown bushes.

When Megan finally came to the end of the path she gasped, "This is absolutely beautiful." She stood on the white sands of the beach with the blue ocean sparkling brighter than diamonds. The golden sun warmed the sand as it danced across the water.

"I have another surprise." Leading her up the beach a little further she noticed a blanket with a picnic basket.

"This is wonderful."

"The rocks on the corners aren't very romantic, but the wind kept blowing the blanket away."

"I think the whole idea is romantic, even the rocks." She smiled as she sat down.

He knelt beside her and opened the basket. "I got subs from the shop." He handed her a sub and a soft drink.

"That's great. I'm in the mood for a good sandwich." She noticed the iPod and speaker. "You brought my songs?"

"Yeah. Rosa said this was your iPod." He pressed a button and country songs sang over the sounds of the ocean and the sea gulls.

"The Petersons bought it for me when they got me all those clothes." He hadn't sounded angry or hurt, but she certainly didn't want to say that Steven had bought it. Besides, he was a Peterson, so it wasn't as if she was really lying.

"I didn't ask where it came from. I just thought some music would be nice."

"I know... I just wanted to explain." However, she didn't know how to explain the rock'n'roll songs downloaded on it. When she'd tried to give it back to Steven, he insisted she keep it and play her favorite songs while they were cooking, but he also wanted to introduce her to the fast-paced beat of rock music as he learned about the boot stepping country.

The tension passed in a moment and they laughed and talked as they ate, then tossed the leftovers to the seagulls, watching them swoop down then up again. After clearing the mess away, they stretched out on the blanket, letting the sun warm their bodies.

After a while, the song "Look at us," started playing. As Vince Gill crooned about loving his wife more over the years, John said, "This song reminds me of us."

Megan laughed as he tried to sing and hum along to the tune.

"How come you're not listening to your oldies list?" she teased.

"Because you like country."

He'd put a lot of thought into this picnic, even planning her favorite music. Now was the time. He pulled her wedding rings out of his pocket and bent down on one knee. "Megan, will you come back home with me? Will you be my wife again?"

She didn't answer immediately. Thinking straight became a hard task. But she had to focus. "John, I...I have to tell you something."

The only thing more unsettling than her tears was the serious note he detected in her tone. His chest constricted and he couldn't feel his heart beating. *I'm going to lose her after all*. "What is it?" He forced the lump out of his throat. "You're choosing Steven, aren't you?"

She shook her head. "That's not what I have to tell you." Taking a deep breath, she continued. "There's something I should have told you a long time ago." Her eyes looked deep into his. "I can't bear the guilt any longer."

"Guilt?" John was perplexed.

"I killed Laura!" she cried. "I'm the reason our daughter is dead."

"Megan, honey, you're not making any sense. You didn't kill her."

"Yes, I did." She furiously nodded.

"The doctor never found any reason for her death. Why are you blaming yourself?"

"Because I fell asleep on my back that night. It cuts off the circulation. I felt Laura kick before I went to sleep. She was alive! Then she was dead by morning. Don't you see - it's the only explanation?"

"I don't understand." Tenderly searching her face, he noticed all the pain and guilt. "Megan, you're blaming yourself for something you had no control over. The doctor said that most of the time, even with an autopsy, they don't have an explanation. It wasn't anyone's fault. It was God's timing."

"I'm responsible," she cried. "I caused all of this pain. I wanted to tell you before but I was afraid you would hate me."

"Is that why you wouldn't talk to me?"

She shrugged. "One of the reasons." Turning tear-filled eyes to him she added, "I thought you'd leave me."

"So, you left first?" He shook his head slowly. "I wish you had trusted me."

"I'm sorry, John." Her mistakes were piling up - soon she'd be buried under them. "I could never find the words. As time went on, it got harder to talk about. I decided to bury everything and not think about it."

"I only want to ask you one thing." His intense blue eyes bored into hers. "Have you dealt with the pain now?"

"I think so." That's all she'd been doing since arriving in Santa Barbara.

"I don't want uncertainty. I want you to know without a doubt that this wasn't your fault."

"I don't know how to do that," she confessed.

"That's what support groups are meant to do, isn't it?"

"And what am I supposed to do there? Sit around telling a bunch of strangers that I killed my baby?" Her friends and family had brought up the subject several times, but she had stubbornly refused to even give it a thought.

"You can talk about your feelings. I'll bet there are other mothers who feel the same way. They can help you work through the grief."

"Now you sound like my mom."

"You've been dealing with the hurt by yourself for too long. It's time to let us in."

"I feel like God is punishing me."

"He's not, Megan. You're punishing yourself unjustly." He wiped away her tears. "It's time to let go of the guilt. Laura is gone and blaming yourself isn't going to bring her back." He pulled his wallet out of his back pocket and flipping it open, he handed her a photograph. "Look at her, Megan."

"No." Tears fell down her face. "I can't."

"Yes, you can. You should."

The hospital had taken the pictures after delivery, but she'd never been able to look at them. "It only reminds me what I've lost."

"I want you to see how beautiful she was."

"I saw her after she was born." The ache in her heart sharpened at the memory of holding the tiny bundle. The dark hair against the white skin haunted her dreams. Her arms ached. She should be holding her now. She should be buying Christmas presents, and planning birthday parties. Not visiting a graveyard!

"Just look at her." John held out the photo stubbornly in silence until she had no choice but comply with his demand. Wiping away her tears, she took the picture from him and stared at her daughter for the first time in over a year.

"She really was real, wasn't she?" she breathed. "She really did exist."

"She was as beautiful as you," John commented. "You gave her life. No matter how short it was. You brought her into this world and you should be proud." He put the picture back.

"You...you don't hate me?" Her lip quivered.

"No, of course I don't. I don't blame you and I never did. I'd never believe that you purposely harmed her." How had she distorted the facts so much? He kissed her gently and added, "Let the past go, and concentrate on the future."

"I'm trying to do that."

"Promise me that you'll go to a support group meeting."

"I promise."

He held up the rings. "Do you happen to see me in your future?"

"Yes!" She threw her arms around his neck, knocking him off balance. "Of course, I do."

He landed on the ground with her falling on top of him. "Well, Mrs. Black, if I didn't know better, I'd say this is a proposition."

"And what if it is?" She arched a tapered brow. "After all, we are married," she looked up and down the beach, "and no one else is around."

"I like the way you think." He embraced her with a passionate kiss.

Unforgiving Ghosts

Chapter 21

Steven entered the dining room, and sat down. Megan came in from the kitchen, set down the bowl of mashed potatoes and took her seat.

Grant started carving the roast.

"I hope the roast is done. I got it in the oven late," Megan said.

"It's just right." Grant smiled.

"Where were you all day?" Steven frowned.

"We had a picnic on the beach." John said.

"How nice," Steven remark coldly.

"Yes, we had a great time." John piled the potatoes on his plate before passing the bowl to Megan. "Can you pass me the roast?" He took the platter from Grant.

Steven wasn't about to be brushed off easily, though. "What exactly did you do on this picnic?"

"It was a picnic, Steven." Megan blushed. "We ate lunch."

Steven was ready to make another smart remark when the reflection from her rings caught his attention. His eyes strained to see the small diamond set in the gold band as he realized she was wearing her wedding ring. He was so horrified at the sight that his grip loosened and he dropped his fork to clatter against his plate. A dismal mood engulfed the room. Although deep down he had always known that she'd honor her commitment, he couldn't avoid the flood of disappointment that washed over him.

"Steven, what's wrong?" Delores noticed his face had suddenly paled.

"I'm not feeling well." His stomach twisted into knots and his heart ached. He'd just lost the girl of his dreams. Those rings on her finger couldn't be a good sign. He couldn't fool himself any longer. He had to face the truth. "If you'll excuse me." He threw his napkin on the table and rose to go.

"Can you wait a minute?" Grant stopped him. "There's an urgent matter I need to discuss with you and your mother."

Steven sat back down without a word. He wanted to be alone, but he didn't like the tone of his father's voice. "This sounds serious."

"I'm afraid it is." Grant looked somberly at his son. "And I'm afraid you're going to be affected the most."

"Honey, you're scaring me," Delores said. "What is this all about?"

"A situation has come up at work that requires our utmost attention."

"If it's work-related why is Mom being brought into it?" asked Steven.

"Because the repercussions will affect the whole family."

"What about Tiffany and William?" Delores asked.

"They're coming by later, but I wanted to give Steven a headsup."

"Dad, what's going on?" Steven's trepidation mounted.

Grant paused for a moment. There was no easy way to say it so he just blurted it out. "Robert brought up the subject of April."

"April!" Steven jumped out of his chair. "How did he find out about her?"

"I don't know. But he did. He more or less threatened to expose the whole sordid matter if we don't agree to his terms on the advertising deal."

"What do you mean by more or less?" Steven asked. "Did he tell you that?"

"Not in so many words."

"Dad, you're confusing me. Please, tell me exactly what was said?"

"Steven, even you said his offer was ridiculously low. Before we started the meeting, he brought up the subject of April. Then, when he made such a low offer, I knew what he was up to. If we don't agree to his terms he'll go to the press."

"Honey, are you sure you're not overreacting? Maybe he won't say anything." Delores tried to console him.

"Then why did he make such a low offer for the advertising package we're trying to sell him?" Grant asked suspiciously. "It's a silent threat hanging over my head. It may be unspoken but it's there." Grant slammed his hands down on the table. "What bugs me is how he found out. I was careful not to let any details get out to the press, or the public years ago." He ran a hand through his silver hair and looked across the table at Steven. "I think you were right all those years ago. We should have fought her in court. If the incident goes public now, it will look like we paid her off to keep her silent about being raped."

"Raped!" John gasped.

"I don't want him to hear this," Steven said defensively.

"Steven, we have a tough decision to make. John's opinion is important."

"Why?" John asked confused.

"Because you're not a family member. You can offer an objective opinion." Grant proceeded to give John all the details.

"Well, paying her off wasn't the smartest move," John agreed.

"I wanted to avoid all the frenzy and publicity that would go along with a trial." Grant shook his head slowly. "Now it seems that decision has come back to haunt me."

John could sympathize with Steven. His first love had betrayed him. And now Megan was leaving. He couldn't help but feel sorry for him, and even almost a little guilty about taking Megan away from him. But, she'd belonged to him first, and he loved her too much to let her go.

"We need to decide what to do next," Grant said to them.

"What can we do?" Delores asked.

"Two things." Grand held up one finger. "We can give in and take his offer." He held up a second finger. "Or we can fight back."

"No way. I'm not giving in this time," Steven insisted.

"How can we fight back?" Delores asked.

"We can go to the press and get our side of the story out first. Maybe then it won't look quite so bad for us."

"The press!" Delores gasped. "Oh, no, we can't do that. People will wonder why we didn't come forward sooner. They'll think we have something to hide, and they won't believe us." Delores vigorously shook her head. "No. No. We can't do that. Why can't we just take his offer? I mean, how much money could you lose on the deal?"

"It's not only the money, sweetheart." Grant reached across the table and took her hand. "If we give in now, he may want more later. He could start extorting money, and even if we pay him off, it doesn't guarantee that he won't go to the press anyway. If that happens, things will look twice as bad for us."

"I don't like it," she insisted. "Besides, you aren't positive about all this. You're speculating." Delores took a deep breath. "We need to pray about it." "Dad's right, Mom," Steven said gently. "We need to go to the press first. If this is going to be exposed, it'll be better coming from us." He couldn't believe his bad luck. Life had punched him in the gut again, one blow on top of another. It seemed fate was determined to bring him to his knees, but that only made him more determined to fight back. He just didn't know if he had the strength to face life by himself. Although his parent's belief in God was strong, he'd never trusted Him. Steven knew he was a sinner, even doing things purposely to anger God, pushing the Lord as far away as possible.

He could recite the verses he needed to be saved. He'd heard them over and over in Sunday school when he was younger. John 3:16 'For God so loved the world that he gave his only son that whoever believes on him should not perish but have everlasting life' kept running through his mind. Even though he knew what he must do to be saved, he'd never opened his heart to God. He wondered if this was his punishment for his disobedience.

"Megan said the same thing the last night." Grant's voice turned Steven's attention back to the subject at hand. "You do realize, don't you, that you'll bear the brunt of all this. Public opinion and gossip will be directed toward you."

"I don't care what people think. I didn't care before, and I'm not going to hide now. People can think what they want. It's no concern of mine. If you had listened to me sixteen years ago, we wouldn't be in this position now." Anger seeped into his voice.

"I know, Steven. I was wrong, but at the time I didn't feel you were old enough to handle everything," Grant explained. "That's why I'm asking for your advice now." His gentle expression showed love and respect for his firstborn. "I believe you can handle anything life throws at you. If you want to make the press statement, I'm behind you. However, you need to know all of the facts before blowing your top."

"What else is there for me to know? People will think I'm a rapist or worse. But I don't care, as long as the people who matter to me know the truth."

"More than likely there will be business repercussions. If customers believe you're a rapist and we covered it up, they might well cancel their advertising contracts."

"I hadn't thought about that," Steven admitted. "Dad, I'll leave this matter up to you. I can't and won't destroy everything you've worked so hard for."

"I won't make this decision by myself. I want everyone to agree." He looked at John. "I haven't heard what you think."

"Well, I would have to say right off the bat that I wouldn't believe these bad things for a second. I've only known you guys for a few weeks, but I'd never think Steven was capable of such a thing, or that you'd all be involved in a cover-up. However, I can see why people would question your coming forward now."

Megan spoke up. "I know people respect you. I think the community trusts you. That may be shaken for a while, but most people will come around."

Grant looked at his wife "What do you think, sweetheart?"

"I don't think it's a good idea, but it seems we don't have any other choices." Her eyes filled with tears. It wasn't the money that concerned her, but the effect this situation would have on the family. She'd witnessed the devastation this woman had brought on them once. And now they had to relive the nightmare in the public eye.

"We'll make a press conference after the holidays," Grant announced. "Steven, do you want to give it, or should I?"

"No, I'll do it. After all I'm the one responsible for this whole mess." He slowly moved to the door looking like a prisoner being led to the gallows. His mom's sobs rang through the air, and tugged at his heartstrings. "I'm sorry, Mom and Dad."

Megan stepped outside into the cool night air. She was so lost in thought that the twinkling stars and the half-moon shimmering in the dark sky went unnoticed. Heading directly for the gazebo, she heard the squeaking of the swing before she rounded the bend.

"I thought I'd find you here." She approached Steven hesitantly. "Do you mind having some company?"

"I'm not in the mood for socializing right now." Steven held out his hand. "However, your presence is an exception."

She took his hand, settling down next to him. The creaking of the chain, leaves rustling in the trees, and crickets chirping sad melodies filled the long silence that ensued.

"I can't believe crickets are still out." Megan laid her head on his shoulder. "Hasn't it been cold enough to kill them yet?"

"They are strong and we haven't had much frost."

"You're strong too."

"I can't believe this stupid mistake is coming up again. My parents are going to be ruined and it's my fault."

"It's not your fault, Steven. April caused all this. She was a manipulator and a gold digger who used you. She caused this devastation." Megan ran her fingers through his messy hair. "Stop blaming yourself."

"You're one to talk." He laughed bitterly, and took her hand, gently pressing a kiss on it. "You've been blaming yourself for something that wasn't your fault at all."

"It feels like my fault."

"You're only looking for someone to blame," Steven said.

"Maybe." Megan shrugged. "I guess people always blame themselves when there are no answers. I found out today that John doesn't blame me either."

"Did you think he would?"

"Yes. That's why I finally left. I let the guilt drive a wedge between us."

"And you also found out he still loves you." His heart twisted at those words, but he kept his emotions buried, not wanting to add to her guilt.

"Yes. It looks like you were right all along." She laid her head on his shoulder.

"Of course, I'm always right." He smiled tightly. "The difference is that you had no control over your situation. But I was stupid enough to fall for her trap."

"Not stupid. You were young and you thought you were in love."

"I really don't care what happens to me. I'm worried about my family."

"You have a good heart." She put her hand over his heart and felt it beating hard and strong.

"It's not a good heart, Megan. It's full of darkness. That's why God is punishing me."

She sat up with a start. "Every heart is full of sin." She could see the wounds of his past surfacing, bringing back the pain, anger and confusion. "If we confess our sins with our mouth, He is faithful and just to forgive us our sins."

"Quoting scripture won't work on me." He smiled ruefully. "I'm a lost cause."

"No-one is a lost cause." If God could forgive her, He'd forgive anyone.

"God has given up on me, that's why he's punishing me. I just don't understand why he would hurt my parents. They have always been good."

Her shrill laugh pierced the night, startling Steven. "We certainly are two peas from the same pod, aren't we?"

"How so?"

Megan took a deep breath. "I've been blaming myself, and directing my anger toward God for the past year. I too, believed he was punishing me. And, now you're doing the same thing."

"My situation is different. You're a good person, Megan.

"No, I'm not. If you see any goodness in me at all, it's Jesus' love." She laid her head on his chest. You are a very special person, too."

"But not special enough for you to stay with me." A strong emotion vibrated in his gut. He fought back the tears burning his eyes. He'd made a big enough mess out of his life, and already hurt too many people he loved. He would do something right, for once in his life. He would let her go, no matter how much it hurt him.

Megan sat up. "Steven, I'm sorry. I never wanted to hurt you. I do care about you, and I always will. But...I've decided to stay with John."

"I know." He choked back the lump in his throat and answered the question forming in her eyes. "I noticed the rings on your finger earlier." He lightly tapped the cold metal bands.

"Steven, I'm so..."

"Don't apologize, Megan. I won't lie and say that I'm not hurt, but I can honestly tell you that I have enjoyed the time we've shared. I won't forget you – never will I forget you."

"I'll never forget you either."

"If there's any good in my heart, it's because of you. I didn't care about anything before. You bring out the best in me."

Megan buried her face in her hands. Tears of regret and remorse ran down her cheeks. "Why are you being nice to me? I'm no better than April."

Steven quickly pulled her hands away from her face. "Don't ever say that!" he protested. "You're nothing like April. You are kind, caring, and the most giving person I know. You'd never be able to betray someone's feelings the way she did." Pulling her against his chest, he wrapped his arms around her tiny body, knowing this would the last time he'd ever hold her. "You've made me a better man, Megan. Before you, I never wanted to be married, or thought about having kids. You made me see there's more to life than just partying." He stroked her silky hair. "I look at my parents and I want a marriage like theirs. I want someone there when I come home. Someone to share my life with. I never wanted that before. I was scared of another woman using me for money that I never got close to anyone. You helped me put the past behind me."

"You did the same thing for me."

"You taught me how to love, Megan. I'll never regret that."

Megan looked through her tears. "Can we still be friends?"

Friends. That word tore his heart apart. How many girls had he said the same thing to? "You bet." The casual words came out with an effort. He forced the dreadful feeling of loneliness away and kissed the top of her head, inhaling her flowery scent for the last time. "I'm going to be all right. Now go find your husband." He watched until her tiny silhouette had gone around the corner. When he felt sure she couldn't hear him, he let all the pain, disappointment, and heartache flow out in a flood of tears.

Steven sat there for a long time. He was a strong, capable, dependable man, who'd always trusted his own abilities and strength. For the first time in his life he felt overwhelmed, almost like Jesus crushed under the weight of the wooden cross. Steven now felt his burdens too heavy to bear alone. He needed help!

"Oh, Lord, please help me." Steven cried in agony.

Chapter 22

The house buzzed with activity as everyone got ready for the big Christmas party. Megan helped Rosa put the finishing touches to the holiday decorations while John and Grant fiddled with the lights outside. Delores went over last-minute details with the caterers. Steven was nowhere to be found.

The house sparkled with excitement and seemed to hold as much anticipation as the occupants. Grand splashes of red, green, and gold adorned every room, while candles and fresh cut flowers were dramatically placed throughout the house. The best chefs had been hired to cater the extravaganza, and even a small orchestra had been assembled for the occasion. No detail went unnoticed.

John and Megan headed upstairs to get ready. She showered first and after slipping into her robe, went into the bedroom, where John sat watching the television.

"Is that what you are wearing?" he teased.

"Do you think I'd make a fashion statement in this?" She held her arms up and twirled around.

John jumped off the bed, stopping her spinning as his arms encircled her waist. "I think you could make a fashion statement in anything." He kissed her lips as he fiddled with the belt on her robe. "As a matter of fact, you look better in even less."

Wiggling out of his grasp, she said, "We don't have time right now. I have to do my hair." She tightened the belt.

"Not even a quickie?" John grinned.

"No." She gave him a small peck on the lips.

He shrugged his shoulders. "It was worth a try."

"The shower is all yours. I have to meet Mrs. Peterson, and get my hair done."

"Is my tuxedo in here?" John called from the closet.

"Did you bring it over from your room?"

"I thought I did. I don't remember seeing anything hanging in that closet."

"I'll go and check." Megan offered.

"Never mind, here it is," he said, emerging from the closet with a black tuxedo."

"I still can't believe you're wearing that tonight."

"I wore a tux for our wedding."

"And that was the only time in your life." She giggled. "What's even funnier is the fact that you actually went shopping for it."

"It wasn't my idea, baby-doll. Grant and Delores insisted. I had to get specially fitted because my shoulders are so wide."

"I know, honey." She couldn't stop laughing. "Wait until I tell everyone back home."

"You better not say a word." John went to grab her but she moved out of reach and ran to the other side of the bed.

"Or what?"

"I'll have to silence you." He chased her around the bed a few times before catching and tickling her.

"All right, all right" she said breathlessly. "I give in. I won't say anything."

The doorbell rang.

"I'll get it," Rosa offered.

"You're a guest tonight," Grant stated.

"*Sí*, but old habits are hard to break." She opened the door. "Andrew. Catherine." Rosa greeted them with a hug. "You're the first to arrive."

"I wanted to get here early so I could talk with Steven." Andrew looked around, "Do you know where he is?"

"No, I haven't seen him all day." Rosa turned her attention to Catherine. "You look beautiful."

"Thanks, Rosa." Catherine's blond hair hung in ringlet curls with diamond and sapphire encrusted barrettes holding up the sides, allowing a full view of the jewels elegantly dangling from her earlobes. The matching sapphire and diamond necklace hung just above the line of her strapless blue satin gown. "You look wonderful too. Teal is your color."

"*Gracias*." Rosa laughed. "I hear there is a little one on the way. I'm so happy for you both."

"News sure travels fast, doesn't it?" Catherine smiled at her husband.

Andrew laid his hand protectively on her stomach. "Yes, and we're very excited."

"Andrew. Catherine. I'm glad you could make it." Grant shook Andrew's hand. "You look beautiful, my dear." He pecked Catherine on the cheek.

"Thank you, Mr. Peterson."

"When are you going to start calling me Grant?" He tucked her hand it into the crook of his arm. "Come with me. I have someone I want you to meet."

Grant introduced Catherine to John, while Andrew went off to find Steven.

"Where is Megan?" John fidgeted nervously.

"Still with my wife." Grant smiled. "Let me tell you something about women, but I bet you've found that out already." He slapped John on the back. "They're always late. They like making a grand entrance." Looking at Catherine he asked, "Am I right?"

"I don't think Megan is the type for grand entrances," Catherine responded.

"No, she's not," John agreed. "I'll feel better when she's by my side."

"I know what you mean," Catherine agreed. "I'll be glad when Andrew gets back."

"Looks like your wish is granted." John pointed his thumb in the direction of the two men walking their way.

"Hello, little mom-to-be." Steven kissed her cheek. "You look radiant."

"She couldn't wait to wear her dress." Andrew smiled. "She's afraid of never being thin again."

"Thanks, Steven." She smiled shyly. "You look pretty good yourself. Why... if I weren't already in love." She winked at him.

"I always look good in a tuxedo." Steven tugged on the ends of his bow tie.

"Speaking of looking good," Grant whispered to John and nodded toward the staircase. Delores and Megan were chatting away as they came down the stairs.

Both women were a vision of beauty: one the picture of youth, and the other of maturity. Megan's emerald green taffeta dress seemed to steal the limelight. Her long hair had been piled on top of her head and hung down her back in large banana curls. Delores wore a simple black velvet gown magnificently accentuated with a large diamond necklace and matching earrings. Her short salt and pepper hair had been teased and curled.

John's heart filled with pride as he watched his wife elegantly descend the stairs. Grant nudged him over to the bottom of the staircase.

Steven watched jealously as Megan took her place next to her husband. He couldn't help recalling Thanksgiving, when it had been him who'd been her proud escort waiting at the bottom of the stairs. It'd been a long month since then, and a lot had changed, including him. He'd loved and lost, but he knew one thing, he would try again. God had a plan for his life, of that he was sure.

"You look beautiful." John kissed her cheek.

Megan blushed. "I just wish I could get ready in time to come down the stairs before everyone arrives. I get nervous with everyone watching me."

"Baby-doll, it doesn't matter where you are in the room. Everyone would stop and stare, no matter when you turned up. You look like a princess." He noticed the emerald and diamond necklace and matching earrings. "Where did you get the jewelry?"

"Mrs. Peterson let me borrow them. She said they matched my dress perfectly." Her hand went up to her throat touching the choker.

"They look lovely on you." *She wears royalty well,* he thought. She seemed to fit right into this crowd.

"There's Catherine. I want to say hi." It eased her nerves having a friend other than the Petersons in the room.

"I'll get us something to drink."

"Just a club soda for me. My stomach is churning like crazy." Walking over to the small group, she gave Catherine a hug. "I'm glad to see you. I hear congratulations are in order." Megan looked at Andrew to include him.

"I can't believe I'm going to be an uncle," Steven broke in, "and the godfather."

"You'll be great at both." Megan smiled.

Steven gave her a casual kiss on the cheek. "You're breathtaking, Megan." He whispered in her ear, "Absolutely breathtaking."

A sorrow tugged at her heart when she heard the pain in his tone. It hurt even more being the cause of his suffering. "You look good too."

Tiffany and William made their way through the crowd, joining the group. Tiffany gave Steven a hug, then hugged Andrew and Catherine. "It's good to see you both," she smiled.

"Wow, Tiff. That is some dress." Andrew whistled.

The form-fitting dress revealed her curves and the shiny red fabric glittered in the dim candlelight. She looked like a bright package waiting to be unwrapped. "Do you like it?" She turned slowly, showing off a very daring plunge in the back.

"You look terrific," Megan said.

"So do you." Tiffany looked around the small crowd. "Where's John?"

"Getting some drinks." Megan smiled awkwardly. "I don't know what's taking so long."

"Drinks sound good to me," William said. "I'll get us some, and see if I can find John." He kissed Tiffany on the cheek and left.

A few minutes later Megan felt an arm slid around her waist. "Did you miss me?" her husband asked her.

"Where have you been?"

"Getting our drinks." He handed her a crystal glass. "Club soda for the lady."

They all talked for a few minutes then John asked, "Do you mind if I steal my wife away for a while? I want to dance."

"No, as a matter of fact, I think we'll join you." Andrew looked at his wife. "Are you feeling up to it, dear?"

She nodded. "But not too much twirling. My stomach has finally settled down."

Both couples headed into the ballroom, where soft music filled the air and couples were already gliding around the floor. Megan melted into John's embrace as they moved to the music. He held her close with no plans of letting her go the rest of the night. After several dances, they went to the buffet table and carried their plates to the huge wood table in the formal dining room. Catherine and Andrew joined them, and soon Steven took a seat.

"I'm tired of making my rounds." Steven wearily smiled. "We have too many business associates."

"You may have fixed that for next year's party." Andrew nudged him.

"Yeah, leave it to me to ruin my Dad's business."

"Come on Steven, I'm only joking. I know things are going to work out. You may lose a few clients, but I'm sure most of these people are going to stick by your side. Look around you." Andrew spread his hands, indicating all the guests. "These people have known and done business with your family for years. You've never cheated any of them and you've always been honest. These are satisfied customers who aren't going anywhere." Andrew winked. "Besides, you have the best lawyer in town."

"I hope you're right," Steven sighed. "I don't want to hurt my parents anymore."

"Steven, your parents couldn't be more proud of you," Megan said.

Steven smiled, longing to hold her one more time. He wanted to dance and feel her body next to his. But she belonged to another man, and he had to find a way to deal with these thoughts and feelings.

Hey, Steven, how about a dance?" Catherine asked cheerily.

"Sure." He smiled and stood. "Do you mind, Andrew?"

Andrew's eyebrows shot up in surprise. "Of course not."

John excused himself to get second helpings from the buffet, leaving Andrew and Megan alone at the table.

"You probably hate me." Megan blurted out.

"Why?" Andrew's brows drew together.

"For hurting your best friend."

"Steven is wounded," he agreed. "But I don't blame you. It's just the way things worked out."

"If only I'd told him I was married from the start..."

"Megan, you can't control someone else's feelings. I don't think knowing that would have made any difference. He would have still fallen for you. I was on the beach that day when he first saw you watching the sunset. He was a goner the moment he laid eyes on you. Nothing you could have said or done would have stopped his heart. Steven is going to hurt for a while, but he'll get through it."

"No wonder you're a lawyer." She smiled. "You're so sensible."

"That's me - Mr. Sensible."

The rest of the night flew by so fast and it seemed impossible that midnight had arrived. Most of the guests had gone home, and only close friends and family remained. Megan made her way around the small crowd chatting with people she knew. Finally joining John, she whispered in his ear. He smiled and nodded.

Steven watched them from a distance as they held hands, clinging to each other like Velcro. They said goodnight to Grant and Delores, then headed up the stairs. Tiffany yelled goodnight from somewhere in the crowd. Megan turned and waved.

Her smile as she waved would forever be burnt into Steven's memory. Her beauty was more radiant than the precious stones dangling from her earlobes and around her neck. His chest tightened at the idea of losing such a precious jewel. The despondency that he'd fought off all evening finally penetrated Steven's defenses, leaving him feeling spent and empty. Craving some time alone, he turned to leave.

"Hey, Steven, where are you going?" Andrew called.

"Back to my apartment. I'm really beat." His eyes drifted to the staircase for one last look.

Andrew caught his gaze. "I'm sorry, buddy." He put a consoling hand on his shoulder. "I know it hurts, but give it time. Your heart will heal."

"Thanks, Andrew." He walked away, his head hanging down.

Catherine slid her arm around Andrew's waist. "Is he all right?"

"He just needs some time." They both watched Steven disappear out of sight. "He's going througha lot right now. I feel bad for him."

"Me, too. I've never seen him so depressed," Catherine said.

"That's because he's never been in love before."

"What did you think of John?" she asked.

"He seemed nice enough. What was your impression?"

"Same as yours, I guess."

"Then why do you sound downhearted?"

"I'm just disappointed. I'd hoped he'd be terrible and mean, so Megan would have an excuse to leave him and stay with Steven." Distress creased her brow as she looked at Andrew. "See what an awful person I am?" Her eyes began to water.

"You don't have an awful bone in your body." He kissed her hand. "You only wanted to see a friend find the same kind of happiness we have."

"But, John seemed nice, and Megan looked happy with him."

"Yeah. Tonight had to be tough on her as well. She feels just as bad for Steven as we do." He wiped a tear from her cheek. "Let's get you home. Your hormones are kicking in."

❧   ❧   ❧

Megan squinted against the bright rays of the sun, closed her eyes again and snuggled up to John.

"Good morning." He pulled her close.

"Merry Christmas." She murmured half asleep.

"Aren't you worried that you're getting up late?" John teased.

"No. Everyone sleeps in on Christmas morning."

"What about the ham?"

"What about it?"

"When do you have to put it in the oven?"

"Is that all you're worried about, when we're going to eat dinner?"

"No, I'm worried about breakfast too."

"Here, eat this." She hit him with her pillow.

"I'd rather eat you." He nibbled on her neck.

Megan put the cinnamon rolls, that she'd made the night before, in the oven. This was her yearly traditional breakfast. The Petersons loved them so much that they wanted to adopt the tradition. However, they would have to buy the rolls from a bakery.

Afterwards, eating the cinnamon rolls and having coffee, everyone went into the living room to open presents.

John handed Megan her present, and she carefully opened the box. "The angel," she gasped, holding up the ornament she'd noticed on their shopping trip. The sun danced through the prisms of the crystal casting a rainbow of colors on the wall.

"It reminds me of Laura, too." John smiled.

"But it's so expensive," she protested.

"You're worth it."

"Thank you. I love it." She gave him a hug. "And I love you, too."

Steven walked in on the touching moment. Although his heart was broken, he put on his best smile. "Are there any presents left for me?"

"Steven." His mom's face lit up "I didn't know if you'd be joining us this morning." She knew how hard it was for him to see Megan and John together. Even though her son was in pain, she knew Megan had made the right choice. Marriage is forever.

"What, and miss my presents?" He sat down next to the tree.

Grant and Delores exchanged looks that told each other their son would be just fine. "This one is from us." Grant handed him a box.

William and Tiffany showed up around five. After a large dinner, there was another round of gift giving. Megan gave Billy and Crystal the presents she'd bought. The kids gave her a gold heart-shaped locket.

"It's beautiful." She gave Billy a hug.

"It's so you won't forget me." He informed her. "See, our picture is inside."

"I'll never forget the best little cookie helper in town."

"I have something else for you too, dear." Delores handed Megan a velvet box.

"Oh, Mrs. Peterson, I can't accept this." She turned the box around and showed John the emerald and diamond jewelry set she'd worn to the party.

"I want you to have them. They looked lovely on you, and I have a ton of jewelry that I don't wear now."

"Where would I wear them? I don't dress up on the farm."

"I insist."

"I'm sorry but I can't accept this, Mrs. Peterson." She handed the box back. "Thank you for the gesture but it's just too expensive. You've already done so much for me, I can't possibly take another gift from you."

Delores raised her eyebrows to Steven, who shrugged back at her. He didn't have an answer he could use to get her to accept the gift, either.

"Well, I think they looked beautiful on you and I'm not taking them back." Delores winked at Steven. "And you know there's no use arguing with me."

"Mom is right, Megan," Tiffany said, "You look terrific in green."

Megan glanced at John. He smiled and nodded his head, knowing she really did want to take the gift but was worried troubled about vanity. "You love sparkly things," John said.

"Yes, but my jewelry isn't real. They don't cost a fortune," she protested.

Grant took the necklace from the box and stepped closer. "If we couldn't afford it we wouldn't be giving it to you." He fastened it. "There, it fits you perfectly and you're going home with it, just a little something to remember us by."

"I could never forget you guys." She touched the emeralds, her favorite gems.

Later that night, Megan lit candles on top of a cake. "When I was growing up, my mom always baked

Jesus a birthday cake. I'd like us all to sing "Happy Birthday" to Jesus.

After they had sung the song, Billy blew out the candles. "Happy Birthday Jesus," he repeated with a smile.

Everyone clapped and cheered.

This Christmas was special for Steven. He realized that Christmas wasn't about presents, or a fancy dinner. For the first time, he truly understood the sacrifice Jesus had made. Giving up the glory of Heaven to be born in a lowly manger. *And He did it for me.* He felt the peace in his heart. He hadn't told anyone about his decision yet. He'd been waiting for the right time. However, his parents had been praying for him all his life. And what better gift could he give them than to finally admit he'd trusted Christ as his savior?

Two weeks later Megan and John said goodbye to their new friends.

"I'm going to miss you." Rosa cried.

"I'll miss you too. The Petersons have offered me the use of their jet, so I can visit whenever I want." She tried to sound positive.

"But it won't be the same." Rosa wiped a tear away. "You better get going." They hugged goodbye one more time.

Megan quickly glanced around. "Have you seen Steven? I wanted to say goodbye."

Rosa shook her head. "No, but I'll tell him for you."

"Thanks, Rosa. You're a good friend." She couldn't blame Steven for not seeing them off. Not after she'd hurt him deeply. Yet, it was unsettling not saying goodbye, and thanking him for all he'd done.

The limousine pulled into the airstrip near a small jet plane. The pilot came over and talked with Grant for a few minutes then boarded the plane and waited for his passengers.

"The plane is ready for takeoff," Grant informed them. "Your brother will be waiting to pick you up."

"Mr. Peterson, thank you for everything." Megan gave him a hug and tried not to cry.

"You don't work for us any longer, little girl. I think it's time you start calling me Grant." He gave her a kiss on her forehead. "I'm going to miss you like my own daughter." His brown eyes misted over and he gave her another hug.

He shook John's hand, and Megan gave Delores a hug. The two women clung to each other, neither one wanting to let go.

"I can't believe you're really leaving," Delores said through her tears. "I kept putting off saying goodbye, because I didn't want to believe it was real. But you really are leaving."

"I have to go." Megan wiped her eyes dry.

"I know. It's the right choice." Delores hugged her. "Promise me that you'll never let anything come between the two of you again. Marriage is sacred and needs to be cherished the way God intended."

"I promise, and if I forget, you can remind me."

"Count on it." Delores smiled.

I'm going to miss you, Mrs. Peterson." Megan clasped her hands. "You mean so much to me."

"To both of us," John added.

"I want you both to come visit us often." Delores hugged John. "The jet will be waiting for your call."

"And you have a standing invitation to Illinois," Megan offered.

"We will take you up on that if you wait too long to come back and see us." Delores nodded towards the plane. "Now go home and have a happy life."

John and Megan started walking towards the plane.

"Wait!" Steven ran up behind them. "Wait a minute," he panted.

"Steven!" Megan exclaimed. "I didn't think you were coming."

"I almost didn't, if you want the truth," he said. "I didn't think I could say goodbye. But then I realized, I couldn't not say it either."

John possessively put his arm around Megan's shoulders. "Steven." He nodded an acknowledgement.

"I only came to say goodbye." He stuck out his hand and John grasped it. "Looks like the best man won, after all."

"I wouldn't go that far." He knew the pain of losing Megan, and empathized with Steven. He'd come to respect him. "Best of luck to you."

"Thanks. You take good care of her."

"Count on it." John smiled at Megan "I'll wait for you in the plane."

Megan was grateful for the time alone. "Steven, I don't know what to say."

"Don't say anything. Just take care of yourself and have a good life."

"You too." She fought the pain in her heart. "I'm going to miss you, Steven."

"Me too, sweetheart." He looked as if he wrestled with a question, finally deciding to ask it. "I need to know one thing." He stared into her blue eyes. "Could you have loved me?"

"If things had been different, and I hadn't already made a commitment to John..." She faltered, as she felt her heart breaking, looking back into his eyes. "How could I not?"

He grabbed her, clinging tight.

"Goodbye, Steven." She tore herself from his embrace and ran to the plane.

"Goodbye, Megan." He felt his soul being ripped out. Tears filled his eyes as he watched the plane taxi down the runway.

Grant walked up beside him and put his hand on his shoulder. "Are you okay, son?"

"It hurts Dad," he said flatly. "This hurts more than anything I've ever known."

"Even more than the press conference you did last week?"

"Even more than that."

"It takes a strong man to admit he made a mistake. I'm proud of the way you handled yourself with the media. But it takes an even stronger man to let someone go. I know you love her, but you're doing the right thing."

"Why does the right thing have to hurt so much?"

"It's part of life. The pain will ease in time and things will work out."

"You sound sure of that."

"I am. God always makes things work out."

"Are you always right?" Steven teased.

"Always." Grand smiled. "I told you things would work out with the press conference." Grant reminded him. "And we got better results than even I'd anticipated. We didn't lose any clients and most of the community rallied behind you."

"Most of the community." His voice trailed off as he watched the plane climb higher in the sky.

Lee waited impatiently for the plane to land, not able to contain his excitement. His sister was coming home. She'd only been gone for a few months, but it felt like years. Finally, the plane touched down and slowed to a stop. He ran out to meet them.

"Megan." He hugged her tight. "You're a sight for sore eyes."

"And look at you. All grown up and running the farm." She couldn't resist reaching up and ruffling his hair like she did when they were kids. "You need a haircut."

After filling in her brother on almost all the details of her time away, she fell silent and watched the snow-covered fields glide by while the guys discussed the farm.

When the small white house came into view she could hardly contain her joy. Her stomach flip-flopped at the very sight. Laying her hand across her belly she whispered, "We're finally home." The car rolled to a stop.

"Be careful, it's slippery." John cautioned as he helped her out.

"I'm fine." Her eyes wondered over the two-storey A-frame house, relishing every detail, while the men carried in the luggage. Looking across the corn fields behind the yard, she noticed the stubble of stalks sticking up through the thick blanket of snow. The sun shimmered across the ground but it didn't hold any warmth. A gust of icy wind tugged at her coat, turning her nose numb.

"Let's go inside," John coaxed.

"Not yet." She inhaled the cold crisp air.

"It feels good to be home." John put his arm around her.

It felt even better, successfully dealing with her grief. Looking around, she didn't feel any remnants from the past. No guilt. No pain. No uncertainty. The unforgiving ghosts had disappeared leaving her free to focus on the future. She also felt God's love and accepted that He was in control of her life. The pain was something she had had to go through. She now felt like a stronger person.

"We're all having supper at Mom and Dad's," Lee informed her.

"We'll be there." She gave him a kiss and waved as he drove off.

"Are you ready to go in yet? John blew on his hands trying to warm them up. "I'm freezing."

"I have something I want to tell you first."

"Can't you tell me inside?" He looked around at all the snow. "One thing I can say for California. It's a lot warmer in the winter."

"I love the cold and the snow." She held her arms out, turning around in small circles then fell into John's arms. "I can't wait to have our children grow up here."

"Children?" She hadn't even wanted to discuss having another baby after Laura died. He'd tried convincing her several times, but she stubbornly refused. "Are you saying that you're ready to try for another baby?"

"No." She softly shook her head, "I'm saying that I'm already pregnant with your child."

"Pregnant? But how?" He looked at the smile on her face. "I mean when?"

"I'm not positive, but I'd guess a little over three months."

His excitement slowly faded. "You knew you were pregnant the whole time you were in California?"

"No. I didn't realize it until a week ago. I wanted to wait and tell you the good news here at home."

"So, you didn't decide to come back with me because you found out you were having a baby and it was the right thing to do?" As much as he loved her, he wouldn't stay with someone who wasn't in love with him.

"I didn't know I was pregnant when I made my decision. There was so much going on that I hadn't noticed I missed my period. When I first realized I was late, I chalked it up to stress." She looked up into his eyes. "When I decided to come back home it was because I love you. This is my life. This is my home. And this," she laid her hands across her stomach, "is our baby."

He stood motionless for a long time as the news slowly sank in. Then with a loud, "Yahoo!" He swept her up and twirled around. "I'm going to be a daddy." With a kiss, he carried her up the steps and kicked the door open with his boot.

"You were right." She smiled up at him.

"About what?"

"It's good to be home."

The End

If you enjoyed Unforgiving Ghosts, visit Inknbeans Press for other books by this author and many others.

Inknbeans.com

www.ingramcontent.com/pod-product-compliance
Lightning Source LLC
Chambersburg PA
CBHW071639260626
47170CB00001B/161